I was very fond of Safdar, but who wasn't?
We liked him for his charming personality,
his easy laughter, sophisticated manners,
effortless articulation, clear-cut views
and tender human values.

HABIB TANVIR

"[*Halla Bol*] has poignantly lurched into our collective conscience at a critical time." RAHAAB ALLANA *The Hindu*

"Moving." ANNIE ZAIDI *HuffPost*

"Fascinating . . . Excellent and authoritative . . . Safdar emerges as fierce and gentle, charming and charismatic." FEISAL ALKAZI *Indian Express*

"Genre-defying . . . Visceral, gut-wrenching, etched-in-detail first-person narrative . . . Enjoyable, revelatory." SHAYONI MITRA *Economic and Political Weekly*

"Moving and provocative." KAUSTUBH NAIK *Frontline*

"A love story between artists and that is a glorious thing to witness." KIRTANA KUMAR *Mumbai Theatre Guide*

"A must read . . . to learn how to write a biography of an activist who lived his life not in isolation, but as part of a collective movement." NITHEESH NARAYANAN *Student Struggle*

"Brilliant and painful." SAYANTAN GHOSH *Scroll.in*

"Magical . . . Vital theatre history . . . *Halla Bol* is a call to (artistic) arms in our times." SADANAND MENON *The Book Review*

"A remarkable achievement." KUNAL RAY *Hindustan Times*

"Combines the two genres of history writing and memoir with other forms such as drama criticism with startling ease." SOURADEEP ROY *Scroll.in*

"I was by turns informed, amused, enraged, and deeply moved." NASEERUDDIN SHAH *actor*

'*Halla Bol* is unputdownable. It is fast-paced, vivid, action-packed, but you know only too well, with sinking heart, it is no fiction. It is the story of a man everyone loved – a man so gifted that all the world could stand up and say: "This was our New Man." And in Sudhanva, he now has his chronicler.'
ANAND PATWARDHAN *filmmaker*

'Luminous. *Halla Bol* is about theatre, culture, politics, and hope, and more poignantly relevant today than at any other time in our county's history.'
SANJNA KAPOOR *theatreperson*

'This is the kind of book we need today, so we can renew our understanding of resistance, and find the strength to put it into practice.' GITHA HARIHARAN *author*

'For a generation that grew up without knowing Safdar Hashmi, *Halla Bol* is a treasure, with stories and accounts that render his passion, humour and humanism into an intimate portrait. To me, this is a book about love.'
NEEL CHAUDHURI *playwright and director*

'*Halla Bol* is several things all at once. A vivid memoir of Safdar Hashmi, it is about intersections between cultural practice and working-class politics, and about lives lived at those intersections. Studded with details about the making of plays and the staging of them at street corners, the book's nimble prose reads like a well-crafted play.
A riveting read!'
AIJAZ AHMAD *Marxist scholar*

'A combination of great storytelling and empathy allows Sudhanva Deshpande to illuminate Safdar Hashmi's rich and deeply committed life. This is also the story of a period of tumult and change in India, and many of the ideas Safdar and his colleagues grappled with are harbingers, for better or worse, of how we are as a society today. *Halla Bol* is an invaluable addition to the sparse body of literature on contemporary theatre in India.'

SUNIL SHANBAG *theatre director*

'A terrible storm is blowing across the page of history we call our present. In *Halla Bol*, Sudhanva Deshpande has cupped his hands around that tender, resilient flame that was Safdar Hashmi.' AMITAVA KUMAR *author*

SUDHANVA DESHPANDE

is an actor, director, and organizer
with Jana Natya Manch, Delhi.
He is Managing Editor, LeftWord Books.
He cycles around town.
This is his first book.

halla
bol

halla bol

The Death and Life of Safdar Hashmi

SUDHANVA DESHPANDE

LeftWord

First published in January 2020
First paperback edition January 2020
Reprinted July 2020, June 2024
Digital print edition, August 2024

LeftWord Books
2254/2A Shadi Khampur
New Ranjit Nagar
New Delhi 110008
INDIA

LeftWord Books and Vaam Prakashan are imprints of
Naya Rasta Publishers Pvt. Ltd.

leftword.com

The photographs in the book are from the archives of Jana Natya Manch.
They are reproduced with permission from the group. Individual photographers are acknowledged, where known. The publisher would be glad to correct any errors in acknowledgement, in future editions of the book.

Royalties from this publication will go towards running Studio Safdar,
Shadi Khampur, New Delhi.

ISBN 978-81-944759-1-0

COVER Safdar and others in *Kala Qanoon*, 1981. Photo: Rathin Das.
P. 1 Safdar, Moloyashree, Lalit in *Machine*, May 1, 1988. Photo: Eugene van Erven.
P. 2 Safdar in *Aya Chunao*, Haryana, 1980. Photo: Surendra Rajan.
P. 227 Sohail and Safdar, late 1980s.
P. 258 *Halla Bol*, January 4, 1989, Jhandapur, Sahibabad.

For Comrade Aai and Professor Baba

CONTENTS

On New Year's Eve, 1988, we were laughing and singing, out in the open, perched on a giant rock amid lush greenery, caring a fig for the bone-chilling cold, and we didn't want the night to end.

On New Year's Day, 1989, we were huddled together, unable to feel rage or grief, in a government hospital corridor with its banal walls, numb to the bone-chilling cold, and we didn't want the morning to arrive.

In between, time stopped. One hand of its clock was an iron rod, the other the barrel of a gun.

My heart was stone. I went through the first three days of January 1989 in a trance. I remember it as one remembers a movie one has watched a dozen times – the picture sharp, crystal clear; the colours vibrant; the soundtrack crisp. I can play the images in slow-motion on my memory's player; but it's a movie, it's not life.

I came back to reality when we went back to Jhandapur to perform *Halla Bol* ('Raise Hell'), the play that was left unfinished when we were attacked three days ago, which had resulted in two deaths. An artist's head deliberately clobbered by blunt instruments, a worker's life snuffed out casually by a bullet.

Theatre is make-believe; theatre is life. It is ephemeral, momentary, fleeting, transient, a wisp of smoke; it is palpable, organic, aromatic, acidic, a bean of coffee.

And it sometimes reeks of blood. The blood spilled on the brick-paved streets of a working-class neighbourhood on a perfect winter Sunday morning.

This is not a story of death. It is a story of life.

The luminous life of Safdar Hashmi, extraordinary in all its ordinariness.

PART ONE

JANUARY 1, 1989. Madras Hotel

I wasn't even supposed to be there.

I had finished my graduation the previous summer and had joined a Master's programme in History at Delhi University. Having narrowly missed a first division in my Bachelor's, I was determined to do well in my MA, and had spoken to Safdar about taking off from performing with Jana Natya Manch (Janam) from January onwards. I wasn't going to be part of the January 1 shows. But New Year's Day follows New Year's Eve, and Jogi, Brijender, Lalit, a couple of Lalit's friends, and I had ended up spending the night together, getting drunk on the legendary Parthasarathi Rock in Jawaharlal Nehru University (JNU), where my father taught and we had a house on campus. It wasn't yet a fortress, the JNU campus, and you could move about pretty much freely.

In the morning, they were going for the performance. It was Sunday. My mum wasn't in town. There was no way I was going to stay behind.

We congregated at the Madras Hotel bus stop. Safdar and Mala were already there, as were a couple of others.

'So, I see you're studying hard,' Safdar ribbed me.

'That's a nice colour. Deep green. I like green.' I deftly deflected the conversation from my studies to Safdar's sweater. Or so I thought.

'Praise is the last refuge of the scoundrel.' We both laughed.

One or two of the actors were a bit late, so we hung around a bit. Safdar scoured the place to see if a tea seller was around. No luck. It was too early.

A drunk ambled up on the opposite side of the street. He looked at us, an odd gaggle of men and women of varying ages, but all clearly together. He kept staring.

'All OK?' Safdar called out to him.

'Happy New Year,' he shouted back, in English.

'And a very happy new year to you, too!' Safdar called back, in Hindi, grinning his goofy grin.

'Don't worry, be happy,' the drunk man shouted to no one in particular, echoing the global hit song that had released a few months ago. The way he said it, it sounded like an order.

'And don't fall in a ditch,' Safdar laughed.

JANUARY 1, 1989. Aiming for the Chair

'I'm glad you've come,' Safdar said as we boarded the bus. 'Let me tell you about the press conference tomorrow.'

A couple of months earlier, in October or November, Safdar had learnt that he was going to be conferred an award by an organization that worked for communal harmony. It was a fairly non-political organization and everything seemed kosher. But Safdar told them he wouldn't accept the award individually, since all his work for communal harmony was as part of Janam. So he'd rather that the organization got the award, not the individual. They agreed.

Then we learnt that the award was going to be handed over by Minister of Information and Broadcasting H.K.L. Bhagat, the Congress party's member of parliament from east Delhi. Now, Bhagat was notorious for his role in the anti-Sikh violence of 1984. There was a discussion in the Janam Executive Committee (EC) on this. Some felt we should boycott the function, but accept the award, because, after all, the organization itself seemed clean and they were honouring us. That the award carried a cash component of Rs 10,000 – quite a sum in those days – was also a factor. Safdar was not in favour of this line. 'No halfway measures. We either accept the award fully, from Bhagat, or we reject it.' We decided to reject the award.

Safdar had planned a press conference on the evening of January 2, Monday, to explain the Janam stand. As we rode in the bus to Jhandapur in the Sahibabad township of Ghaziabad, he told me about the preparations and showed me a copy of the press release.

We got off at the wrong stop, so we had to walk a bit to get to Jhandapur. I saw election posters on the walls.

'Yes,' said Safdar. 'They are having corporation elections in UP after some 18 years or so. The people are fed up. All the parties are scared to face the electorate, so their candidates are contesting as independents. Only we [he meant the Communist Party of India (Marxist)] are contesting on our party symbol. In fact, our performance today is in support of our candidate, Ramanath Jha. He's a militant trade unionist. He was there when we came here in December. Do you remember?'

'Yes,' I half lied. I remembered the performance, but not the man.

'It's so much fun to see election symbols, don't you think?'

'Yes.'

'Oh, look at this! This guy is absolutely clear what he's fighting for. His symbol is the chair!' Safdar laughed.

'*Kissa Kursee Ka*,' I laughed, quoting the name of the movie that had been banned during the Emergency because it mocked Indira Gandhi.

'This is so funny. Just this morning I read a fantastic short story – really short – in *Hans*. Here's how it goes. "What do you see?" asks Drona. "I see the capital, Delhi, my guru," says Sahdev. "You're useless," says Drona and calls Nakul. "What do you see?" he asks. "I see the Parliament House in Delhi, my guru," says Nakul. "You're useless," says Drona and calls Bhim. "What do you see?" he asks. "I see the council of ministers, my guru," says Bhim. "You're useless," says Drona and calls Yudhishtir. "What do you see?" he asks. "I see the prime minister's chamber, my guru," says Yudhishtir. "You're useless," says Drona and calls his favourite pupil, Arjun. "What do you see?" he asks. "I see the chair, my guru," says Arjun. "Good," says Drona. "Shoot."'

'Looks like this candidate also reads *Hans*.'

Safdar chuckled. 'That'll be the day. When our politicians start reading literary magazines.'

Vishwajeet was also walking with us. He was from Allahabad, and had come to Delhi to audition for a part in a TV series, a part he finally got. But with the shoot delayed, he had found his way into Janam.

'See my new shoes?' Safdar beamed as he pointed to them. They were black leather shoes, fresh and gleaming. 'Guess how much they're for.'

Having known Safdar for a while, I knew this game, and wasn't going to fall for it. Vishwajeet didn't, so he did.

'Nice, Safdar bhai. I would say 200, 225. In that range.'

'Ha! I got them for 75.'

'No way! They look really expensive.'

By now we were nearly at the office of the Centre of Indian Trade Unions (CITU), from where we were to go to the performance spot.

'Listen,' Safdar said. 'I may not remember later to remind you, but do come for the press conference tomorrow. You are a member of the EC. It'll be good for the press to see that Janam has young leaders too.'

'Sure, I'll be there.'

As it happened, I was. Safdar wasn't.

JANUARY 1, 1989. The Performance

The CITU office in Jhandapur was a one-room affair with a small courtyard. The adjacent plot at the back was empty, and a wall, about four feet tall, separated the two plots. The front wall of the courtyard was taller, about seven feet maybe. A somewhat rusty iron door led from the street into the courtyard.

It was a crisp, sunny winter day, perfect for street theatre. Comrades were waiting for us at the CITU office when we arrived. They had tea and biscuits ready. The actors got into their black kurtas, and those who had carried bags decided to leave them at the office. The performance site was a short walk away, on the main street that led into Jhandapur from the main road.

The spot we were to perform at was at a three-way junction. The main street that led to it came from the north. It swerved to the east, where a temple stood. A smaller street led to houses on the west. To the south was Dr Ambedkar Park, which, at the time, was a big garbage dump. Today, we hold the Safdar Hashmi Memorial Day performance and public meeting here on January 1 every year.

Some spectators were already present when we reached. Mala and a couple of other actors laid out the properties. Jogi took out his dholak and started playing. This immediately attracted more spectators, especially children.

Safdar asked me to speak before the performance. 'You may as well, since you're not performing today.'

'I can, but you don't let me do the role I really want to do. And do better than anybody else.'

This was the role of the cop, which Vishwajeet and Lalit would perform alternately. Since they were both there that day, Vishwajeet was to do the first performance, after which Lalit and he were to alternate. We had three performances lined up that day.

Soon, there was a sizeable crowd of a hundred and fifty or so, and the performance began after I had spoken, exhorting the people to vote for Comrade Ramanath Jha. I exited the acting area and joined Safdar and Lalit. There was a tea shack at the corner, and we sat there, sipping tea. We were barely fifteen feet away from the performance space, so we could hear everything clearly.

About 10–12 minutes into the performance, we heard sloganeering from the north, from beyond the temple. A couple of minutes later, a cavalcade of campaigners arrived. In front was a car carrying some four–five men. Behind the car was a tempo decorated with campaign material. Between the car and the tempo were a dozen or so men, carrying lathis and shouting slogans. The tempo itself carried about as many as were on foot. Behind the tempo were more people.

'I'll talk to them,' Safdar said, and walked up to the car.

I saw him bend down and talk to the man in the front, next to the driver. He pointed to the performance, which had stopped, given the noise.

'Let me go there too,' Lalit said, and went to join Safdar. I followed a few steps behind.

Safdar was speaking to the man. 'Sir, we are doing a small play here. Why don't you stop and watch the play? There's only ten minutes more to go. You'll enjoy it.'

The man said something I couldn't catch.

'Then why don't you take an alternative route, and come back here after a short while? Our play will be over by then.'

The man seemed to agree, and the car and tempo started backing off. As they reached the temple, Safdar went into the acting area and spoke to the audience.

'Sorry about the interruption, but we're starting the play again.'

Jogi played the dholak for a short time, and once the attention of the audience was back on them, the actors re-started the play. The interruption must have lasted some five to seven minutes at most.

And then, before we knew it, all hell broke loose.

JANUARY 1, 1989. The Attack

They came upon us with lathis and iron rods. The spectators scattered in no time. We had nothing to defend ourselves with, except the half a dozen bamboo sticks on which we mounted our flags. These were light and thin, easy to carry, but hardly enough to withstand the solid, oil-fed lathis and iron rods they had. Our sticks broke somewhat comically into two in no time.

We picked up whatever stones we could find and threw them in an effort to keep the attackers at bay. But it was pandemonium, our aims were pathetic, and the attackers were hardened goons. We pushed them back a little bit, but it was clear we could not beat them back.

Safdar was in the middle of all this, shouting instructions to us. His hair dishevelled, he still looked striking, arm raised, his voice rising above everyone else's. He was the leader, and he had taken charge.

One of the CITU comrades, Jadumani Behra, was hit on the head and was bleeding. Some of us got hit by lathis on our backs or arms.

I was throwing stones at the attackers when I heard Safdar's voice. 'Come to the CITU office. We are going there.' I looked back to see Safdar, Lalit, Mala, Prachee, Shikha, and some others take refuge in a dhobi's shop at the corner. From there, they started moving towards the CITU office.

I wanted to join them but couldn't. A couple of attackers blocked my way.

I looked the other way and saw Brijesh and Vishwajeet at the corner of the small street on the south side.

'Sudhu, come!' Brijesh yelled.

I scampered free of my attackers and joined them. We ran as fast as we could into the winding gali, hoping we'd soon be out of sight. All three of us were relative strangers to each other. Vishwajeet had come to Delhi a couple of months ago, and Brijesh was one of Safdar's young doctor friends. He knew Mala and Safdar well, but I had met him only recently.

Vishwajeet was a tall guy, about six foot three. He was easy to spot, and his policeman's costume made him even more conspicuous. Brijesh asked him to remove his khaki shirt.

'But I'm not wearing anything underneath.'

'Take my shirt,' I said. I removed my jacket and sweater, and gave him my shirt. I put back my sweater on my bare body and started wearing my jacket.

'Don't wear that,' said Brijesh. 'It looks too much like the police shirt he's removed.'

It was true. My jacket was khaki coloured. I held it in my arm.

'What do I do with this?' Vishwajeet asked, holding up the baton he carried as part of his police costume.

'Let's leave it with that paan wallah,' I said.

We gave the baton to the paan wallah, thinking we'll come back and pick it up later.

That never came to pass.

JANUARY 1, 1989. Finding Our Way

We had no idea of the layout of the basti. We needed to reach the CITU office, where Safdar had asked us to congregate.

We made our way to the main road, from which we knew the main street entered Jhandapur, culminating in the three-way junction we were performing at. As we started walking down the main street, a man ran past us.

'Don't go down this way. They are there, looking for you.'

Clearly, our attempts to be inconspicuous had been unsuccessful.

We came back to the main road and looked for another entry point. We found one a little further down the road, on our right. We entered, and found ourselves in a maze of alleys. We knew the general direction of the CITU office, but not the exact way.

'Let me find out,' Brijesh said. 'You guys wait here.'

He returned a few minutes later. 'This is the right way. But they're saying the CITU office has been attacked.'

'Well, let's go there and see,' I said.

We reached the CITU office and saw the signs of the attack. Riyaz's scooter lay prone outside. The gate hung open, things were strewn about, there were a few stones here and there, which the attackers had thrown at those inside. I saw a mark on the brick-paved floor that could've been blood, but then it could've been some other stain as well. There was not a soul in sight.

As we stepped out of the office compound, a woman emerged from the house opposite. 'One of your men is dying on that street,' she said, pointing to the main street of the village, which led to the performance area. 'Five people have been killed in the area. There are corpses all over.'

Brijesh and I looked at each other. Despite having experienced violence just some time ago, despite having seen the ravaged state of the CITU office compound, it was hard to believe that people had been killed. And five corpses? That seemed hyperbole. We decided to look.

Brijesh led the way. I was behind him. Vishwajeet brought up the rear. Brijesh went to the head of the alley and peeped into the main street, to his left, where the performance spot was. And he was off like an arrow.

I ran to where he was, to figure out what he had seen and what he was running towards. At the corner where he had turned, I saw a figure lying on the ground, up ahead, and Brijesh running towards that figure. For a microsecond, it looked like Vinod, one of the actors.

Then I saw the green sweater. Safdar.

JANUARY 1, 1989. Saving Safdar

I ran towards Safdar, shouting to Vishwajeet behind me to come fast. When I reached the spot, I looked at Safdar. He was unconscious, breathing through his mouth in violent spurts. There was blood all over his head, his hair was dripping wet, but his face was relatively clean. Brijesh had put his finger in his mouth and was clearing it of blood and saliva. I realized he was clearing the passage for air.

Brijesh looked up at me. My face must have had a question written on it, because he gave the slightest shake of the head. I knew then that this was serious, possibly fatal.

'Pick him up,' Brijesh said.

I took hold of Safdar's ankles and Brijesh held his wrists. We tried to lift him, but it was hard. Safdar was a big guy.

'Hold him by the armpits,' I said.

'You come this side, but make sure his head stays upright. Or he could choke.'

As we traded positions, I looked for the first time at the spot where we had been performing. It was about 25–30 metres away. A couple of men stood there. One had an iron rod in his hand, and was shouting menacingly at nobody in particular.

The other had a gun, which he fired in the air.

'Drag him,' I said. 'Vishwajeet, move!' He stood somewhat paralysed by the shock of it all.

The three of us managed to drag Safdar into a tiny side alley before the killers spotted us.

Now, we lifted Safdar. I held him under the armpits, with his head resting on my stomach. Brijesh lifted him by the legs. Vishwajeet supported the middle. Brijesh's hands kept slipping on Safdar's socks.

'Take off his shoes and socks,' I said. 'It'll be easier to grip his ankles.' Initially we tried to carry the shoes with us, but at some point, I don't know when, Safdar's new, shining shoes, were abandoned. I hope they made their way to some worker's feet. Safdar would've liked that.

It was tough going. Safdar kept slipping from our hands, and trying to keep his head up made it harder still.

'This is going to be difficult,' Brijesh said. 'Let me try and get a vehicle from outside. You people wait here.'

We sat Safdar on the ground, his torso and head on my chest. I tried to clear his mouth, but it wasn't as easy as it looked when Brijesh had done it.

Then, out of nowhere, a stranger appeared. Wordlessly, he joined us. Now Vishwajeet took his legs and the stranger picked up Safdar from the middle. He was a worker, and his powerful arms held up Safdar in a way that none of us had managed. Suddenly it became much easier to walk.

Soon Brijesh joined us. 'There's a car waiting on the main road. They'll take us to the hospital.'

When we reached the main road, we found it deserted. Brijesh told me later that the car had Bharatiya Janata Party (BJP) flags on it. It was nowhere to be seen.

Then, who knows from where, a cycle rickshaw appeared. The man took one look at Safdar and agreed to take him to the hospital. 'But the Mohan Nagar hospital is far from here. It'll take a long time,' he said.

We managed to prop up Safdar on the cycle rickshaw, with Brijesh sitting next to him, holding him up, trying to keep his head upright, periodically clearing his mouth of saliva and blood. Vishwajeet and I didn't know what to do, so we jogged behind the rickshaw.

The stranger who had helped carry Safdar vanished as he had appeared, without a trace, wordlessly. Much later, days, maybe weeks later, Brijesh and I realized we hadn't thanked him.

Then a bus appeared from behind us. Vishwajeet and I almost blocked the way, forcing the bus to stop. The conductor refused to let us board with Safdar, our entreaties falling on deaf ears.

'Let me go up to Mohan Nagar and get an ambulance,' I said to Brijesh. 'You carry on in this direction. I'll find you.' I boarded the bus.

'What should I do,' Vishwajeet asked, as the bus started moving.

'Go with him,' Brijesh said.

At the hospital reception, I asked for an ambulance. The guy looked at me blankly. 'It is Sunday. No ambulance.'

I ran out, Vishwajeet behind me. I spotted a taxi stand on the opposite side of the road. There, I was able to get a driver to agree to come with us. He drove a private car as a taxi.

I had no idea how far Brijesh would have reached with Safdar on the cycle rickshaw by now. In fact, I had no sense of how much time had passed. I was keeping my eyes peeled for a cycle rickshaw coming from the opposite side.

As we descended the Mohan Nagar flyover, I saw a car on the other side. It had broken down, and the driver was out, trying to flag a vehicle. In the car, on the back seat, I saw two figures.

The green sweater.

We turned around, and transferred Safdar to the taxi. Brijesh sat with him on the back seat, while Vishwajeet and I squeezed in at the front, next to the driver. They didn't have bucket seats back then, thankfully.

Neither Brijesh nor I spoke. It didn't occur to me to ask how he had found his way into a broken-down car at the foot of the flyover.

I looked back. Safdar looked like a child in Brijesh's arms. I couldn't make out though if his body was being rocked by small spasms, or whether it was the car driving jerkily.

JANUARY 1, 1989. Mohan Nagar Hospital

Safdar was lying on a bare metal bed. His breathing was still spasmodic. The first thing Brijesh had done upon reaching was to take off all his clothes to see if there were any other injuries apart from on the head. There were none. I emptied Safdar's pockets. There was a packet of cigarettes – Charminar plain, as always – a matchbox, a phone diary, and a little bit of money. I kept the money in my pocket, thinking I'll give it to Mala when I see her. I never did, but I can't remember what I did with it either.

Brijesh went to fetch a doctor. I asked Vishwajeet to be with Safdar while I went to make a call.

'Don't be long, please!'

I said I wouldn't.

Fortunately there was a pay phone in that hall. I called my home and spoke to my father. My mother was away, in Trivandrum, as an interpreter for the French delegation that had come for the Party Congress of the Communist Party of India (Marxist) – CPI (M) – ongoing at the time. My sister was also there, with the song squad Parcham.

'We are at the Mohan Nagar Hospital in Ghaziabad. Safdar is seriously injured. There are three of us here. Call the Party office and ask them to send help.'

I got back to Safdar. Vishwajeet said a cop had come around and was looking for me. 'He looks like Sadashiv Amrapurkar, the same bloodshot eyes,' Vishwajeet said, referring to the actor who had essayed a number of villainous roles in Hindi films. I stepped out of the enclosure, and there he was.

'So, you guys think you'll get away, is it? You've killed three people there. You'll hang, each of you.'

I looked at him incredulously. 'There's an injured man in there.

He's dying. We brought him to hospital. What are you talking about?'

Behind me, I heard a thud. I looked back to see that Vishwajeet, all six feet three inches of him, had slumped on the wooden bench. When I interviewed him for this book, Vishwajeet recalled he had been terrified and nervous, and had passed out from fear. I hadn't realized that. I thought he had suffered a blackout as one sometimes does when getting up suddenly, especially if one hasn't eaten anything, as he hadn't. In the interview, he said something astonishing: He remembered being with Brijesh that day but has absolutely no memory that I was there as well. Even after I prodded him with several details, nothing came back to him. Trauma filters memories, and what it keeps out, it wipes clean, I guess.

'Sir, my friend here has also been hit on the head,' I lied. 'He needs a doctor. Please get one, fast.'

'Don't try to run away, OK? We have eyes everywhere.' This guy watches too many Hindi movies, I thought to myself.

Brijesh came back with a doctor. He was a young man, maybe a junior resident. He took one look at Safdar and realized things were serious.

Brijesh flashed his ID to prove he was a doctor too, a government servant at that. 'We must get a CT scan done, immediately.'

'You are right, Sir. But our scan machine is not working.'

'Then I'm taking him to Delhi. Right now.'

'But Sir, this is an MLC [Medico-Legal Case]. The police will insist on an FIR here.'

'I don't care. This man is very serious. I'm taking him to Delhi. Sudhu, get a cab. Fast.'

I rushed out and got a cab. It was an Ambassador. As we were transferring Safdar to the back seat, we saw Comrade Ved Gupta walk in to the hospital. He was in the CPI (M) office when my father had called there. He took a cab and rushed to the hospital. He was a tall, silver-haired, soft-spoken man, who taught at Zakir Husain College in Delhi. I knew him a little bit, because he used to conduct study classes for us in the Students' Federation of India (SFI).

Brijesh told Comrade Ved he'd take Safdar to Irwin Hospital (renamed Lok Nayak Jai Prakash Hospital) in Delhi.

'Yes, Brijesh. Do that. I'll go to Jhandapur and find the others. Do you know where Mala is?' Shit. It hadn't occurred to me that Mala probably had no idea what had happened to her husband.

We had no clue where anyone else was. Brijesh drove off with Safdar.

'Comrade Sudhanva, you two should also go to Delhi. You'll get buses to Shahdara from outside. Do you have money?'

'But comrade, a cop told us not to move from here.'

'Don't worry. Go. I'll handle the cops.'

I later learnt that he made short shrift of the cop, claiming he was a member of parliament. He wasn't.

When Comrade Ved died a few years later and they needed volunteers to stand vigil through the night with his body, Brijesh and I raised our hands. We went to the Party office, where his body lay covered with a red flag. Ved's wife Babli was there, and so was Brinda Karat. We spent that refrigerated winter night in the office, Brijesh and I in red shirts, standing on either side of Ved, while Babli spoke of Ved and Brinda held her in an embrace.

'Ved really loved Safdar. You see this Hindi typewriter? Safdar bought it for this office shortly before he was killed. He had got some money for a television assignment. Ved wouldn't normally talk of office stuff at home. But that day, I remember how he spoke about Safdar, his dedication to the Party, his cheerful disposition. Do you know how Ved used to describe Safdar? "Rangeen mijaz fakir" [fakir of colourful disposition]. He was so angry they killed him. Can you picture this gentle, quiet man angry? The only time I saw him really, truly, furiously angry was then. When they killed Safdar.'

JANUARY 1, 1989. Delhi Hospitals

Vishwajeet and I went directly to Irwin Hospital. As we reached, we saw Brijesh going off in an ambulance. We learnt that Safdar was being shifted to Ram Manohar Lohia Hospital.

When we got to RML, I saw Mala for the first time. I saw her from a distance, surrounded by comrades. Her parents, Aparnadi and Baba, and Safdar's mother Ammaji, were also there. I was surprised to see how many people had gathered. It was then that I learnt that everybody else from the group was safe, except that nobody had any news of Brijender. I also learnt that a worker had been killed.

Brijesh emerged from the Intensive Care Unit (ICU) and spoke to Mala and the others. I was standing some distance away with Jogi, Lalit, and a few other Janam friends. The older members of Janam, Subhash Tyagi, who had been in Jhandapur with us that day, and Manish Manocha and Arun Sharma, were standing in a group near us.

As soon as Brijesh came to us, we huddled around him. 'The scan shows his brain is smashed. His brain fluid is coming out of his nose. It is very unlikely he will survive. And even if he does, we don't know what state he'll be in.'

The hospital kept filling up with people. Comrades were arriving, as were a number of other people. My father came as it was getting dark. I hugged him. There was nothing to say. A short while later, theatre director Habib Tanvir arrived with his wife Moneeka. He hugged me wordlessly.

Moneekadi held my face. 'Be strong. Be strong.'

The evening wore on and the crowd swelled. Everybody was looking shell shocked. No one was speaking much. It was well after dark when we learnt that Brijender was safe. He came to hospital a short while later. He told us he had gone to the police station in Jhandapur to get help. Rather than send out a team to rescue the actors, they had held him in the station till late evening before finally letting him go. He made his way to the Party office, from where he came to the hospital.

We learnt more details of the other killing: The worker shot dead was Ram Bahadur, a young migrant from Nepal who worked in one of the factories around. That killing was random. It was purely to spread terror; they had no beef with him.

At about 10 or so at night, Mala came to us. 'There's no point waiting here. Go and get some sleep. Have you people eaten anything? No? Then get some food. Do you have money? Come back in the morning.'

Brijender, Jogi, Lalit, and I left the hospital. Nobody had an appetite, but Lalit insisted we eat something. We found a dhaba and nibbled on daal and roti. It was the first time we were eating after the biscuits in the morning.

We spent the night at the Democratic Youth Federation of India (DYFI) office in Vithalbhai Patel (V.P.) House, which Lalit got opened for us. A comrade, brother of our Janam friend Soman, was a wholetimer there. He gave us a couple of quilts. Jogi, Brijender, and I spent the night there. Lalit stayed with the comrade.

I didn't think I'd be able to sleep. I was wrong. I was out like a light the moment my head hit the pillow.

JANUARY 1, 1989. Escape

Among those who met us at the Madras Hotel bus stop that morning, there was one guy I had never met before. He was a short, sprightly man, with a nice smile. He came with us to Jhandapur, but in the course of the day's events, I don't remember thinking about him.

His name was Muralidharan. He had shifted from Ahmedabad to Delhi recently as a Party wholetimer, and Safdar and he had worked together to coordinate the arrivals and departures of the international delegates attending the CPI (M) Congress in Trivandrum. Kerala didn't have an international airport at the time, so the delegates had to pass through Delhi. Since all the international delegates were now in Trivandrum and the Party Congress was underway, Murali was at a bit of a loose end, and when Safdar suggested he join us that day, he readily agreed.

When the attack started, Murali moved with Safdar, Mala, and others, none of whom he knew, to the CITU office. When the attackers came there, Comrade Ramanath Jha, Brijender, and Safdar initially held the compound gate shut. One of the attackers hurled a brick at them from over the wall. It hit Ramanath Jha on the head. He had already been injured on the knee before. He staggered. Safdar asked everyone to escape. Ramanath Jha jumped the wall. With killers on his tail, he ran for his life, and was given protection by a worker who locked him up in his house. Unable to find him, the killers pulled out Ram Bahadur from his room, and shot him in cold blood, at point blank range, in front of his wife, Pavitra.

Murali jumped the wall. He knew nobody, and he had no idea where he was. He saw some people peeping out of a window, afraid to step out. He found himself with Brijender, and the two ran, strangers bound together by circumstance. Murali, having spent his life in warmer climes, had never worn shoes before. To cope with the Delhi winter, he bought Gola sports shoes, and was wearing them the first time that day. He found he could run faster in them.

Brijender and he ran together for quite a bit before they reached a main road, where they saw a tea stall.

'I'll go to the police station,' Brijender said. 'You wait here.'

Some men arrived carrying sticks. They were the attackers, but they couldn't have recognized Murali because he wasn't wearing Janam's black kurta. He sat there, hoping that Brijender wouldn't come back while the attackers were there. But Brijender didn't come back at all. Murali waited a long time, and then made his way back to Delhi. He no longer remembers how.

As Brijender ran, a man on a bicycle offered him a lift to the police station. There, he told a cop, Bhag Singh, and a couple of others, about the attack.

'Yes, we know,' Bhag Singh said. 'We have the report. You relax. Sit down. Or you can go back. Our force has already gone there.'

Brijender was relieved. He sat on the bench and considered his options. May as well leave, he thought. If the police have reached Jhandapur, I can look for the others. Just then, a number of the goons arrived in three–four cars. They pointed to Brijender.

'This bastard attacked me with a lathi,' one of them said, pointing to a tiny scratch on his forehead. 'He's one of the people who attacked us. They've come from Delhi. Many of our people are grievously injured.'

Brijender protested. A cop slapped him on the face four–five times.

'Sit on the floor, motherfucker. This isn't your house.'

Then he thought the better of it and put Brijender in the lockup. After a few minutes, Brijender was taken out of the lockup and made to sit on the floor again.

The cops wouldn't let Brijender go. He saw the attackers hand over what looked like a wad of cash to one of the cops, Ram Swarup. Brijender was detained till evening, and not allowed to even go to the bathroom. He was finally allowed to leave when a PAC (Provincial Armed Constabulary) jeep arrived.

Out on the main road, he saw an empty Delhi Transport Corporation (DTC) bus going to Hasanpur Depot. He flagged it and told the conductor that he had no money because he had been mugged and robbed. Since he was only wearing a kurta and jeans on the cold winter evening, the story seemed credible. He got a lift and eventually made his way back to the Party office in V.P. House.

That morning, when the play was interrupted for the first time, Jogi didn't think much of it. 'Safdar is here,' he thought, 'he'll handle everything.' So, when the attack started, he was taken by surprise. He saw the audience scatter in no time; women, children, men, all running helter-skelter. He was part of the group that went with Safdar to the CITU office. He remembers going with Diwakar, Vinod, Brijender, Mala, Shikha, Prachee. When the CITU office was attacked, Safdar asked them to scale the back wall and escape. As Jogi ran, still holding a stick from the props, he saw a man chasing him, baying for his blood. Jogi flung the stick at him, catching his legs. The man stumbled and fell, which allowed Jogi to escape. Someone pulled him into a little room and shut the door. A shot was fired somewhere. Jogi was scared. He could only hear his own breathing, nothing else. A little while later, the man pushed in Diwakar into the room, and soon thereafter, Vinod.

The three actors, Jogi, Diwakar, and Vinod, were absolutely quiet, not talking to each other. They got out of their black kurtas and put on their own clothes, which they had got from the office. The man shoved in a bucket of water and a mug into the room, presumably for drinking. How long they were there, locked up, nobody knows. It could have been twenty minutes; it could have been two hours. Eventually, the man opened the door.

'Comrade, they have gone. You can escape now. Take that lane. Be careful.'

When the attack began, Tyagi was one of the first ones to be hit. He got two blows from a lathi on his back. Within seconds, there was pandemonium. Some comrades tried to fend off the attack by throwing stones at the attackers. Tyagi ran. I'd better take off my kurta, he thought. He handed it to a woman standing nearby. But he realized his baniyan was spotless white – too white for a worker. The woman pulled him into her house and locked it from outside. Another Janam actor was with Tyagi – he says it was Diwakar, but Jogi also remembers being with Diwakar, so I'm not sure. They could see through the cracks in the door – the goons arriving with guns and asking whose house it was. The woman said there's no one in; the owner had gone to the factory. The woman opened the door after the goons left. Tyagi reckoned that if they left by the main door, they might encounter the goons down the road. So, they climbed on to the terrace, and kept going from one terrace to the next, till they reached the last house.

Tyagi and the other actor jumped down from the terrace of the final house to find they had landed amongst foes – the house belonged to one of the goons.

'Here they are, catch them!'

But Tyagi, at 47, was still sprightly enough to outsprint them. The other actor was younger anyway. Somehow, they lost their attackers and reached the main road. Here they learnt that three people had been killed. They had no way of finding out if this was true; nor, if true, who the victims were. They got on the first bus that came by. It dropped them to Shahdara, from where they made their way back to the Party office. Here they learnt that Safdar was seriously injured and that he was in Irwin Hospital. When they reached the hospital, they learnt that the CT scan machine wasn't working, and that Safdar was being shifted to RML Hospital. Just then, some reporters landed up. The doctors at Irwin Hospital said that if the photographers took any pictures, they'd have to keep Safdar there, and the transfer wouldn't happen. Tyagi spoke to the press and requested them not to take pictures. They complied.

Lalit had gone with the others to the CITU office. With the attackers relentlessly trying to get to them, he, along with Mala, Shikha, and Prachee, jumped over the back wall and found refuge in a house. They spent the next several hours there.

JANUARY 1, 1989. Hiding

On December 31, 1988, Mala and Safdar had gone to the performance of *Halla Bol* at Tehkhand Mode in the Okhla Industrial Area. After the show, Safdar told the group that he won't be there for the show on January 2, because of the press conference. New Year's Eve was no big deal for Mala and Safdar. They weren't a partying couple. They went home.

The next morning, January 1, they walked down from their house in Laxmibai Nagar to INA Market, and took a bus to Shivaji Stadium. Many of the actors were late, but one, Riyaz, was so late that Safdar and Mala were trying to see who could replace him. Fortunately, he arrived on his ramshackle scooter just as the bus was about to leave. He decided to carry on on the scooter, and meet the rest in Jhandapur.

Mala remembers the long walk from the bus stop to the Jhandapur CITU office. Besides Safdar, she, and I, there was Brijender, Brijesh, Diwakar, Jogi, Lalit, Murali, Prachee, Riyaz, Shikha, Tyagi, Vinod, and Vishwajeet. Fifteen in all. When the play began, Mala remembers Safdar and Murali standing at the tea shop with Ramanath Jha.

When the first interruption took place, Mala didn't think it was anything dangerous. From inside the acting area, she didn't even think there were that many people. The play had stopped, and she saw Safdar and Ramanath Jha go over and talk to some people. Within a few minutes, she saw Safdar signalling them to resume the play. Jogi played the dhol a bit, and the actors picked up the action from where they had stopped. They had performed for maybe two or three minutes when Mala realized that something was happening. The audience seemed unsettled; she caught a glimpse of a large number of people with iron rods and lathis, and then everything was a blur. She saw someone pick up a bench and hit Ramanath Jha with it, on his legs.

In the bedlam, Mala's focus was on the properties; she collected them and retreated to the istriwali's shop, in front of which the play was happening. She ensured that Prachee and Shikha were with her. Safdar came in, and Mala realized that he had either been pushed, or he had fallen, because she saw his spectacles on the ground. Picking them up was pointless. They were crushed.

Mala felt a sense of menace.

Safdar said, move to the CITU office. At the office, she saw Jadumani Behra, whose head was injured. Mala looked at the injury and realized it was a bad one; to date, his skull is dented. She attended to his injury, and tried to staunch the blood flow. She wasn't thinking, only responding.

She heard the attackers approaching. The metal gate didn't bolt from inside. Safdar turned to Mala.

'*Main darwaza andar se pakadta hun. Tum ladkiyon ko le ke peechhe se bhago.* (I'll hold the gate from the inside. You take the girls and escape from the back.)'

Mala, Prachee, and Shikha jumped over the wall. The others followed. From there, people split up and ran in different directions. Lalit joined Mala, Prachee, and Shikha. Mala remembers the houses being low – mostly single-storied. The walls were low, and there were many empty plots between houses. They cut across one empty plot and tried a house. Nobody opened the door. Mala tried two more houses. No response. She saw another house, where the door looked open. She pushed it open, they all entered, and Mala bolted the door from inside.

A woman with a little child was sitting there. Another room was locked. There was a kitchen to the left and a toilet to the right, but to get to either, you had to come out of the room.

Mala turned to the woman. 'We are being pursued by goons. Please open this other room and lock us inside. We won't make a noise.'

The woman complied. The locked room, it turned out, was rented to a tenant, who had gone to his village. It was bare. No furniture, just a mattress on the floor.

Locked in the room, the four of them tried to figure out what was happening outside. It was hard. They could hear noises, incoherent shouts.

Half an hour later, they heard a gunshot. The room had a skylight, which the women helped Lalit climb up to, to see. It was no use. The skylight had a cement grill with tiny openings. He could see nothing. At some point, they realized a man had arrived, maybe the woman's husband.

Then they heard noises outside, close by. Some men, maybe half a dozen or so, were walking up and down, asking for the women in black kurtas. Two of the actors were wearing sweaters under their kurta. They took them off and put them on over the kurtas in a futile attempt at camouflage.

The woman came into their room and said she wasn't going to let them go. Mala said they weren't planning to either.

The four of them sat quietly for the most part. An hour and a half after the first gunshot, they thought they heard another. But this came from farther away, so they couldn't be sure. For long periods in between, they heard nothing.

The woman came in.

'One of your men has been killed.'

'What was he wearing,' asked Mala, trying to find out if it was a black kurta.

'A sweater.'

At some point, they heard the sound of a scooter. It was Riyaz's. Mala stepped out three hours or so later, and went into the toilet. She looked out through the chinks in the window. She saw Riyaz go by, as well as Diwakar, but they didn't seem to be together.

Things became quiet again. There was still tension in the air. Mala didn't feel fear, but she felt the anxiety of the others. They didn't know where they were, how long they were going to be there, or what was going to happen. Mala said they'd leave only after dark, when they'd be less conspicuous.

The actors wanted to use the bathroom. The woman got them a bucket. Then she gave them a little something to eat, maybe chickpeas.

It must have been about five in the afternoon when Ved arrived, because Mala remembers it wasn't yet dark. By now, things had quietened down. The goons had left, there was no longer menace in the air. Mala heard Ved outside, talking loudly – on purpose, so if anyone was hiding, they'd hear him. They came out, and Ved immediately took them to the car.

As they drove to Delhi, Mala asked Ved about each person. Most of them had been located.

'What about Brijender,' Mala asked.

'He's not been located.'

'And Safdar?'

'We'll talk about it when we get to Delhi.'

Mala didn't push him but realized that Safdar was probably injured. At that point, she was more concerned about Brijender.

Mala saw many people when she arrived at Irwin Hospital. Safdar's mother, Ammaji, was there, as was her mother, Aparnadi, and some comrades. She saw Safdar on the stretcher, and was told he was being taken to RML Hospital for the scan. Brijesh was with him. She realized that his injuries were serious.

I asked her what her thoughts were when she saw him then.

'There was suspension of thought. I just saw.'

At RML, Safdar was first taken to the Emergency unit. Many people were there already, among whom Mala remembers theatre director Bansi Kaul, who gave his shawl to cover Safdar. She also remembers science activist Prabir Purkayastha, who was trying to push the hospital to do the scan soon.

After the scan, Safdar was taken to the ICU. One of Brijesh's doctor friends, Kantoor, who also knew Mala and Safdar, worked at RML. Kantoor and Brijesh told Mala that Safdar's brain stem was broken, that his condition was serious, but that they were watching. There was nothing else to do but wait. At some point, she found out that Brijender was safe. A comrade from Ghaziabad came to the hospital and met her. He told her about the killing of Ram Bahadur. She told him that CITU must organize a public meeting in Jhandapur, soon. Maybe in a week's time. And Janam will perform, she said.

Mala spent the night in the hospital, in some kind of an office, with Ammaji, Aparnadi, Pushi (Safdar's brother-in-law and comrade), Brijesh, and Kantoor. There was probably one more person, but she can't remember who. They spread out sheets on the floor and tried to sleep.

JANUARY 2, 1989. Safdar's Death

I was back at the hospital in the morning. Soon enough, the crowd had swelled to well beyond what was there the previous evening.

The news of the attack had made it to the front pages of many newspapers. By now we knew that the attackers had been led by Mukesh Sharma, a Congress leader in Sahibabad, and a goon. The Congress party was in power at the Centre, Rajiv Gandhi was prime minister, and the chief minister of Uttar Pradesh, where Jhandapur is located, was Narain Dutt Tiwari, another Congressman. Thus, when Buta Singh, the union home minister, visited the hospital that day, he was confronted by a furious crowd, which didn't let him visit the ICU and see Safdar. So, he met the doctors, and apparently said that the government would pay for whatever treatment Safdar required, including brain surgery.

Whether it was before or after this, I'm not sure, but looking at newspaper reports now, I see that about three hundred artists and intellectuals held a demonstration at the residence of Buta Singh. The delegation that met him, the papers report, included noted artists such as Bhisham Sahni, Habib Tanvir, Nemichandra Jain, Reotisharan Sharma, M.K. Raina, Bansi Kaul, Manohar Singh, and Sudhish Pachauri. The enraged theatre community had decided to boycott the Sahitya Kala Parishad's theatre festival that was to commence on that day, and Buta Singh directed Delhi's Chief Executive Councillor Jag Pravesh Chandra (Delhi didn't yet have a chief minister) to cancel it. Following long-established ritual, the Home Minister assured the delegation that a high-powered enquiry would be conducted into the causes of the attack. That was the last anybody heard of it.

From there, the protesting artists marched to Rabindra Bhavan, about a kilometre and a half away, and in an impromptu meeting, decided to observe January 9 as a protest day all over the country.

Later that afternoon, the press conference that Safdar had called for took place. The room was packed with journalists, activists and artists. I struggled to find place to even stand. The people who addressed it included theatre artists Govind Deshpande, M.K. Raina, and Habib Tanvir. From among the Janam actors, Brijender spoke and described what had happened to him.

Govind Deshpande (or GPD, as he was called; my father) spoke about how the Congress had degenerated even further from the Emergency days. 'Now they don't put people in jail or black out news. They simply kill. This is the worst form of censorship.' He spoke about the incredible talent that Safdar was, and about his political commitment.

M.K. Raina couldn't contain his fury. 'We have walked together in processions because of Safdar Hashmi. Because he was a pivotal force in binding artists together. For 13 years, I have seen his plays.

These are plays which are relevant, which question all the time the status quo. Communal harmony, national integration. What more do you want from a citizen? That this kind of a poet, artist, intellectual, painter, writer – the kind of work he's done, the potential – can be hit by a goon, and he is to be dead? Just outside Delhi? Only 14 kilometres distance from here? If it happens to Safdar Hashmi, what is left in this country?' I remember his blazing eyes.

Habib Tanvir was not given to shouting. Not for the most part, anyway. But his words that day were burning embers. 'And, if it is so, if this is the situation, one would like to say, arm the whole people. Then we will defend ourselves. Because a hundred goondas against one unarmed man, or a band of artists, performers – they cannot possibly cope with this. It should be then – let's all be given weapons. We perform; we have our own guns. We kill; or we get killed. Otherwise, we must put an end to this.'

One only read about press conferences in the newspapers those days, so I had no idea what a real one looked like. This was my first, and I was surprised by how trenchant and angry the speakers were. Illogically, it seemed to me that they were breaching some protocol. Yet, it seemed to mirror what I was feeling but was unable to express.

We went back to the hospital after the press conference. Even late on that winter evening, there were many people there, and fresh faces kept turning up. I sat in a corner with Jogi, Brijender, and a couple other Janam friends. Many people sought out Brijender in particular. The poor guy had to recount his ordeal many times. I was thankful for being left alone. Once in a way, I'd see Brijesh emerge from the ICU and speak to Mala and Sohail, Safdar's brother, who arrived late that evening from Trivandrum.

Later that night, at maybe around 10.30, Brijesh emerged one last time from the ICU. Safdar was dead.

For a few minutes, there was silence. Then someone raised a slogan: 'Comrade Safdar *amar rahe*! (Long live Comrade Safdar!)' There was muted response to this. Then another: '*Khoon ka badla khoon se lenge!* (We shall avenge blood with blood!)' Mala shot him a sharp look and raised her hand in admonition. The man withered and slunk away.

I sat numb, staring at nothing.

After a while, Mala came to us. 'Go get some sleep. Come to the Party office tomorrow morning.'

Brijender had gone home earlier in the evening. Lalit, Jogi, and I went to the DYFI office. None of us spoke. Lalit smoked incessantly. We sat, the three of us, staring into nothingness. Then Lalit got up, spat out a couple of abuses, and left. Jogi and I got under the one quilt we could find. I slept like a log.

JANUARY 2, 1989. Mala

Early in the morning on January 2, Mala went home. She was back at the hospital by nine. She knew Safdar was not going to survive. This was confirmed by the senior doctor, probably the head of neurology, who spoke to her. She remembers him being a calm and balanced person. He said the chances of survival were extremely slim, but they were trying to do everything they could. Given the nature and extent of the injuries, surgery was ruled out. If the family wanted to employ any other treatment, he said, he would cooperate fully. Mala said no.

Through the day, a large number of people came to the hospital, some of whom met Mala. She remembers Buta Singh being driven away. She also remembers that many Doordarshan employees visited the hospital. Safdar had befriended them when he had worked on a number of short documentaries a few years ago. Artists kept streaming in. She remembers Bhisham Sahni, as well as Ebrahim Alkazi, who came in the evening. Sohail arrived from Trivandrum late in the evening, with CPI (M) Delhi Secretary Jogendra Sharma.

The day was spent waiting. Shabnam and Shehla, Safdar's sisters, arranged for food. At one point, Ammaji and Mala were allowed inside the ICU, and they saw Safdar from a distance. He was on a ventilator.

The previous day, since Janam was to do three performances spread through the day, Mala was carrying the manuscript of a school textbook she was writing, hoping to find some time between the shows to work on it. Now she wondered if she'd ever get it back. She did, later that day, when she went to the Party office.

After Safdar was pronounced dead, Mala waited for the eye donation procedure to be completed before going home. She had wanted the organs donated and the body given for medical research, but there were legal hurdles.

The post-mortem report noted what we saw when we carried him to the hospital, that there was bleeding from his ears, nose, and throat. It said that he had sustained 'deep lacerated wounds' on the scalp and forehead. He had been 'beaten on the head at least 20 times with iron rods'.

JANUARY 3, 1989. The Funeral Procession

A large crowd had started building up even before Safdar's body arrived at the Party office in V.P. House that morning. By the time it was kept in a pandal, draped in a red flag, for people to pay their respects, the crowd had swelled to a few thousand.

On the soundtrack of my memory, I can hear only two things from that morning. Slogans, and wailing. Both rent the air, piercing the sky. I was one of the Red Volunteers that day. Standing vigil next to the body, wearing an ill-fitting red shirt I had been given at the Party office, looking at hundreds of people file past. Many opposition leaders, including V.P. Singh, who was to become prime minister later that year, came to pay their respects. The only parties that were unrepresented were the Congress and the BJP.

The Congress denied that the attackers had anything to do with them.

A line of volunteers, the men wearing red shirts and the women wearing white sarees with red borders, carrying red flags at half mast, led the funeral procession. The tempo carrying Safdar's body followed. Sohail, M.K. Raina, Bhisham Sahni, Mala, her father, and

Ammaji were on the tempo. Also on the tempo were Prakash Karat, Jogendra Sharma and P.M.S. ('Pushi') Grewal, the former, present, and future secretaries of the Delhi state CPI (M), respectively. Janam actors, including me, walked behind the tempo, carrying the Janam banner. Behind us was a sea of humanity.

There were at least 15,000 people in the procession that day. I had no idea who most of them were. Many came after reading the news, which was prominent on the front pages of all Hindi and English national dailies. Already on that day, through my state of shock and grief, I had begun to comprehend that Safdar's killing had touched a raw nerve in the country. It had become a cause larger than Janam, larger than Safdar, larger than the Left. It seemed to me to crystallize the feeling of dissatisfaction and anger that was to sweep aside the Congress in the upcoming elections.

The procession started from V.P. House on Rafi Marg, went up Sansad Marg to Connaught Place, going around the circle to exit on Barakhamba Road, went past Mandi House to ITO and all the newspaper offices on Bahadur Shah Zafar Marg, turned right at Ferozeshah Kotla, went past Gandhi Samadhi at Rajghat and up the Ring Road till it came to the electric crematorium at Nigambodh Ghat.

As we were walking on Bahadur Shah Road, I felt a hand on my shoulder. I looked back. It was a stranger. He looked like a bank clerk or someone who worked at one of the newspaper offices.

'Excuse me, can I ask you something?'

'Yes.'

'Were you at the Central Park in Connaught Place about a month ago, one afternoon, singing songs?'

'Yes.'

'So he was the one singing that day?' the stranger asked, pointing to the tempo.

'Yes.'

'I was there too. I didn't know who you people were. But Hashmi saheb's personality stayed with me. I told many people about him. I've never heard anyone sing Ghalib like he did. He was a good man.

Please don't give up your work. We are with you. I just wanted to pay my respects.'

And the man melted away in the crowd.

After Safdar's body was consigned to the electric furnace, Mala came to where a bunch of Janam actors were standing.

'There is a proposal that we should perform *Halla Bol* tomorrow at Jhandapur. What do you people think?'

I guess we just nodded.

'OK, so then let's meet tomorrow morning for rehearsal.'

I went home that night. As I took off my clothes, I realized that my sweater and jacket had Safdar's blood stains on them. I had my first bath in three days that night. Then I got into bed and cried.

JANUARY 4, 1989. The Performance

Less than 48 hours after Safdar's death, we performed the interrupted play at Jhandapur, at the same spot. It remains, to my mind, perhaps the single most important performance of a street play in Indian history.

We gathered at 6 Talkatora Road, where CITU had its central office; we used to rehearse our street play on its lawns. The same cast that had been in the interrupted performance was to perform again. With one change. Vinod had a job interview that day. Since I knew his lines and moves, I was to be his replacement. I had been in Jhandapur on January 1, quite by chance. Now I was to perform, again by chance.

We did a quick line rehearsal. It was all business-like. I was told I was to speak before the performance.

We got into a hired bus. When we reached Mandi House, I realized there were many more buses carrying people to Jhandapur. I counted 15; maybe there were more. Each bus was jam packed, without even any standing space. Hundreds of workers had gathered in Jhandapur. More than 5,000 people crammed the narrow streets. Many of them were artists, writers, activists, professionals. There were so many familiar faces, but much of it was a blur for me.

The one person who wasn't there, though, was Sohail. I learnt, decades later, that the reason was that he had been asked to stay back in the Party office, to take the many calls they expected to receive from journalists. Someone senior and responsible was needed to take those – no mobile phones then, after all. It was a horrible miscalculation. All the journalists were at the site of the performance, and Sohail had to answer a total of zero calls.

We first went around the basti in a silent procession. We went past Ram Bahadur's house, paying our respects to him. He had been married a year or so before, and had just had a child about a couple of months earlier. I later learnt that Mala spent some time with his young wife Pavitra and their infant, consoling and giving strength.

Parcham, the song squad led by Safdar's old friend Kajal Ghosh, sang two songs.

Tu zinda hai, tu zindagi ki jeet mein yaqeen kar
Agar kahin hai swarg to utar la zamin par
You are alive, so trust in the triumph of life
If there's a heaven somewhere, then bring it to earth

and

Laal jhanda lekar, comrade, aage badhte jayenge
Tum nahin rahe, iska gham hai par, phir bhi ladte jayenge
Onwards we march, comrade, holding the red flag
We mourn your loss, but pledge to fight on

I had no idea then that '*Laal Jhanda*' had been translated from Bangla to Hindi by Safdar.

When they sang '*Hazaar bhes bhar ke aayi maut tere dwar par / Magar tujhe na chhal saki, chali gayi voh haar kar*' ('Death came to your door in a hundred guises / It could not deceive you, and retreated, defeated'), I choked.

There were people everywhere, in every nook and cranny, on

rooftops, and even on the garbage dump. I had never seen such an audience before. Many carried hastily made placards that said 'Safdar lives' and 'Safdar died, but not in vain'. There were red flags everywhere.

My mind was blank when I rose to speak. And then, I don't how or from where, the words came.

'We are here to perform our interrupted play. We are here to fulfil our commitment to our audience. We are here to say that they can kill us, but they can't stop us. We are here to honour Comrade Ram Bahadur. We are here because Comrade Safdar Hashmi is not dead. He lives here, among us, and he lives among countless young women and men all over the country.'

The play began sombrely. The actors seemed to merely go through the motions. The first few minutes of the play are humorous, requiring us to laugh as well. But everybody was grim. There's a moment when, in response to the cop character trying to stop the play, the actors go into a huddle to decide what to do next. As we went into the huddle, I was right opposite Mala. She looked at everyone sharply.

'What's wrong with you all? Come on, laugh!'

As we broke the huddle, she twirled back, laughing.

It was as if we'd been given a glucose shot. The play came to life, and in seconds, the audience was in splits too.

That performance, and photos of Mala performing, were on the front pages of newspapers all over the country the next day. In that simple act, of leading us in a performance at the spot where her comrade and friend, the love of her life, had been felled, she, more than anyone else, captured that incandescent moment. In the coming days, there were protest demonstrations all over the country, in small towns and large. Mala travelled to Bombay, Tripura, and Kerala, and addressed large gatherings. In late January, she went to Calcutta, where we joined her a couple of days later to perform *Halla Bol*. At the first performance at Calcutta University, where Safdar was conferred a posthumous honorary doctorate, we were mobbed by students. It's the only time I've signed autograph books.

That tour culminated with a performance at the basketball court of Salt Lake Stadium, where some 25,000 people came to express solidarity. Poems, songs, and plays were written about Safdar and Mala, artists made paintings and posters, intellectuals and activists gave speeches. Within a few days of the performance on January 4, the Safdar Hashmi Memorial Committee came into being. It was the first step towards the formation of the Safdar Hashmi Memorial Trust (Sahmat), which has played a stellar role in mobilizing artists and intellectuals against communalism and the rise of the Hindu Right.

From Satyajit Ray to Ravi Shankar, from Adoor Gopalakrishnan to Utpal Dutt, from Krishna Sobti to Rajendra Yadav, the list of artists, big and small, known and unknown, who came out in public displays of solidarity and support, was virtually endless. In a stirring gesture, on January 8, Shabana Azmi used the stage of the International Film Festival of India being held in Delhi to read out a protest note on Safdar's killing. Outside, on the overcast, breezy winter day, Dilip Kumar stood in protest with Safdar's photograph. The following day saw coordinated protests all over the country. Later, on April 12, Safdar's birthday, which was celebrated spontaneously as National Street Theatre Day, over 30,000 street play performances took place.

Rajendra Prasad ('Rajen'), who's been the chief organizer in Sahmat since its formation, told me years later that in his opinion Sahmat wouldn't even have come into being but for Mala's action that day.

It is true. Mala was the picture of quiet defiance that day. I remember her eyes – determined, without a trace of the grief that ravaged her soul. Her slender body seemed to have a spine made of steel. She stood erect, ramrod straight. Her slight frame seemed incredibly tall.

And that voice.

Clear, resonant, ringing, sailing over the audience, and into their hearts.

SUMMER 1987. My First Time with Janam

I had just finished my second-year college exams and had the whole summer in front of me. I didn't think I'd do anything but watch international art house movies at Shakuntalam theatre and the various cultural centres in the city, with my friend Sanjay Maharishi.

One afternoon, the phone rang. It was Safdar.

'We have some shows coming up and are a couple of actors short. Can you come?'

I had seen many Janam performances, both in JNU, where I lived, and in Delhi University, where I studied. My sister Ashwini, who was an SFI activist and a singer, was also part of Parcham, and my mother, Kalindi, a Communist and feminist, was an activist of the All India Democratic Women's Association (AIDWA). Safdar had helped my mother when she had organized a women's theatre group, Buland, to do street plays for AIDWA. I had known Safdar for about four–five years before I worked with him, regularly bumping into him and Mala at various film screenings and play performances.

'Which play is it?' I was hoping he'd say *Raja Ka Baja* ('The King's Band'), Janam's play on the education system, which had a delicious role, of the protagonist Rameshwar Dayal, which I'd been eyeing. It was performed, even then, by Subhash Tyagi, who was well into his forties by now.

'*Samrath Ko Nahi Dosh Gosain* ('Blame Not the Powerful'). It's a small role, you'll pick it up in one rehearsal.'

I knew the play. It was on price rise and corruption in the Public Distribution System.

Small role, I thought. Ah OK, the cop. Yes, Safdar was right, I could learn the lines and the moves in one rehearsal, no problem.

Safdar had seen me perform in the plays we JNU kids did on campus, as well as plays I'd done in Ramjas College, where I studied. He had asked me more than once to join Janam over the years. I would always say, yes, soon.

'You keep saying you'll join. When are you going to carry out your threat?' he'd joke.

'Soon, Safdar, one day very soon.'

'Your "one day" is like the revolution. It is always round the corner.'

When I turned up for rehearsal that evening, Safdar gave me a piece of paper.

'Come, let's rehearse the song you've to sing.'

'What? Sing? Me? Why? The cop doesn't have a song.'

'Who said cop? You've to do the Bora.'

The play has a street magician, the Madari, who goes around showing tricks to the audience with his assistant, the Jamura. Since the people are hungry, they decide to produce a sack of grain (Bora) as part of their magic. The Bora sings a song explaining how the labour of the peasant brought him into being, but how the Lala (trader) subsequently imprisoned him. Now that he is free, the Bora says, he will be with the people. Normally, Manish Manocha would do the Madari, Subhash Tyagi the Jamura, and Safdar, who sang well, would do the Bora. Manish and Tyagi, though, were not available to perform on the same day for these shows. Safdar would do Manish's role when he wasn't available, and shift to Tyagi's when he wasn't. So, they needed an actor to do the Bora. An actor who could sing.

Mala, who taught at Sardar Patel Vidyalaya, the school I had studied in, had seen me sing as part of the school choir. And Safdar knew Ashwini sang well. So he assumed I could too. He was wrong. Very wrong.

'But I can't sing, Safdar!'

'Oh come on, don't be shy. Come, sing after me.'

I did.

'Ah, OK. Very good. But let's try again. See, this is the note.'

I sang again. And again. And again. Not once did I seem to catch the right note.

'No problem. Let's do the lines and the actions. Then later we can go to Kajal's. He'll identify your scale. You'll be OK when you practise it with the harmonium.'

We did. Kajal tried this and he tried that. But he could not make me pick up the song on the same note twice running. We were to perform the next day.

Safdar said, 'OK, no problem. See, you just pick up the first line of the song. I'll join you from outside. And on days that I'm doing Jamura, Manish can join as well. He sings well too.'

Our first performance was near a temple. Within ten minutes of the play beginning, the temple bells started ringing. Tyagi and Safdar, both seasoned street theatre actors with great throw in their voices, just about managed to make themselves heard above the cacophony of the temple bells.

Just before my entry, Safdar signalled to me to take it easy. I'll join you, he gestured.

But I was about to do my first street performance. I fancied myself as an actor. How could I let some silly temple bells spoil my debut? So I entered, adrenaline raging through my body, and started the song on a heroically high note.

Safdar winced, signalling me to come down a scale or two. As if I knew how to! I kept looking at him, wondering why he wasn't joining me. He was to take over, wasn't he?

Then it happened. My voice cracked. I strained more. It cracked more. Safdar held his head in his hands. He never joined me. I was left all alone, trying desperately to strain my voice beyond what it was capable of. By the end, I was reduced to whispering hoarsely.

My street theatre debut was an unmitigated disaster.

SUMMER 1987. Faridabad

The shows of *Samrath* were for the election campaign of Comrade Mohan Lal, who was contesting for the Haryana state assembly on a CPI (M) ticket. As a kid, he had performed in a local nautanki company. Originally from Mirzapur, UP, he got a job in the weaving department of the Modinagar textile mill. He was radicalized into Communist politics during the 1967 agitation and firing on workers, and was dismissed from work. He went away to Kanpur for a short time, and finally got a job in Bengal Suiting in Faridabad in 1969. He became a trade union wholetimer in 1984. He was a lovely man, kind and generous, and we would often call him to Janam to speak to us about the challenges and issues facing the workers. His insights and experiences were crucial to the making of many of our plays. Years later, when we opened Studio Safdar, our own space in Shadipur, New Delhi, on April 12, 2012, we requested him to inaugurate it. He was frail and ill, in the last stages of cancer, but he accepted.

'How can I say no to Comrade Safdar?'

The shows themselves went well, though Comrade Mohan Lal lost. I was new to politics, and couldn't understand how the best candidate, honest and upright, a fighter for the poorest, with the best programme, could lose. Honestly, I still don't fully understand. I've just stopped being surprised.

I had gone with Safdar from V.P. House for the first performance. I realized over the next few days that I could just as well take the bus to Faridabad from Ashram Chowk, but I didn't, because I'd look forward to long conversations with him on the journey. You could chat with Safdar about all kinds of things.

One day, I don't know how, the conversation drifted towards the Russian Revolution. We had a paper on the history of the Soviet Union in our second year, and I had read voraciously for that. From Alec Nove to Maurice Dobb, from Trotsky to Lenin, from Mayakovsky to Blok, I had read them all. I was surprised to find, therefore, that not only had Safdar read a lot of what I had, but that he could recall it as well. Our argument on the collectivization of agriculture in the 1929–33 period ended not with me vanquishing his line, as I expected, but on an even keel. Or perhaps he had the upper hand, but I was too proud to admit it. Another time, we got chatting about modern Indian playwrights, and he offered one of the most incisive analysis of Vijay Tendulkar's work I'd heard. Another time, he did a comparative analysis of the work of Satyajit Ray (which I knew something of) and Ritwik Ghatak (about which I knew nothing).

He loved to talk, and in me, he had an eager listener. But I didn't get the feeling that he was showing off, nor was he ever patronizing. He genuinely wanted to know my opinions on things, and was always curious about what I was reading. I urged him to read the Latin American magical realists, Garcia Marquez, Vargas Llossa, and the rest, of whom he had read hardly anyone.

And it wasn't all heavy stuff either. He'd recount the most banal incident that he'd seen or been part of, with the liveliest turns of phrase, facial expressions, and gestures. He was always observing people, trying to figure out why they were doing what they were doing. We soon developed a little game where we'd look at a person on the bus and construct an entire back story for them.

It would be six of us in *Samrath*: Safdar; Manish or Tyagi; Arun Sharma (an underrated actor who played the Lala delightfully); Lalit (the politician); Jitender Dagar (the cop); and I. At 19, I was the youngest. Safdar was nearly 14 years older; Tyagi was 12 years older than him, so a quarter century older than me; Manish and Arun were about the same age as Safdar; Lalit was about five years older than me; and Jitender must've been about Lalit's age, or a couple of years older. But more than age, I guess it was class and upbringing that prevented me from connecting with any of the others. I was a middle-class kid, I read English books, and I had pretensions of being an intellectual. I found it hard to have a conversation with anyone except Safdar.

One day, Safdar said he'd be staying back in Faridabad after the performances. He had to help put up campaign stuff. He was somewhat surprised when I asked if I could stay back too, but agreed readily. Vijay Kalia accompanied us that day to help with the work. I'd seen him act in some Janam plays but didn't know him personally.

We started by sticking posters. Kalia and Safdar, along with some comrades, would spread out along a wall, in teams of two. One person applied the glue, the other stuck the poster on the wall. I was also assigned to a working-class comrade. He applied the glue, and I stuck the poster. But I would either stick it crooked, or folds or bubbles would appear. So the comrade took over, and asked me to apply the glue. I either applied too much or too little, and never evenly in any case. I would also often leave parts of the poster unglued. To his credit, the comrade I was with was always encouraging, giving me little tips, and I think I improved a bit over the couple of hours that we did it. Even so, it was a relief when the task finished.

After this, it was time to do wall-writing. The working-class comrades looked at us to do most of the writing, helping mostly to carry the paint and brushes, and preparing the wall by giving it a coat of white. Despite having the text written up on a piece of paper in front of me, I made mistakes. I blamed it on the brush, which I was finding hard to handle. In the time it took me to do one wall, Safdar would finish two, and his would inevitably look much better than mine.

Around four in the morning, we shifted to the last task, which was to put up three–four hoardings at strategic points around a basti. I say hoardings, but they were more like signboards, about four feet by three feet. They were handpainted on a tin sheet that was mounted on a wooden frame. The signboard had to be affixed with long nails to two wooden poles, and then two holes had to be dug into the ground, about a couple of feet deep each, into which the poles had to be inserted. Then the holes had to be packed with stones and soil to make it all stand firm. Safdar asked the rest of the comrades to leave, since it was nearly morning and they had a working day ahead. Only one comrade stayed back with us.

By now I knew that nothing was as easy as it seems when a skilled person does it, but digging a hole seemed pretty easy when the comrade and Kalia did it.

I looked at Safdar. 'Why aren't you doing it?'

He smiled. 'You try.'

I did. And realized that handling a sledgehammer effectively is no less a skill than anything else I had done that night. If I used full force, I'd either get the aim slightly off, or the thick, iron rod with a pointed end (a gigantic nail, really) would go in at an angle, not straight. Safdar laughed.

When we finished, we found a roadside tea seller. A cycle rickshaw wallah was also there. Safdar started chatting with him, as we waited for the tea to be ready. Then he turned to me.

'Mala told me you used to bicycle to school. Is that true? All the way from JNU?'

'Yes.' Finally there was something I could be proud of.

'Ever ridden a cycle rickshaw?'

'No.'

'Want to try?'

'Yes, of course!'

After asking the rickshaw wallah, I mounted the vehicle and stepped on the pedal with all my body weight. The rickshaw turned left. I straightened it and tried again. No matter how many times I tried, the rickshaw kept turning left.

By the time I got back, Kalia was in splits. 'A rickshaw always runs to one side. You have to use your body weight correctly to keep it straight.'

'And this rickshaw is Communist. Keeps going left.' This was a joke from *Samrath*, and Safdar couldn't resist cracking it. Reluctantly, I had to laugh at my own ineptness.

I had noticed, though, that apart from writing, Kalia was really good at everything else we'd done that night. I mentioned this to Safdar in the bus coming back.

'Ask him how many things he's done in his life.'

I did. He had sold lottery tickets; filled matchboxes with matches; cut excess rubber from chappals; cleaned baking trays in a biscuit factory, and prepared them for the next lot of baking; assisted a carpenter; sold home-made ice cream; worked at a small provision store; and, because his father died when he was 16, and the economic condition of his family was dire, he had to quit his studies and get a compensatory job in the Indian Railways as a

Class IV employee, basically as a labourer. He was in the ninth standard when it happened. One of his teachers encouraged him to study on. Somehow he juggled a full-time job with going to school, and finally completed not only school, but also got a BCom degree from Delhi University, which enabled him to appear for the railways departmental examinations, after clearing which he became a clerk. In the meanwhile, his participation in the 1974 railway strike had not gone unnoticed, and, as punishment, he was demoted. When I spoke to him that day, he was still fighting that case in court. It was only in 1990 that he won the case, and the railways had to give him three promotions simultaneously, to compensate for promotions that would have come his way had he not been victimized.

SUMMER 1987. The State of Janam

On the day of my first performance in Faridabad, I knew I wouldn't be getting Janam's signature black kurta, because my costume was going to be a jute sack. But I did expect the others to be dressed in black kurtas and blue jeans or trousers.

'Why weren't you guys dressed in black?' I asked Safdar after the performance.

'Ah well, you know, these guys come from work. ... It's hard for them.' And he changed the subject.

But the reality was that Janam was in a state of disarray. For the past couple of years or so, it had been hard to pull together actors for performances. Some of the earlier actors in Janam had moved on to other things. Of those that remained, some were paralysed by the changed circumstances of their lives, as well as a sense of ennui. They were now in their thirties. They were all married. Many had children. Their parents were growing older. They had done this stuff for a decade or more, and were no longer as inspired as before.

It is typical at such times that personal issues start to crop up, and, over time, they become important. When they had begun as idealistic youngsters, it was a small group; everybody was equal, and there were no hierarchies. There wasn't even an organizational structure, even though the group was registered. Soon, though, as was natural, some started developing as artists as well as activists. The others didn't, for various reasons. This led to resentments.

Janam had had three truly creative writers and directors. One was Rakesh Saksena, who co-wrote some of Janam's early street plays with Safdar, including classics such as *Machine* and *Aurat*. He had a superb command over language, and he and Safdar worked well together as a team. The third was N.K. Sharma, who wasn't a writer, but had a strong visual and dramatic sense. Rakesh Saksena left the country in the early 1980s because of his job. By the time I got to see Janam first, in the mid-1980s, I heard it being referred to in the Delhi theatre circles as 'NK–Safdar's group'. NK had a passion for cinema, and he left to try his luck with filmmaking. By the time I came in, Safdar was the only creative leader in the group, writing and directing plays.

Mala also played a big role in Janam, but it was never fully acknowledged in those days. She was always a fabulous actor, and for long stretches, she was the only female actor in Janam. Organizationally as well, she played a crucial part, working on logistics, making and maintaining costumes and properties, and performing myriad other tasks that an active group requires. Most of these tasks, however, were performed out of sight, at home, and mostly at night. Besides, in her own estimation, she was first and foremost a teacher, and only secondarily a theatreperson. Safdar knew what she brought to Janam, but others neither saw nor gave it importance.

An older Janam actor from the time candidly told me, on record, when I interviewed him for this book, that they thought Safdar had become too big for his boots, since he had started working in television, and had hopes of becoming a scriptwriter in the Bombay film industry. 'He became too elite,' he said, using the English word. That it was connected to his dream of raising money for a cultural centre in a working-class neighbourhood is a different story, and one that his comrades didn't appreciate. 'We wanted to sideline him,' he told me. That never came to pass, fortunately.

I saw some of this dynamic play out when I joined Janam in the summer of 1987. There was a desultory air about the group. Another actor always made sure that I knew that they were the 'seniors'. About a year or so after Safdar's death, this entire lot left Janam. They held a press conference, in which they lamented that 'one person' was being turned into a hero, and said they were unhappy with Janam being so closely aligned with the Left movement. Their real resentment, however, was reserved for Mala, who had deservedly acquired a towering stature, even though she herself continued being the person she's always been, down-to-earth and plain-speaking. I guess it was hard for them to reconcile to being led by a woman. I was pained at what they did, and how they did it, but I was hardly surprised.

Safdar realized that Janam was dying. He had to resuscitate it.

But he also had other, grander, plans.

PART TWO

The Early Years

Safdar's parents, Haneef Hashmi (1924–1976) and Qamar Azad Hashmi (1927–2013), were married in 1948. Sabiha, their first child, was born in 1949, followed by Sohail in 1950, and Shehla in 1952. Safdar was born in 1954. The first four children were born in Delhi. Abbuji, as Safdar's father was called, shifted to Aligarh in 1952, followed by the family in the winter of 1954–55, when Safdar was about ten months old. Shabnam, the last sibling, was born there in 1957.

Abbuji was a man of many parts. A Communist by political leaning, he had dabbled in archaeology before setting up a furniture workshop in Aligarh. Qamar Azad, or Ammaji, was a school teacher. The family was not economically well-off, and lived through hard days, especially in Aligarh, where Safdar lived till he was about ten. Ammaji, a school teacher, had a quiet, understated, but deep influence on the family. Her interest in literature and the arts rubbed off on the children. Safdar's childhood was spent surrounded by books, and Ammaji, even though exhausted at the end of the day, would tell him stories. She managed to maintain a balance between respecting their space, while always being there for them. She was the lodestar that steered the family through the difficult days. But children are children. They find ways of creative exploration wherever they are. Poorer children tend to be especially enterprising in figuring out ways to amuse themselves. The Hashmi children, too, despite economic want – or perhaps because of it – had fun. Deeply attached to each other, they have hilarious anecdotes of their growing up years. Safdar – called Rajju affectionately, which Shehla still sometimes does when reminiscing about their childhood – grew up in a happy atmosphere.

Sabiha and Sohail read Urdu, and so they read Premchand, Ismat Chughtai, and other progressive writers in the original. Sohail had read *Mother* by Gorky in Urdu by the time he was in Class 4 or 5. He also read a lot of Tolstoy in translation. Abbuji would subscribe to literary magazines – *Shahrah* ('The Highway'), which was virtually a Progressive Writers' Association (PWA) magazine, though not officially; the more arty *Kitaab* ('Book'); *Shabkhoon* ('Night Attack'), which Shamsur Rahman Faruqi brought out from Allahabad; the progressive magazine *Savera* ('Morning'); and the children's magazine *Khilona* ('Toy'). Sohail doesn't remember Safdar being a bookworm in Aligarh, but certainly when the family moved back to Delhi, Safdar would be found immersed in books. By the time he was in college, he was reading stuff that none of the other siblings had read; he introduced Sohail to John Dunne ('No man is an island ...'). Through the 1970s, Safdar was reading whatever he could lay his hands on – American literature, literary criticism, whatever he could find of Brecht – and most of it was outside what was required for his college courses.

Literature, yes; cinema, no. Rather, cinema was a rarity. The family had no money. Moviegoing was a big occasion. When *Ben Hur* released in Delhi, Abbuji sent the family from Aligarh to watch it. They also watched *The Ten Commandments* in Delhi, and *Jhanak Jhanak Payal Baje* at Tasveer Mahal in Aligarh. When Sohail came back to Delhi at the age of 14, he had seen only five films in his life. Abbuji bought a radio with his first salary when he started working at the Russian news agency TASS, and his second salary went towards a record player and three LPs – one of K.L. Saigal; one of Pankaj Mullick; and the third, of Ravi Shankar's ten short pieces. Abbuji would sing Ghalib and Mir and some Persian poets as he worked, so the children picked them up.

After the family's move back to Delhi in 1964, Safdar first went to the New Delhi Municipal Corporation (NDMC) School, Sarojini Nagar; then to Dayanand Anglo-Vedic (DAV) School, Baird Road; and finally to Delhi Kannada Senior Secondary School, Lodhi Road, from where he passed his Higher Secondary in 1970. He was a bright kid, and got a double promotion, from Class 1 directly to Class 3. The NDMC school was co-educational till Class 5, after which the boys and girls had to go separate ways. When Sohail cleared Class 5, he had to change schools. Simultaneously, Shabnam had to join nursery, and since there was a nursery in DAV, she was sent there. Now Safdar was left alone in the old school, so he was also shifted to DAV, so all three children could go in the same rickshaw and save money. A few days after Safdar joined, some of his new friends in Class 3 were given a promotion to Class 4. Safdar went to the Principal and demanded a promotion too, which he was given. As a result, Sohail, who was four years older than Safdar, was now only two years senior to him in school. And then, when he reached Class 10, Sohail failed because he had spent time organizing a strike in the school rather than studying, so he was now only one year senior. It was almost like in Premchand's delightful short story, *Bade Bhai Sahab* ('The Elder Brother'), where the hardworking and studious elder brother keeps failing, and the younger brother, despite loafing about, keeps passing, till, originally five years apart, they end up in the same class.

Sohail joined Kirori Mal College in 1969. Safdar followed in 1970. Abbuji and Sohail both wanted him to go to Hindu College, but he ended up joining English Honours at the elite St Stephen's. Though he read English, he didn't speak the language well at this time, and he was only accepted in St Stephen's because someone on the interview committee – he wore a kurta-pyjama for the interview – recognized that the boy was intelligent, and permitted him to speak in Hindi. He did, and impressed the committee with his mind. They figured he'd learn to speak English soon enough, as indeed did happen. But he hated the college, its elite, English-speaking atmosphere, and couldn't even eat in the canteen because he couldn't afford anything on the menu there, even though it was subsidized. And oh, St Stephen's was the only college in Delhi University where you referred to the canteen as a café.

Sohail had become politicized by now and was an activist of the SFI. In my interviews with them, both Madan Gopal Singh and M.K. Raina remembered Safdar from this time as a good looking, tall, slim boy, shy, and quiet, but well read. 'Sohail was very proud of his younger brother,' Raina said. Even as Safdar was getting politicized, he was attracted to a group of Naxalite students in St Stephen's. More than anything else, what made him gravitate towards them was that they too had no money to buy anything in the canteen. Sohail was angry and ticked him off. Safdar argued back, and the brothers didn't speak to each other. The infatuation wore off in maybe ten days, and Safdar was back with the SFI.

Nearly a decade later, Safdar was to write to Prabhat Upreti, who had become his closest friend in Srinagar, Garhwal: 'I have no desire to pick up a stengun and kill a few bastards. I pity people who think or act like this. I feel like explaining things to them, to open their eyes. ... They've erected barricades of fake bravery and glory on the path of the revolution. If you seek inspiration from them, you'll be destroyed.'

This, and all his letters to Upreti, were in Hindi. Neither Abbuji nor Ammaji spoke English with any degree of facility. Both spoke beautiful Hindustani. Abbuji, in particular, had the gift of understated humour. Once, a friend of Safdar's happened to be travelling in the same Delhi Transport Corporation (DTC) bus as Abbuji. The bus was horribly crowded. The young man and Abbuji chatted a bit, after which Abbuji had to get off.

'*Agar aap ijaazat dein to mein chalun?* (May I get off, with your permission?),' Abbuji said.

Flustered with this extreme politeness, the friend mumbled a goodbye. But Abbuji wouldn't move.

'*Aapke saath aapke pair ki ijaazat bhi chahiye* (Along with yours, I also need your foot's permission).'

It turned out that the young man was standing on Abbuji's foot all the while.

EARLY 1970S. Delhi University

What was the university like, when Safdar joined St Stephen's?

In the mid-1960s, Delhi University looked markedly different from what it does now. Where now the Students' Union office building stands, close to the Arts and Law faculties, there stood a row of barracks. Wenger's, the bakery and confectionaries shop which still runs in Connaught Place, ran a restaurant out of those barracks. You could get a pot of tea, serving four cups, for 84 paise. If you were generous, you added a 16 paise tip, taking the price of tea per cup for a group of four to 25 paise. Citing inflation, Wenger's decided to increase the price of a pot of tea to nearly double.

The 1950s had been a period of relatively low inflation in India, thanks to the Five-Year Plans. Inflation started to creep up in the early 1960s, and between June 1963 and June 1964, the prices of food articles rose by 13.4 per cent. In August 1964, the socialist leader Ram Manohar Lohia proposed to the Jan Sangh (the erstwhile avatar of the current BJP), and the left and right factions of the Communist Party to initiate what came to be called the Price Rise Resistance Movement (PRRM). The Jan Sangh was sceptical, as was the right faction of the Communist Party, but the left faction joined enthusiastically. The main site of the struggle was the Indian Coffee House in Connaught Place, outside which protesters set up a makeshift stall to serve cheap coffee. The boycott of ICH proved spectacularly successful, drawing support from writers, journalists, politicians, artists, and ordinary citizens, and after about two months, the ICH was forced to revert to its pre-agitation rates. The agitation had an effect on other items as well, and succeeded in lowering prices for all consumers, not just coffee addicts.

When Wenger's decided to increase its prices in 1966, a group of students, inspired by the success of PRRM, wrote in protest to C.D. Deshmukh, Vice Chancellor of Delhi University. Deshmukh knew a thing of two about economics – he had been the first Indian appointed as Governor of the Reserve Bank under the British, and went on to become the finance minister of India under Nehru, from 1950 to 1956. He probably didn't want an agitation on campus, for which he knew there would be popular support in the city. He invited five students to meet him. One of them was Rajendra Prasad ('Rajen'), who was then pursuing a PhD in philosophy. Deshmukh asked the students what they wanted. They proposed running a cooperative canteen on campus. He agreed, and appointed a teacher as their advisor. Rajen and his comrades started the cooperative canteen, where they served a full meal for one or two rupees. Hundreds of students would come to have that meal, and the cooperative canteen became a centre of student organizing.

The All India Students' Federation (AISF), the student front of the Communist Party of India (CPI), didn't have much of a presence on campus then. The opposition (to the Congress, that is) space was dominated by socialist groups, of which the Samajwadi Yuvjan Sabha (SYS) was the most prominent. The CPI split in 1964, resulting in the birth of the CPI (M), but it wasn't until 1970–71 that the mass fronts of the party split. As Rajen tells it, the three individuals who built the CPI (M) on campus in the late 1960s were all teachers – Kumaresh Chakravarty, Zahoor Siddiqui (both former presidents of the Delhi University Teachers' Association), and Kitty Menon.

Kumaresh Chakravarty, in particular, played a stellar role in democratizing the university. In August 1967, he led a revolt of teachers during the general body meeting of the Delhi University Teachers' Association (DUTA). Till that point, DUTA was a pocket body of a handful of powerful administrators and principals, who got their cronies elected year after year. Sensing the mood of the teachers, who were galvanized by Chakravarty's fiery speeches, the authorities agreed to hold an open election. The democratic group won a resounding victory, with Chakravarty getting elected to the executive. In 1971, he was elected president of DUTA, defeating the Jan Sangh-backed candidate. Under his leadership,

DUTA made common cause with the karmacharis, championing their demands, as well as with the school teachers' agitation in neighbouring Haryana. Among other important democratic victories of the teachers' movement was the ending of the tenure system for department heads; instead, a rotational system ensured that every department head held the post for a limited period. The teachers' movement also got the central government to withdraw a bill in Parliament that would have replaced teachers' unions with 'college councils'. Till these struggles took place, English-speaking professors and principals from elite backgrounds dominated the university. Now, a number of teachers from humbler backgrounds became leaders of DUTA. It has always been a bit of an anomaly that in a city politically dominated by the Congress and Jan Sangh/BJP, and lately the Aam Aadmi Party, the largest university has always had a sizeable Left teachers' movement.

The SFI came up around 1970, but even before that, Left students organized artistic activity. One such was a production of Bertolt Brecht's play, *The Exception and the Rule*. At a time when Camus, Sartre, and existentialism were the rage, Rajen came across a book that contained this Marxist play, which impressed him deeply. He asked Mansur Saeed to translate it. Mansur bhai, as he was called, was Safdar and Sohail's cousin, who later migrated to Pakistan and set up the theatre group Dastak in Karachi. His daughter Sania is a celebrated actress there. The cast for the play included the future filmmaker Ketan Mehta. They also organized an exhibition on Brecht in the Hindu College foyer. Rajen played an important role in getting Sohail into the SFI. He also got the artist Vivan Sundaram's pencil sketches on Pablo Neruda's masterpiece, *The Heights of Macchu Picchu*, for exhibiting at Kirori Mal College. Then there was a programme on the Cuban Revolution, held in what was then called the Tutorial Building, next to the Sri Ram College of Commerce library.

Sohail remembers that the Communist stalwart Hare Krishna Konar, a hero of the anti-colonial struggle who was imprisoned at the notorious Cellular Jail on Andaman Islands in 1933 for six years and who later became the chief architect of the Left Front's land reforms in West Bengal, Operation Barga, was invited to speak about the agrarian crisis to Kirori Mal College by the SFI. It is astonishing how some crises never seem to go away. Noam Chomsky says somewhere that when he's invited to speak and the date is set, say, a year in advance, he safely gives the title, 'The Current Crisis in the Middle East', because there is always a *current* crisis there, thanks to Israel and the Americans, and their assorted clients. So it is with India. You can be sure there will always be an agrarian crisis of massive proportions here. (For as long as the ruling classes comprise of the monopoly capitalists and the big landlords, that is.) Konar spoke no English, and he could barely speak Hindi. The electricity went off sometime during his speech, so the public address system wouldn't work, nor the ceiling fans. Three hundred people were crammed in a lecture hall that was supposed to hold a hundred and fifty. Many were Economics students, but there were others as well, and they were all engrossed as Konar dissected the agrarian crisis, the need for land reforms, the Congress's approach versus the Left's, and so on, over three hours. 'Nobody left,' recalls Sohail.

Then there were talks organized regularly by the Delhi University Discussion Society (with the playful acronym DUDS) at the lecture hall of Delhi School of Economics. These would be delivered by scholars and activists such as Kitty Menon, Bipan Chandra, Harbans Mukhia, Romila Thapar, and others. Rajen mentions another regular, perhaps weekly, study circle. It comprised of radical students, some of whom were of socialist persuasion, some of whom were Communist, and some undecided. The study circle was addressed by, among others, historians Nurul Hasan and Satish Chandra, who came all the way from Aligarh for it. Aroon Purie, founder-publisher of *India Today*, was a part of this study circle, and some of its sessions were held in his office in Connaught Place.

A number of young women gravitated towards the Left, and some of them became active in the SFI: Madhu Prasad, who returned from England to join Delhi University, already politicized; Babli Gupta, whose house in Old Delhi was a hub of Left cultural activity, and whose brother Vinod Nagpal became a well-known actor; Ranjana Narula, who has dedicated her life to the women's movement, and later, the trade union movement; Indira Jaisingh, one of India's outstanding lawyers, who has taken on the might of the current Modi government; Darshana Bhogilal, who, among other things, later took up the cause of Mumbai's pavement dwellers through her work with the People's Union for Civil Liberties; Madhu Kishwar, founder of the feminist magazine *Manushi*, who today is a fan of Modi, but who became president of the Miranda House Students' Union as a Left candidate back then.

Young activists on the Left would have raging debates on the character of the Indian ruling class. Was it the national bourgeoisie, or an alliance of the monopoly capitalists and the big landlords, or the comprador bourgeoisie that ruled India? Those who argued the national bourgeoisie line wanted to see a National Democratic Revolution in India; those who argued the monopoly capitalists–big landlord line wanted to see a People's Democratic Revolution; and those who argued the comprador bourgeoisie line felt that a socialist revolution was imminent and that one spark would light the prairie fire. These lines corresponded to the CPI–CPI (M)–CPI (Marxist-Leninist) differences. Even though the RSS's student front, the ABVP, was strong in Delhi University (the late BJP union minister Arun Jaitley was elected president of the Delhi University Students' Union on an ABVP ticket in 1974, for example), and the Jan Sangh had a base in Delhi, the Hindu Right was a peripheral force in Indian politics as a whole. For young people in the 1970s, then, the socialist leader Jayaprakash Narayan, with his slogan of 'Total Revolution', was one pole of attraction, while the various Communist formations were the other. Even though there was much difference among those on the Left on the question of the characterization of the ruling class, and therefore on the stage of revolution, what was common to all factions and tendencies was opposition to American imperialism, particularly in the context of the war on Vietnam. With this also came the cultural influence of the American counter-culture – Bob Dylan and Joan Baez; Pete Seeger; Andy Warhol and pop art – and the American hippie culture.

By 1970, the SFI was a presence on campus. That summer, during the college break, Rajen and Sohail were among a large number of young men and women from Delhi, Haryana, and western UP, who came together for a training workshop at Rohtak, Haryana, conducted mainly by Ved Gupta and Mahender Singh, along with M.A. Javed. All three taught in Delhi University colleges, lived in Old Delhi, and the first two, in particular, played a stellar role in teaching generations of young people the basics of Marxism. The veteran Communist kisan leader Harkishan Singh Surjeet, a major figure on the national political scene, came to take a class, throwing the police deployed there into a frenzy.

For that generation of student activists, then, if anti-imperialism was a cardinal belief, so was the defence of democracy in India, alongside trying to understand the causes of the terrible poverty suffered by India's poor. It is assumed today that the Left students' movement began in the Jawaharlal Nehru University. However, the fact is that the more influential JNU Left students' movement follows that of Delhi University.

It was in this atmosphere that Safdar joined St Stephen's College in 1970, at the age of 16, thanks to the two double promotions he had got as a schoolboy.

EARLY 1970S. Reviving IPTA

Subhash Tyagi was a young man who lived in Delhi's Gole Market area and worked in the Delhi Electric Supply Undertaking (DESU), which he joined in 1968. One day in 1970, when he was hanging around playing cards with his friends in front of Birla Mandir, he learnt about a theatre group that operated out of Shankar Market. Excited, he landed up there, and was asked to sweep the room. Angered at what he considered an insult, he slunk away, determined never to return. One of his friends from the cards group explained to him that sweeping the floor was an essential part of learning to be an actor, and that everybody did it. So Tyagi went back, and joined the Delhi chapter of the Indian People's Theatre Association (IPTA).

IPTA, which had been a dynamic all-India movement that pulled together the who's who of the Indian performing arts scene in the anti-colonial and anti-fascist struggles of the 1940s, had been defunct in Delhi for over a decade since the late 1950s. Shyamal Mukherji, a young Communist activist from Calcutta, took the initiative to revive the organization in July 1971 by gathering around him a group of youngsters, including Safdar. They began their work in V.P. House on Rafi Marg, where many Left MPs stayed and several Left organizations were given rooms for their offices. In September 1971, this group went to Rurkakalan in Punjab for the All India Kisan Sabha Conference and presented a cultural programme there.

IPTA had an office in Shankar Market, adjoining Connaught Place, in flat no. 33, which was used by the secretary of IPTA to conduct private business. The young activists commandeered a part of this space to hold rehearsals and other activities. A number of non-students also joined now, and many of the IPTA old-timers started visiting again, though the activities were conducted by the younger lot.

One of the old-timers was Aparna Roy, who had been office secretary and had also acted in a few plays in the earlier phase. Her daughter Moloyashree (Mala) had visited 33 Shankar Market as a child and remembers meeting Niaz Haidar there on several occasions. Niaz Haidar, who lived in Delhi's Walled City, owned nothing except command over eight languages, the gift of poetry, a sharp Marxist outlook, and a legion of followers who ensured his well-being – to the extent anyone could ensure anything about him. A lover of bhang (root of the cannabis plant, which was available in licensed shops), he was a cantankerous critic of mediocrity – in art, politics, life – permanently at odds with the literary establishment. Called 'Baba', Niaz Haidar, a contemporary of Faiz Ahmad Faiz,

Kaifi Azmi, and Ali Sardar Jafri, also translated several plays. He had a younger sister, Murtazai, who he encouraged to become a Communist. Hopefully, one day someone will write a book on this impudent atheist, vagabond poet, rebel fakir, insolent scholar, revolution's pilgrim, who surely could have been nothing but a novelist's creation.

One day in late 1970 or early 1971, Mala went to 33 Shankar Market after classes in Miranda House, where she was studying Zoology Honours, to see her mother. She found the place buzzing with the energy of young people. Even though some of the older lot visited the office more or less frequently to give support and encouragement, it was clear that IPTA was now a young people's organization; they were in charge, they decided everything.

It was a motley bunch of young people who reactivated IPTA. Shyamal Mukherji was politically astute and a superb organizer; someone who, in Mala's words, 'kept things together'. His death, in a road accident in March 1972, was a big loss, something Safdar would often talk about. Another exceptionally good organizer was Uday Chatterji, a Bengali who grew up in Delhi. Outwardly quiet, he had a tremendous sense of humour. Safdar learnt a lot from watching Uday's organizing skills. He went away when he got a job in the Damodar Valley Corporation. Bijoy Samajdar, whose father was a Communist, liked to act and sing. He was what Mala described as 'a great talker'. Kajal Das, who wore glasses so thick that he was virtually blind without them, was intellectually sharp, vibrant, and always up for a good, passionate argument. He later joined the Indian Information Service. He introduced Safdar and others to the cinema of Ritwik Ghatak, whom he knew personally. Subhash Tyagi, older than the others, soon developed a reputation as one of their best actors, spontaneous and energetic. Rakesh Saksena studied part-time while working in the New Delhi Municipal Corporation, where his older colleague Jogendra Sharma recruited him to IPTA. Possessed of slight frame, a serious expression that was at odds with his jovial nature, and a razor-sharp intellect,

Rakesh spoke Hindi beautifully. Over the years, Safdar and he became close friends. Kajal Ghosh came to Delhi right after he finished school in Batkula (Nadia district) in West Bengal, where he had been part of a revolutionary song squad. By the time he came to Delhi, he was already proficient on the harmonium. He came from an underprivileged family that belonged to the Namashudra community, a Dalit caste in Bengal. Both his parents were part of the Communist movement. His mother later became a member of parliament in the Lok Sabha. In the 1980s, Kajal became the chief creative force in the song squad, Parcham. Recipient of the Sangeet Natak Akademi Award, he is one of India's leading theatre music composers, and continues to be closely connected with Janam. The other musical talent in IPTA was Gaurishankar, who preferred to call himself Amit Sengupta, and who held Naxalite beliefs. There were other singers too, not all of whose names people recall now. Young writers would come too, many of whom are well known today – Ashok Chakradhar, Ramesh Upadhyay, Kanti Mohan, Chanchal Chauhan, and others – and read their works.

And there was Safdar, who Mala remembers as 'tall, lanky, who spoke well, and had a beautiful voice', but the two didn't become special friends in any way.

In January 1972, IPTA Delhi held a General Body meeting, which elected an eleven-member ad hoc Steering Committee, consisting of people close to both, the CPI and the CPI (M). Despite Shyamal Mukherji's death, IPTA Delhi continued to be active, presenting cultural programmes for the trade union wings of both, the CPI (All India Trade Union Congress, or AITUC) and the CPI (M) (Centre of Indian Trade Unions, or CITU). They also performed on the platform of many Indo-Soviet Friendship Societies. In June 1972, IPTA joined CITU and SFI in organizing a demonstration outside the United States Information Service (USIS) office, which operated then from Bahawalpur House on Bhagwan Dass Road, which today houses the National School of Drama (NSD) and the Kathak Kendra. Many artists took part in this demonstration, one of whom was M.K. Raina, then freshly out of NSD. IPTA performed a short skit, entitled *The Nixon–Kissinger Dialogue*, which was Safdar's first brush with street theatre. He played Nixon.

They also did larger plays: *Kimlish*, an old IPTA play translated from Bangla, about a landless labourer in Bihar who goes to the city, becomes a worker, gets politicized, and returns to the village to organize the rural working class; *Durbar* by Kanti Mohan, a wordy play about politics and politicking; Brecht's *Qanoon Ke Aqa* (*The Exception and the Rule* in Mansur bhai's translation). These were all performed on makeshift stages in front of mass audiences numbering hundreds, sometimes thousands. Mala remembers a late-night performance of *Kimlish* in Chandni Chowk, near Fatehpuri, where they had erected a stage by blocking off the road. Then there was that performance of *Qanoon Ke Aqa* at Kirori Mal College, which Safdar would tell us about with great amusement. Tyagi was playing the Judge, who has to deliver a long judgment at the end. Rather than memorizing the lines, Tyagi would keep a file in front of him with the dialogues, which he could refer to. In this show, he opened the file on stage to find his paper missing. Without missing a beat, he grandly announced that the court needed time to think, exited, saw Mala who was prompting from the wings, grabbed her script, and re-entered with absolute nonchalance.

None of the plays had a long run. *Kimlish*, the most successful, had maybe a dozen performances. There was another play, *Mia Ki Jooti, Mia Ka Sar*, which they read but probably never performed. Well-known IPTA artists such as Habib Tanvir would sometimes visit. Mala remembers a workshop he conducted on the terrace of 33 Shankar Market, in which he gave them words to enact, including *pyaas* (thirst) and *saanp* (snake).

Mala left IPTA and joined another theatre group, Mukti ('Liberation'), which was her only dalliance with Naxalism. Among others, Shamsul Islam, who later led Nishant Natya Manch, was part of this group. Gaurishankar, and Bijoy Samajdar's younger brother Sapan also joined them. Srilata Swaminathan, who was an NSD graduate, and later became a leader of the CPI (ML), would help them.

IPTA continued performing intermittently on student, trade union, and Indo-Soviet Friendship Society platforms. They also performed at the cultural programmes of Durga Puja celebrations in October 1972. By the time the year ended, though, it was becoming increasingly clear that the CPI sympathizers within the group were uncomfortable with the more radical younger members who were close to the CPI (M), who wanted to perform more and more for the working class and farmers. The CPI group wanted to give IPTA a more 'artistic' orientation and turn it into a professional, not activist, group. Sometime towards the end of March or early April 1973, Safdar wrote that 'we propose to leave this organization at the earliest, carry as many general members [he meant those not connected to either the CPI or CPI (M)] along as possible, and start work on a completely new footing'.

Probably because they got wind of this, the CPI group evicted the young radicals in dramatic fashion, and recaptured the Shankar Market office by literally throwing out their stuff from the first-floor window. Undeterred, the young activists got together and formed Jana Natya Manch in April 1973. IPTA Delhi again became defunct, and the premises reverted to being used for private business. Safdar, now 19 years old, was one of the founder-members of the new organization, along with Subhash Tyagi, Kajal Das, Rakesh Saksena, Uday Chatterji, Rathin Das, Kajal Ghosh, Shehla Hashmi, and others.

The torch had passed, from IPTA to Janam.

1973. Janam Comes into Being

A press note hastily put together after Safdar's death says that he joined the CPI (M) in 1976. I'm not persuaded by this date, since he was teaching outside Delhi at the time, and not active politically. It is more likely that he joined the Party in late 1972 or early 1973, going by the tone of a note he wrote to the Party at the time. Thus, it is likely that when Janam came into being, he was already a Party member. In the absence of firm evidence, though, one can't say with certainty.

The early rehearsals of Janam took place at many places. Kavita Nagpal's house was one. Kavita and Vinod Nagpal were established theatrepersons in their own right. Kavita had started doing theatre in 1964, first in Kanpur, then in Bombay, where she worked with Satyadev Dubey, the iconoclastic young theatrical prodigy. Later, Kavita had a long and distinguished career as a theatre critic, admired and feared in equal measure for her outspoken reviews. Vinod was well known as an actor and singer on the Delhi stage. I remember watching him play the Sutradhar in Rajinder Nath's production of Vijay Tendulkar's classic *Ghashiram Kotwal*, singing his way into our hearts. Although I was a small child, maybe four or five, my impressions of the play are surprisingly strong because my father acted in it, and my sister Ashwini and I were dragged by our mother to watch rehearsals. To date, we can recite passages from the play. Vinod attained national fame in the mid-1980s as the lovable father in India's first television soap, *Hum Log*, and he continues to appear in Hindi films.

Janam also rehearsed in the school where Ammaji worked, in Lodhi Colony; on the lawns of V.P. House, sometimes even in the office of the Delhi CPI (M), and in Kajal Ghosh's house upstairs. Jaipal Singh, affectionately called Comrade Major, was the Party secretary in Delhi. Comrade Major had lived an extraordinary life, almost out of a movie. An officer in the British Indian Army, he was attracted to the Freedom Struggle. In 1942, he spread the message of the Quit India Movement among army personnel, and in 1946, when he was posted in Assam, he exposed British conspiracies against Nehru. Faced with the prospect of a court martial, which would surely have resulted in his execution, he went underground. While underground, he trained revolutionaries in places as widely apart as Assam and Pondicherry. He became one of the main military commanders of the legendary Telangana peasants' armed uprising against the feudal rulers and the colonial state in the mid-1940s. After Independence, he surrendered to the army authorities, who, instead of feting him as a hero, imprisoned him in Fort William in Calcutta. He escaped after a year's imprisonment. He was again imprisoned the night Emergency was declared. When he died suddenly in Vijaywada in January 1982, thousands of peasants poured in from all over Telangana to pay tribute to their hero.

By all accounts, Comrade Major was a simple, warm-hearted, and humble man, who won the affection of everybody who came in contact with him. Belying the stereotype of a Jat peasant, he was sensitive and generous in his handling of cultural and artistic matters. Perhaps this was due to the influence of his wife Usha, a dancer and actress in Bengal IPTA, or perhaps it was the result of his own sophisticated understanding of Marxism. Either way, it was lucky for Janam that when the group broke away from IPTA, he was at hand to provide rehearsal space, advice, encouragement, and logistical support. Even those in Janam whose primary motivation was more artistic than political, respected him. As Kavita Nagpal said, 'Comrade Major was very cooperative and sympathetic to our efforts. He used to help us organize most of our shows. He never interfered, only facilitated our work.'

It took a few months to get Janam going, though. Rathin Das remembers a meeting at Kajal Das's house at what was called Market Square in Gole Market (where Bhai Veer Singh Sadan stands today) in mid-September 1973, when they decided to do a play. As part of IPTA, they had already performed at one or two Durga Puja celebrations the previous year. They decided to produce a Bengali play for the upcoming Durga Puja. This was *Mrityur Atit* ('Beyond Death'), based on Irwin Shaw's *Bury the Dead*. There were many non-Bengali-speaking actors in the group. The language of the play was tweaked to accommodate them: Tyagi played a lower-caste Dom character who speaks in Hindi with some Bengali words thrown in; Safdar played a doctor, which required him to use medical terms in English such as 'left ventricle damage'; and Rakesh probably played a policeman who spoke Hindi. The play didn't earn them much, but the group announced itself as a carrier of the IPTA legacy.

Their next play was *Bharat Bhagya Vidhata* ('The Creator of India's Destiny'; a phrase from the National Anthem) by the young Hindi writer Ramesh Upadhyay. It was a musical satire that took pot shots at the Congress and Indira Gandhi, with music by Mohan Upreti, who was an established composer. It had a large cast, and they travelled by bus. Kavita and Vinod Nagpal had joined Janam by then. Kavita directed the play; Vinod played the narrator, and Safdar the counter-narrator. In the play, a landlord is pitted against a capitalist in the elections. Ordinary people, sick with electing the same exploiters over and over again, put up a cobbler as their candidate. When it appears that the cobbler, a Dalit, might win, the other two candidates gang up and get him killed. The play ends with the narrator and counter-narrator singing a song that says that even though he is dead, the struggle he represented is alive.

Janam performed as part of the CPI and CPI (M) campaign for the 1974 Uttar Pradesh assembly elections. The CPI (M) won two seats (Jalalpur and Mainpuri) and came second in one, while the CPI won 16 seats. The CPI was placed fourth overall, behind the Congress, the Bharatiya Kranti Dal led by Charan Singh (which later merged into the Janata Party), and the Bharatiya Jan Sangh. Though I don't think Janam performed in any of the constituencies where the Communists won, Communists were enough of a force for the other parties in Amroha town to spread a rumour that a team from Delhi had arrived and were organizing 'randi naach' ('prostitutes' dance'). The young actors laughed when they heard this, because they were now certain that they would draw a big crowd. A young woman of the cast took it to heart, though, and refused to perform. Kavita had to pacify her. By the time the play was to commence, thousands of people had landed up and there was total pandemonium. That was when Vinod got on to the stage and started singing Faiz Ahmad Faiz. Astonishingly, the crowd quietened down. Later, Safdar would claim that Vinod's heroic singing that night had something to do with the 'liquid spirit' he had imbibed, but Vinod would claim that he was sober as a judge. Either way, it was magical.

At more than one location, they had to reconfigure the acting area creatively to be able to perform – at one place, even doing some action on the balcony of a house; at another, because there was no arrangement for lights, getting the bus to shine its headlights on to the stage at an angle; at yet another, performing in the illumination provided by petromax lamps.

The next play was *Bakri*, by Sarveshwar Dayal Saxena, directed by Kavita. Sarveshwar was already a major poet and a firebrand Marxist considered close to the Naxalite movement. Kavita asked him to write a play in the nautanki style. He wrote a shorter version, which was first done by the students of NSD, and then he expanded it and gave it to Janam. The play was a huge success. Vinod played the Sutradhar in this too, enthralling audiences with his wonderful, sonorous singing and commanding stage presence. Pankaj Kapoor, who went on to become a film and TV actor, was then freshly out of NSD, and did one of the central roles. *Bakri* got many 'call shows', i.e. performance invitations. Rathin Das remembers travelling to Chandigarh and performing at the massive Tagore Theatre. The play ended up having some fifty performances, many more than the half a dozen which was the norm for most plays. *Bakri* announced the arrival of Janam as a serious theatre group in Delhi, which was both artistically strong and politically committed.

1975. Emergency

In May 1974, about 14 lakh (1.4 million) workers of the Indian Railways went on strike. The Indian Railways was then, and continues to be today, the largest employer in India. The political significance of the 1974 strike transcended the railways; it affected the entire country. The Indira Gandhi government crushed the strike with massive use of brute power. Thousands were put behind bars; many more lost their jobs.

The growing militancy of the working class, along with a

coming together of non-Congress bourgeois opposition parties, led Indira Gandhi to declare a state of national emergency in June 1975, though the proximate cause was the Allahabad High Court judgment that found her guilty of using unfair means to win her election. The government suspended elections, curbed civil liberties, censored the press, and imprisoned thousands of opposition leaders and activists during the Emergency, which lasted until March 1977.

When Indira Gandhi refused to resign despite the High Court judgment, Janam did a short skit called *Kursi, Kursi, Kursi* ('Chair, Chair, Chair'). An elected ruler sits on a chair, but loses the election. The ruler gets up, but the chair sticks to him. No matter how hard anyone tries, it is impossible for the ruler to be separated from his chair. This short skit was Janam's second foray into something like street theatre. It was performed on Boat Club lawns, where central government employees, then as now, loll about playing cards and suchlike at lunchtime. Over the few days that they performed it, the skit kept changing, as they kept adding new jokes and gags.

Kavita mentions another play, *Janata Pagal Ho Gayi Hai* ('The Public has Gone Mad'), in which she played Indira Gandhi, who seduces the Public, played by Vinod. She says they did one performance, on June 21, 1975, but her mother died that night, and then the Emergency was declared four days later, so the play was never performed again. Safdar mentions this play too in an article from 1980, but says it was 'performed about 20 times in different parts of Delhi'.

Theatrically, this type of street theatre was a pretty spontaneous exercise, without any consciousness that they were doing anything new in terms of form. That was to come later, after the Emergency, when Janam turned to street theatre with seriousness.

The Emergency years were wasted years as far as Janam was concerned. Safdar was candid about these lost years in his 1988 interview to the Dutch theatre scholar Eugene van Erven: 'When the Emergency was declared on June 25 [1975] and many of our friends were arrested we got scared like hell. We thought we were a great danger to the Indian state. We exaggerated our own threat and thought we were bound to be arrested and tortured. So we disappeared. We didn't perform any more; we didn't go to the Party or trade union office any more. ... But in a sense it was all bogus. We could have continued working in different ways.'

What could those 'different ways' have been? In an undated, handwritten, telegraphic, and tantalizing note, written in all likelihood during the Emergency, Safdar says:

'1. The long delay. Need to begin immediately.

'2. Fields of work limited. (Song squad and street-theatre has to be immobilized)

'3. Plays with old content no more possible. Even if they are permitted it is not advisable to attract undue official attention at such a time as this.

'4. This is the time when we can reshape ourselves. Consolidate our strength, start working with renewed vigour. Song squad can begin purely musical classes to raise artistic competence; Drama section can take up classics, classics with progressive content if possible, and stage them on a large scale. Build up a totally different image of Jana-Natya [*sic*] Manch, increase professional standard and attract various elements to Janam and operate as a purely theatrical organization.

'5. Organizations with an image of a professional or purely art-orientation are being allowed to put on progressive plays; we lack that image.

'6. We can take up plays like Bhavabhuti's *Uttar Ram Charit*, Sudrak's *Mrichchakatik*, Tolstoi's *Power of Darkness*, Girandeux's *Madwoman of Chaillot*, or purely theatrical pieces like *Sakuntala*, *Ramlila*, *Oedipus*, or plays by Shakespeare.

'7. This is an opportunity to take great art to the culturally starved working classes and peasantry.

'8. (Premchand) Hori – Laxminarayanlal + Bharatendu (Vishnu Prabhakar – *Godan*)

'9. Submitting a number of scripts for approval.

'10. A list of less objectionable songs to be submitted to censors.'

None of this came to pass. Janam remained dormant for the entire duration of the Emergency.

JUNE 1979. Safdar Roy and Moloyashree Hashmi

Safdar finished his MA in English Literature and took up a teaching job in Delhi University, but he found life in Delhi dull. He joined the newly formed Garhwal University (subsequently named after Hemwati Nandan Bahuguna) in Srinagar, Garhwal, where he stayed more or less the entire duration of the Emergency. Here, he discovered his love for the mountains. He would go for long treks in the Garhwal Himalayas with his friend Prabhat Upreti. Safdar stayed there till May 1977, when he took up a job in the better-known Srinagar, in Kashmir, to teach at the university. He organized a dramatics society in the university, directed an English production of Büchner's *Woyzeck* with a massive cast, and followed it up with a double bill featuring Brecht's *The Exception and the Rule*, of which over 40 shows were performed in the open, and an ancient Chinese play, *Orphan of the Chow*.

In the meanwhile, Abbuji died in 1976. He was 'wise like a sage', and his heart and endurance were amazing, Safdar wrote to Upreti. 'The realism, the stark-naked realism of that man is apparent in a clean and total acceptance of death.'

After sorrow, exhilaration. He found love.

Mala had left Delhi in 1975 to join a teachers' training course at Neel Bagh in Kolar district, about a hundred kilometres from Bangalore. It was started by the British-born educationist David Horsburgh, who had first come to India with the Royal Air Force in 1943. Along with his wife Doreen, he set up an innovative, experimental, rural school, which built upon many theories of a democratic approach to learning. They placed a great deal of emphasis on preparing innovative teaching materials, using locally-found objects, such as blocks of wood, cigarette packets, etc. Over the years, I've met scores of students taught by Mala in Sardar Patel

Vidyalaya. Without exception, 'Moloyashree Aunty' is one of their most favourite teachers. A part of the credit for this goes to David Horsburgh and the Neel Bagh School, where, for two years, she was 'learning to help children learn'.

After Neel Bagh, David involved Mala in a project he was running for the Department of Education in Kashmir, for which he was to write a set of English textbooks. Mala went to Srinagar in 1977 with an associate to conduct workshops. She had heard, possibly from her mother, that Safdar was in Srinagar. Perhaps she didn't know that there was a Srinagar in Garhwal too, but as it happened, by the time Mala went, Safdar had moved from the Garhwal Srinagar to the Kashmir Srinagar. So, by a curious alignment of the stars, the two ended up in the same city, when they should've been mountains apart.

Safdar initially stayed as a paying guest with T. Jayaraman, who headed the English department in the university. When Mala mentioned Safdar's name to her host in the Education Department, he knew exactly where to find the young man from Delhi. Mala visited him, and ended up also becoming friends with Professor Jayaraman, a man whose sharp tongue was matched by the sharpness of his intellect. Mala reminded him of his niece, Gargi Bhatt, who, again by a curious alignment of the stars, later became her colleague in Sardar Patel Vidyalaya. Gargi, delightfully crazy and unhesitatingly warm to everybody she met, died of cancer, much too young.

Mala spent about five weeks in Srinagar, came back to Delhi, returned to Srinagar and spent about a month there, this time travelling to remote villages to meet teachers, before going to Jammu for the same work. She remembers being welcomed with love, affection and respect everywhere – being an 'ustani' (teacher) was a big deal – but it was also clear that she was 'from India'. Safdar wrote to Prabhat Upreti in December 1977:

'I was utterly delighted to receive your letter. I lifted up Moloyashree higher than my shoulders; I planted dozens of kisses on her. The poor thing was totally stumped. She was here till 13 November. Time passed like a storm. ... My love for Moloyashree has left me in a feverish state, unable to do any work during that period. ... Moloyashree! How do I describe her to you? At times, she is like the flow of Alakhnanda, bouncing off rocks (not angrily – I don't know if she knows anger); at times, like the soft afternoon light filtering through Pipal leaves; at times, like the silence of the Kedarnath valley; at times high like the Tungnath peak; at times dense like Dugalbitta; at times deep like the sky; sometimes near, sometimes far; sometimes happy, sometimes sad; sometimes wild, sometimes peaceful; sometimes mischievous, sometimes serious. But always full of love, and always lovely. Weeps at the pain of the world, but is solid and strong as a rock. Only, she is scared of dogs. Smokes away dozens of Charminars from morning to night. Gets excited when she speaks of children. And her eyes – darker than a desert storm, deeper than the night. But most important – she loves me truly, my friend!'

In 1978, Mala went back to Srinagar, but this was what she calls a 'personal visit', to be with Safdar. They decided to get married. Safdar was impatient to get back to Delhi – to theatre, to politics. 'Even though he was doing theatre in Kashmir with his students,' Mala says, 'Janam was a very large part of his concern. He didn't know what to do, but it was something he constantly talked about. And the fact that he needed to do political work. Politics was something that was very important to him. His commitment to the CPI (M) was unshakeable. He said it in so many words, that there is no compromise on that. But he didn't know what to do. "If I go back to Delhi to take charge of Janam" – because that is something he had now started thinking, that somebody needed to push it – "how can I go back to Delhi without a job?" Clearly, he wanted to go back. That was definitely there. And he didn't think getting married and living in Kashmir was a very good idea, because of the so-called difference in identities – one carrying a Muslim name, the other a Hindu name. I said, why not? It is a very good idea. Sometimes these things are upheld as examples. By July 1978, it was pretty certain that he was coming back.'

In his letters to Prabhat Upreti, Safdar expressed the same concern, that he didn't have a job, and had no idea what he was going to do to earn a living. Then, one day, he decided to up and leave. He resigned from his job. Earlier, in the winter, when Safdar was still employed in Kashmir, he and Mala had gone to Anand in Gujarat, where he had applied for a job as editor for the in-house magazine of the National Dairy Development Board (NDDB). He was offered the position, but he didn't take it, because even though the campus was beautiful, he said to Mala, 'I'll be able to do nothing here,' by which he meant political work. After he came back to Delhi from Kashmir, Safdar got a job in *Vidura*, a news magazine of the Press Institute of India, where Rathin Das also worked.

Much later, Safdar would tell Mala that once, while they were in IPTA and didn't know each other too well, when they had gone in a large group for a meal to Safdar's house, Abbuji had pointed to Mala and told Safdar, 'This is the girl you'll end up marrying.' Mala doesn't believe this story. She thinks it's one of the many stories Safdar was in the habit of cooking up. Abbuji died in 1976, before Mala and Safdar met up again in Kashmir. They married on June 18, 1979. Safdar was two months over 25, Mala was four months older. It was a simple court marriage, with Aparnadi and Sohail as witnesses, and Baba (Mala's father, J.C. Roy, who was a trade unionist at the Reserve Bank of India), and Ammaji in attendance. Baba had asked Mala if she wanted a reception, but she refused. The only reception that took place was a simple affair hosted by Ammaji and Sohail for their friends. Before they were married, they had found a small, low-income housing flat in Posangipur, near Janakpuri in west Delhi. Within months, rats drove them out, and they shifted to a barsati (a small rooftop apartment, usually with a larger terrace) right opposite Mala's uncle and aunt's house in Patel Nagar. They lived there for a little over two years.

Safdar proposed that they both change their names: he would

be Safdar Roy, and she Moloyashree Hashmi. Armed with name change application letters, copies of the marriage certificate, proofs of identity and address, and photographs, the newlyweds went to their respective banks to effect the change. At Mala's bank, the bank officer looked, cursorily, at the marriage certificate, and signed her application for name change. Done.

At Safdar's bank, the official screwed his brow, peered at his application, read it carefully, thought hard, read it again, consulted a colleague, who, in turn, consulted a rule book, and finally pronounced, no, the bank didn't have the authority. You'll have to get your name changed officially. OK, so what do I do for that, Safdar asked. Hmm, said the official, chewing on his pencil. You'll have to get an affidavit made on official stamp paper, giving your current name and address, your new name and address, and the reason for change – astrology, numerology, marriage, etc. But you are not a woman, so I don't know if 'marriage' is acceptable as a reason for name change. Anyway, after you have the affidavit, you have to get an advertisement printed in two newspapers, one an English daily, the other a daily in the official language of your state, in this case Hindi. Once these are published, write an application for name change in the official gazette, attach the original advertisements, attach two attested copies of your passport photos, and copies of your identity and address proof, and submit to the office of the Controller of Publication. Once your name change is published in the gazette, even God cannot take it away from you.

Thus it was that Moloyashree Roy came to be Moloyashree Hashmi, but Safdar Hashmi remained Safdar Hashmi.

OCTOBER 1978. The Turn to Street Theatre

The Emergency was lifted in March 1977. During his winter break at Srinagar University in 1977–78, Safdar came to Delhi and got involved in efforts to reorganize Janam, and met N.K. Sharma. NK grew up in the mohalla known as Chudiwalan in Old Delhi, where he went first to an NDMC and then DAV school, after which he joined

Hindu College in Delhi University. But his father, an industrial officer in Delhi Administration, died suddenly. The family didn't own any house in Delhi. NK applied for, and got, a job in Delhi Administration on humanitarian grounds, enabling them to retain the government accommodation. He was just about 18 then. He quit Hindu College because of the job, and enrolled as a distance learner, completing his graduation. NK had first been in the touch with Janam in 1975, but the Emergency was clamped down before he could get active. When things moved again after Emergency, NK joined. By this time, Arun Sharma, from Meerut, was also part of the group.

The Hindi poet Kanti Mohan was connected to Janam at the time, and NK remembers a meeting at his house in Naya Bazaar, Old Delhi, attended by Safdar, Tyagi, Manish, Arun, and himself. Maybe they met more than once, because Kavita Nagpal also remembers a similar meeting at Kanti Mohan's house, but NK is emphatic she wasn't there. Either way, nothing concrete came out of it. The young men were nevertheless upbeat. Since Rakesh Saksena hadn't been part of the meeting NK mentions, they met again a few days later on the lawns of Sapru House, which in those days was an intellectual and cultural hub, with a fine library. Rathin Das was also part of this meeting. Rakesh Saksena played an important part in Janam's reorganizing efforts.

Janam regrouped with a production of Asghar Wajahat's *Firangi Laut Aye* ('The Colonizer Returns'), directed by Kavita Nagpal. After this, they took up an Utpal Dutt play, *Ebaar Rajar Pala*, a critique of the Emergency, and did it as *Ab Raja Ki Bari Hai* ('Now, the King's Turn'), directed, NK says, by Utpal Bannerji. It was translated from Bangla to Hindi by Aparnadi, and Rakesh and Safdar then worked on that text. These were plays in the old mould: large, and with big casts. Safdar didn't act in either, because he was back in Kashmir. It was hard to get performances. The trade unions, kisan sabhas, and students' organizations had all been working underground and were short of money. They also needed financial resources to fight court cases against their activists. They needed Janam's theatre in their reorganizing efforts, but couldn't afford it.

Safdar had quit his job and come back to Delhi in the summer of 1978. The group was wondering what to do, and how to go forward. If big plays are not feasible, Safdar said, let us make small plays that are inexpensive to produce, mount, travel with, and perform. Janam already had some experience with a rough-and-ready sort of improvised street theatre. Could this be developed further, the group wondered. NK had seen street sellers in Old Delhi, showmen who could entertain crowds of a hundred or so as they performed little tricks and sold their wares. Why can't we do something like that, he said.

A decade later, Safdar told Eugene van Erven, 'Someone suggested that we write our own plays, things that could be easier and cheaper to produce. We felt we didn't have the confidence for that. Then an older Communist leader called me one day and told me about an incident that had happened in Ghaziabad … in a chemicals factory called Herig-India. The workers didn't have a union. They had two very ordinary demands. … They wanted a place where they could park their bicycles, and inside the factory they wanted a canteen where they could get a cup of tea and heat up their food during a recess. … For these simple humanitarian demands, the workers had to go on strike. … The guards opened fire, killing six workers. … We decided to try writing a play about this.'

Six people lost their lives for what were not even economic demands, and they were killed by private guards, not the police. Why?

After Emergency, there was an upsurge in working-class struggles. The police and administration are always with the owners in any case; owners also have goons in their direct or indirect employ. In Ghaziabad, however, traditionally, the role of goons and criminals as strongmen of capitalists has been high. In some cases, the owners themselves are strongmen with criminal records, who run factories as fronts for all kinds of illegal activities. Many factory owners are also part of the land mafia. Herig-India was not the only factory where workers faced repression. In the same period, there were about a dozen factories in the region where the workers had to go on strike, because the owners wouldn't even talk to the workers about their problems.

The larger context was also important. The Janata Party government, which came into power at the Centre after Emergency, was trying to bring in a new Industrial Relations Bill to curb the growing militancy of the unions.

When Janam decided to make a play around these issues, they were clear that the play had to (a) be simple to mount; (b) be general enough to appeal to workers at large, not only those from a single factory; (c) talk about capitalism as a system, rather than about the cruelty of individual owners; (d) bring out the inhumanity of the capitalist class; (e) suggest that no matter how terrible or kind individual owners might be, the way out was to abolish capitalism. Safdar and one or two others met a number of trade unionists to understand the situation, both at the larger, macro level, and also at the ground level. K.M. Tiwari, then a CITU activist and worker, now Delhi CPI (M) secretary, says that he remembers speaking to Safdar and others along with a senior trade unionist, and answering their questions, many of which were quite detailed. Jogendra Sharma, who too was a CITU activist then, also recalls meeting Safdar and others and discussing at length the industrial situation in Ghaziabad. With all this background research buzzing in their heads, and after discussions in Janam about the form and content of the play, Rakesh Saksena and Safdar sat down one day to write and, as Safdar told van Erven, 'practically on its own something started emerging. We started speaking the dialogues almost naturally'.

Machine was the result.

It is a short, 13-minute piece. Five actors enter and create a machine with their bodies. The machine has three component elements: the workers, the owner, and the guard. Each of them emerges from the machine and talks about their role in the production process: The worker creates value, the owner enjoys the economic fruits of the workers' labour, and the guard enforces discipline and compliance from the workers with an iron fist. The narrator links the various elements. At one point, the machine breaks down. The narrator asks, who is responsible for this? The workers step forward: We are. On one side, we face the stone wall of the owner, on the other side, we have the iron fist of the guard. They have no option but to strike. The owner unleashes repression; in the end, the workers win.

This schematic representation captures nothing of the power and beauty of the play. The human machine is a simple, yet powerful visual metaphor for capitalism, and the language is lyrical and poetic, full of word-play, rhyming, and alliteration, conveying pathos and humour. I first saw the play at a street theatre festival in Pragati Maidan in the mid-1980s, before I joined Janam.

It was also the first time I saw Badal Sircar's work. What struck me was this: Badal Sircar's work was more physical, and, despite being minimalist and spartan, had a spectacular quality about it. I admired it deeply, but it left me feeling a little confused. I didn't get what the plays were really trying to say. I put it to language – my familiarity with Bangla was sketchy, at best. But Safdar was at hand – he had told me about the show in the first place – and when I asked him, he seemed a little lost too. Badal Sircar's plays appealed to me viscerally – they communicated a sense of anger and outrage, of illogicality and absurdity. Having read many of Badal Sircar's plays now, I also realize that a certain tension permeates his plays with regard to meaning – they seem solid and within reach, but turn to sand and slip away when you try to grasp them. I saw *Machine* the next day, and was struck by how similar it was to Badal Sircar's plays, and yet how different. It was spartan and physical, just as clever with language, but there was no ambiguity about its meaning.

Machine was first performed on October 15, 1978, at a writers' conference in Satyawati College, then in Timarpur. The play had been designed for a circular acting area, with spectators all around. The first performance was on the conference stage, with the audience on one side. The actors found they could adapt pretty easily. The Hindi poet Manmohan was present at the show, and he once told me that he was gobsmacked on that day. 'It was as if someone had condensed Karl Marx's opus, *Capital*, into a 13-minute treatise.' NK remembers senior writers like Dr Mahadev Saha and Chandrabali Singh being bowled over.

Machine became a phenomenon after its fifth performance, at an all-India trade union session to discuss the proposed Industrial Relations Bill at the Talkatora Indoor Stadium on November 19, 1978, with a big rally planned the next day on the Boat Club lawns. Safdar recalled a decade later:

'We went to the stadium early in the morning and we pleaded and pleaded with the organizers to allow us to present our play to them. But they couldn't see what a play could have to do with a serious trade union session. We kept on pestering them. They didn't even know us. We stayed until evening. Finally, they got sick and tired of us and told us we could perform it after the final resolutions had been passed. "We are not even going to make an announcement. If you can do it on your own you can go ahead," they said. The way the stadium was built helped us. It's an arena. There is a big basketball court in the centre with seats all around. ... The moment the final slogans had died down and people were beginning to file out of the stadium we ran inside, six people in black, and quickly started operating the machine in the centre with that hissing, rhythmic sound. People turned around to watch what the hell was happening. Normally we run the machine for twenty seconds at most but since there was a lot of noise in the hall we went on running it for two minutes. We had to do it at a very high pitch, so we were exhausted after that. You see, the nearest person in the audience was at least sixty feet from us. Then they finally became silent. I was the narrator. I gave a signal to stop the machine and started speaking. It was an incredible success. After we sang the final song, the trade union delegates jumped over the rails. The leaders were like kids. They lifted us on their shoulders. We became heroes. People took our autographs on cigarette packets. And they invited us to come and perform during the rally on the next day.'

When they performed at the Boat Club rally to an audience of tens of thousands the next day, perched up high on the stage, people heard the play more than saw it. The effect was electrifying anyway, and they got invitations to perform from all over. A number of performances, now finally in working-class bastis and industrial areas, followed. Safdar said, 'The workers absolutely love this play. I still do not understand why, for it's so simple. There is nothing in it. It is schematic, except that the dialogues are interesting. Everywhere they love it, though. It is something very difficult to explain. Perhaps it is something subliminal or abstract that appeals to them.'

Comrade Mohan Lal of Faridabad recalled *Machine* like this: 'Safdar had spoken to many people about workers' agitations. I had told him about the firing in 1967 at the Modinagar agitation, because that is when I started. How the police attacked, how firing took place. When I saw *Machine* for the first time, I was reminded of 1967, of Modi Mills, what happened at the gate. I said, you've shown the same thing, but in short. In reality, it was a huge affair. It was a short play. But when the play was performed at the factory gates, workers would feel strong within themselves, because it was a play connected to the movement. It gave strength to workers to unite. I liked the play a lot, because I felt that they'd shown the things connected to my life as a trade unionist. Every worker, every organizer felt that this was about them.'

Janam was on a roll after *Machine*, producing 22 street plays in ten years. When we marked a decade of work in street theatre in November 1988, Safdar estimated that Janam had 4,000 performances over this period. Mala feels this is an exaggeration. She puts the number at a more modest 2,500.

The turn to street theatre was not a conscious artistic decision. It was not an attempt at experimentation. It was occasioned by something simple – what one would call today a lack of funding. Janam's large plays were possible to perform because trade unions, kisan organizations, and student groups spent money for erecting the stage and basic sound and light equipment. When these organizations were themselves impoverished because of the Emergency, they could no longer do so. Janam was at a crossroads. Either it could continue doing its artistic work by seeking alternative audiences, or it could adapt its work to suit the needs and financial capabilities of its working-class audience.

In today's arts management terms, one could say that the choice was between amending its vision to continue with its mission, or adapting the mission to stay true to its vision. Too many artists, too many non-governmental organizations (NGOs), too many radical activists today do the former – they chase the funding and adapt their work to it. Janam did the opposite. It put politics in command.

THE 1980S. A Theory of Street Theatre

As they walked back to V.P. House after the Talkatora Stadium performance of *Machine* that November evening in 1978, surrounded by throngs of people asking for their contact details, Mala remembers Safdar saying excitedly, 'We've hit upon something new. What is this? How does it work? We have to discover it. We need to work on this. We need to develop it. We need to find a grammar for it.' Everybody in Janam was excited by the success of *Machine*, so in itself Safdar's excitement was hardly unusual. What is striking is that this was only the fifth performance of the play, and he was already analysing it, in the middle of that tremendous high. 'But this was not unusual,' Mala says. 'Whenever something new happened, Safdar would be the first to note it and try and see patterns – we did this, and that happened – even during performances.'

Soon after, Safdar wrote a 'Draft Paper on the Nature and Need for Street-Theatre' to share with 'actors, directors, playwrights, musicians and artists', who might be interested in exploring this new, exciting form. Janam had been doing street theatre for four months. Street theatre, Safdar wrote, is 'documentary and brief, shocking yet familiar', and so its impact is 'not only emotional but also rational – and therefore a lasting one'. The form is not subtle or 'minutely analytical'. It is 'loud and spectacular, and funny', and 'its timely appearance is a comment in itself'. But 'loudness and clownery in actual practice meant not a multiplication of antics but rather a sureness of touch where precise and clear details established a situation or a mood with an economy of gestures and postures'. He saw it as a sort of newspaper-in-action, 'to make explicit our stand on contemporary events from day to day'. Beyond this agitprop role, street theatre also had a larger function: 'of taking healthy entertainment to the culturally starved people'. For those doing street theatre, it is a means to not only train themselves artistically, but also politically, because 'it helps them, indeed it forces them, to think sharply, clearly and analytically'. This note was not published, but it was certainly circulated, because the Janam papers have Kumaresh Chakravarty's neatly handwritten response, dated February 28, 1979, appreciating Safdar's insights.

While discussions on the nature, form, and politics of street theatre were frequent in Janam, so far as I can find, Safdar was the only one who attempted to theorize the group's experiences in writing. I found one article on street theatre by Rathin Das in *Vidura* magazine, but nothing else. Apart from unpublished notes, Safdar wrote a number of articles that lay the foundation for a theory of street theatre: 'Concept of People's Theatre' (1980); 'The Enchanted Arch' (1983); 'The Tradition of Street Theatre' (1986); and 'The First Ten Years of Street Theatre' (1988).

There is a remarkable continuity in his thinking over the decade. One, Safdar traced, in broad strokes, the history of street theatre. Modern, political street theatre began with the Bolshevik Revolution in Russia and was subsequently a part of numerous movements – the Chinese Revolution; IPTA and the Indian freedom struggle; the Civil War in Spain; the anti-colonial struggles in Vietnam, Latin America, and Africa; struggles of the Mexican farmworkers and the civil liberties movements in the US; and so on. In doing so, he went against the grain of common sense. Instead of arguing that street theatre has always existed in India – since many of our traditional forms of theatre were performed in the open, in fields, or in other non-theatre spaces – he gave it a modern lineage. Safdar argued that to call 'any drama performed in the open' street theatre, is as ridiculous as 'calling any play in which the hero dies at the end a tragedy'. Street theatre is a product of the workers' movements against capitalism: 'All over the world, including India, the political pamphlet, the poster, wall writing and the agitational speech have all gone into creating the form of street theatre. Street theatre had become inevitable when the workers began organizing themselves into unions in the mid-nineteenth century. Its arrival became imminent with the emergence of political demonstrations in the late nineteenth and early twentieth century. As such, it is a twentieth century phenomenon, born out of the specific needs of the modern world,' even if, in terms of form, it draws 'in equal measure from our folk and classical drama as well as from western theatre'.

Two, he saw street theatre as a part of the Left movement, emerging from it, and giving back to it. 'It is basically a militant political theatre of protest. Its function is to agitate the people and to mobilize them behind fighting organizations.' Janam's plays such as *Machine*, *Aurat*, and *Chakka Jaam/Halla Bol* are excellent examples of this.

Three, he was also concerned about the artistic quality of street theatre. If it remains at the level of a poster or pamphlet only, it will become clichéd, stale, and predictable. He looked forward to the 'development and flowering of street theatre into a full-fledged art form'. Therefore, he didn't see street theatre as a 'rebellion against the proscenium theatre, or as standing in opposition to it', because 'both belong equally to the people'.

Four, he was against appropriation of theatre by the ruling classes, whether it is 'the proscenium theatre which has been appropriated by the escapists, the anarchists and the revivalists', or the 'reformist and sarkari street theatre'. This latter has become a full-blown epidemic since he wrote this, with government agencies,

NGOs, bourgeois political parties, and even corporates using street theatre in an entirely utilitarian, transactional way to communicate this or that message. Ironically, Safdar's killing, and the spurt in street theatre immediately after, played a role in drawing attention of these agencies to the form.

Safdar was not a slave to what he called the 'implements and devices of artistic expression', arguing that 'drama is born with force and beauty in any empty space whether square, rectangular or circular. The play comes alive whether the spectators are on one or all sides, in darkness or in light'.

1978. **Samudaya and Belchi**

As Janam discovered street theatre in the north, Samudaya discovered street theatre in the south.

Formed in 1975 in Bangalore by left-wing theatre activists, Samudaya, the group, rapidly became Samudaya, the movement. It expanded spectacularly. By 1982, it had 18 units all over Karnataka. Samudaya's first productions were directed for the proscenium stage by Prasanna: K.V. Narayana's *Huttava Badidare* ('Beating the Anthill'), an adaptation of Samsa's *Vigada Vikramaraya* ('King Vikrama the Wicked'), with music by B.V. Karanth, followed soon after by *Paata Ondu* ('Lesson 1') and *Paata Yeradu* ('Lesson 2'), two short plays. In the second of the two, the actors were the residents of Bangalore's slums. Prasanna also directed two Brecht plays, *The Mother* and *Galileo*. For the former, the CPI and CPI (M) helped to sell tickets. For the latter, Samudaya constructed a small portable stage, facilitating more performances in the open.

In the meanwhile, Samudaya had also started film societies and a library movement, besides publishing booklets of revolutionary songs and poetry, and pamphlets on political and cultural issues. The first street play by Samudaya was *Belchi*, based on the ghastly burning of Dalit agricultural labourers in May 1977 in Bihar. *Belchi* was first performed in 1978, and it notched up some 2,500 shows. The parallels with *Machine* are striking: Both were prepared in the same year, both were based on real-life killings, both allied themselves with the revolutionary classes – *Machine* with the urban proletariat and *Belchi* with the rural – both were theatrically innovative, using a degree of stylization, both were responses to the Emergency, and both were soon widely translated and performed all over the country. *Belchi* was written by C.G. Krishnaswamy and had songs by the Dalit poet Siddalingaiah. It was performed extensively in slum areas, and the actors were also drawn from slums. There were two more street plays: *May Day*, written by Krishnaswamy close on the heels of *Belchi*, and *Struggle*, a docu-drama on a strike in a Bangalore factory, dramatized by the striking workers themselves under the direction of Laxmi Chandrashekhar and M.C. Anand.

More plays were produced later: *Patre Sangapanna Kole* ('The Killing of Patre Sangappa'), the dramatization of the brutal murder of a Dalit bonded labourer by his master in Shimoga district; *Chasnala*, on the death of 380 coal miners due to flooding of a mine in Bihar in 1975; *Beledavaru*, on superstition and godmen; *Bharata Darshana*, on the Tarkunde Commission Report on police killings in Andhra Pradesh; and *Jeethadahatti Ranga*, on bonded labourers. I'm not sure if all these were produced by only the Bangalore unit or by several units. Either way, within the first year of street theatre, by October 1979, there were eight plays in the Samudaya repertory.

That Samudaya became a people's movement is seen, most spectacularly, in the 'jathas' (caravans) that they organized periodically. The first of these jathas was held between October 15 and November 15, 1979. Rati Bartholomew wrote: 'The purpose was twofold; to get to know people at the grassroots level, to learn, experience and evaluate the scene at first hand, and to use theatre as an instrument of education, as an attack on feudal and semi-feudal values'. The money required for the venture was raised by the sale of 20,000 greeting cards made by artists, and through individual donations. The jatha covered 17 of the 19 Karnataka districts, performing 450 shows, singing countless songs, selling literature, and conducting discussions with audiences, who also provided local hospitality. The second jatha, from January 15 to 31, 1981, was of shorter duration but more intensive and decentralized. There were ten groups this time, with 20 to 25 permanent members, which started from ten towns and ended in ten others – there was no central convergence at the end. In the first jatha, they had travelled in vans; this time they used bicycles.

Even from the sketchy description here, the significance of Samudaya's work should be obvious. It was the first major, and largely successful, effort to build a truly people-oriented, democratic, secular, mass cultural movement since the IPTA days. It not only took progressive, even revolutionary culture to the people, it drew the people themselves into the act of creating and nourishing this culture. The expansion of Samudaya's activities – from a single unit to a state-wide network of units; from initially doing only proscenium theatre to doing street theatre as well; from theatre to other arts; from single instances of creative collaborations with the people to massive, state-wide jathas – was made possible by the belief that people are the real heroes of a people's cultural movement. In the years to come, organizations such as Chennai Kalai Kuzhu in Tamil Nadu and Praja Natya Mandali in the Telugu states were to emerge as significant practitioners of the street theatre form, with the latter becoming a mass movement with thousands of members drawn from the poorest and most marginalized communities.

THE 1980S. The Actors

Mala joined Sardar Patel Vidyalaya, a progressive school run by the Gujarat Education Society, in July 1981. The school is located in Lodhi Estate, right next door to the Delhi Kannada School, where Safdar had been a student. By this time, Mala and Safdar were living in West Patel Nagar. Bhisham Sahni, the celebrated Communist novelist, brother of the Communist actor Balraj Sahni, lived with his wife Shiela in East Patel Nagar, a short walk away. Safdar and Bhishamji had earlier been colleagues in Delhi College (now called Zakir Husain College), where Safdar taught English

Literature briefly after he returned from Kashmir, and even though four decades separated them in age, they became friends. Mala remembers Safdar and Bhishamji discussing literature, art, and politics. Ved Gupta also lived nearby, and Safdar and Ved also became friends now, where earlier they had been only comrades.

By the time Janam's street theatre began, Kavita and Vinod Nagpal had moved on from Janam. Kavita wanted Janam to continue doing proscenium theatre and 'be the vanguard of the theatre movement', as she put it, while the younger lot, Safdar, NK, Rakesh Saksena, Mala, and others, were searching for ways to reach their core audience, the urban poor. In 1982, Rakesh, co-writer with Safdar of the early street plays, left for Ethiopia on a job assignment. I met him only once, after Safdar's death. He died in 2008, aged 51.

New members joined. Vijay Kalia, who worked in the railways, saw Janam perform at a loco workers' conference, and approached Safdar, who asked him to come to a rehearsal. Lalit Ratan Girdhar, son of a small businessman who grew up in the Karol Bagh area, saw Janam perform at the Art Mela that would spring up every Saturday in Central Park, Connaught Place, to enable young and struggling artists to sell their works, and for the public at large to purchase contemporary art. He joined the group thereafter. Kunwar Deepak Gulati, a bank employee and theatre lover, had been a friend of some Janam members before he came into the group. Diwakar Pandey, who was part of the SFI, joined when he was a student in Delhi University. A character if ever there was one, he was two years my senior in Ramjas College, and was about a decade or so younger than Safdar and the rest.

Through the 1980s, Mala was the only regular woman actor in Janam, with others going in and out. Sonya Surabhi Gupta, a student of Spanish at JNU, joined Janam in 1980. She was part of the SFI group that did a Hindi version of Samudaya's *Belchi* on the campus. She was a good singer, and stayed in the group for a couple of years. Later, she taught at the Central Institute of English and Foreign Languages (CIEFL), Hyderabad, and then at Jamia Millia Islamia,

New Delhi. Rajni Palriwala, now professor of Sociology in the Delhi School of Economics, was then a student in Delhi University. She was in Janam for a year or so. Abha Dayal was a friend of Janam's who acted in a couple of plays off and on, and travelled with the group to Assam in 1981. The journalist Javed Naqvi, who acted in Janam's *Ab Raja Ki Bari Hai* in 1978, remembered a chance meeting with a co-actor, Nimmi, now an air hostess. When he asked her if working in a political theatre group tarnished her image with her family, her response was, 'I am not sure which is more difficult – to be a Communist or to be a woman in our society.'

Banter, leg-pulling, and pranks were part of Janam's culture, with Tyagi, Manish, NK, and Safdar himself being experts. You didn't want to be the target of their leg-pulling. Kajal Ghosh remembers the time he used to compose commercial jingles, earning Rs 200 for one. If he did one a week, he'd earn Rs 800 a month, quite a sum in those days. He once did an underwear jingle. One day, when a group of them were chatting outside the SFI office in V.P. House, Safdar began ragging Kajal about how, on the road to the revolution, they were now to sell underwear. Embarrassed, Kajal decided to quit doing jingles. Soon thereafter, he bumped into Safdar at All India Radio. When asked what he was doing there, Safdar said he'd come to give voice for a radio spot.

'Then why did you rag me so much! I gave up doing jingles because of that.'

Safdar cracked up. 'You're an idiot. You actually gave up doing lucrative work because I made a joke of it?'

Kajal went right back to composing jingles.

Then there was that occasion when I walked into rehearsal wearing rather fancy shoes. There was a gleam in Safdar's eye when he saw them.

'Oh my! You're stylish, eh?'

'No, no. Someone gave these to my uncle, and they didn't fit him too well. So he passed them on to me.'

My uncle was a dentist, and knew both Safdar and Mala, who

consulted him. After that, I was forever introduced as the guy whose uncle had a cupboard full of shoes from which I got an endless supply. I could never live that down.

THE EARLY 1980S. Ritwik Ghatak

In May 1981, Janam was one of the organizers of a protest march against the prevention of a street play by the police in Nandpur village, Bakhira Bazaar, Basti (UP), and the subsequent sexual harassment of protesting women, again by the police. Later that year, Janam was involved in organizing a series of protest actions by artists, against a police notification enjoining upon all performing groups (in theatre, music, and dance) to seek police approval of their scripts. The artists constituted, initially an ad hoc, and then a steering committee, of which Janam's Rathin became a spokesperson.

Much of the organizing effort for these protests took place from the West Bengal Information Bureau (WBIB) in the State Emporia Complex on Baba Kharak Singh Marg. Only once in the history of WBIB was it a truly active, vibrant, and vital organization, and this was when Safdar worked there as Information Officer, from 1980 to 1983.

Shohini Ghosh, documentary filmmaker and scholar, was a student in Lady Shri Ram College in the early 1980s, who was feeling lost in Delhi after leaving the comforting familiarity of Calcutta. Interested in cinema, she became part of the college film society. In those pre-digital – and pre-VHS – days, film societies had to source the large cans that carried the film reels, and rent projectors to screen films. In Delhi, the cultural centres and embassies of various countries were one source, or you had to write to the National Film Archive of India (NFAI) in Pune to get films. So film societies were always on the lookout for alternative sources of films.

At her father's instance, Shohini showed up at WBIB looking for films. 'I went there, and saw this good-looking man sitting at a desk, with two large posters behind him. One was Ritwik Ghatak, the other was Aparna Sen in Satyajit Ray's *Teen Kanya*. He spoke to me in Bangla, but with an accent, so I couldn't really make out if he was Bengali or not. And he had all the time in the world for me. He chatted with me, made me feel comfortable, and gave me a bunch of films to screen. I happily carried those cans back with me.' One of them was a rare gem: *Palanka* ('The Bedstead', 1975), an Indo-Bangladesh joint production directed by Rajen Tarafdar, starring Utpal Dutt and Anwar Hossain. Shohini later learnt that Safdar also got into some trouble for this – 'his bosses were cross that he had given the cans to a completely unknown college kid. But he didn't care'. She started dropping in to WBIB off and on, 'just to see Safdar and chat with him. He had a range of interests, and, remarkably, was never patronizing, even though I was just an undergraduate'.

She wasn't the only one. A group of young doctors from Maulana Azad Medical College (MAMC) had set up a film society, and they came to Safdar seeking help in getting affiliated to the Federation of Film Societies of India (FFSI). Safdar sent them to Raina, who had contacts in FFSI, with a note: '*Guru, inki madad karo*' ('Boss, help them'). Brijesh was a part of this group of young doctors who became Safdar and Mala's friends, and Safdar would send comrades, and others who couldn't afford private medical treatment, their way.

Singer Madan Gopal Singh, scholar of film and art and an expert on Sufi poetry and music from Punjab, had been Sohail's friend in Delhi University, and their friendship continued when they moved to JNU. In the meantime, Madan had also become friends with Safdar. He remembers WBIB, when Safdar was there. 'It became the most important meeting point for filmmakers, theatrepersons, musicians, folk artists, what have you. Safdar had no facilities there; he would sit at a simple table with a large Ritwik Ghatak photograph behind him, under which he had written, "The unparalleled film genius", or something like that. Alongside that was also a poster of a Satyajit Ray film. We used to have these biases then. If Brecht was your playwright, you had to despise Beckett. If you liked Vilayat Khan, you ran down Ravi Shankar. If you were a fan of Ghatak, you couldn't like Ray. We were very rigid in those days. But Safdar never fell into this trap. When filmmaker Mani Kaul visited Delhi, WBIB became his de facto office, as it did for a number of others. They'd have endless cups of tea, lunch, tea again. Safdar started organizing film screenings and press conferences. It became by far the most exciting space. There was hardly a day when I didn't go there. I would leave JNU and would drop in to Safdar's office on the way home. I had so many discussions there about cinema, theatre, and the role of the artist – I had recently read Sartre, and his idea of "littérature engagée" [socially engaged writing]. All types of artists would come there, not only Leftists. They all knew Safdar. And he'd organize lectures there. I heard architect Romi Khosla for the first time there.'

Safdar organized three festivals of Bangla plays in Delhi during his years at WBIB. He invited Utpal Dutt to perform *Daraon Pathikbar* ('Halt, O Traveller') for one of them. Utpal Dutt, already a bit of a legend on the Bangla stage, and a star of Hindi commercial cinema, had a clown's soul – he would make a joke of everything, be sarcastic and irreverent, and give a symbolic middle finger to figures of authority. But beneath that buffoonish exterior was a deep thinker, a committed Marxist revolutionary, a powerful artist who wanted to make a change in the world with his art. The older man perhaps saw a bit of himself in the younger one, and took a shine to him. When Utpal Dutt came for the festival, he made it a point to have long discussions with Safdar on theatre and politics, and Safdar was deeply influenced by his conception of the popular revolutionary theatre. Safdar also screened Utpal Dutt's films on Henry Derozio and Michael Madhusudan Dutt at the WBIB office.

When Mala and Safdar visited Bombay in 1982, they stayed with Mani Kaul for about ten days. It was a somewhat unlikely friendship, Mani Kaul's with Safdar. Safdar was nine years younger, but that didn't matter. Mani Kaul had a spiritual bent of mind, while Safdar was an atheist and materialist. Yet they hit it off. One point of convergence was their shared admiration for Ritwik Ghatak's work. One of Safdar's crucial contributions was the first Ritwik

Ghatak retrospective organized in Delhi in 1981, at Pyarelal Bhavan, alongside a seminar on his films. But he did something else as well. Madan Gopal Singh has this story to tell:

'Mani Kaul had introduced Ghatak's work to Hubert Bals, who was founding director of the Rotterdam Film Festival. Bals wanted to put in some money into the restoration of Ghatak's prints. He was a well-endowed man. The other chunk of money had to come from the Ministry of Information and Broadcasting. Safdar knew the Director of the Directorate of Film Festivals, who also used to drop in at the WBIB. There was also a Secretary from I&B ministry, a very erudite man, who came by. I think his name was Chakravarty. Mani Kaul approached Safdar. Till then, the only two directors from Bengal known internationally were Satyajit Ray and Mrinal Sen. Nobody was willing to take Ghatak. The problem was that the prints were in a pathetic shape, not worthy of being shown at an international festival. Safdar wrote to the Director of Film Festivals, who wrote back curtly, saying we can't do this. Safdar met I&B Minister Vasant Sathe, who repeated the Director's line. We were distraught. We wanted Ghatak to become an international figure. The French Marxist critic George Sadoul had seen his films, and was impressed. After that, nothing. Safdar then got an idea. He wrote to former I&B Minister Inder Kumar Gujral asking for a meeting. Gujral happened to be a friend of Ghatak. He immediately dictated an official letter to Sathe, and also called him up. Sathe said, "Done, Sir!" I think Mr Chakravarty also had a hand somewhere in this – maybe he suggested Gujral's name. Safdar was delighted, like a child. "Maddi," he said, "it's done!"'

THE EARLY 1980S. Audience Testimony

Today, with so much street theatre being done across India, it is hard to remember how the first spectators reacted to it. Here is a testimony of one.

'I first saw a street play in the early 1980s. I had been fond of plays since my childhood. I had seen many plays and even acted in some, but they had all been traditional proscenium plays. These plays – on mythological, historical, social, psychological subjects – would last for two–three hours. Naturally, these plays had all the necessary paraphernalia required for theatre, such as a stage, appropriate sets, costumes for the actors, sound and light, and an audience mentally prepared to take in the subject of the play! For me, this is all that a play meant.

'Thus it was that when one day I saw a notice for a play called *Aurat* on the notice board of Jawaharlal Nehru University's School of Languages, my curiosity was aroused. The title of the play was itself attention grabbing, but it also said that it was going to be a "street" play which would be staged on the lawns in front of the School (JNU was then in its Old Campus). All this intrigued me and I resolved to watch the play that day. In fact, though, the timing of the play was very inconvenient for me, for it was precisely then that my children got back home from school, hungry, thirsty, and cantankerous. I debated for a long time – play or home? Domestic duties of a housewife, or the yearning of a woman? And what if the elders at home got to know that I had neglected my children – and nobody worse than children to squeal on an occasion such as this! Looking at me today, it might be hard for people to imagine the struggle I went through, but at the time, it was something for me to cross the boundaries of middle-class domesticity. It seemed like a real battle! In the end though, I decided to revolt. I can't recall what arrangements I made for the children, but the memory of the play is still fresh in my mind.

'I reached the venue of the play before the announced time. I kept waiting for the stage to be set up, so I could grab a place in the front, but there was no visible movement. I thought, maybe I've misread the notice. I checked the notice again – no, there was no mistake. I got back and waited. After about five–seven minutes, suddenly students started gathering. I heaved a sigh of relief. Imagine, ignoring the children, and then missing the play as well! People kept coming and forming themselves into a big circle, as if that was rehearsed too. Ah well, here are the audience, but where are the actors? Then some youngsters started keeping what looked like small props along the inside periphery of the circle, and I became even more curious. What on earth is happening? And then, suddenly, there was this slim, dusky girl who appeared in the middle of the circle. She had no make-up, nor was she in any special costume. She wore a dark blue khadi kurta and perhaps a black salwar. In these utterly plain looking clothes, she stood in the middle of the circle, raised her arm and her voice rang out, "I am a woman ..." That gesture, those words – my heart stopped beating. I had goosebumps. I was stunned, just stunned.

'I watched, entranced. The central character, "Woman", had neither a name, nor a specific religion or region, nor was she a specific age. The actress moved effortlessly from being a small child to being a college student, to a newlywed, to an old factory worker, and while none of these had any direct connection to my own life, each resonated with me. It was amazing – I was none of the characters being portrayed, but there was a part of me in each of them. The preconceived idea of what a "heroine" is was most pleasantly shaken up by this portrayal. Sometimes, even after three hours of watching a character complete with all the theatrical accoutrements, you are left indifferent and wondering, but here, in a mere 30–35 minutes, the eternal, ancient, never-ending frustrations, suffocations, and pains of being a woman were portrayed succinctly. It was universal, but it was specific to time, place, context. As I watched, my soul tingled and I was filled with an unusual self-confidence. I was so entranced that I knew not when the play finished. The red flag, which the old woman picks up at the end of the play with such pride, kept dancing in my eyes. And then, suddenly, there was a young actor standing in front of me, collecting donations. I don't know how much money I had on me that day, but I do remember that I emptied my purse in the Janam coffers that day.'

The spectator, here, was my mother, Kalindi Deshpande, who went on to become an activist of the Janwadi Mahila Samiti (JMS);

member of the Communist Party of India (Marxist); founder of the JMS's street theatre group, Buland, and writer-director of all its plays. And the 'cantankerous children' is me, since my sister was neither cantankerous, nor quite a child anymore.

THE EARLY 1980S. The Spread of Street Theatre

In the late 1970s, there was a group in Delhi called Workshop Theatre, which included some who later migrated to the Bombay film and television industry, such as Sudhanshu Mishra, Sudhir Mishra, Sushmita Mukherjee, Bina Pal, and Anil Mehta, and some who didn't, like Anamika Haksar and Manohar Khushlani. This was the time Badal Sircar was conducting workshops across the country, teaching techniques of what he then called 'Third Theatre'. His effort was to leave behind an active theatre group after the workshop, and Workshop Theatre was one such group. They did a production of *Fanshen*, based on William Hinton's classic account of a village during the Chinese Revolution, and Badal Sircar's *Bhoma*. Many of the group's members worked with M.K. Raina, when he produced a street version of Badal Sircar's *Juloos* ('Procession') and, later, *Spartacus*, and Brecht's *The Mother*.

Sometime in 1979, with reportage of dowry deaths on the rise, feminist activists Urvashi Butalia and Subhadra Butalia of Stree Sangharsh asked theatrepersons Maya Rao and Anuradha Kapur to create a street play so that it could be used as a platform to generate discussion around the issue. Anuradha Kapur and Maya Rao together devised the street play with activists drawn from a few women's groups, a group of college-going students from Delhi University, and students from the medical colleges of Delhi. *Om Swaha*, as the play was named, had its first performance at Indraprastha College, where it had been invited for performance and discussion by scholars Kumkum Sangari and Sudesh Vaid. *Om Swaha* was subsequently translated into several Indian languages.

Responding to the popularity of *Om Swaha*, Anuradha Kapur, Manohar Khushlani, and Maya Rao decided to form a group. It came to be called Theatre Union, and *Om Swaha* was thereafter performed under its banner. Ein Lall, Ragini Prakash, and Vinod Dua joined the group. Sudesh Vaid and Kumkum Sangari continued to be involved in researching material for plays, and were actively associated in researching issues around the rape law. The other key person was Rati Bartholomew, theatreperson and scholar. Theatre Union created some of the finest street theatre I've seen.

The group's second play was on the proposed Rape Bill, called *Balatkar Qanoon* ('Rape Law'). Some doctors from Safdarjung Hospital joined in and became part of the team that devised the play. I didn't see it, but I did see *Marz Ka Munafa* ('Profiteering from Illness'), created by Theatre Union in partnership with the Voluntary Health Association of India. It was humorous, satirical, but also informative, and exposed the pharmaceutical companies that profited from people's misery. Theatre Union also experimented with taking classic plays out to the street, and they performed *Inspector General*, inspired by Mudrarakshasa's *Ala Afsar*, with music derived from nautanki, in and around Delhi. The late Asheem Chakravarty, one of the founder-members of the fusion rock band Indian Ocean, joined the music team for this production.

Without doubt, Theatre Union's masterpiece was *Toba Tek Singh*, based on Saadat Hasan Manto's short story. Over the years, I've seen several adaptations of the story on stage and screen, maybe over a dozen, but Theatre Union's production stands out for its spartan artistry and its economy of expression, which produced immediate emotional affect. The fact that I saw the play in the mid-1980s, while the wounds of the anti-Sikh violence of 1984 in Delhi were still fresh, heightened its political impact. It was truly a powerful and inspiring piece of theatre.

In the mid-1980s, the Delhi unit of AIDWA started their own street theatre group, Buland, and did four new plays in a year, all written and directed by Kalindi Deshpande. She consulted Safdar on the scripts, direction, music, choreography, and even the casting, and I remember that one of the most powerful scenes, the burning of the bride, came together because of Safdar's idea to create flames through the use of red and yellow strips of cloth. Later, when Safdar wrote the television series *Khilti Kaliyan* on literacy and women's empowerment, he gave the name Kalindi to one of the characters.

When Janam observed ten years of street theatre in late October 1988, we invited Theatre Union, and they performed *Marz Ka Munafa* and *Toba Tek Singh*. That was the last time I saw Theatre Union in action.

There were many other groups coming up in other parts of the country. The first major spurt occurred in the early 1980s, when street theatre groups sprang up all over India. In several cases, progressive writers inspired the birth of street theatre groups – reminiscent of IPTA growing out of the PWA in the 1940s. Many journals also published street plays, helping their wide dissemination. The Hindi journal *Uttarardh*, for example, brought out a special issue on street theatre in 1983. Published from Mathura by Savyasachi, the 450-page single issue played a crucial part in disseminating street plays in north India. It carried 23 street plays, including seven by Janam, five by Asghar Wajahat, two by Gursharan Singh, and a Hindi translation of a Samudaya play. *Uttarardh* continued to publish street plays regularly until Savyasachi died. The journal's contribution to the growth of street theatre cannot be overstated.

Janam's contribution, too, was crucial: Plays like *Machine* and *Aurat* reached far and wide, through journals such as *Uttarardh* and through photostats of handwritten scripts. Many groups started calling themselves Jana Natya Manch – without any organizational link with the original Janam. Several others, needing to call themselves something, took on the name of IPTA. Beyond a point, however, these names hardly mattered. What mattered was that hundreds, perhaps thousands, of young and not-so-young people felt the need to do theatre amongst, for, and of the people, and become a part of movements on the Left. Street theatre became their natural vehicle.

Some groups would turn to Janam for advice. This would happen a lot face-to-face – still does – whenever Janam travelled to another city, but some would write. For example, on February 27, 1986, an Indore-based theatre enthusiast, Parshuram Tiwari, wrote to Safdar informing him that they had formed Janam. Safdar's response of March 11, after expressing happiness and offering whatever help Janam could give, also offered two pieces of advice:

'Street theatre is a genre without an evolved grammar. This form is being continuously developed on the basis of experience. Every group is doing so in its own way. …

'Second, like every art, street theatre too demands discipline and practice. To improve, the actors need to put in their own effort. They'll need to train their voice, learn to sing, play instruments, dance, consciously deliberate on the correct use of "space" in a circular performing arena, and to rehearse seriously and systematically. No matter how potent your message, how scientific your understanding, without artistic merit, you won't move your audience.'

Safdar enclosed a copy of Janam's latest play, *Apaharan Bhaichare Ka* ('Amity Abducted'), with the letter, but also told Comrade Parshuram that the suggested contribution for the script was ten rupees, which he could send by money order.

The second major spurt in street theatre activity took place in 1989, after Safdar's murder. When artists decided to observe April 12, Safdar's birthday, as National Street Theatre Day, the response was staggering: 30,000 performances were done on that day in 1989. The figure was compiled based on the information Sahmat received; many more performances took place, though no one knows how many.

APRIL 1982. The 'Harijan' Play

'How come Janam doesn't have a play on the caste issue?'

I don't remember when I asked Safdar this, but I remember we were walking on the wide boulevards with their leafy canopies in Lutyens' Delhi.

'Well, honestly, it's a devilishly difficult issue, terribly complicated. Just think of how we name the oppressed castes. People used to use derogatory terms like "achhoot" or "chudah". Then Gandhi came along and coined "Harijan", to give them dignity. For a long time, that became the default term, except if you were speaking in a technical way, in which case Scheduled Caste was used. Today, the more politically aware sections among the oppressed don't like "Harijan", and they prefer "Dalit". Is Dalit a Marathi term?'

I was embarrassed that I didn't know – but in case you're wondering, no, it's not. It is a Sanskrit word, meaning 'broken' or 'split', and was the term preferred by Ambedkar, who thought 'Harijan', which Gandhi thought bestowed dignity, was an attempt to annex those who were outside of the four-fold varna division to Hinduism. Interestingly, the first major theorist of caste, Jotirao Phule, used the term 'Atishudra'; he also used 'Shudratishudra', which is a compound of 'Shudra', the fourth varna, and 'Atishudra', those outside of the varna division, the so-called untouchables. Moreover, Phule included all women, including Brahmin women, in Shudratishudra, since all women were victims of the inhumanities of the caste system. The other popular term, 'Bahujan', was probably coined by Ambedkar's older contemporary Vitthal Ramji Shinde, sadly a much-neglected figure in caste studies.

Safdar was thoughtful. 'We tried once to make a play on the caste issue. We failed. There were so many aspects, and we failed to bring them into a single play. We should make a proscenium play on this issue. Might be easier to deal with on a wider canvas.'

As it happened, after Safdar's death, Janam made two proscenium plays on caste, both directed by me: Govind Deshpande's *Satyashodhak*, on Jotirao and Savitribai Phule's life, in 1992, and Brijesh's *Shambukvadh*, on the episode from the *Ramayana* where Ram kills a Shudra for the 'crime' of reciting the Vedas, in 2004. We've also done street plays: Janam member Komita directed *The Last Letter* in 2016, based on the Hyderabad Central

University scholar Rohith Vemula's final testament before he took his life; and Bangalore-based theatreperson Abhishek Majumdar was invited by Janam in 2018 to write and direct *Tathagat*, the story of a shudra sculptor's supposed transgression, set in an imaginary Buddhist kingdom in ancient India.

The still-born play mentioned by Safdar was discussed in April 1982. The notes in Janam's files indicate that there was a vigorous discussion around the issue, and some attempt at writing the play. We have, in Safdar's hand, a schematic plan for a play with three episodes; in someone else's hand, about three pages of dialogues for a scene; in Safdar's hand, but entirely crossed out, a page of dialogue from the same scene. The three episodes in Safdar's schematic notes are:

'I. Landlord moneylender demands immediate settlement or eviction from land. Murder and arson. Song of cause and effect.

'II. Labourer asks for wages. Is told to wait till completion of work. Arguments lead to dismissal. Son rebels. Murder at night. Song of cause and effect.

'III. Mother wants her son admitted. Headmaster and other parents and sons protest. Arguments lead to lynching. Song of cause and effect.'

Brecht's influence is clear: 'Song of Cause and Effect' is something Brecht might've written (but didn't). The fragments of dialogue, in both Safdar's and the other person's hand, are probably from the first episode above. What is fascinating, however, is the discussion, or what can be gleaned of it from the telegraphic notes we have.

Lalit spoke of the humiliation of Dalits at the hands of caste Hindus, and of how reservations and other facilities due to Dalits are often hard to access; moreover, the dropout rate for Dalits is high in educational institutions because of economic as well as social factors. Asif felt that conversions to Christianity or Buddhism reflected a yearning for security. Vijay said that the deprived included the non-Scheduled Castes as well. Safdar made a lengthy intervention – or maybe it's just that Mala's notes were more detailed than Safdar's – and spoke of the oppressions faced by all the exploited, but also warning that in order to show the extent of oppression faced by all the poor we may tend to undermine the specific problems of Dalits. He spoke of an unnatural hiatus between the poorest Dalits and the poorest non-Dalits. Caste violence and democratic movements have an inverse relation – caste violence is more where the democratic movement is weak, and vice-versa. He spoke of the sexual exploitation of Dalit women who worked in fields and in middle-class homes. The salvation of Dalits lay not in seeking discrete, separate identities – which was a conspiracy of the ruling classes who want to divide the people on the basis of caste, religion, language, etc. – but in identifying with the toiling masses and forging a larger unity. Rajni Palriwala, the sociologist, who was in Janam then, warned against conspiracy theories, because in villages, the differences between Dalits and non-Dalits can be real, and talked of the social boycott of Dalits. Tyagi recounted in detail a situation in his village where, he claimed, some Dalits had large houses but no land to farm, leading to backlash from the upper castes. He felt that reservations were not the cause of caste conflict, as is often argued. NK reminded everyone that the discussion was to understand the situation, not on how to depict it in the play. In a bit of poetic hyperbole, he made a point about how the caste system is a weapon to outlaw the rebel. Mala said that when the poor transgress caste boundaries, so-called caste carnages are unleashed upon them. It was the social aspects of the problem they had to explore. Arun reminded everyone that even untouchability was not a thing of the past, and so must be taken up as part of the play.

The two sharpest interventions come from someone called Ravi – neither NK nor Mala have any recollection of who this person was – and Manish. Ravi warned against using the term 'Harijan', and recommended 'Dalit' instead; Dalits, moreover, he argued, were not a monolithic group. He said the Indian Renaissance of the 18th–19th centuries brought about superficial reforms that did not help the Dalits. Missionaries did not accept untouchability and brought education to the Dalits. He also said that reservation led to the creation of a comfort loving group of beneficiaries. He made a mention of Jotirao Phule, though what he said about Phule is not noted. Manish made the astute point that an attack on caste is an attack on religion, echoing Ambedkar's belief that there is nothing called Hindu religion if you take away caste.

This is a summary of what was clearly a lengthy discussion. The only record we have is in the form of hastily-scribbled bullet points. To the best of my knowledge, none of the people in the discussion were Dalit. In 1982, the vast literature on caste that we can now summon up, virtually at the click of the mouse, was simply not available. Except one, all of Gail Omvedt's published works are from the 1990s and later; Rosalind O'Hanlon's study, the first academic work of note on Phule, was published in 1985; the first volume of *Subaltern Studies* was published in 1982; the multi-volume *Writings and Speeches* of Ambedkar, edited by Vasant Moon and published by the Government of Maharashtra, first came out in 1979. But when I was an undergraduate student in the mid-1980s, I remember how hard it was to find the texts, despite having access to some of the best libraries in Delhi.

Even though scholars came to it somewhat later, the caste question was very much on the table in the Left movement. B.T. Ranadive's influential article, 'Caste, Class and Property Relations' was published in the *Economic and Political Weekly* in 1979. He argued that if the anti-caste movement did not put at the centre the question of social relations in the countryside, it would drift into casteist reformism; on the other hand, if Communists neglected caste, the Left movement would slide into class-based blindness. BTR urged both, the Left and the anti-caste movements, to conduct more joint struggles. E.M.S. Namboodiripad had also published three important pieces in this period: 'Caste, Classes and Parties in Modern Political Development' (1977); 'Caste Conflicts vs. Growing Unity of Popular Democratic Forces' (1979), 'Once Again on Caste and Classes' (1981). These essays are included in EMS's *History, Society and Land Relations: Selected Essays*, published by LeftWord Books in 2010. Like BTR, EMS too emphasizes joint struggles, and comes out strongly in defence of reservations.

In the end, Janam didn't make this play, despite all the discussion, and despite coming up with something of a structure for the play. I think what Safdar said to me was key. They struggled to capture the various levels of complexity of the caste question in the abbreviated, terse form of a street play. The early Janam plays tried to capture the essence of the totality of a phenomenon in their plays. When they succeeded, they came up with masterpieces like *Machine* and *Aurat*. They are plays of the grand sweep and a panoramic view. Sometimes, however, as in the case of the 'Harijan play', Janam struggled to reconcile the various opinions within the group, or to integrate them into an organic whole, and the play was eventually abandoned.

THE MID-1980S. Writing for Children

I was in school, in Class 11, and it was November 14, 1983, Children's Day. Most schools celebrated the day with children's performances, and teachers in the audience. Sardar Patel Vidyalaya was different. Here, teachers were on the stage, and children in the audience. I remember how our two music teachers, Uma bhai and Shahane sir, along with an art teacher, had us in splits as they sang '*Ek chatur naar, kar ke singaar*' from the Hindi film *Padosan*. This was followed by a play, *The Disappearing Act*, performed by six teachers from primary and middle school. It was about six sisters who live together. One day, a postman arrives to deliver a letter for one of the sisters. The other five sisters look for her everywhere, but cannot find her, because the postman is played by the actor playing that sister, who has now disappeared. The next day, a milkman appears at the door to deliver the milk ordered by one of the sisters, but she's disappeared too. And so on, till all the sisters have done the disappearing act.

It was an utterly charming play, and its madcap logic was

evident the moment the first sister transformed into the postman. Everybody knew what was going on, except the sisters themselves. Some of the younger kids were shouting delightedly at the actors, telling them where the missing sister was, whom the remaining sisters were simply unable to find. Watching your teachers being silly on stage is fun, the inversion humanizing what is normally a strictly hierarchical relationship.

Gargi and Mala played two of the sisters, and the play was written by Safdar.

Mala joined SPV as a primary school teacher in July 1981. It had already acquired quite a reputation in Delhi as a progressive school, and its principal, Vibha Parthasarathi, encouraged students to take part in arts activities and performances conducted by the teachers. Mala would often chat with Safdar about what she was doing with her children, and he would give ideas on how to perform a particular story or poem.

Possibly the first time Safdar wrote something specifically for children was when a parent, who was a dancer, wanted to create a performance with the students using one of the Akbar–Birbal stories written by another of the parents. The existing text was in English, and SPV was one of the rare schools that encouraged the use of Hindi without being chauvinistic about it. The medium of instruction at the primary level was Hindi, switching to English when children got to the secondary stage, and for three years they also had to learn a third language. Mala asked Safdar to translate the story into Hindi. He turned it into a poem, called '*Duniya Sabki*', and gave it a democratic twist at the end, with Akbar realizing that this earth either belongs to all or to none at all.

Safdar wrote a number of poems and plays for the SPV children, for all kinds of occasions, on request from many teachers. So, when a middle-school teacher wanted a play for children of Class 7, Safdar wrote *Girgit*, a play adapted from Anton Chekhov's short story 'The Chameleon'. Mala remembers another play, *Murtikaar* ('The Sculptor'), again written for Children's Day, in which teachers acted alongside children from Classes 2 and 3. It was about adults fighting amongst each other while children show the way through art.

Mala reckons that one of Safdar's best works for children is the poem '*Kitaben*' ('Books'). SPV had separate buildings for the primary and senior schools, which were a short walk apart. The junior school library was part of the main library in the senior school building. Mala asked Vibha Parthasarathi if the space under the staircase in the junior school could be turned into a dedicated children's library. Vibhaben said yes, but only if Mala could figure out a system for the logistics involved in accessing, keeping track of, and returning books from the main library. Gifted organizer that she is, Mala worked it out, and now the primary school had its own library. It was called 'Kitabghar' ('Bookhouse'), was easily accessible to children and teachers, and was created with contributions and ideas from teachers and parents alike. Children would sit on the staircase and read. There was also a display board, on which Mala and the other teachers would put up things related to books.

One day, Mala asked Safdar to write a poem on the wonder of the world of books. Usually, she gave him a fairly detailed brief when she asked him to write for her children. Safdar would expand the brief with his own ideas. This time, he began writing before she could say anything else.

'He didn't even take time to think,' Mala remembers. 'He wrote it at one go, with no rewriting. Normally, he worked a lot on what he wrote – editing and rewriting. For "*Kitaben*", he made very minor changes. Ninety-eight per cent of the poem you read today is as he wrote it that day, at one go. I put up the poem on the board, and the kids enjoyed it. I didn't tell them anything, or ask them to go read it. They just read it on their own, and loved it. I remember one Class 5 boy who came to me and said, "I want to write like that."'

'*Kitaben*' was later turned into a poster by the National Book Trust, and, separately, Sahmat published a poster of the poem illustrated by Mickey Patel. The poem travelled far and wide, and is easily available on the internet. It is a fine example of Safdar's use of language, which had what Mala calls 'a penetrating simplicity'.

Between about 1983 and 1987, Safdar wrote a lot for children, sometimes translating or adapting something he read and happened to like, but mostly he wrote at the instance of Mala or one of the other SPV teachers. He also helped Mala by coming up with words, and making sketches for the learning material she created for activities with children. 'He often added his own ideas and made my mad ideas madder.' Though Safdar himself never worked with children, nor was he a trained pedagogue, Mala feels that he must have imbibed something from Ammaji, who was a passionate school teacher. For her part, Mala spoke to Safdar about how children learn, and how adults can help them, not by patronizing them, but by treating them as human beings with a brain, because children have a seemingly magical ability to glean what they need from what they get.

As Safdar picked up Bangla, he started reading Sukumar Ray, and he was also fond of the other master of nonsense verse, Edward Lear. He attempted to translate Sukumar Ray into Hindi, but found it hard. He decided to try writing something new. '*Gadbad Ghotala*' ('Topsy-Turvy'), another poem that children love, was the result. Mala got her children to perform it. He also adapted Satyajit Ray's film *Gupi Gayen Bagha Bayen*, itself derived from a story by Sukumar Ray's father (and Satyajit Ray's grandfather) Upendrakishore Raychaudhuri, into a children's play.

Then there were other stories, jointly created by Mala and Safdar for this or that activity in school, which were never written down. Many of them featured animals such as a snake, black buffalo, hornet, earthworm, crow, and frog – not exactly favourites of children's literature writers – who end up playing an important and positive role in the narrative. Gender roles were routinely reversed – so the plain-looking female bird goes out to rescue the pretty male bird, who, upon being rescued, preens and says, 'Oh, you're late. I'm hungry.' Another story was about a land where the king forbids singing. A child is born here who cannot speak, but only sings. Never written down, it was converted into a play by

Janam, *Natak Jari Hai*, which we performed at Jhandapur on the first anniversary of the attack, in 1990.

Safdar's children's works were not written to be turned into books. They were written for use by teachers, or for family and friends. They were written for particular contexts, with specific readers in mind, with no thought of creating something for posterity. As a result, though he worked hard on many of them, there's a lovely casualness about them, a sense of ease, and a spoken rather than written quality – even though Safdar himself regretted that he couldn't write like Sukumar Ray. After Safdar's death, Sahmat made his writings available for wider audiences by publishing them as books, beautifully illustrated by leading artists.

THE MID-1980S. Taking Theatre Seriously

In Safdar's papers, there is a handwritten note, titled 'Adhocism in Street Theatre', written in 1983, in which he laments 'the recklessly casual manner in which most of us have taken to street-theatre'. From *Machine* onwards, a great deal of debate and discussion took place in Janam on the form of street theatre and its grammar. When you perform with the audience on one side only, the part of the stage further away from the audience, towards the back, is called upstage, and the area closer to the audience, towards the edge of the stage, is downstage. Similarly, stage-left and -right refers to the audience's perspective, not the actors'. The acting area is clearly delineated – there are wings or curtains to mark it out. What does it mean to perform with the audience on all sides? What might be upstage for one section of the audience is downstage for those on the opposite side, and similarly stage-left or -right become meaningless. There is no concept of wings or curtains which can hide or reveal the actors and the action. Performing in a circular acting area, then, had to be accompanied by its own grammar. NK, Tyagi, Rakesh, Safdar, Lalit, and others, were reminded of the street sellers they had seen, especially in the Walled City of Delhi. They sold all kinds of medicinal and aphrodisiac concoctions made of, it was claimed, roots, leaves, herbs, flowers, seeds, besides mentionable and unmentionable body parts of assorted animals. They had their audience all around them, but no spectator felt excluded. Using word play, innuendo, wit, and repartee they could hold an audience for a long time. Safdar and others admired their skill and artistry.

'Is it only this circumscribed perspective of certain established proscenium theatre people that is responsible for a near universal censure of street-theatre as little more than sloganeering? I don't think so. Part of the reason, and the major part I should imagine, is the recklessly casual manner in which most of us have taken to street-theatre. How many of us have tried to discover and develop the specific grammar and language of street-theatre? How many of us have made consistent efforts to train and equip ourselves according to the nature and exigencies of street-theatre? How many of us have tried to determine the tradition of street-theatre? Not many, I'm afraid. Our plays are clumsy, shabby, unentertaining, predictable and stale. When we sing we are out of scale, when we dance we're out of step, when we speak we can't be heard above the street-noises. Our situations are hackneyed and typed, our characters are caricatures, even our humour is singularly unfunny. We are a pain to watch. Yet, it must be noted, we're flourishing. Because we're the only [illegible; perhaps "guys"] out performing on the streets and our audiences are hungry for art.

'It is my feeling that we have taken our success for granted. This is going to be fatal as far as any possibility of the positive development of this genre is concerned. Our commitment to the emergence of an alternative theatre easily accessible to the people, a theatre responding dynamically to everyday issues of our life is going to remain a pipe-dream unless we take the specific needs and demands of our medium seriously into consideration. Let us always remember that we are theatrical workers. Unless our work is viable theatrically, it is quite meaningless. A well must be dug deep to draw clear water. If we stop when we touch the sub-soil water our efforts would have been in vain.

'There is this tendency of casualness and ad-hocism in our work. It is very often felt that street-theatre can be done by anybody. Practice, training and discipline are not really necessary. This is very harmful. There's no place in street-theatre for anyone who is not prepared to work hard to train himself/herself mentally as well as physically. Those who jump into it without any native talent and/or without any desire to develop it, harm street theatre more than those who attack it as being innately inartistic.'

In all likelihood, this note is the result of having attended a ten-day National Street Drama Festival and workshop in Bhopal, organized by the Sangeet Natak Akademi and the Madhya Pradesh Rang Mandal, in February 1983. The Janam archives include the festival handout, which lists 27 theatre groups. They included groups from cities such as Ujjain, Ambikapur, Dewas, Thane, Rajnandgaon, Arrah, Gorakhpur, Bikaner, Jabalpur, Chennai, among others. Apart from Janam, there were two other groups from Delhi: Ahsaas, which included Deepti Priya Mehrotra, author; Rahul Roy, filmmaker and activist; Vrinda Grover, lawyer; Sanjoy Roy, best known for managing the Jaipur Literature Festival; and a group known simply as 'Akhilesh Group', which was a hastily collected bunch of young Delhi actors who went to Bhopal in the hope of adding to their CVs, with neither love nor passion for street theatre. Also invited were some of the leading lights of Indian theatre, a total of 66 playwrights, directors, critics, and others. The invitees included Shombhu Mitra, Kamladevi Chattopadhyay, Govind Deshpande, Tripurari Sharma, Prasanna, Pearl Padamsee, M.K. Raina, Bansi Kaul, Kamlakar Sontakke, Rati Bartholomew, Namwar Singh, Mahesh Elkunchwar, Anuradha Kapur, Sarveshwar Dayal Saxena, Shyamanand Jalan, M.S. Sathyu, and Rajinder Nath, but I can't be sure who finally attended.

Although no group from Manipur is listed, Heisnam Kanhailal and Sabitri Heisnam are mentioned in the list of speakers and observers, and Mala is certain that she saw their classic play *Pebet* in Bhopal during this festival. Mala remembers that the Janam team was blown away by this wordless production of a simple folk tale about how a mother bird protects her young ones from the clutches of a sly and conniving cat. The play is elemental and lyrical, and anyone who's seen Sabitri as the mother bird is unlikely to ever forget this actress of extraordinary power and grace, who brings together a simple yet sophisticated gestural language and a wide vocal range of expressions in a seamless amalgamation of acting, dance, and singing. In Sabitri, the player, the instrument, and the expression become one in a way that you see rarely. Today, people are used to all kinds of experiments in theatre. In the early 1980s, when even Janam's street theatre was a stylistic and formal departure from the theatrical mainstream, Sabitri and Kanhailal's theatre, at once cerebral and physical, explosive and restrained, musical and gestural, elemental and modern, and all of this executed with matchless precision and sophistication, was a world apart. It left people gaping. For years afterwards, I heard stories of this peerless actress from Safdar and Mala, and finally, in 2010, a bunch of us from Janam packed our bags and went to Manipur to spend ten days with the maestros and their young actors. It was an incredible learning experience for us.

Probir Guha, also an exponent of physical theatre, was in Bhopal with his Living Theatre from 24 Parganas, near Calcutta; as was Atamjit Singh with Kalam, Lucknow; Gursharan Singh with Abhinaya Natya Kala Kendra, Amritsar; Ratnakar Matkari with Sutradhar, Bombay; and one of Samudaya's units, the rural troupe from Puttur. The groups would perform in the morning at the festival, and discussions and talks by experts would follow.

Through the 1980s, NK and Safdar in particular made efforts to develop their theatre skills. They watched plays, discussed them with fellow theatre workers, attended talks and seminars, and made friends with theatre artists. A year before the street theatre festival, NK and Safdar had gone to Bhopal when the director Peter Brook was visiting and wanted to interact with fellow theatremakers. This was long before his celebrated Mahabharata project, for which he visited India several times in the mid- to late 1980s.

'We need a trained theatreperson,' Safdar told Lalit. 'Someone who can train us, and others. Someone who can take the work forward.' Safdar tried to get Lalit admitted to the National School of Drama. Safdar got him the form, helped fill it out, submitted it, and even got intelligence on the entrance test from his contacts in NSD. Armed with insider knowledge, Lalit cleared the written paper, but didn't clear the practical exam.

On several occasions, Janam took a stand on controversies. For example, Janam criticized the withdrawal of Prasanna's production of *Tughlaq* from the Festival of India in London in 1982. And when, on February 8, 1986, the police stopped the performances by Janam and Parcham near Madras Hotel, and picked up NK and Safdar, a number of artists issued a statement on the same day. They called it an act of 'barbarian suppression' and demanded that the Janam actors be released immediately. The signatories included, apart from Janam, Bhisham Sahni, M.K. Raina, Dadi Pudumjee, Ramnath Pasricha, and Manjit Bawa. The actors were let off in the evening.

Many theatrepersons also became personal friends of Safdar. Among them was Seema Kapoor. She was dating actor Om Puri in the 1980s, whom she was to marry later. Safdar and Om Puri hit it off instantly, and when Om Puri learnt weaving for his role in Shyam Benegal's *Susman*, he gifted Safdar a piece of cloth he had woven. Om Puri flew to Delhi to be part of the first anniversary of Safdar's killing, travelled to Jhandapur to watch us perform, and read Pash's poem '*Ghaas*' ('Grass') at the memorial event at Rabindra Bhavan the next evening. When Mala and I met Om Puri years later, his first question was, 'What did he do with that cloth?' and became moist-eyed after learning that Safdar turned it into a shirt, which he wore with great pride.

THE MID-1980S. Committee for Communal Harmony

Prime Minister Indira Gandhi was assassinated by her Sikh bodyguards on October 31, 1984. The anti-Sikh pogrom that followed, which claimed over 3,000 lives, shattered many long-held assumptions about our society, about Hindu–Sikh relations, about the city of Delhi, and about the Congress party. Thousands of Sikh victims had to move to camps set up at various locations across the city, having lost their dear ones, their homes and businesses destroyed.

The embers were still smouldering, the wounds still raw, when one of the first peace marches took place in Delhi University's North Campus. The march wound its way across the campus, touching every college and some of the main faculties. It culminated at Khalsa College with a public meeting. Some speakers were to address the gathering, which had swelled to several thousands as the students of the host college joined in large numbers. Many of them were young men. They were angry, full of rage. Their eyes burnt with pain, hatred and sadness. Talk of retribution was in the air.

Parcham was to perform before the speeches began. But it was impossible to sing. The students were far too angry. Much of their anger was directed at the large posse of policemen. The police had been more than complicit in the bloodletting and destruction visited upon Delhi over the past days. The students were hardly unaware of this. An ugly situation was building up. The organizers of the peace march were apprehensive of what might happen.

Safdar turned to the youngest member of Parcham, Sumangala Damodaran, a frail looking, first-year undergraduate student. He asked her to take the mic. 'Sing "*Jaanewale sipahi*",' he told her. This is an anti-war song of the 1940s by the Communist poet Makhdoom Mohiuddin, and composed by Salil Chaudhury for the 1960 Hindi film *Usne Kaha Tha*. Till then, Parcham had only sung collective songs. This was their first solo song, and they had never performed it before.

The young singer, waif-like, was nervous. Safdar prodded her.

'Don't worry, sing. Just sing.'

Sumangala hesitated, but, with Safdar behind her, she started to sing. Her mellifluous voice was unexpectedly powerful. It seemed to emerge from some place deep inside her, and the fullness of her voice belied her slight build. It carried across the assemblage, which, amazingly, quietened down. As her song soared, the angry young men and women were transfixed. Something moved in them. The song spoke of a soldier as he goes to war, leaving behind his grief-stricken wife and hungry children. There is the stench of burning corpses all around; it is as if life itself is crying.

Someone in the audience started sobbing. Then another. And another. In a matter of a minute or so, many were sobbing. Women and men. Those who were not, were still overcome with emotion. There was hardly a dry eye to be seen. The cops, readying for action a few minutes before, were amazed to see the complete transformation of the mood.

It was an utterly unlikely happening. An anti-war song from forty years ago by a Hyderabadi Communist poet with a Muslim name, composed for a 1960 film by a Bengali, sung by a young Malayali undergraduate with a Hindu name, leading to catharsis among hundreds of angry Sikh youth in the wake of a communal pogrom. Nothing matched, nothing fitted. And yet, the song, soulful and searing, connected the pain of one set of victims with another, generations, geographies, and violences apart.

The anti-Sikh violence of 1984 had been a rude wake-up call for me. It occurred when I was still in school. On November 1, the day after Indira Gandhi's assassination, we didn't get the morning newspaper, and since we stayed on the JNU campus – at the time, a small island off the coast of Delhi – we had no idea what was unfolding in the rest of the city. My father asked me to cycle down to the newspaper vendor to fetch the paper. I cycled, and cycled on, wide-eyed, mesmerized by the grotesque reality unfolding in front of my eyes, as I went past the burning shops in Munirka, on to the Ring Road, to Safdarjung Hospital, where I saw a Sikh man being chased off a bus by a bloodthirsty crowd, and further to Malviya Nagar, where my then girlfriend stayed in a house owned by Sikhs, before reaching which I saw a couple of taxis on fire, spewing toxic fumes. It was a ghastly morning. Then, in the weeks following, my mother took me to some of the refugee camps, where I heard horror stories from survivors.

Two years later, on December 18, 1986, I walked with thousands of others through the streets of Delhi in what was called the People's March for Communal Harmony. I was in the second year of my undergraduate studies, and was on the fringes of the SFI, flirting now and then with activism, but really only interested in theatre, cinema, and girls. By the time the 1986 march came about, I was no longer a naive schoolboy – I had seen the campaign for Ram Janmabhoomi pick up, and I had encountered RSS cadre on the university campus – but I was still stunned to see how many people had turned up for the march: over 30,000.

This wasn't spontaneous. About one-third of those who marched were workers, mobilized by CITU. The full scale of the organizing effort became apparent to me as I researched this book. The Committee for Communal Harmony, which had called for the march, was formed on April 6, 1986, 'at the initiative of some prominent citizens of Delhi', as the brochure put it. But they were not alone. They received organizational backing from the CPI (M).

The Committee held mohalla-level meetings over six months, followed by a convention against communalism in October. Then, from mid-November, there was a month-long, concerted, final push for the march. Over twenty large public meetings were held, as well as more than a hundred and fifty street-corner meetings and door-to-door visits. Meetings were also organized in schools, colleges, and office buildings. The Committee sold about 20,000 badges with the interlocking three-hands logo designed by artist Manmohan Bawa, distributed ten lakh (one million) handbills, and pasted over 40,000 posters in the four major languages of the city: Hindi, Urdu, Punjabi, and English. It organized at least 15 screenings of M.S. Sathyu's classic film *Garam Hawa*, and Parcham sang at numerous places. Nearly 1,000 school children from 39 schools took part in a painting competition. Several eminent artists took part in a poster-making workshop, and more than eighty top artists donated their works to raise money for the campaign. The auction was held on the lawns of Rabindra Bhavan in Mandi House. I remember that former minister I.K. Gujral was the first auctioneer, who passed on the baton to artist Krishen Khanna, but the auction really took off when senior journalist Romesh Thapar took over, adding humour and verve to the proceedings, often shaming his friends to bid for higher figures than they had possibly intended to. The cause was impeccable, and nobody took offence.

The artists who had donated their works to the Committee included Anjolie Ela Menon, Arpana Caur, Arpita Singh, B.C. Sanyal, G.R. Santosh, Jatin Das, Jogen Chowdhury, Latika Katt, M.F. Husain, Madhavi Parekh, Manjit Bawa, Raghu Rai, Rumana Hussain, Sankho Chowdhury, and Vivan Sundaram. The auction raised about Rs 2.40 lakh (0.24 million) a substantial sum back then. The brochure for the march included greetings messages from President Giani Zail Singh; Supreme Court Chief Justice P.N. Bhagwati; and the vice-chancellors of Delhi University, Jawaharlal Nehru University, and Jamia Millia Islamia.

Via this massive effort, it is estimated that the Committee reached out to no less than 15 lakh (1.5 million) people.

Safdar was possibly the youngest member of the Committee for Communal Harmony. He plunged himself into organizational tasks. He had, by now, a large number of contacts in the press, among artists and intellectuals, and he drew them all into helping disseminate the message of communal harmony. He mobilized his group of young doctor friends to set up a medical camp during the march.

Janam made a new play for the campaign. Called *Apaharan Bhaichare Ka* ('Amity Abducted'), this was Janam's third play on communalism, after *Hatyare* ('Killers'), on the Aligarh riots of 1979, and *Veer Jaag Zara* ('Arise, O Brave'), on the situation in Punjab. Janam previewed *Apaharan* for friends and comrades. Babli Gupta was part of the teachers' group in the Committee and later wrote about that preview performance:

'The play was then called *The Great American Circus*. In its first version, it wasn't very effective. Comrades felt that foreign powers were being held responsible for communalism in too one-sided a manner. Alongside imperialism, the role of domestic communal and political forces was not brought out in a balanced way. Even more, comrades felt, the play was unsuccessful in inspiring people to struggle for bhaichara (amity). Safdar heard everyone out and said, OK, come back after two days to watch the revised show. In just that short time, the play underwent a fundamental transformation. I was astonished at how rapidly the Janam team was able to revise its play with such maturity. ... Now, instead of the American ringmaster, it was Bhaichara that became the focus of the play.'

She also described Safdar's organizational role in the committee. 'You could see him everywhere, carrying out a number of tasks, before the Peace March. Getting school and college principals to organize meetings in their institutions, arranging for speakers like us to go speak there, to organizing audiences – Safdar was at the forefront of all this. Then he would push us to the fore and retreat to the background, all the while assuring us that we were excellent speakers. ... When he was praised, Safdar would laugh it off. Indeed he wore his extraordinary talents very lightly.'

THE MID-1980S. Television and Documentaries

On February 2, 1988, Safdar signed a Deed of Particular Partnership under the name Vartamaan Film Makers with Gurbir Singh Garewal. The two had worked together on *Khilti Kaliyan* ('Blooming Buds'), the 24-part serial on adult literacy aired by Doordarshan. Safdar was the writer, and Garewal, a 1975 batch passout of the Film and Television Institute of India, was the director. The two had become friends and established an easy working equation.

A particular partnership is something you create for a single project, to be dissolved once the project is over. The project that Safdar and Gurbir were planning was a '13-part television serial in Hindi on the theme of Communal Harmony'. Two days later, Safdar wrote to Director-General of Doordarshan Bhaskar Ghose, saying that he had submitted a proposal for the serial, and that 'If you like my concept and the screenplay of the First Episode, I would be very pleased to have an opportunity of explaining ... how we propose to treat the subject'. It is not clear if the meeting took place.

With the working title 'Ummeed' ('Hope'), the proposed serial was the story of two families in Punjab, racked by extremist violence. Harbhajan Singh, a farmer, is a retired soldier and a veteran of the 1965 and 1971 Indo-Pakistan wars. He lives with his widowed mother, his wife, his married daughter and younger son. One of his closest friends is Jugal Kishor, a retired middle-school teacher, whose wife is a trained midwife. The two families, one Sikh, the other Hindu, are connected in all kinds of ways – for example, Jugal Kishor's wife delivers Harbhajan's daughter's child; Harbhajan's son and Jugal Kishor's elder daughter are in love. Over 13 episodes, the destinies of the two families criss-cross each other, as extremist violence, killings, migration, the rise of divisive politics among both Hindus and Sikhs, take their toll. And yet, the essential love and fraternity of the two families, and the communities they represent, not only stays intact but also grows.

Safdar's papers contain the proposal for this serial submitted to Doordarshan, which includes the concept note, the synopses of 13 episodes, and the typed screenplay of the first episode. The papers also contain the handwritten screenplays of episodes two and three. The concept note explains that the serial will: 'a) honestly record the strong links between the Hindus and the Sikhs in all aspects of life in Punjab; b) glorify the heroic and dauntless struggle of those committed to secular values in Punjab and elsewhere; c) highlight the dangers of the communal approach towards this problem'. Does it sound a bit didactic? It probably is – but then television itself, in the pre-liberalization age, was didactic. What gives the story narrative flow is the forced migration of the Hindu family to Delhi, where we encounter, among others, a Hindu nationalist property agent. The note acknowledges that the serial would be a 'somewhat idealized account of all that is positive and inspiring in the life of the ordinary people of Punjab'. The serial was never made. I haven't found a response from Doordarshan among Safdar's papers, and 1988 turned out to be an incredibly busy year for Safdar, as we shall see.

Khilti Kaliyan, the previous production that Safdar and Garewal had collaborated on, was commissioned by the Directorate of Adult Education (DAE) and UNICEF. It was based on an experimental literacy primer by the same name, and was aimed particularly at rural women in the 15–35 age bracket. The serial focused on the social, economic, and political deprivation that women faced, thus moving from literacy per se to critiquing patriarchy.

Safdar began each episode with the madari–jamura (street magician and his sidekick) act, but inverting tradition, both roles were now played by women. Each episode ended with a song on women's empowerment. The last frame of each episode was a close-up of a woman's face, with a positive and confident expression. Traditional literacy material, including the primer on which the serial was based, depicted women as homemakers and caregivers, and with bowed and covered heads. The serial, then, made a marked departure by showing women as strong, thinking individuals. Each of the characters comes across as a credible person. Avik Ghosh reports that in the evaluation study done by the Centre for the Development of Instructional Technology (CENDIT), 'it was found that the younger women in the sample villages identified closely with the characters and saw them as their inspirational role models. The older women disapproved of their forthright manner and outspoken dialogue but agreed with the substance of the issues raised. … The serial succeeded in generating a conscious thought process that was necessary before meaningful change could be brought about.'

Safdar wrote songs for specific situations in the serial. One was about a girl child having to help at home while her brother is free to play. Another song addressed the woman who finds it hard to remember the alphabets, and shows how she can recall them with the help of things she uses in her daily life. Yet another song celebrates the victory of women drawing water from a 'high-caste' well, defying the norms. Instead of using only chalk and blackboard to teach adults, each episode used everyday objects like sticks, bread, sand, grain, string, etc., to create alphabets and words – clearly something Safdar had picked up from watching Mala prepare her teaching materials. This made learning a fun activity, and was a nudge to literacy instructors to be innovative and creative. When a women's organization, Mahila Samiti, is formed in the village, there's a puppet show about a woman abandoned by her husband, who is supported by other women. Each episode emphasized the collective – to give strength to each other, to secure rights, and to earn a living. Ghosh reports: 'In the survey ... many women found these aspects of adult education more interesting than literacy and wanted to initiate similar activities in their own environment; in fact, some of them had already initiated such group-based activities'.

By creating spunky and vivacious characters, dramatic situations, and lacing his writing with humour, Safdar injected verve into what would ordinarily be a dull subject. As the serial progresses, most of the rural women gain confidence and skills – one of them, Rashida Bai, a tailor's wife, comes out of the purdah to take on the thakur. The urban characters in the serial are also women who struggle against their circumstances. The relationship between the urban and rural women is marked by warmth, respect, and camaraderie, 'without any hint of patronage towards the poor and illiterate village women', as Ghosh puts it.

The drama of the narrative derives from class, caste, and gender conflicts – the antagonist is a landlord arraigned against the progressive forces, which are represented by the health worker, the literacy movement, and the farmers' and agricultural workers' organizations such as Kisan Sabha and Khet Mazdoor Union. The serial, then, conceptualized the adult literacy movement not as a bureaucratic exercise, but as part of a genuine empowerment of economically and socially oppressed rural women.

Safdar knew the work of Paulo Freire, the Brazilian Marxist

educator whose landmark book *Pedagogy of the Oppressed* had appeared in English in 1970. Freire spoke of conscientização, or consciousness-raising, which for him was not a one-way process where middle-class educators 'raise' the consciousness of the unlettered poor. In fact, the educator is themself educated as their own objective reality is unveiled and the contradictions of that reality revealed. The middle-class educator might know how to read and write the word 'plough', but would typically have no idea how to use it. The poor farmer who does not know how to read or write 'plough' not only knows how to use it, but is also knowledgeable about myriad other things associated with it, including soil types, crops, flora and fauna, the weather, not to mention local languages, songs, and stories. For Freire, just the dissemination of existing knowledge was not enough – after all, existing knowledge had been created within existing oppressive structures. For a society free of oppression, one needed to work towards the creation of new knowledge. In this, the oppressed would become as much the knowledge creators as the educators.

But the unveiling of the structures of oppression would not automatically lead to their transformation; one needed social and political movements for that; and thus organizations of the oppressed played a crucial part in transforming societies. Through his work in theatre, in the Communist Party, and through his reading of Paulo Freire, Safdar was acutely aware of this, and therefore the conflict between the landlord and the rural poor in Safdar's writing is not a tale of woe and tragedy, but of empowerment and transformation, because the Kisan Sabha and Khet Mazdoor Union organize the poor. Some episodes of *Khilti Kaliyan* are available on YouTube, and make for compelling viewing. You might enjoy watching a young Seema Biswas as one of the central characters, and I certainly enjoyed reading slogans such as 'Kisan Sabha Zindabad', 'Khet Mazdoor Union Zindabad' written on village walls in a television show produced by a government and a UN agency, and telecast on the national broadcaster.

Safdar was not unique in conceptualizing the literacy movement in this way. Most left-wing radical activists who went into literacy work in the 1980s shared the belief that it was part of the struggle against gender exploitation, patriarchy, superstition, regressive social practices, feudalism, and caste. It was a struggle for rationality and the development of a scientific temper, and for the creation of a just and equitable society.

There's a little, personal postscript to this. I was to play a landless labourer, Kalua, in *Khilti Kaliyan*. The character appeared at the end of the first episode, and was to grow in subsequent episodes, with a love angle included. If you watch the episode, you'll see that short sequence filmed from afar, with Kalua (me, making my screen debut) with his back to the light. Even I cannot recognize myself in that shot. The reason? I stammered and stammered and stammered when we shot that. Safdar tried this and he tried that, but I just wasn't able to deliver my two lines. It held up shooting for a couple of hours. In the end, Garewal decided to go for the backlit long shot, and I recorded the lines separately. The character was dropped from subsequent episodes. When I asked him, Safdar wouldn't say it was because of me.

'The story changed. We decided to take out the love angle.'

I chose to believe him.

Perhaps Safdar's most popular work ever is the song '*Padhna Likhna Seekho*' ('Learn to Read and Write'). Ghosh says the song was 'written for' the National Literacy Mission (NLM), but Mala recalls that Safdar wrote it independently, perhaps as part of the writing for *Khilti Kaliyan*, or maybe for no particular purpose. Either way, it became the NLM's rallying song, an anthem, became wildly popular, and was translated into several languages. Paulo Freire's spirit is again present in these lines: '*Padhna likhna seekho, o mehnat karne walon / Padhna likhna seekho, o bhookh se marne walon*' ('Learn to read and write, you who toil / Learn to read and write, you who die of hunger'). The song itself is an adaptation of Bertolt Brecht's song 'Praise of Learning' from his play *The Mother*. Not only was the song taught and sung extensively all over the Hindi-speaking region as part of the literacy mission work, it was also telecast on Doordarshan, gaining it audiences in the millions.

The politics of the song challenged traditional hierarchies. Objections were raised, apparently by some viewers, but most certainly by some officials of the adult education directorate, that the words 'you who die of hunger' ran contrary to the government's claim of having eradicated starvation. I recall there was an alternative version of the song broadcast as well, in which the offending line was dropped and the first line repeated. But what went uncensored was this:

Poochho, mazdoori ki khatir log bhatakte kyun hain?
Padho, tumhari sookhi roti giddh lapakte kyun hain?
Poochho, ma-beheno par yon badmash jhapat-te kyun hain?
Padho, tumhari mehnat ka phal seth gatakte kyun hain?
Ask, why do people have to wander looking for work?
Learn, why is your meagre bread snatched away by vultures?
Ask, why are women sexually exploited?
Learn, why are fruits of your labour pocketed by the rich?

Padho, likha hai deewaron par mehnatkash ka nara
Padho, poster kya kehta hai, vo bhi dost tumhara
Padho, agar andhe vishwason se pana chhutkara
Padho, kitaben kehti hain, sara sansar tumhara
Padho, ki har mehnatkash ko uska haq dilwana hai
Padho, agar is desh ko apne dhang se chalwana hai
Read, the workers' slogan on the wall
Read, what the poster says, for it too is a friend
Learn, to break the shackles of superstition
Read, books say, the whole world is yours
Learn, if toilers are to win rights
Learn, if you are to run the country in your own interests

Idiotic bureaucrats, then, obsessing about a reference to poverty and hunger, paid no attention to the references to capitalist and gender exploitation, and to socialist revolution.

'*Padhna Likhna Seekho*' was adopted spontaneously by nearly everyone who was involved in any literacy-related work, including in the Total Literacy Campaign and by the activists of the Bharat Gyan Vigyan Samiti. It was also taught to children in municipal schools of Delhi. The appeal of this song, however, transcended the specific government campaign that had adopted it, striking a chord among the people at large, becoming a rare example of a government-transmitted song gaining wide popularity on its own.

Safdar wrote songs for documentaries as well. In 1985, six graduates of the recently established Mass Communication Research Centre (MCRC) in Jamia Millia Islamia came together to form a filmmaking collective, Mediastorm. They were Shikha Jhingan, Sabina Gadihoke, Sabina Kidwai, Ranjani Majumdar, Shohini Ghosh, and Charu Gargi. It was probably India's first documentary collective, and the fact that it was an all-woman group made people sit up and take notice. They made three films – *In Secular India* (1986), *From the Burning Embers* (1988), and *Whose Country is it Anyway* (1991).

Shohini, who Safdar had been generous in sharing film cans with in his time at the West Bengal Information Bureau, recounts, '*In Secular India* was a film on the Shah Bano Judgment and its consequences. It started as a student project encouraged by the founder of the MCRC, Anwar Jamal Kidwai, after whom the Centre is now named. But, soon we had to pursue this as an independent film because the university took a different position on the Muslim Women's Bill. A.J. Kidwai helped us find support from other independent filmmakers like Mike Pandey. After the shooting was completed, we asked Safdar to write a song that would help us depict the journey of an indigent Muslim woman who would have to bear the consequences of the Muslim Women's Bill. He protested, saying that he had never written standalone songs which were not part of a play or serial before. But we persisted. What he wrote was a beautiful, narrative song, that captured perfectly the essence of our film. Ranjani remembers him struggling with the song for two or three days, after which it suddenly happened. The song flowed. He wrote it while sitting in a dhaba and sipping tea while the rest of us finished our final projects at MCRC. He also wrote three powerful songs for the second Mediastorm film, *From the Burning Embers* (1988), on the incident of Roop Kanwar's "sati" in Deorala. Janam performed a play within the film about sati, which is an important recurring motif. That play was written by Kalindi Deshpande and Mala played Roop Kanwar.'

Over time, Shohini remembers, Safdar became a 'regular figure' at MCRC. Ranjani did a studio-exercise on the Bhopal Gas tragedy in which the guests in conversation were Prabir Purkayastha of the Delhi Science Forum and Safdar. He also taught the street theatre module at MCRC for a year. Later, in 1993–94, Mala taught it for a year, after which I took over for a decade.

In 1987, Safdar conceptualized a series called *Paanch Minute* ('Five Minutes') for the Press Trust of India's television wing PTI-TV, to be written and directed by him. These were short, five-minute fiction films revolving around one family, and each episode, around a single issue, would feature one guest actor. I was present when he shot the pilot episode in June 1987 at a flat in Munirka, adjoining JNU. Safdar asked if I'd like to see how things are shot and I went along since I had nothing better to do. The episode was shot on one night, and edited the next day, so effectively Safdar worked twenty-four hours at a stretch. I had never before seen anybody work that long without a break and I remember I was having a tough time keeping awake during the editing. As I recall, the series revolved around a family consisting of the parents and two children, and a grandmother. The father was played by Manish, and Lovleen Misra, fresh from her success on India's first soap *Hum Log*, was the daughter. The episode was around the issue of senior citizens feeling useless to society. The guest in the pilot was Virendra Saxena, who was superb as Jarnail Singh in Govind Nihalani's adaptation of Bhisham Sahni's series *Tamas* the previous year, and whom Safdar knew from earlier through his theatre work. The series was never shot, even though the pilot may have been approved.

Between 1985 and 1988, Safdar worked extensively in video and television. In these three years, he was involved, as scriptwriter, songwriter, and/or voiceover artist, in at least 13 documentaries of varying lengths, all for Doordarshan. These included short, five-minute films on progressive icons such as Charlie Chaplin, Albert Einstein, and Jawaharlal Nehru, as well as Shakespeare; also other films on subjects as varied as a wildlife film festival; energy; world peace; rural India; and the First War of Indian Independence. In addition, he voiced a large number of documentaries for various agencies, and directed some as well, including one on communal harmony for the Committee for Communal Harmony, *Mil Ke Chalo* ('Walk United'), and one on public health for the Delhi Science Forum, *Rog Puran* ('Illness Saga').

These were early years of home video, or VHS technology, in India, which had originated in Japan and had arrived in the US and Europe in the late 1970s. Suddenly, the technology made video a consumer product – the cameras became smaller, therefore more portable, and cheaper; and you could record, store, and play back video on tapes, much like what you could do with music. Just as many of the first generation of IPTA stalwarts moved to the Bombay film industry in the hope of reaching mass audiences through the cinema, Safdar believed that left-wing cultural activists must embrace technological change. This and other ideas formed a large part of his dream of establishing a cultural centre in a working-class neighbourhood, to which we shall come later.

1988. Pakistan

Safdar had been to Pakistan once as a child to meet family, but as an adult, he had no passport, for the need had never arisen. So, in December 1987, when he got a letter from Kamla Bhasin, then with the UN's Food and Agriculture Organization (FAO), inviting him to travel to Lahore for a six-day street or people's theatre workshop from February 6 to 11, 1988, he had to scramble around and first get a passport. The letter said that participants could stay on for the Faiz Mela from February 11 to 13.

Badal Sircar, at 63, was the oldest member of the Indian team, followed by Rati Bartholomew (59), Anuradha Kapur (37), Maya Rao (34), and Safdar (33).

Fortunately, we have a video record for large parts of the workshop. I had seen bits of it in Sashi Kumar's film, including that hilarious part where Safdar laments that in Janam most actors go off tune – but in full volume, in their powerful, well-oiled, street-theatre voices. Later, when Lalit Vachani made a film on Janam, he used this bit for further hilarity, by intercutting an utterly tuneless Vijay Kalia and a moderately tuneless me singing the Bora song from *Samrath* with a tuneful and melodious Safdar.

The workshop videos are wonderful to watch. There are, as one can expect, no barriers between the Indians and Pakistanis. They look the same, have the same habits, speak the same languages, and smoke as many cigarettes. Even though the Indians emphasize more than once that they've come to learn about theatre in Pakistan, they are looked upon as teachers by the Pakistanis. For good reason, because each of the Indians had more experience than any of the Pakistanis. Badal Sircar, in fact, led a full session only for the Pakistanis, talking at length about his own theatre practice, and explaining how the human body was used in his work, by getting the Pakistani actors to do small bits from his plays.

The overall mood was one of open engagement, frank discussion, and even, at times, gentle critique. Of the Indians, Badal Sircar was a silent, nearly invisible, observer for the most part, except when he's leading the workshop, when he springs to life, animated and passionate. Rati Bartholomew was not as vocal as I had expected, but she can be seen taking extensive notes and following the discussion keenly. Anuradha Kapur made brief, but sharp, interventions.

Maya Rao and Safdar were the most vivacious participants, taking notes, keenly following every point made by others, contributing with questions, comments, and sharing their experiences. Nobody seemed like they were projecting or pushing themselves, or looking for further networking or travelling opportunities. Early on, when Nighat Saeed Khan, their host in Lahore who had partnered with Kamla Bhasin for this workshop, proposed that they spend the last session concretizing a programme for the future, Safdar clarified that 'I've not come here to be part of any programme. I've come here for an interaction with Pakistani theatre workers. I want to make that very clear. I represent a group. If a programme emerges, I'll have to talk to my group and get their mandate'. Maya was also not sure: 'If there's a pre-designed programme, I'd like to know what it is.'

Perhaps because Badal Sircar put it on the table while explaining what he means by 'Free Theatre' (by this time, he had abandoned his earlier term, 'Third Theatre'), there was a fair bit of discussion early on about the practicalities of doing theatre and mobilizing the resources required for it. Madeeha Gauhar, 32 at the time, who went on to become a leading theatre and women's rights activist in Pakistan, spoke at length about their group, Ajoka. Her husband and collaborator Shahid Nadeem was a mostly quiet presence, making an occasional factual intervention, or asking questions. The members of Punjab Lok Rehs and Saanjh also shared their experiences.

Some of the most exciting parts of the workshop were when the Indians explained the craft of their street-theatre work, and connected it to their politics. Anuradha and Maya, with help from some volunteers (including Safdar), demonstrated a couple of scenes from *Om Swaha*. They spoke about, and showed how, they tried to convey those parts of women's experiences that are typically not considered important – the silences and the sighs – by the techniques of amplification and its opposite, concentration. Maya spoke about the experience of a predominantly female team performing in the open about issues that are particularly private –

dowry and rape. 'Rape is real, but in showing it in street theatre, you have to use styles and forms that are non-realistic,' she said. She also spoke about how in street theatre, since time was limited, priorities had to be absolutely clear. For instance, they had to decide if their play was going to be on dowry, or on dowry deaths. 'Dowry is a vast subject, and goes into all kinds of issues, including fundamental ones of women's status in society. So we decided to focus on dowry harassment and dowry deaths, not so much on dowry itself.'

Safdar shared Janam's experiences and gave insights into craft – he spoke of performing with and for mass organizations; the use of traditional metres like Alha and Beher Taveel; the use of film song tunes; about the difference between campaign plays and plays about abiding issues; about how the same device – the madari–jamura act – works well in one play (*Samrath*), but doesn't in another (*Apaharan*). Anuradha and Maya had spoken earlier about the difficulty of ending a play. Safdar added a formal dimension to the issue: 'Ending the play is always a challenge. We don't have the formal devices of the proscenium stage to signal the end of the play, like a curtain falling, or blackout, or lights in the auditorium going up. We just have a circular acting area, often not even formally marked out. So the play has to have a sense of completion. We all agree that street plays should end with a call to action. But there are many subjects that don't lend themselves to a simplistic call to action. So sometimes you end with a question or a set of questions that you want the audience to take back with them.' He gave the example of *Samrath* and *Raja Ka Baja*, which both end with questions.

When Madeeha spoke about working with traditional forms because they were familiar to the people, Safdar gently brought in a balancing perspective: 'There is tradition and there is tradition. Every thinking person has to establish a critical relationship with tradition. All kinds of obscurantist and backward values are also part of our tradition. Ideas that pull us back. You see, it is very easy that in an effort to discover your tradition, you become its slave. In the performing arts, there are many forms that are vibrant and part of tradition. It is at times possible to use these forms, with changes, creatively. Sometimes the form brings with it its content, bundled together. One has to be careful. In India, it has played havoc with our culture. This "going to the roots" has really played havoc with us. Today it's being used by government organizations like the Sangeet Natak Akademi and by imperialist agencies like the Ford Foundation, and the motives behind such use are not very clear.'

Safdar was firm on his politics. When Kamla Bhasin asked him about propaganda and theatre, and how Janam steers clear of the former, his response was candid and honest: 'There is no simple answer possible. Sometimes you need a clear-cut "line". In a situation of riots, for example. Sometimes the play is directed towards the consciousness of the people. Sometimes the play only raises certain questions. Sometimes the play only poses a problem. I am not shy of putting forward the group's position in front of the people.'

For me, one of the moving moments of the workshop was when Badal Sircar recounted the events leading to the death of the young theatre worker Prabir Datta of Silhouette. This happened in Calcutta's Curzon Park in 1974, at the height of the semi-fascist terror of the Congress government in West Bengal. There was consternation and anger about his death, and many theatre and other artists and intellectuals came together to protest. 'I insisted,' Badal Sircar told the participants, 'that the real reply is not to send a letter to the prime minister – do that by all means – or to send a delegation to the chief minister – do that by all means – but, over and above that, go to Curzon Park next Saturday and establish our right to do theatre'.

Mala made sure we did exactly this when the time came.

LATE-1980S. Ennui

The year 1986 was the centenary of the historic May Day struggle in Chicago. More than anything else, it was this struggle that normalized the idea of the eight-hour working day with the slogan,

'Eight hours for work. Eight hours for rest. Eight hours for what we will'. Trade unions all over the world were gearing up to observe the centenary, so also CITU. Janam decided to do a play to commemorate this occasion and to take the legacy of May Day to workers. Safdar wrote a play called *Mai Divas Ki Kahani* ('The Saga of May Day'). It dramatized three historic moments: the trial of the May Day martyrs in Chicago in 1886; the 1905 parade in Russia, based on Brecht's May Day scene from *The Mother*; and May Day in Nazi Germany. Though the settings and names were foreign and unfamiliar to workers in Delhi, they responded to the play with enthusiasm.

While the play was successful, it was hard to do – not for any other reason but simply because Janam didn't have enough actors available, even though it was written such that it could be done with only six actors. Safdar sought to compensate for the lack of actors with innovative use of properties, including masks. *Mai Divas* is probably one of Janam's most visually interesting street plays, using nearly ninety different pieces of properties in an intricate choreography of who picks up what object from where in the circle, and keeps it down where.

Sometime around then, Safdar saw an American actor do a single-person performance on Mark Twain's life and work. That excited him. Solo performances were not at the time as common as they've subsequently become. He thought maybe Janam could develop such performances as well, and Premchand seemed a good figure to start with. He had started reading Premchand to try and develop this idea. He said to Mala that maybe they could do it as a two-person piece, if nobody else was available. He had also seen his old friend Jayanta Das, one of the finest actors on the Bengali stage in Delhi, do a dramatized reading with a group of actors. Safdar thought this was also something to look at. On the other hand, he would surely also have wondered whether, while the idea of such a performance was exciting in itself, it would not make the problem worse, rather than solving it.

And it's not as if the drift had only recently begun. Among

Safdar's papers, there is a note from April 1982, in which there is a reference to the need to make plays on 'broad and general issues', such as caste-based reservations, communalism, unemployment, and population. The note mentions a report by Rathin Das, which said that after the 1980 tour to Calcutta, the group seemed to have moved away from its core audience, the working class, especially in and around Delhi. Safdar observed that there was a tendency among Janam actors to be unavailable for working-class shows, which led to cancellation of these shows, and that this tendency was 'pronouncedly more compared to shows for middle class audiences'. He lamented that 'general feeling of participation is absent', and underlined the need to maintain and prepare accounts 'scrupulously and meticulously'. The other bullet points include the need for new plays to be prepared regularly; review of each performance; and planning performances at Janam's initiative – that is, to not wait for organizations to invite them. The last point, which seems to go counter to Safdar's repeated emphasis on collective functioning, is tantalizingly brief: 'Establish the leader completely.'

Over the next few years, the problem only got worse. The conclusion was inescapable. Apathy and ennui had set in.

PART THREE

1988. Reviving Janam

In 1987, the Janam that I came to was dying.

Safdar figured that the only way to resuscitate it was to anchor the group's politics more firmly. Janam had to become, once again, part of the actual movements on the ground.

This could hardly be done with a tired, demotivated, and aging group of actors. It needed youthful minds and young bodies, fresh new actors who'd bring new energy and ideas with them, and who'd be willing to learn. Perhaps Safdar was reminded of his own time in IPTA. He went on an aggressive recruitment drive. The only way to retain young people was to give them exciting things to do, to challenge them creatively, and for the whole group, new and old, to learn new skills as theatremakers. These young people had to be made leaders, for which Janam's internal organizational structure had to be revamped. Janam had to build closer ties with other Left cultural organizations. And all this was in service of the greatest need of the hour: to strengthen Janam's ties with the working class and to take active part in struggles on the ground.

In retrospect, it seems extraordinary to me that he managed to do all this in the space of about half a year, from the summer of 1988 to the end of the year. And he did all this without making a big deal of it, always with good cheer. The abiding impression I have of him from this time is that of a man who walked with a spring in his step, a goofy grin pasted on his face, which, for all its goofiness, nevertheless managed to enhance, rather than compromise, his good looks.

SUMMER 1988. Aurat

One day the phone rang. It was Safdar.

'I know you're preparing for exams, but we have a performance of *Samrath* coming up in Deshbandhu College. I'd like you to come. I'm trying to see if we can attract some of the students to Janam. It'll be good for them to see some young faces as well, not just old fogies like us.'

Since Manish and Tyagi were both available for the show, Safdar was back in his role as the singing sack of grain, so I didn't have to act. I was relieved.

Deshbandhu was for long considered a somewhat rowdy college. In the mid-1980s though, it had seen a remarkable turnaround. It was now known for two things – left-wing student activism and theatre. SFI had built a strong organization there, and, if memory serves, had not only won the president's post three years running, but held all four central office bearers' posts that year.

As Left ideas started circulating among students, and as the SFI stood up to the student organizations of the Congress and the RSS, the college became a safer place, especially for women. An overall atmosphere developed that valued intellectual development, involvement in activism, and cultural activities. In this context, the theatre society of the college also took wings.

The performance was a success, and the theatre society students were impressed. They'd never seen anything like this before – a play in the open, performed in daylight, without fuss, and with a minimum of properties, yet so inventive, clever, and funny. After the performance, the theatre society students took us to the canteen for tea and samosas. Safdar was chatting with the students.

'Don't any of you play any instruments? Who are the singers?'

One played the dholak, and another sang.

'I'm not going to let you go. You have to join Janam. Where did you learn to play the dholak? And are you a trained singer? No? Great, so you have natural talent. Here's where we rehearse, take down the address. When can you come?'

The dholak player was Jogi, and the singer was Brijender. They were friends from before college. They were so thick that they had even developed a secret language that they used with great felicity. It sounded like Hindi, but when you listened carefully you realized it wasn't. They shared the same surname, Singh, so people assumed they were brothers. As they both developed into good singers, I used to affectionately call them the 'Singh bandhu' of Janam.

With them came Rakesh Sharma, an actor who later developed interest in direction as well. When we worked with Habib Tanvir later that year, more actors from Deshbandhu College joined Janam: Arun Kalra, Praveen Vadhera ('Lamby'), and, later, Joy Sengupta. Another person to join was Shikha Sethi, whose connection with Deshbandhu College was that her husband taught there.

Safdar also held a theatre workshop in JNU, looking to attract young actors. Despite the strength of the Left students' movement in JNU and the fact that we perform on campus frequently, few students there have been part of Janam over the years. One reason is that JNU has a more rigorous academic schedule. Also, JNU students have a tendency to stick to their campus and not travel out too much. But the JNU workshop was successful in one special respect: Three young women joined Janam, all at once. One was Ayesha Kidwai, who brought along her friend Shikma Pandit. Everybody assumed that Shikma was a JNU student, and she was happy to let them. The third was Prachee Doval. No longer was Mala the solitary woman actor in Janam. I dragged my friends Sanjay Maharishi and Nandita Das to Janam. We'd been classmates in school, and had kept up our friendship through college, made easier by the fact that we were all on North Campus. My colleague from the Ramjas College drama society, Aishwaraj Kumar, also joined.

But that was later. Earlier in the summer, Safdar directed a production of *Aurat* with an almost entirely new cast. *Aurat* is a little gem; the street version of the well-made play. In a sense, you could read it as having three acts, preceded by a prologue and followed by, not quite an epilogue, but a sort of 'brahmavakya', or concluding statement. The 'acts' are stories of three characters, which together combine to tell the story of Woman. The stories of the three characters are not told in full biographical or psychological detail. Rather, we see scenes that typify the lives not of three unique women, but the experiences of multitudes of women who find themselves in similar situations. In that sense, the scenes don't tell what is different about these characters that sets them apart from the rest of society; we learn what is common to many women who live in our society. The women are not heroines, they are emblems of our world.

When people think of 'street theatre', the structure they have in mind, is like that of *Aurat* – a general statement of the problem, followed by short, pithy scenes that explicate different aspects of the problem. These scenes are not part of a single narrative, nor a single character's story. They are linked together like spokes of a wheel – each pointing in its own direction, but each emerging out of the same central hub. Thus, the girl child's story (who grows up to be married to an alcoholic husband), the middle-class young woman's story (who is sexually harassed when she appears for a job interview), and the worker woman's story (who is thrown out of her job by the capitalist because she allegedly cannot work as hard as the male workers) are all connected to, and grow out of gender oppression in Indian society, which is the central problem.

The songs, Brechtian in character, comment on the action, sometimes signal the end of the section, and take the action forward to the next scene. The play has superb, biting humour, in the best tradition of political theatre. When the girl is married, the priest chants a series of dos and don'ts of a woman's life, as holy mantras; when the second woman seeks admission to study physics in college, she is asked hilariously ridiculous questions.

The prologue to the play is a poem – Marzieh Ahmed Ooskooi's 'I am a Woman'. Ooskooi was an Iranian Communist school teacher, who was assassinated by the Shah's police. Safdar read an English translation of the poem somewhere and was determined to include it in the play. He translated it beautifully into Hindustani.

In Janam's new production, Mala did the various roles of the woman, and I, like the rest of the male cast, played a number of roles, including that of the girl's father in the first scene. It was the first time I was acting with Mala, and I played her father.

SUMMER 1988. Raja Ka Baja

Before the university opened for the new term that year, Safdar directed a production of *Raja Ka Baja* ('The King's Band'), again with a fresh cast. It was a dream come true for me. I had eyed the central role of Rameshwar Dayal for the longest time and was thrilled when Safdar asked me to play that. Since we had two singers in the group now, the Sutradhar's role was split in two, and Jogi's dholak added an extra something to the play. Shikha was now part of the group, so she replaced Mala, and even Safdar's niece Sania Saeed, visiting from Pakistan, and going against visa regulations, acted in some shows.

When the university opened, we did performances in several colleges. Safdar would speak before the performance, telling students that we were an open group that they could join too, and asking for donations at the end. After every performance, a few students would take our contact details. Some of them landed up at rehearsal as well.

Safdar and I were walking to rehearsal one day.

'I want you to speak before the play as well. It shouldn't only be me.'

'But Safdar, you know I stammer. I'll never be able to.'

'You never stammer when you're acting. Or singing. Or what you think is singing.' I never lived down my sensational singing debut with Safdar.

'That's different. There I know my lines. It's all rehearsed.'

'So learn these lines as well. Write them down. I'll help you.'

Then, a day or two later, as we sat in the bus, going for the performance, Safdar helped me prepare my speech. I didn't write it down, but I pretty much memorized it.

And when the time came, I delivered it without a hitch. Not even the hint of a stutter.

'See? I told you you'd be OK.'

In the coming weeks and months, I started speaking more and more frequently before the performance, and no longer felt I had to memorize the lines. I could just get up there and extemporize.

MAY 1988. Habib Tanvir

It was with bouncing steps and a grin wider than the Bay of Bengal that Safdar arrived at rehearsal one day.

'You'll never believe this. Habib Tanvir has agreed to direct a play for us. It's going to be a proscenium play. And I'll be writing it!'

After a whole decade of only doing street plays, Safdar felt it was time to take up more complex theatrical challenges. He had never written a proscenium play. He had adapted Maxim Gorky's *Enemies* sometime around 1982–83, but it had remained unproduced because Janam didn't have the means – we neither had the actors, nor the financial resources, nor the theatrical skills. Now was the time to take the plunge and change that. *Dushman* ('Enemies'), which remained unperformed in Safdar's life, was eventually directed by Habib Tanvir for the National School of Drama Repertory Company in 1989, after Safdar's death. Habib Tanvir wrote fresh songs for it. It was a marvellous production, but the NSD Repertory only did a few performances of it. Habib sa'ab later told me that the NSD bosses found it politically too radical, what with all the red flags and revolutionary songs, and killed it. Habib Tanvir was never again asked to direct another play for the Repertory.

Habib sa'ab had known Safdar's father, Haneef Hashmi, as a colleague and friend at the Soviet Information Department in the 1960s, and remembered being introduced to the young boy.

'He is already a Communist, and his colour is much deeper red', Haneef Hashmi, himself a member of the CPI, told Habib sa'ab. 'He is trying to follow in your footsteps,' he continued, alluding to Safdar's early school days' interest in theatre. Some time before we started working with Habib sa'ab, his associate, the legendary Naya Theatre actress Fida Bai Markam, got badly burnt in an accident. 'Everyone admired her talent, Safdar no less,' Habib Tanvir later wrote. 'She barely managed to recover after several months of treatment but ended up with a hole in her throat. She was staying with our group at our Ber Sarai headquarters in Delhi when Safdar dropped in one day and had a look at her. He suggested that she be shown to some young doctors of his acquaintance at Safdarjung Hospital where in any case she was still undergoing treatment at the Burns Unit for cosmetics. We went to another section of the hospital, where I was amazed to see such a lot of young surgeons summoned by Safdar within minutes, who had gathered round Fida and got busy examining her with some new sophisticated machines. There we spent a good part of the day with the doctors – I was wondering all the time whether this man had anything else to do at all in life other than what he was focused on at that moment.' Habib sa'ab was struck by Safdar's 'irrepressible humanitarianism', and noticed how many doctors had gathered when Safdar was in hospital after the attack, which 'set me thinking that he must have, apart from knowing them helped so many needy patients in his life who did not have the wherewithal for treatment'.

Safdar had written a sympathetic but critical review of Habib sa'ab's *Hirma Ki Amar Kahani* in 1985. He had not only watched the play, but had also attended many rehearsals and interviewed Habib sa'ab at length about it. Safdar's review, Habib sa'ab wrote, had 'more depth than any review I have ever seen.'

In the summer of 1988, Safdar and Mala requested Habib sa'ab to direct Janam in a proscenium play. Safdar told him of Janam's plan to mount big plays to provide training to actors who had done nothing but street theatre for the past decade. 'I was the first man he approached in this connection, and I was thrilled. I was very fond of Safdar, but who wasn't? We liked him for his charming personality, his easy laughter, sophisticated manners, effortless articulation, clear-cut views and tender human values,' wrote Habib sa'ab.

Safdar contacted other Left cultural organizations, the writers' organization Janwadi Lekhak Sangh, the song squad Parcham, and Jansamskriti, an organization of Malayalis in Delhi, and proposed a festival around the most popular Hindi writer of the century, Munshi Premchand. Called the 'Premchand Samaroh', it was to have a seminar on the writer and a production based on his works. It was this that Safdar was to write and Habib Tanvir direct.

He had planned to do a short play on the issue of communalism, of about forty-five minutes to an hour. Hindu and Muslim communalisms had grown as twin monsters in the last few years. Rajiv Gandhi had become prime minister riding the wave of the Hindu backlash that followed Operation Bluestar, Mrs Gandhi's assassination, and the anti-Sikh pogrom of 1984. The following year, the Supreme Court delivered a progressive judgment in the Shah Bano case, recognizing the right of Muslim women to get maintenance from their former husbands after divorce. The Congress government effectively annulled this by passing the Muslim Women (Protection of Rights on Divorce) Act, 1986. The Hindu Right started conducting a vicious campaign against the government alleging minority appeasement – and appeasement it was, but not minority appeasement; it was appeasement of minority communal forces. In response, the government opened the locks of the Babri Masjid in 1986, giving a fillip to the Hindu right-wing forces that had been campaigning on the Ram Janmabhoomi issue. Communal passions were on the rise all around. Safdar felt that a cultural response to this could be shaped through the writings of Premchand.

While Premchand is justifiably celebrated as a novelist, he was also an ace short-story writer, and Safdar began looking for stories that could be adapted for the stage. He started reading *Mansarovar*, Premchand's seven-volume compilation of short stories. I asked if I could also get involved in some way. I wasn't a writer, nor had ambitions to be one, but I was keen to observe Safdar and Habib Tanvir at work. So I began reading the stories too. Safdar passed on the volumes that he had read, to me. I read them with zeal, but

I had no idea how a story could be adapted into a play, so all I was good for was to act like a more or less silent bouncing board for Safdar's ideas.

Safdar identified about half a dozen short stories from *Mansarovar* which he thought might provide material for our play. Since Habib sa'ab read Hindi slowly (he read and wrote in Urdu), he asked us if we'd read them out to him. So one Sunday morning, Safdar and I landed up at Habib sa'ab's house in Ber Sarai.

I was startled to see how tiny it was. You entered through the kitchen, went into a small drawing room with books, files and writing material strewn all over – as well as Habib sa'ab's trademark pipe, tobacco, a big box of matches and an ash tray. There was no door between this room and the only other room in the house, their bedroom, which had a double bed, where Moneekadi sat reading. Habib sa'ab sat on the wooden and jute sofa, and we were given two moodas.

Safdar read one story, and asked me if I'd read the next. Somewhat nervous to be in the presence of the legendary Habib Tanvir, I didn't even have the guts to say no.

Bad idea.

I began reading, but I was stammering as much as my heart was thudding in my chest. Safdar kept up an encouraging prattle. 'He's a very good actor. Once he gets going, you'll see.' Habib sa'ab nodded, an unmistakable twinkle in his eye. I smiled weakly and soldiered on. Habib sa'ab lit his pipe languorously. I became even more nervous. After five minutes of stuttering, I had not even managed to finish the first paragraph.

'Hmm. Safdar, right now we need the Rajdhani Express, not a goods train, or else we'll be here for the next two days. Why don't you take over?'

So Safdar read for the next three hours, one story after another. Moneekadi and Habib sa'ab listened, Habib sa'ab occasionally jotting down a note or two in his diary. After the first few minutes, I relaxed and forgot my embarrassment, drawn into the worlds that

Premchand created for us. When he finally finished with the last one, Safdar looked at Habib sa'ab.

'What do you think? Which of these can we use?'

'Well, they are all superb. What do you think? After all, you have to write, not me.'

'I think we might be able to punch together two of them: *Hinsa Parmo Dharmah*, and *Satyagraha*.'

'Explain.' Habib sa'ab lit his pipe for the umpteenth time.

The protagonist of *Hinsa Parmo Dharmah* ('Violence is the Supreme Religion') is Jamid, a village simpleton. An orphan, he is forever taken advantage of by the villagers. A well-wisher finally tells him to go the city, and make a life for himself. In the city, he lands up at a temple, where the cunning priest takes him under his wing. But Jamid cannot remain silent when he sees injustice, and soon enough he's thrown out of the temple. Now, he is picked up by the maulvi and paraded as a victim of Hindu oppression. But here too, he speaks up when he sees injustice, and is again thrown out. Disillusioned, he makes his way back to the village.

Satyagraha is one of the half a dozen or so stories that Premchand wrote with Pandit Moteram Shastri of Banaras as protagonist. Each of these stories is hilarious, and the plots centre round Moteram's voracious appetite. In *Satyagraha*, the Viceroy of British India is to visit Banaras, but the Indian National Congress announces a strike to coincide with his visit. The Magistrate goes into a funk and seeks advice from feudal and religious potentates on how to prevent the strike. They hit upon a plan – why not get someone to go on a hunger strike against the nationalist strike? The person chosen is Pandit Moteram Shastri. Against the advice of his wife, he consents, and gorges himself silly before sitting down on hunger strike. But hunger is hunger, and Moteram's hunger is gargantuan. Eventually, a young Congress worker lures him into breaking his strike, by waving the choicest mithais in front of him. The colonial plan fails.

Safdar felt that there could be a way we could begin with *Hinsa*, and the communal elements of the first story could become the Magistrate's allies as we segued into the second story. And it could be Jamid, not the young Congress worker, who gets Moteram to break his fast. Habib sa'ab agreed, and Safdar started writing.

This was in mid-June. The rehearsals were to start on July 1, and the play was to open on July 30, with a follow-up performance on July 31, Premchand's birth anniversary.

JUNE 1988. Adapting Premchand

I would land up at their place in the evening. We'd have dinner, and then Mala and Safdar would each get down to work – Mala to prepare for school the next day, and Safdar to write. An hour or so later, Safdar would read out a scene to us. We'd offer comments, he'd make some changes, and then get to writing the next scene. He churned out scenes like a machine, including songs. The next day we'd go to Habib sa'ab's in the morning. He'd read out the scene and leave a carbon copy with Habib sa'ab. From there, Safdar would go to the Party office, and I'd get back home, exhausted, and crash. So it went, every day.

Till he got stuck.

The Jamid story was fine, and the play began well. Then, at some point, Safdar had to segue from Jamid to Moteram, and figure out how Jamid comes in contact with Moteram, and get him to break his fast. Safdar tried one approach. It didn't work. He tried another. It didn't work. Late that night, an hour or so before dawn, he tried a third version, and we thought he'd cracked it.

But on the bus to Habib sa'ab's the next morning, Safdar wasn't so sure.

'It's not working. Neither Jamid nor Moteram are any more the characters that Premchand had created. We're losing something.'

He read out all three approaches. Habib sa'ab listened, deep in concentration, filling his pipe, lighting it, puffing, lighting it again, in an endless mesmerizing cycle. His brow was furrowed. He discussed each approach, and spoke about what he thought was wrong with each. Every time, something like a glimmer of hope would appear, but we'd be back to the deadlock within minutes.

After about an hour or so, when Habib sa'ab offered yet another possible solution, Moneekadi, who had so far been dozing semi-reclined on the bed, boomed.

'You're a fool, Habib. You can never solve this problem. This Jamid story is a tragedy. The Moteram story is a farce. If you mix the two, either you have to make the tragedy into a comedy, or you have to turn the farce into a tragedy. If you do either, Premchand goes out of the window. It's like oil and water. They will not mix!'

Silence.

'Hmm. Moneeka, I think you're right.'

'He thinks I'm right. Safdar, look at this stubborn man. He thinks I'm right. Of course I'm right!'

'So Moneekadi, what do you think we should do?'

'Choose one story, for God's sake! The Jamid character is nice, but the story is clichéd. I like Moteram. Lovely character, unusual story. And it's a farce. Habib is good with those. Stick to that. I like your sense of humour, Safdar. Habib and you will get on like a house on fire.'

It was settled, then. Safdar wrote the entire play in about a week. In reading, it took about 35 minutes. So, we thought, we'd have a 45-minute play in performance.

But we hadn't reckoned with Habib Tanvir.

JULY 1988. Hanuman's Tail

A single sentence in the story, 'The Magistrate, astride his horse, went around the marketplace threatening shopkeepers with dire consequences if they went on strike', conjured up for Safdar the image of a comically inept Magistrate and his seven Officers. He wrote several scenes that elaborated on this image. Premchand's story spends a short time, maybe a couple of paragraphs, introducing the basic conflict – which is that the Congress has declared a strike on the day of the Viceroy's visit to Banaras – before introducing us to the character of Pandit Moteram Shastri, who agrees to go on hunger strike against the Congress strike.

In Safdar's script, those introductory paragraphs became about half the play. But when the script passed on to Habib sa'ab, he stretched out every comic potential, milking it to the maximum. Like Hanuman's tail, the play kept lengthening. For instance, after a short introductory exchange between two Orderlies where we learn that the Magistrate has called for an emergency meeting with his officers at the break of dawn, the seven Officers enter, followed by the Magistrate himself, who tells them that the Viceroy is going to visit and that they must put their best foot forward.

MAGISTRATE: Morning, morning. Sit down. Orderly, are all the Officers present?

ORDERLY: Yes Sir.

MAGISTRATE: Then let us commence the meeting. Dear Officers, at the crack of dawn today, I received a telegram from His Excellency the Viceroy of India. What is important is not that the telegram is from His Excellency, because as the Magistrate of Banaras, I routinely get instructions from His Excellency. It is an everyday affair. What is important is that Viceroy saheb is visiting us for a day next week.

The Officers faint. The Magistrate claps. The Orderlies come running and revive the Officers.

OFFICER 1: Water, water …

OFFICER 2: I need some air …

OFFICER 3: Someone please hand me my smelling salts …

OFFICER 4: Sir, I'll just be back … (*He's off to the toilet*)

OFFICER 5: Orderly, get me another pajama …

OFFICER 6: I'm having palpitations, someone pass me the brandy …

OFFICER 7: Where am I? Where is my pillow? Chamelijaan, where are you?

The Orderlies get everybody to sit again.

MAGISTRATE: I am happy to see that you've taken this news so seriously. I am certain that you will prepare for His Lordship's welcome with the same seriousness and alertness. I want Viceroy saheb to be welcomed with such pomp and splendour that this will become a truly memorable visit for him.

OFFICERS: Yes Sir, yes Sir.

MAGISTRATE: So what suggestions do you have? Inspector of Works?

After this, the Officers each come up with more and more crazy and outlandish ideas.

In Habib sa'ab's hands, the scene became this:

MAGISTRATE: Is everyone here?

OFFICER 1: Well, I'm here, for sure.

OFFICER 6: You think I'm absent?

OFFICER 1: I never said that.

OFFICER 7: So let's say everyone is here.

OFFICER 5: How can you say that? How do we know who all have been invited?

OFFICER 4: I don't see Three-Nought-Three here.

OFFICER 6: He hasn't been invited.

OFFICER 3: Well, forget about the others.

OFFICER 2: All we know is that we are all here.

MAGISTRATE: Very good, very good. Please listen carefully to what I have to say. The situation is very serious.

OFFICERS: Serious, Sir?

MAGISTRATE: Yes, very serious. At the crack of dawn today, I received a telegram from His Excellency the Viceroy.

OFFICER 1: Viceroy saheb himself?

OFFICER 6: I told you!

OFFICER 5: No, you didn't!

OFFICER 4: Shut up and listen to Sir.

OFFICER 3: But this is amazing news.

MAGISTRATE: What is amazing about this? After all, I am the Magistrate of Banaras. I keep getting instructions from His Excellency. It's a daily affair.

OFFICER 1: Yes Sir, it's a daily affair.

OFFICERS: Yes, yes.

MAGISTRATE: The important point is this. His Excellency, the Viceroy of India, is visiting Banaras for a day next week.

The Officers all stand up, and start speaking simultaneously.

OFFICER 2: He's coming to Banaras?

OFFICER 3: The Viceroy himself?

OFFICER 4: What, what did you say, Sir?

OFFICER 5: See, I told you it was big news.

OFFICER 6: Impossible!

OFFICER 1: We're in deep trouble!

MAGISTRATE: Yes, the Viceroy is going to visit Banaras.

The Officers all collapse, unconscious.

MAGISTRATE: I am happy to see that you've taken this news so seriously. I am certain that you will prepare for his welcome with the same seriousness and alertness. I want Viceroy saheb to be welcomed with such pomp and splendour that this will become a truly memorable visit for him. I want suggestions from each of you. Inspector of Works? (*The Officers are unmoving, unconscious. The Magistrate bellows*) Officers, attention! (*The Officers get up with alacrity. The Magistrate barks, military style*) Give suggestions, one by one. Inspector of Unemployment!

And so it went. If Safdar had created situations and characters that were suggested to his fecund imagination by Premchand's text,

Habib sa'ab teased out every farcical possibility that lay latent in Safdar's text. Safdar insisted that Habib sa'ab get equal credit as co-author. Habib sa'ab was pleased, but his own view was clear.

'You invented. I elaborated. You are the primary author of the play. I am secondary.'

JULY 1988. Chamelijaan

And then there was the Chemelijaan episode.

In Safdar's script, the Inspector of Entertainment suggests that the Viceroy's visit to Banaras culminate with a visit to the famous courtesan Chamelijaan. Safdar got the courtesan's name from another story by Premchand, and wrote a short scene. It is in this scene that the Magistrate, and we, the audience, learn that the Congress has called for a strike to protest the Viceroy's visit. So, in terms of narrative, it was a crucial scene. When we started rehearsing it on the floor – with Safdar as the bumbling Magistrate, Mala as an utterly seductive Chamelijaan, myself as the hyper-energetic Secret Agent Three-Nought-Three – the scene kept expanding, with both Safdar and Habib sa'ab coming up with more and more hilarious twists and turns, with minor contributions from some of us. Eventually, the Magistrate is discovered in a semi-dressed state with the courtesan by the full posse of his officers – causing him discomfiture, but also suggesting that she knows them well anyway. As Habib sa'ab later wrote: 'The scene was exceedingly funny. Actually, Safdar himself had advanced some most obscene suggestions during the rehearsals to enhance the comic effect, which I had lapped up. Safdar had a brilliant sense of humour.'

Some of the older actors, the 'seniors', were opposed to the scene. It was not 'political' enough for them, but really, they were just uncomfortable with the unbridled sensuality. While Chamelijaan remained fully dressed right through the scene, it was the men around her who undressed – the Magistrate undressed, so did Three-Nought-Three, and later in the scene, an anonymous man draped only in a bed sheet appeared from under the bed. The scene was 'obscene' in the sense that it evoked sex and sexuality, and thereby challenged the propriety of middle-class audiences.

Mala's Chamelijaan was delightful – sexy, playful, free, completely in control of her sexuality and of the narrative in the play itself, with her tingling laughter filling the auditorium. Safdar played the awkward, excited, smitten Magistrate, all hands and legs, to perfection. They were electrifying on stage – she seemed like a trapeze artist, throwing herself at the role with abandon but always in supreme control, he like a comic maestro, each ungainly stutter, twitch and jerk pitched just right, neither overdone, nor underplayed. I should add that I got to play Three-Nought-Three with three Magistrates – after Safdar's death, Habib sa'ab stepped in, and when we revived the play in 1991 with a largely new cast, with the marvellous Jayanta Das – and, apart from Mala, I also rehearsed the scene with Shehla Hashmi, Shikha Sethi, and Nandita Das as Chamelijaan, though none of them performed it in a show. But of all these combinations, there is no question that the Mala–Safdar chemistry in that scene was simply unmatched. It was sheer joy being on the stage with these two delectable actors.

I saw the scene as scoffing at bourgeois morality and the middle-class hypocrisy about sex, and that was enough to make it political for me. With hindsight, I see the scene as being political in other ways as well. It showed a free-spirited woman twirling around her little finger the entire bureaucracy of the colonial state. Her unabashed sexuality is itself a liberating image. The song described her as the 'pride' of Banaras, as the one who sets hearts aflutter, as a cultured, sophisticated aesthete in tune with the feelings and aspirations of the city. It is through her that the Magistrate, and we, the audience, learn of the impending strike. And while both, the Magistrate and the head of the secret service, faint in the course of the scene, she remains entirely in command of her wits. She is an empowered presence surrounded by weak-kneed, idiotic men.

Perhaps it was this that was threatening, I don't know. But when the 'seniors' raised the issue of this scene, Safdar was faced with a dilemma. They wouldn't speak to Habib sa'ab directly, but would grumble and complain behind his back. Safdar, who upheld the democratic principle, needed to let Habib sa'ab know what was happening, but personally he felt that the scene was an artistic and political triumph. He also wanted to protect the objectors and didn't want them to come across as narrow-minded. So when Safdar spoke to Habib sa'ab about the misgivings of some of the actors, he invented a more credible argument – that the scene was so funny that it was standing out too much, and the main theme of the play, of the need to separate religion from politics, was getting obscured.

Habib sa'ab wrote an alternative scene where the news of the impending strike is revealed to us in the marketplace by the Kunjdan (woman vegetable-seller). We rehearsed the scene in a day, and did the first four scenes of the play with both variations, to see which worked better. Again, there was a split, with the vocal minority preferring the new version and the silent majority the Chamelijaan version. In the end, it was left to Habib sa'ab to decide, and his own preference had been clear from the beginning.

In performance, this was one of the high points of the play and, as I said above, one of the most politically potent scenes. With the praise the scene garnered, the murmurs of complaint faded away.

JULY 1988. Guru and Shishya

Safdar had recently turned 34 when we began working on the play. He had a decade and a half of serious theatre practice behind him, including a decade of doing only street theatre. Habib sa'ab was 65, at the peak of his career, having created some masterpieces such as *Charandas Chor*, *Mitti ki Gadi* and *Shajapur ki Shantibai* in the decade and half before – not to mention his much earlier classic, *Agra Bazaar* – while some of his later outstanding plays, such as *Dekh Rahe Hain Nain* and *Kamdev ka Apna Basant Ritu ka Sapna*, would be created in the half decade following. Safdar wanted to learn, and Habib sa'ab was keen to teach. I was the fly on the wall, soaking up what I could.

If Habib sa'ab had expanded the earlier parts of the play – which was all basically Safdar's creation, suggested by Premchand's story but not directly from it – a somewhat opposite move took place in the latter half. In the scene where Moteram is persuaded by the Magistrate and his feudal allies to go on a hunger strike, Premchand had some marvellous comic dialogue. Safdar added a little bit to it, which Habib sa'ab cut out. Again, in the final scene, where the young Congress worker lures Moteram with the fragrance of mithai to break his fast, Safdar had expanded on Premchand's dialogues. Again, Habib sa'ab cut out the excess, and restored the brevity of Premchand's dialogue.

'Premchand is a master, Safdar. See how tight his dialogue is. He is miserly with words, but achieves maximum impact. Why should we meddle with it? Best to let it be.' I should say, though, that his reverence for Premchand only went so far. The original story is called 'Satyagraha', as was Safdar's draft, but Habib sa'ab changed it to *Moteram Ka Satyagraha*. He explained, '"Moteram" is such a perfect name for a petu [gluttonous – though without the Christian sense of sin attached to it] Brahmin. It immediately evokes an image. You know it's going to be a humorous play. And you also know that the satyagraha is going to fail – how can someone called Moteram sit on a fast! Just "Satyagraha" is too dry – it could well be a serious story of a martyr. Premchand is a great short story writer, but not the best namer of his stories. When I did a stage adaptation of "*Shatranj Ke Khiladi*" long ago, I renamed it "*Shatranj Ke Mohre*", which seemed more apt to me. The story is not about some expert chess players. The story is about these two men whose fate is controlled by forces of history, like pawns in a chess game.'

Habib sa'ab reworked Safdar's draft meticulously. He fused shorter scenes to make longer, composite scenes; he eliminated some characters and made other characters perform those actions; and at a couple of places he wrote short scenes to show in action something that was only being described second-hand.

Then there were the songs. 'Safdar was a poet alright,' Habib sa'ab wrote, 'in so far as his imagination was concerned, and some metres, in which he was adept. But he was familiar with only a few metres. However, his greatest quality was his lack of conceit and his self-awareness. He would say in so many words as he did during our work on *Moteram* that his mind would not work on the metre I had chosen for the song about the courtesan Chamelijaan, as much as to suggest that I went ahead and composed the song myself, which of course I did. The reason for this was his inadequate, weak background in prosody. Which made him commit mistakes even in metres he was best familiar with, such as the Pingal – the Alha Udal metre, in which he was on the whole most at home. That is one reason I deeply regret his passing away so soon. I had the gumption that in time I would point out to him these lapses in his handling of his metres in a manner that he would comprehend, for he had an extremely intelligent mind. I used to think of Niaz Haider, who during my initial years of poetry writing had given me such valuable tips about metre. We tried, but he was already so preoccupied with so many organizational matters, Party affairs, and other aspects of the play itself that I had to put off such an exercise for a future time, which unfortunately never came.' Habib sa'ab had encountered Niaz Haider's genius when the two collaborated – as well as fought – in Qudsia Zaidi's Hindustani Theatre in the 1950s.

I remember two instances of Habib sa'ab pointing out to Safdar errors in his poetic metre. The first line of Safdar's opening song was:

Premchand ne likha tha qissa, natak humne diya banaye
Premchand had penned a tale, we turned it into a play

Habib sa'ab changed this to:

Katha likhi thi Premchand ne, natak humne diya banaye

Similarly, in a song towards the end of the play, Safdar wrote:

Baasi roti hi kha lunga agar kahin vahi mil jaye
Stale bread gladly will I eat –
Tell me where it's found

Habib sa'ab changed this to:

Baasi roti bin paani ke kha lun kahin vahi mil jaye
Stale bread without water gladly will I eat –
Tell me where it's found

In both cases, the moment he sang the new lines, it was clear to Safdar that they sat better in the metre and flowed more musically off the tongue. In the second instance, they also accentuated the plight of the hungry, fasting Brahmin. When Kajal Ghosh and Devilal Nag refined the tunes, the effect was even more startling.

Astonishingly, all this happened in a space of merely 29 days, from the day of the first reading to the day of the final dress rehearsal. And except on Sundays, we would work only in the evenings. Fortunately, Mala had been able to get permission for us to work in the auditorium of Sardar Patel Vidyalaya, so we had a lovely working space. Thanks to Vibhaben, and the manager of SPV, Pathakbhai, we always felt entirely at home there.

On the Sunday before the first performance, the play was still nowhere near ready. Shehla, with Shivani Chander's help, was still working on the costumes under Moneekadi's supervision; Safdar had still not finalized the words of one crucial song that appeared in the play twice, in two different versions; the actors were still fumbling with the lines; the singers were still reading the songs; and the set had still not been coloured. Most importantly, I thought the climax was just not working. I worried that we had perhaps made the audience laugh too much earlier in the play, and that maybe therefore nobody would find the end funny. Is there something like laughter fatigue, I wondered. And if so, could the Chamelijaan scene be the culprit?

I was stage manager (besides doing two roles – Three-Nought-Three and the Congress worker), and had to liaise with Habib sa'ab to work out the rehearsal schedule. We were having tea in the school canteen. Safdar, who was refining lines for the final song, had half an ear on our conversation.

'There's only five days to go, Habib sa'ab. How on earth are we going to be ready?'

Habib sa'ab lit his pipe and was thoughtful.

'You're right, there's very little time. But let me tell you a little trick I learnt when I was at the Old Vic. One of my teachers there used to say that if you don't have the time to work to your satisfaction on every scene, work hard as hell on the opening and the closing. The middle takes care of itself. That's what we're going to do. Our opening works well. The end is a little flat. We need to heighten that.'

'Do you think we've made the audience laugh too much earlier in the play, and that's why the end seems flat?'

'Hmm. That is an interesting thought. I don't think making the early part less funny will somehow make the latter part funnier. But we know that laughter is contagious. So we need to do something extra at the end.'

And that day he cracked it. As the Congress worker lured Moteram into breaking his fast and the audience saw Moteram eat like a ravenous pig, the chorus stepped in and began singing the song, and one by one all the actors came on to the stage and just laughed at the sight of Moteram eating. So Habib sa'ab created an audience on stage which, by laughing its guts out, gave the cue to the real audience of the play, which, even though they had laughed a lot by now, still found the energy to laugh at their loudest yet and create a rip-roaring climax.

JULY 1988. Zohra Segal

'Zohra is back in India and looking for work. She wants to work with me. Do you think we can cast her in this play?'

Habib sa'ab, Moneekadi, Safdar, and I were chatting at the end of rehearsal one day, when Habib sa'ab sprung this on us. I had no idea who he was talking about. But Safdar jumped with joy. His excitement was to be seen.

'Zohra Segal? *The* Zohra Segal? Of Prithvi Theatres? She needs work? Of course! It would be a privilege for us to work with her.'

After working for eight years with Uday Shankar and 14 years with Prithviraj Kapoor, Zohra Segal had lived in England for a quarter century working mainly in television, and had faded from public memory in India. It was only in the late 1990s and after, that she again became known in India through her work in Hindi films. She was born in 1912, so she was 76 when she worked with us, making her second debut in India, in a sense. She was cast as Moteram's wife, the Panditayin. Tyagi, who played Moteram, was exactly thirty years younger than her. She matched him step for step. Her agility and lightfootedness were to be seen to be believed. I also marvelled at her vocal skills. She could perfectly hit any note she wanted, every time, and she could project down to the last syllable of a long line, right to the back of the auditorium. When I asked her about it, she told me nonchalantly that she did vocal riyaz.

'Oh. Every day?'

'You mean you don't?' Her eyes widened in disbelief and I wished the earth would swallow me.

Her professionalism was exemplary. She would arrive precisely on time every day. I would announce the coming day's rehearsal schedule. Now, Habib sa'ab being Habib sa'ab, he would pay scant attention to his own plans. He'd often get obsessed with that one tiny detail and could spend an hour or more getting just that speck of action right. Zohra aapa was a perfectionist too, but she always came fully prepared from home, and in any case her level of skill was so high that Habib sa'ab would barely need to spend any time with her, even when he wanted her to do something differently from what she had come prepared with. As a result, the time she had to spend on the floor was very little, and it would only lengthen if her co-actors couldn't deliver. For the most part, she had to just sit around and wait. I would get nervous about this, and once, when she had waited over an hour doing nothing, I went to her and apologized.

'Don't worry about it. I know you are all amateur actors. I can't expect here what I can from a professional company. But I love to see your enthusiasm and dedication. I know you are all working very hard. I'm enjoying this – working with Habib, with Safdar, with all of you. Do you know Habib is a decade younger than me? But look at him, you'd think he's my grandfather. He was always like this, even back in the '40s, when I first met him. Full of ideas that none of us ever understood. But always a genius.'

She acted with us for the first two shows. When the play had to be repeated, Safdar approached her again, but she politely said no. She writes in her memoirs that she declined because of two reasons: one, that she had to dye her hair – 'I felt I looked a right cartoon!' – and two, because she never acted for free, and though we had paid her for the first two performances, she knew our economic position and didn't want to embarrass us. She took part in the protests after Safdar's killing, and on the first anniversary of his death, at the poetry reading at Rabindra Bhavan, she opened the evening with Faiz's '*Intisaab*' ('Dedication'). The others to read that evening included film personalities Shabana Azmi, Javed Akhtar, Om Puri, and Roshan Seth, dancer Indrani Rahman, and painter Krishen Khanna.

JULY 1988. Moneekadi

Before I came to Janam, I had worked with Dramatech for a while. It was one of those short-lived groups on the Delhi theatre scene, made up of IIT graduates. I was the youngest in the group, and not an IIT-ian. I was made stage manager, which was a fancy title for the odd-jobs boy, and made to do things nobody else wanted to, including hiring the tempo to transport sets. In retrospect, I learnt a lot handling those big sets full of hundreds of real props, and in particular I learnt how useless it is both artistically and financially to have big sets full of hundreds of real props. Even after doing three plays with Dramatech, when I found that not only was I handling props, the roles I was getting were no more than glorified props – including, in *Witness for the Prosecution*, the guy who calls out the next witness's name in court – I quit working with them.

Habib sa'ab didn't know any of the Janam actors. He knew Safdar, but I doubt that he had seen him perform before. He came to some of our shows before we began work. We were performing *Aurat* at the time, so getting him to see that was no problem. But *Aurat* didn't have Manish, Tyagi, and Arun, so Safdar got them to rehearse *Samrath* for a couple of performances, which were arranged so Habib sa'ab could see them. I'm sure he also wanted to impress Habib sa'ab with his singing, as he was doing the Bora. The shows were in Rani Bagh in west Delhi, and I was to bring Habib sa'ab. It was still early days in the writing process of *Moteram*, so I didn't know the Tanvir family well. It came as a bit of a surprise to me that when I reached their house in Ber Sarai, Habib sa'ab was dressed in jeans and a natty shirt with a colourful bold print; Moneekadi was in a lovely saree and putting on make-up; and their daughter Nageen was fussing over what to wear.

'Do you have to go somewhere after the show?' I asked, worried that I wouldn't get the ride back with them.

Habib sa'ab looked at me quizzically, wondering why I had asked the question.

'I mean, you're dressed up as if to go to a party.'

'No, but we are going to the theatre!' Nageen said excitedly.

'Yes, but it's only a street play in a basti.'

'But it is theatre, isn't it?' Moneekadi chimed in happily.

Later, over the years I knew them, I learnt this about the Tanvirs – that going to the theatre, any kind of theatre, anywhere, one had to dress up; and that theatre is theatre, whether it happens in a fancy auditorium or on a village square. It is always joyfully, cheerfully, exhilaratingly, serious business.

Moneekadi and Nageen came to every single rehearsal of *Moteram*, and Moneekadi in particular was integral to the creation of the play. She used to handle costumes and properties in Naya Theatre, and her expertise was more than useful to us now. But there were three other priceless contributions she made.

One I have already spoken about – the choice of story for the play.

The second was spirit. Towards the end of the rehearsal process, there was a day when we'd had a long, exhausting rehearsal. At about 9, when we thought we were about to wind up, Habib sa'ab said we had to do a run-through. I looked at Safdar.

'Habib sa'ab, it's 9 already … ,' he said, tentatively.

'Yes, and we'll finish by 10.30.'

Well, that was that. As stage manager, I had to break this news to the actors. I don't think I've ever been hated more in Janam. Anyway, the run-through began, and the actors went through the motions, desperate for the torture to end. After the dreariest run-through of a hilarious play, we sat around Habib sa'ab, who used to write notes in his diary and give what he'd call 'points' about each scene to the actors. But before he could begin, Moneekadi stood up.

'Forget your points, Habib.' Habib sa'ab shut his diary. She turned to us. 'What are you doing? Have you come to a funeral? Where's the energy? Where's the joy? You should see our Naya Theatre actors. They are grameen [rural] people, unschooled, unlettered, uncultured in urban etiquette. But, for them, theatre is joy. Whether they are playing on a village chaupal [square] or in the fanciest theatre in England, whether it is their first show or their hundredth, whether they are performing or rehearsing, whether they've just started working or worked through the entire night, they do it with joy. The actor must give energy to the darshak [spectator]. Fling yourself at them. You have a ruddy good play. Play it!'

I'll never forget how she said 'fling'. Small and rotund, she who shuffled rather than walked, heaved her entire body and flung it into that word. Our playing changed after that.

It was she who pointed out to me something that may seem

obvious, but which I had been oblivious of till then. As stage manager, it was my job to marshal the team that came in for set changes, and arrange whatever few props were required for each scene.

'We don't have a front curtain. If we can, we dim lights during set changes, but if you're performing in flat lights – as we have to in small towns – or in daylight, that is not possible. So, you see, the set change is seen by everyone. You have to do it like actors, not technicians. Keep the tempo of the play in mind. Rehearse everything. Each little thing. Set change should be like clockwork. It should be done with aesthetic precision. And always enjoy it. *Mazaa aana chahiye.* Your joy will communicate to the darshak.'

This was the third lesson: Everything on stage – and behind the stage – is part of the play, and therefore has to be enjoyed, because enjoyment is contagious.

It was only in subsequent years that I learnt that Moneekadi started out as a director in her own right, before, as so often in Indian theatre, the wife took a backseat as the husband rose to prominence and became the scaffolding that enabled that monument to be built.

JULY 1988. What is Acting?

The 'points' that Habib sa'ab would give actors after a run were to be kept in mind, and remembered. By itself, this is standard practice: You do a run-through, and the director then gathers the actors and gives feedback. As an actor, I've been part of this ritual countless times, and have conducted it myself as a director numerous times. Why is it that in my head this feedback session is indelibly connected to Habib sa'ab?

Partly, I guess, it was the charm, wisdom, and humour of the man. He was incapable of encountering any situation without seeing the amusing side of it. His feedback to actors was laced with humour – sometimes gentle, sometimes subtle, but equally, sometimes, utterly devastating. But what really stood out for me was how he instructed actors. He would say, for instance, 'You are moving too fast when you discover your child is dead. Move slowly.

With heavier steps.' Or, 'Puff out your chest more after you fool the cop.' Or, 'When he rejects your overture, call out to the soldiers on a higher note, with more volume.'

Nothing remarkable about these instructions, you might think, till you realize that in none of them does Habib sa'ab speak about emotions or feelings. Over the years, I saw this again and again. Habib sa'ab never ever spoke to actors about that thing called 'feeling'. He would never tell you, 'Bring more emotion into this', or 'Do it with more feeling'. Consider the situations above. For other directors these same instructions could well be, respectively, 'Show us more sorrow'; 'Walk away cockily'; and 'Show more anger'.

This focus on 'doing' rather than 'feeling' went to bewildering levels sometimes – bewildering for the actor, that is. In 1990, Habib sa'ab was directing Asghar Wajahat's *Jis Lahore Nai Dekhya Voh Janmya Hi Nai* ('If You Haven't Seen Lahore, You Haven't Lived') for the Shri Ram Centre Repertory. Set during the Partition, it is the story of an old Hindu woman who refuses to leave the Lahore mansion she lived in, even though the rest of her family had migrated to India. When a Muslim family from India gets allotted this mansion, they discover the woman there. As the play progresses, the old woman becomes everybody's darling except the Islamic fundamentalists'. One character in the play is a poet who roams the streets at night. At one point he wakes up a roadside tea vendor, who curses, but realizes, embarrassedly, that it is the poet, for whom he has great regard. The spontaneous abuse was pretty funny, as was his double take, and I chuckled the first time I watched it in rehearsal. Then Habib sa'ab made them do it again. And again. And again, about a dozen times. Every time, he would ask them to get some minuscule detail right – 'Slap your thigh harder as you utter the abuse', or 'No, don't rub your eyes three times. Twice is enough'. When the tea vendor got his part right, Habib sa'ab focused on the poet. 'No, don't bend backwards so much when you laugh', or 'Don't keep your mouth open when you wake him. Open it when he abuses you, but open it to let out a small laugh'.

I am not exaggerating when I say that he spent about two hours on just this tiny exchange. Nothing seemed to satisfy him. The actors were at their wits' end. Finally, the actor playing the poet said, pleadingly, 'Sir, I've done this so many times, in every possible way. What is the feeling you want?' To which Tanvir responded with a silent, slightly amused look. He got up, replaced the actor, and demonstrated what he wanted. And there was no question – it was just funnier. Then he turned to the poet and said, 'You worry too much about feeling. Just move your muscles correctly, and it will be fine.' After which he demonstrated, step by minuscule step, exactly what he did with which muscle, how he shifted his weight from one foot to the other and back again, how much his elbow went back as he arched his back, and so on. To his credit, the exhausted actor took this all in, and proceeded to do it pretty much perfectly.

The point of the story, however, doesn't end there. In the play, this little exchange – which always got a loud laugh – was followed by an encounter between the poet and a fundamentalist goon. This was a serious scene, but the poet had witty lines, and again evoked laughter, though this was a different kind of laughter. About a couple of years after the rehearsal I described above, in an entirely different context, I was chatting with Habib sa'ab about how laughter can be of different types, and how sometimes new actors in our street theatre troupe get rattled when people laugh at the protagonist of the play being beaten up by the police or the industrialist's goons. Habib sa'ab then started speaking about *Jis Lahore*, and the various types of laughter in the play. I recalled the rehearsal, and asked him why he had driven the actor to frustration that afternoon.

'The chai wallah's embarrassment is funny if the poet doesn't take it personally. But it's not funny if the poet thinks it is exceedingly funny, because then it will appear as if the poet is mocking the chai wallah. The poet sees the humour of the situation, but for him, it is class neutral – he doesn't care about his higher status vis-à-vis the chai wallah. The chai wallah, on the other hand, is doubly embarrassed because he is aware of the poet's social status. It is this social status, the fact that he is so learned, which gives the poet his self-confidence when confronting the fundamentalist. He makes mincemeat of him, but wittily. We want the audience to laugh at that point, because that is political laughter, through which the audience express their disapproval of the fundamentalist's politics. But this laughter will not come out right till the tension in the scene builds up to a point where we fear that the fundamentalist might attack the poet, which is the eventuality that the poet's wit forecloses. And this tension, this real fear for the poet, in turn, will not build correctly if the laughter at the tea vendor's embarrassment is not just right.'

And this, to my mind, was the key to Habib sa'ab's approach to acting. The audience had to feel the threat of the fundamentalist towards the poet as a real, visceral feeling, because the poet represented, in a sense, the conscience of the ordinary folk who wanted to live in harmony and without violence. But this threat was not to be realized as much by the actor playing the fundamentalist as by getting the audience in the right frame of mind, for which you had to get the humour of the preceding part spot on.

To put it differently, the actor was the vessel that carried the emotion to the audience, but did not necessarily feel it, like the glass that carries wine without getting intoxicated itself. The analogy of the wine and the glass is from the *Natyashastra*. I had never understood what it really meant, till I encountered Habib sa'ab.

Many of the Naya Theatre actors, including Bhulwa Ram, Deepak Tiwari, Uday Ram, Chait Ram, Govind Ram, Mala Bai, and Agesh Nag were involved in the rehearsals of *Moteram*. Devilal Nag, the musician and singer, was co-composer for the songs along with Kajal. It was the first time I was observing these actors at close quarters, though I had, over the years, seen them perform. Safdar knew many of them well. In particular, he was sad that Fida Bai was no longer able to act because of her burning accident.

One day, we watched Uday and Govind nonchalantly improvise a short situation, for which Habib sa'ab had given them barely any instruction at all. It came out just right the first time, and became part of the play. I remember Safdar's utter delight as he watched this little bit of a scene being improvised. 'I've read everything there is to read of Brecht's,' he said. 'But I swear I could never demonstrate "distancing" in acting as well as Habib sa'ab's actors could. This is what we have to learn for street theatre.' Safdar used the word 'distancing' rather than 'alienation'. He felt it was closer to the Brechtian idea of *verfremdung*. 'Alienation' has a dry, unfeeling, unemotional connotation, he felt.

AUTUMN 1988. Training Ourselves

We opened *Moteram* at the Gandhi Memorial Hall in Pyarelal Bhavan on July 30, and had our second performance on Premchand's birth anniversary the following day. The play was an instant success, as was Premchand Samaroh, of which it had been a part. The seminar on Premchand that was part of the Samaroh was an education for me. I hadn't read many of his novels, but as part of preparing for *Moteram* I had read all the *Mansarovar* volumes, and now I learnt so much more about Premchand, the preeminent progressive writer, the founder of the journal *Hans*, and the nationalist. The Samaroh was the first time that the four Left cultural organizations – Janam, Janwadi Lekhak Sangh, Parcham, and Jansamskriti – worked together. We brought out a brochure for the Samaroh, and the advertisements therein – almost all mobilized by Safdar – funded the play, as well as the rest of the festival.

In August, we continued doing performances of *Aurat* and *Raja Ka Baja*, and in September we repeated *Moteram* at the All India Fine Arts and Crafts Society (AIFACS) auditorium. As a kid, I had seen some plays at AIFACS, and this was the first time I was performing there. It used to be a lovely little auditorium, with perhaps the best acoustics in Delhi. We did three performances there, the last of which was in the afternoon. The Janwadi Mahila Samiti brought in their members from the various bastis for the show. What a lovely, boisterous, expressive audience it was, and the play worked wonderfully with them. The Chamelijaan scene in particular was appreciated with prolonged applause, drowning out the song that followed. Moneekadi's eyes wouldn't stop twinkling with delight. 'These women are exactly like our grameen audiences. So spontaneous.'

There used to be an actor in the NSD Repertory those days, Yuvraj Sharma, who was trained as a mime. Safdar requested him to do a workshop with us. Yuvraj's workshop ran for about ten days, and Safdar had managed to get an air-conditioned room in the Soviet Cultural Centre on Ferozeshah Road for the workshop, free. About a dozen of us took part in the workshop. Yuvraj was late on one of the days. Safdar asked Rakesh Sharma to conduct some exercises. A couple of the 'seniors' kept giggling as Rakesh led us through exercises. Rakesh remembers that Safdar was angry, and expressed it.

'Is this how you encourage young people?'

Perhaps it was the same day, or later, but Soman also remembers Safdar being irritated during this workshop.

'This is a great workshop,' Soman said to Safdar. 'We should have more like this.'

'Why? For these jokers, who can't appreciate what they're getting?'

Around the same time, in September, the legendary mime artist Niranjan Goswami visited Delhi, and Safdar proposed that he work with us. Safdar and he had become friends when Safdar was at WBIB. Goswami was thrilled at the idea of collaborating with Janam. Safdar followed up the conversation with a letter, in which he proposed:

'We are thinking of a production in which the elements of pantomime can be integrated with theatre. In other words, we are thinking of a full-length theatrical production in which pantomime is used as a major artistic device. We are not thinking of a mime show. However, we are conscious of the fact that such a production will involve disciplined and concentrated training in mime under your direction. What may emerge ultimately can be a production in which you direct the mime and one of us directs the theatre part. A kind of collaborative venture.'

The Janam files from the period have a letter from Lovleen Misra to Safdar, in which she asks about how plans were coming along for the 'scheduled play to be directed by Bansi Kaul'. This was Safdar's adaptation of Gorky's *Enemies*. The Janam files also have drafts of letters in Safdar's hand. One is addressed to a senior person in Doordarshan, asking if they'd be interested in considering *Moteram* for their scheme of filming plays. A second draft is to the Sahitya Kala Parishad, which had given Janam a grant of Rs 5,000 to help produce *Moteram*, to now support performances in the open for mass audiences, in Mangolpuri, Jehangirpuri, Nand Nagri, Dakshinpuri, and Shakur Basti, for which Safdar had calculated a cost of Rs 6,555 per show. A third draft is to an unnamed interlocutor, which might have been the Sangeet Natak Akademi, asking for a grant to cover workshops with Yuvraj Sharma on pantomime, Bansi Kaul on the body, M.K. Raina on acting, and Devendra Raj Ankur on the history and theories of theatre. The letter states that future workshops were being planned with Habib Tanvir, Anuradha Kapur, Guru Janmejaya, and Pandit Narendra Sharma. In my interview with him, Raina mentioned that Safdar was speaking to him about doing a production of *Mother* under his (Raina's) direction. A reference to this is found in a fourth handwritten draft letter, again to an unnamed interlocutor, which speaks about an ambitious plan to mount two proscenium plays a year with fifty shows each in auditoriums and bastis, while continuing with the street theatre work, besides other activities like festivals. 'In preparation of this ambitious programme we wish to hold a number of workshops for our actors to raise their artistic standards.'

I don't think any of these letters were sent, because there's no copy of the final typed letters, nor a record of a response from any of these bodies. But what the letters show is that Safdar wanted us – all of us, youngsters as much as older actors – to be creatively challenged, learn new skills, and claim our space in the larger theatrical landscape. And there were myriad other ideas, plans, dreams bubbling up in his mind, for the long run.

However, none of this could happen without putting in place a robust organizational structure for Janam.

OCTOBER 1988. Reorganizing Janam

'We'll finally have a General Body meeting,' Safdar told us one day. 'We'll have a report on what we've been doing, we'll present the accounts, and we'll elect a new Executive Committee, which will elect a Convenor and a Treasurer.'

'New EC?' I asked. 'You mean we have an old EC?'

'Oh yes we do. And we've kept it a closely guarded secret. We only reveal it on very special occasions.' We laughed.

Later, as Jogi, Brijender, and I were standing at the bus stop to get home, I wondered aloud. 'Who do you think is going to be in the EC? And who is going to be the Convenor?' I can't remember who we each thought was going to be in the EC. But we were split on who was going to be Convenor. Jogi and Brijender were certain it would be Safdar. 'Who else can it be?'

I wasn't sure at all. 'Well, haven't you seen how Safdar always promotes other people? He'll be in the EC, he'll do all the work, but he'll have one of the "seniors" as Convenor. You wait and see.'

They were both not convinced, but agreed with me that if this was suggested in the GB, we would stage a little mutiny.

Thus it was with some excitement that I arrived at V.P. House on the morning of October 2, 1988, for Janam's first-ever General Body Meeting. The minutes sheet records that 29 people attended, including six women. Eleven of those present were older members, having been with the group for two or more years, while 18 were new, a majority of whom having joined in the last six months. Jogi, Brijender, and I exchanged silent glances. In case of a vote, there was no question at all, we'd be able to get Safdar elected as Convenor.

The proceedings began. First, Manish informed us that the existing, and now outgoing, EC consisted of himself (Convenor),

Tyagi (Treasurer), and Lalit. Manish gave a verbal report of some of our recent activities, and said we needed a larger and more organized EC now that we had many more members and were doing so many activities. He admitted that Janam had been unable to do anything on some of the recent issues that had come up, including the horrific murder of 18-year-old Roop Kanwar in a so-called sati the previous year. Safdar said we had neglected our own education and training for a long time, and was glad that we had taken steps to rectify that. Lalit felt that we could make different types of plays in the future – perhaps a play on Bhagat Singh, or a play for children, considering so many children form part of our audience in every show. Manish felt that with so many more members now, we could form two teams, something we had always wanted to do. The report was passed unanimously, though the minutes also record me as saying that we should have been given the report in written form before the meeting. 'We'll now finalize the report in written form and circulate it,' Safdar said.

Then Tyagi, as Treasurer, told us that Janam had Rs 10,819.15 in its kitty – and all of it was cash. A clerical error in Janam's registration had made Natya into Natak, which meant we weren't able to open a bank account. He said that the new EC must take this up on a priority basis. I was stunned – the organization had functioned without a bank account for 15 years.

Manish then proposed the new, seven-member EC panel: Safdar (Convenor), Vijay Kalia (Treasurer), Lalit, Arun, Brijender, Shikha, and I. Jogi and Brijender both looked at me with that superior grin – see, we were right! I was excited to be in the EC, but I must say I felt marginally let down that our little mutiny had not come to pass.

Then Safdar spoke, as the newly elected Convenor.

'One of the main issues is, how do we intervene in the theatre world of Delhi. We see a decline in the quality of mainstream proscenium theatre in Delhi, and this is also true of other parts of India. It would be wrong to blame television for this decline – for example, the decline of theatre in Bengal has a long history and reasons other than the electronic media. The main reason for the decline is political – the Sangeet Natak Akademi, as well as the Ford Foundation, have vigorously promoted revivalism in theatre through an emphasis on the "ethnic", the so-called Theatre of Roots. But this is not an organic movement, this is funded and promoted by these two agencies with specific schemes and lots of money. There is excessive preoccupation with "form", and almost none with content. A socially aware theatre group such as ours has to study this phenomenon, and work out our role in this. The crucial question is: What should be the connection between tradition, indigenous forms, and modern ideas?

'On the other side, there are progressive groups. In their plays, there is an excessive preoccupation with "content", and virtually no attention is paid to stagecraft and technique. Their plays can be deathly boring.

'Groups like Janam have emerged as a distinct cultural stream in north India – not only are we seen as "political", but our theatrical skills are also recognized by other theatre people. We need to think about our role in the larger theatre landscape.

'Communalism has emerged as a grave danger in the social life of Delhi. There are now active communal senas [armies] in Delhi. This has to worry us. Our shows of *Apaharan Bhaichare Ka* were a mere drop in the ocean. We have to do much, much more. There are many theatrepersons in Delhi who are progressive, democratic, and secular. We have to reach out to them, organize them.

'To meet all these challenges, we have to continuously educate and train ourselves – we have to learn about social history, culture, stagecraft, the history of theatre, and so on. We also need to work out a process of raising funds for our work. We need a central rehearsal-cum-office space, or at least a store on hire for our properties.'

The first meeting of the new EC was held immediately after the GB, and I was nominated the minutes keeper. With the tenth anniversary of Janam's street theatre coming up on October 15, we set about planning for that.

Between October 2 and November 30, we held six EC meetings. Our seventh EC meeting was held on January 5, 1989, when we co-opted Mala in the EC and nominated her Acting Convenor. It was the most sombre meeting I've ever sat in. Many of us were having trouble just focusing and not tearing up. Mala plunged right into work, into the minutiae that any kind of organizing entails. Sometimes, heroism takes the plainest form.

But all this lay in the future. For the moment, I was looking forward to learning organizational skills from Safdar, just as I was learning theatre from him and Habib sa'ab. That afternoon, some of us – I remember Nandita, Jogi, Brijender, Rakesh, and myself – had been volunteered by Safdar for a TV film that M.S. Sathyu was shooting in Kusumpur Pahadi, the slum cluster atop a hillock next to the wealthy neighbourhood of Vasant Vihar. Afterwards we walked across to JNU, where we met up with Ayesha and Shikma. It being Gandhi Jayanti, there was no chance of getting alcohol, but we were high on the optimism of a new beginning. We spent the evening, and much of the night, on Parthasarathi Rock, singing and laughing.

OCTOBER 1988. Ten Years of Street Theatre

The new EC set about planning the tenth anniversary event. We organized a street theatre festival, and a round table on street theatre. Both took place in 35 Ferozeshah Road – the performances on the lawns, then part of the JNU City Centre, and the seminar in a conference room of the Indian Council for Historical Research (ICHR) in the main building. We decided to create an exhibition of photographs, and write a paper for discussion, for which we created separate sub-committees. Shikha was the convenor of the exhibition sub-committee, with Shehla, Mala, Rakesh, and Jogi as members; I was convenor of the other sub-committee, with Safdar, Sanjay, Shikma, and Nandita as members. Shehla put her cartographic skills to good use by creating a map of India showing all the villages, towns, and cities where we had performed. The exhibition had some 75 photos of Janam's work over the years. In other words, the exhibition sub-committee did a lot of work. The sub-committee I was heading volunteered Safdar to write the approach paper for discussion. He did.

There were five performances on the evening of October 15. Safdar gave a general introduction to our ten-year journey in street theatre, and invited theatrepersons to come and work with us. *Samrath*, the first play, was introduced by Mala; Shikha invited Theatre Union to perform *Marz Ka Munafa*; Manish introduced *Raja Ka Baja*, after which we had a short break; then Lalit introduced the production of *Girgit*, which had come out of the workshop that Safdar had conducted in JNU; and finally, I introduced *Aurat*.

I have three distinct, and inter-related, impressions of the evening. One, that it was a long evening, and watching five street plays one after another, no matter how good each of them was, can be tiresome. Two, the worst thing you can do is to put the longest play first up, especially if it also ends up being the worst performed. We had first decided that we'll open with *Machine*, but under pressure from the 'seniors' Safdar insisted we replace it with *Samrath*. That gave them more scope to showcase themselves, I guess. The EC's review later noted that 'Disregard for some of the basic rules of street theatre acting, complacency, and over-confidence of some actors were ... the cause for *Samrath* not clicking'. It was embarrassing to see actors hamming their way through the play. Fortunately, they were followed by Theatre Union, who managed to revive the audiences' interest. Three, concluding the evening with *Aurat* was the best thing we could've done. The combination of young, energetic actors supporting Mala's magnificent performance lifted the evening. A number of theatrepersons attended that evening.

Of those who attended the round table on street theatre on October 29, I remember Rati Bartholomew, Raina, G.P. Deshpande, Madan Gopal Singh, and Ram Gopal Bajaj. Safdar presented the approach paper. We had circulated cyclostyled copies in advance, so he spoke extempore, expanding on some of the main points. I marvelled at the ease with which he moved from English to Hindi – Hindustani, actually, laced with beautiful Urdu words that I was learning for the first time, such as mukhtalif (varied) and israr (request). Rati was generous, as always, in her comments, and argued for the need to break fresh ground after a decade's work. Raina was blunter: 'Look at all these photos, they all look the same. Why don't your plays look different? What have you done to break up the space? Till you break the space, nothing will happen.' GPD made the point that we needed to move beyond IPTA in our aesthetics, and in our politics. 'Look at the Shiv Sena in Bombay. They do their communal politics as if they're running an industrial enterprise. It's all streamlined; it's all about input and output. Where is the Marxist analysis of communalism? All one hears is a sort of humanist, liberal analysis of communalism. Our plays merely say, "Be good boys, don't kill each other." But this message is increasingly hollow, because all "secular" parties, from the Congress to all the splinters of the Janata Party, say this. They have no problem with it. A Marxist position should hurt the communalists, but it should also make liberals uncomfortable. I don't find that happening.'

What Rati, Raina, and GPD were saying was that we needed to reorient ourselves, to think afresh, to break moulds. Safdar was excited by these critiques. Creatively, he was poised to take a big leap forward. We saw the first signs of it in the play we created for the seven-day strike of the working class in November that year. The play was called *Chakka Jaam* ('Strike'), and it was the first version of what was later called *Halla Bol* ('Raise Hell').

To understand what *Chakka Jaam/Halla Bol* achieved, though, we have to first understand the nature of Delhi's working class in the late 1980s, and why it decided to go on a hitherto unimaginable seven-day strike.

THE 1980S. Delhi's Working Class

Workers don't need to be told that they are exploited. Domestic workers know they work too much for too little; when a lecherous employer harasses one, she knows it is a violation. Rickshaw pullers know brutality when they strain every sinew to pull the rickshaw in Delhi's 45-degree crackling, dry heat. Home-based workers who polish a hundred and forty small industrial parts a day to make them reusable, know that the chemical they dip the pieces in also claws into their own body. A daily wage-earning mason knows that to wait at the roadside, hoping someone will turn up and buy his labour, is to turn time into one's enemy. Sex workers sell gratification to men knowing well that the giver is stigmatized, not the buyer. Manual scavengers descend into sewers resentfully, aware that their humanity is of no value to the rest of the world.

The poor, the marginalized, the exploited, the oppressed, rise up in disgust sporadically, when they feel they cannot take it anymore, but these episodes can be like froth on sand. For the oppressed to organize themselves into a movement for lasting change, they have to believe they can win.

I was witness to one such moment, in November 1988, when 13 lakh (1.3 million) workers across Delhi, Ghaziabad, and Faridabad, the vast majority of whom were not organized in unions, rose up to demand what was justly theirs. They went on a historic seven-day strike, not because they were finally convinced of the justice of their demands, which was self-evident to them more than anyone, but because something gave them the belief that the demands could be won. Those who led the strike had a nuanced understanding of the nature of the working class, and evolved appropriate strategies and slogans to mobilize workers across the spectrum.

The 1988 strike remains the most successful and militant action by the working class as a whole, in the history of Delhi. For that reason alone, it is worth reminding ourselves of this historic struggle, the memory of which has all but vanished from the minds of even workers, let alone the middle classes and others. I might also note that the 1988 strike, preceded by strikes in 1986 and 1987, was in part also a conscious response by the Left to the growing communalization of Delhi's population. The memories of the anti-

Sikh pogrom of 1984 were still fresh, and the Hindu Right had begun mobilizing on the Ayodhya issue in a big way. Communal divisions were not absent among the working class. I have written earlier in this book about the Left's initiative in mobilizing large sections of the people on the anti-communalism platform through the Committee for Communal Harmony. The strike actions of the 1980s were the other side of that coin.

The Hindu Right is ascendant today, and the secular and progressive people are groping to find ways to fight the menace, to protect India's Constitution and social fabric. Quite apart from the centrality of the 1988 strike to Safdar's story, today's context makes it imperative for us to understand the strike in some detail.

The population of Delhi, which stood at just over nine lakh (under one million) in 1941, increased over ten times in the half century that followed, to reach 94 lakh (9.4 million) in 1991. The first mass migration into the city occurred at the time of Partition, when mainly Hindu and Sikh refugees from the Punjab poured in. They played a major role in giving the city its character, and their resilience, creativity, and fortitude shaped the city's economic activity. Over time, other migrants also arrived. These were predominantly rural migrants seeking to escape the crushing poverty of their original locations. Initially, Delhi grew not as an industrial centre like Bombay or Calcutta, but as an administrative centre.

Till the early 1980s, Delhi's industrial landscape, and its working-class struggles, were dominated by the five large textile mills – Delhi Cloth Mills (DCM), DCM Silk, Swatantra Bharat Mills (SBM), Ajudhia Textile Mills (ATM), and Birla Mills (BM). Of all workers employed in large enterprises, about half worked in these five mills alone. While there were some medium-scale factories (for instance the Delhi Flour Mills, which employed about two hundred and fifty workers), the vast majority of industrial units in Delhi employed thirty workers or less. In 1988, about thirty per cent of all industrial units employed four workers or less. Shockingly, less than seven per cent of all industrial units in 1988 were registered under the Factories Act. This meant that the overwhelming majority of Delhi's industrial workers had no legal protection at all, however tenuous it might have been even for those who had it. Labour inspectors and labour courts were generally amenable to bribes and corruption; they ended up, unsurprisingly, mostly on the side of the owners, not workers.

Effectively, all workers faced the brutish exploitation of Delhi's capitalist class. Not only did the capitalists extract increasing levels of surplus value, workers were also at the mercy of their overt and covert violence, both on the factory floor and in the bastis and slums where they lived. Wages were low, and living conditions pathetic. The working hours were interminable with 12-hour shifts quite the norm, with some even having to work 16 hours. Injuries and deaths resulting from accidents at work were common, and the idea of compensation virtually non-existent. Many workers got no holidays at all. For most, employment was precarious, and they were forced to change jobs frequently. Many stayed on factory premises – not in workers' quarters – cramped together in tiny rooms. At the first sign of dispute with the owner, they risked losing their job as well as a place to stay. A large number of workers were not on the muster roll, being employed through contractors. Over the decades, more and more women joined the workforce. They got lower wages than men for the same amount of work. Many women also faced sexual and other forms of harassment; being pregnant meant losing one's job.

Things were tougher for fresh migrants from villages. Young men, many illiterate or barely literate, would leave their familiar, if precarious, surroundings in the village and arrive in the city. The crowds, noise, traffic, buildings, languages – everything would be unfamiliar and intimidating. They would get absorbed by circles of kinship or community, which would provide them accommodation and food for a few weeks, but they knew they had to get employment fast. Rather than dazzled, they'd be traumatized by the city. It was not uncommon for fresh migrants to withdraw into a shell or become lethargic for a while. In extreme cases, some would even lose speech for a week or so. Even though I write in the past tense, the conditions are no better today; in many ways, they are worse, and with the introduction of a slew of 'labour reforms' by the Modi government, workers stand to lose rights their predecessors fought for and won.

Factory owners had little to complain about, although capitalists as a class perennially complain and demand more. Delhi in the 1980s ensured three things for capitalists: there was always a steady supply of unemployed labour, which helped to keep wages low and exploitation high; workers had little to no protection from the legal framework that was supposed to protect them; often, because workers found a degree of comfort and social insurance in networks of kin, region, language, and religion, these same networks also formed the fault lines along which workers could be divided.

Organizing Workers

K.M. Tiwari, the current secretary of Delhi CPI (M), has been a full-time unionist and Communist organizer. As a boy, he had spent time in a nautanki troupe in Gonda in eastern UP, before going to Jamshedpur, where his father was a member of the Congress-affiliated Indian National Trade Union Congress (INTUC). He migrated to Ghaziabad in 1969–70, where he found a job in a polyester fibre plant. He was dismissed in 1978 for his union activities. He explains how they organize workers:

'There are always accidents in an industrial area. Someone loses his hand, someone a finger, someone gets injured. We keep letting workers know that if they have a problem, they should come to us. As soon as we hear of an accident, even if the worker is not part of a union, we get his name, his father's name, and go to the Karmachari Rajya Bima Nigam [Employees' State Insurance Corporation] to register his case, to get compensation and treatment. I remember an instance from 1979–80. There used to be a factory called Rathi Udyog in the South of G.T. Road Industrial Area. It was a big factory.

One night, I was sleeping in the union office when a worker came running, and said, "Comrade, there's been an accident. A worker has died." He was afraid that they'd cut up his body, put it in a sack, and throw it into the furnace. I woke up the others and asked some of them to go to the Collector's house, and wake him up. And I went to the factory gate along with some others and created a ruckus. So the workers get to know that you'll stand by them. The workers talk among themselves and come to join us. Then we talk to them about other things – about getting their names on the muster roll, about getting labour laws implemented. This is one way to get an entry into the factory. Sometimes, when workers don't get wages, or bonus, or holidays, they look around to see who can help them. If we are there in the area, they come to us. Then we talk to those workers, even if they are only four or five of them. Slowly, with their help, we try and build an organization. When there is repression from the owners and the police, we demonstrate in front of the police station. We go to the factory gate at the time the shift gets over. When we demonstrate with the red flag, the workers see that they can get protection.'

Journalist Subodh Varma studied at St Stephen's in Delhi University, became an SFI activist, and then joined CITU as a wholetimer in the run-up to the 1988 strike. He was arrested on the first day of the strike at the G.T. Karnal Road Industrial Area in north Delhi, and spent three days in jail. He underlines the issue of trust:

'You might raise a demand with a general sense of acceptance. Workers agree with the demand. But mere agreement is only the first step. They may have some intellectual convergence with what you are saying, but it's not sufficient. The step forward from that is, is there something on which a fight can be carried out. Which raises questions of confidence, of trust, in the organization leading or dealing with it. Is it [the organization] really capable of doing it? The biggest question is security. Will this imply a blowback later, which an individual worker is unable to face? Is this organization sufficiently strong to fight back? These are issues that are nebulous, but definitely exist in workers' minds and hearts, and especially so in small-scale industries. There is no job security. Most people don't get appointment letters. Their names are not in the registers, and so on. It is a daily life of insecurity and humiliation. So in these conditions, these are life and death issues.'

An organization, to get a mass base, needs to build leadership at the intermediate levels. Leaders are not trained only by giving them classes, speeches, and ideological education, though all of that is also important. They need to be engaged in concrete agitational activity, to get experience of organizing struggles, and the chance to discover their own strengths. Building confidence is a painstaking, step-by-step process, and rarely proceeds in a straight line. There are ups and downs, ebbs and spurts. People try different approaches, different methods, and in the process they make mistakes. Leadership building is not only about giving responsibilities, it is also about reposing trust. The person must feel that if they make a mistake, the higher level of leadership will stand by them, not crucify them, and, collectively, everybody will learn from failures.

Crucially, confidence-building is also about winning victories. You start with a small struggle where your assessment is that a victory can be won. You identify the issues, evolve slogans that will resonate with workers. In every struggle you include demands that you think can be won, but also demands that you think will not be granted. Why? Because each struggle is preparation for the next; workers must see that our canvas is not limited. A victory, even a partial victory, is celebrated and publicized. It attracts more workers and widens the scope of the struggle.

Not all unions work like this, though. Most unions, whether independent or controlled by bourgeois parties, don't even believe in struggle. Workers call these the 'ten per cent unions'. The emphasis of these unions is on going through the conciliation process, and getting the worker compensation, from which they would pocket ten per cent (or more) for themselves, besides getting a cut from the owner. The union leadership makes a living out of this. Such unions have zero interest in conducting actual struggles for the betterment of workers as a whole. An agitation here, another there, is useful only inasmuch as it helps build their profile as troublemakers, which gives them a bargaining chip with the owners. Some unions are literally paid by the owners so workers don't get radicalized. Why do workers go to such unions? Partly because they know it has the owner's backing, so the chances of victimization are reduced, and partly because the entire legal process is so long and tedious that workers can't hold out. It is tempting to have a private settlement with the owner, brokered by the union leader.

A trade unionist's life is hard and unglamorous. Aditya Nigam, professor at the Centre for the Study of Developing Societies in New Delhi, was an SFI activist in Delhi University before becoming a CITU wholetimer for five years. He took part in the 1988 strike as an organizer in the Jhilmil Industrial Area in Shahdara. He recalls the daily life of a union organizer:

'Apart from the strike period, most of the activity would be the drudgery of conciliation activity. There used to be a labour office in each area, with labour inspectors. So, periodically, one had to write letters against the owner on whatever issues were there. Even the legal process requires you to go through the conciliation process before initiating any other activity. For example, if someone was dismissed, the matter would first have to go for conciliation. This involved writing letters, and being present on the requisite dates. Then, if something got sorted out, fine, otherwise you challenged it in the labour court. That's another tedious process. Only when it didn't work at these levels did you go to the next stage of struggle. Sometimes there was a spontaneous conflagration in a factory, even without a union. Say a senior management official misbehaved, and this galvanized the workers. Then the union would also get involved. We'd hold gate meetings and so on. But this didn't happen more than five per cent of the time. The rest of the time was conciliation activity. In CITU, our position was that we won't get out of court settlements done. There were the 10–15 per cent unions who would get the deal done with the owner. They'd pocket 10–15 per cent of it.'

Sometimes, Aditya points out, they had to fight against these tendencies in their own organization as well. 'Wholetimer wages are so low, and wholetimers don't work in a factory, so they don't even get that minimum wage or anything. The ones who come from working-class backgrounds don't have any financial backup. Middle classes have a backup. For them, the wage doesn't really matter. You can be holier-than-thou and say that this is upright and uncompromising, but for the wholetimer who comes from a working-class background, there is no financial backup whatsoever. Owners realize this. They say to the wholetimer, "Yaar, you take ten per cent and get the work done." Eventually some get sucked into that trap.'

Being a trade unionist is also a tremendous learning experience. Radicalized by the protest movements of the late 1960s, Brinda Karat quit her job in London and came back to Calcutta to join the CPI (M) in 1970. She came to Delhi when the Emergency was imposed. She entered the trade union movement as an underground activist under the name of Rita, and became a popular leader at textile mill gates in north and west Delhi. She became secretary of the CPI (M) North Delhi local committee, and played an important part in the growth of the General Mazdoor Union. During the 1988 strike, she was the Delhi secretary of Janwadi Mahila Samiti. She went on to become secretary of All India Democratic Women's Association (AIDWA), and is currently a member of the CPI (M) Polit Bureau.

She recalls her early trade union experiences:

'When I came to Delhi and met Comrade Harkishan Singh Surjeet, he asked me what I would like to do. I said I would like to work with the trade unions. He said, well, the biggest trade union in Delhi is the textile union. He never felt that it was strange for a young woman to want to work with the trade union without having worked in any other mass organization in Delhi. He welcomed it. At that time, the secretary of the Delhi State Committee, Major

Jaipal Singh, was already in jail. Comrade Surjeet was sort of semi-underground. I met him at someone's home, not in the office. He spoke about me to the senior trade unionist Chacha Shadiram, who was looking after Delhi in Major sa'ab's absence.

'My first meeting with the textile workers was at the Karampura office. Comrade Sriram was there in that meeting. He was a dismissed textile worker. He was an extremely knowledgeable and militant worker, and very supportive. It was decided then that I should work in north Delhi through the Kamla Nagar office.

'At that time, it was very difficult to work because there was a very big attack on workers' rights. There were new productivity norms for textile workers. Union activity was disapproved of. When anybody was found working in the unions, there would be consequences. You were not allowed to hold gate meetings. In textiles, the main way of communicating with the workers on any issue is to hold a gate meeting. Our union was never given permission to hold a gate meeting. INTUC used to hold gate meetings. Then we used to have blackboards outside the textile union office on which we used to write messages for the workers. Now we were not allowed to write on blackboards unless it was something in support of the Emergency. Sitting at the gate to collect membership was also circumscribed, because they used to look at which worker was joining which union. Workers themselves were not very confident. The management was mechanizing the mill and bringing in the two-loom system. They were trying to increase the machines that each worker could work. It was a very big issue at that time. There was a brewing discontent among the workers.

'We used to hold meetings in the living quarters of the workers. Not only in official workers' colonies, but also all the surrounding slums where workers lived. At that time, many of the jhuggis were bulldozed and were shifted to Nand Nagri. I spent weeks there, very often nights as well, because it was very difficult to return in the middle of the night. We got to know the families of the workers. We got to understand the different cultures of workers. It was a huge learning process for me. I was also working with the handloom workers. I was fortunate to be deputed to work in the North Local Committee of the Party, under Comrade Sriram's leadership. It was one of the most politically active committees. During the Emergency we couldn't work in an open way, but there was a huge, spontaneous coming to the red flag by the workers. The suppressed discontent of the workers was out in the open. There were so many strikes, struggles, and militant actions in which our union was involved. It was at that time when we felt that this really is the heart of the changes that we envisaged in the political scenario in Delhi.'

OCTOBER 1988. Organizing for the Strike

Before the seven-day strike in 1988, the working class in Delhi took part in two other major strike actions in the 1980s – a one-day strike in 1986 and a 72-hour (three-day) strike in 1987. The central demand of these strikes was that of minimum wage. The official minimum wage for unskilled workers in Delhi had gone up from Rs 300 in 1982 to Rs 562 in 1988 – an increase of Rs 262 – while the consumer price index for Delhi had gone up by 334 in the same period. Simply put, while the nominal wage had increased, the real wage had decreased. The seven-day strike demanded an increase in the minimum wage from Rs 562 to Rs 1,050, and a dearness allowance of Rs 2 per point rise in the price index.

The second major demand concerned the living conditions of workers. A vast majority of Delhi's workers lived in jhuggis (slums) considered 'illegal'. This is hardly unique to Delhi; it is a global condition. As the American theorist Mike Davis reminds us, we live on a 'planet of slums'. Urban elites, typically, need the labour that slums provide, but hate the people whose bodies provide the labour. While mainstream discourse views slums through the lens of criminality and pollution, slums are sinews of any city's social, economic, political, and even cultural life. They are universities of the poor, where they learn to negotiate the tough art of survival in a metropolis. Quite simply, capitalism cannot survive without slums. The strikes demanded permanent settlement rights for slum dwellers.

Other demands included abolition of the contract system, and giving permanent jobs for permanent work as well as equal pay for equal work. The provision of crèches in establishments that employed twenty or more women workers was also on the agenda. The repeal of anti-worker laws, and the implementation of existing labour laws was also demanded.

The first time I saw an industrial strike firsthand was in 1986, when I was among a team of SFI activists. At the time, the common sense among trade unionists was that you could only sustain a one-day strike in Delhi; anything longer was bound to fail. Strikes in individual factories, or even specific industries, were one thing. But a multi-day general strike across industries? No way. There was a political reason for this as well. When the Communist Party of India split in 1964 and the CPI (M) came into being, in Delhi, unlike in many other states, no important CPI leader came with the CPI (M). Until CITU was formed in 1970, the only real Left union was the AITUC, which was with the CPI. However, the AITUC would shy away from militant struggles due to CPI's pro-Congress approach. The other unions were not interested in struggles either. So, in 1987, when CITU proposed a three-day strike, none of the other unions joined. They felt that workers would not respond to the unions' call for further revision of the minimum wage after it was revised from Rs 414 to Rs 489 in May 1987. But CITU went ahead, and conducted a successful 72-hour strike.

The same story was repeated in 1988. Once again, other unions were sure that the CITU had overreached itself, especially since the government announced a further revision of the minimum wage to Rs 562 in March 1988. The Delhi working class would never be able to sustain such a long strike, they felt. But the workers were angry. The slogan that most resonated with them was '*Jeena hai to ladna hoga*' ('To live, you have to fight').

CITU Delhi Secretary Suraj Bhan Bhardwaj sensed the seething anger of the workers and knew they were ready. Comrade Bhardwaj was politicized during the Freedom Struggle. Originally from Muzaffarnagar district in Uttar Pradesh, he worked in JK Cotton in Kanpur, and became a leader of AITUC. He joined the CPI in 1961, and when the party split in 1964, he went with the CPI (M). He was brought to Ghaziabad by Comrade Major to build CITU. Of working-class origin and a veteran of many a battle, he, more than anyone else, galvanized CITU.

Spontaneity without organization is a shooting star; organization without spontaneity is quicksand. The CITU leadership evolved a multifarious strategy to ensure the success of the strike. CITU's actual membership was infinitesimal in comparison to the size of the working class. It was relatively strong in Ghaziabad, but in Delhi it was a marginal force.

'We decided to go alone,' Jogendra Sharma, who was then Delhi CPI (M) secretary and CITU vice president, tells me. 'But we had to plan meticulously. We had to think of the timing. What kind of attacks are workers facing? How ready are they to fight? And if they do fight, what assurance can we give them? The leadership had to think about all this. Workers don't join a strike simply because of your call. A man will fight if he can hang by a peg. We had to be that peg. We had to prepare the organization. This took four to five months of work.'

By the late 1980s, the five big textile mills of Delhi were downsizing their labour force, and in the following decade they shut down altogether, one after another. This meant that the striking power of the working class was adversely affected, since the organized and powerful unions of the textile sector had been the spearhead of all industrial working-class action till then. The major trade union leaders had also cut their teeth in these mills, where it was relatively easier to reach out to and organize workers. In an innovative tactic, CITU decided to consider an entire industrial area as a unit, rather than reach out to the myriad units in an industrial area separately.

The CITU leadership realized that workers had to be met at their homes in order to reach out to the industrial area. This meant going in a big way into the jhuggi bastis adjoining the industrial areas. Janwadi Mahila Samiti activists played a crucial role. As women, they could enter the jhuggis in the afternoon, when the men were at work. Also, since a large number of women had entered the workforce by now, in industrial areas too, they could speak to the women workers in a way that the men couldn't. This was because the JMS, as Brinda put it, 'was rooted and grounded in the working-class bastis'. In recent years, intersectionality – the overlapping interconnectedness of various forms of social, economic, and political discrimination with gender – has been an important idea in feminist organizing and studies. The organizing effort behind the seven-day strike is a fine example of it.

The Delhi State Conference of the CPI (M) took place from October 8 to 10, 1988. The upcoming seven-day strike was a major point on the agenda of the Conference. The leadership exhorted all Party committees to work towards it. Safdar was a delegate to the Conference.

'We called Party general body meetings and reached out to every member, who had to be prepared politically, ideologically, and organizationally,' Jogendra Sharma tells me. 'We explained: Why was this struggle necessary? What were workers fighting for? And what did we need to do? The second step was to prepare the trade union leadership. If that didn't happen, the workers would not come out. The third step was to mobilize the mass organizations and Party sympathizers. The Janwadi Mahila Samiti, Democratic Youth Federation of India, students, teachers, white-collar employees, cultural front, sympathizers – everybody had to be prepared. This was not something CITU could have pulled off on its own. We didn't have that kind of strength. We would take professors, lawyers, retired judges, and artists to working-class areas to address meetings. This was something we had done during the campaign of the Committee for Communal Harmony as well. This gave confidence to workers.

Workers were finding their peg now. As we were doing this, we were also reaching out to workers who were not with us.'

The Party, through its various fronts, including CITU, JMS, and DYFI, launched a massive propaganda campaign for the strike among workers. Indrani Majumdar's report provides figures: 'All told 6,80,000 leaflets, 40,000 posters and 24,000 poster strips were used in the campaign. ... Over a thousand street corner meetings spearheaded the campaign into the heart of industrial and working-class residential areas. Apart from these area-level meetings, a central hartal rath or a mobile platform on a tempo carrying central leaders, went to every area from the 11th of November till the 21st. The mammoth meetings addressed through this sweeping tempo campaign had a powerful charging effect on the workers and raised the pitch of the preparations to new heights.' Her report contains a rich discussion of 'the hundreds of small details of preparatory work, of tedious, and sometimes confusing, organizational processes that were finally welded together in a unified and common endeavour'.

At the time, I was unaware of the scale of the preparations going on, nor was I alive to the historic significance of the coming strike. Safdar was. He would spend every morning in the Party office, doing whatever was required of him. Activists from various fronts would troop in and out of the Party office all day. Safdar was soaking in their conversations, and particularly seeking out trade union comrades to learn more about the living and working conditions of workers, the specificities of their demands, their struggles, their aspirations and hopes.

There was electricity in the air, and Safdar was the lightning rod who transmitted it to Janam.

OCTOBER 1988. Writing Chakka Jaam

'Listen to this. I've written an opening for the strike play. It's going to be a love story.'

Safdar was grinning from ear to ear as we met for rehearsal. He took out his papers, and began reading: A bunch of actors start the play with slogans for workers' rights. A man emerges from the audience and interrupts the play. What are you people doing, he wants to know. We're doing a play, the actors tell him. Well, this ain't no play, he says. These are slogans. This is a play for the working class, he is told. There are bound to be slogans. The man is not satisfied. Why can't you do a simple, regular play? With stories of love, with fun and frolic? The actors think about it, and say, yes, why the hell not. Let's do a love story.

The actors sing a parody of an old Hindi film song as we are introduced to the lovers – a worker named Jogi and his sweetheart Ashsho. The boy has to ask for her hand in marriage, so he has to meet the parents. The lovers rehearse the scene, with Ashsho playing the father. Jogi is confident he can crack the interview. When he comes up against the real father, though, he turns into a nervous, bumbling wreck. The father asks him how much he earns. Five hundred and sixty-two rupees, says Jogi. The father then starts subtracting all his monthly expenses from this, and we see how it is impossible for a couple to survive on this paltry wage. Nothing short of 1,000–1,100 rupees will do, the father says. Jogi says yes, that's what the CITU is also saying. They're demanding 1,050 and are planning a strike. So join them, says the father, and come back to me when you win that demand. At this point, the actors address the spectator who had stopped the play to begin with.

'Why doesn't it enter your thick skull that if you do a play on the life of workers – whether you raise the red flag or not, whether you raise a slogan or not – it doesn't matter, because the fact is, *jeena hai to ladna hoga. Aur pyar bhi karna hai to ladna hoga.* (You have to join the struggle if you want to live. Or to love.)'

This then segued into a scene where two or three actors have a conversation about living conditions in slums. A bulldozer arrives to demolish the slum. The actors appeal to the neta (political leader) for help. He refuses, and instead, his goon threatens them. The workers realize that rights are not granted, they are fought for and won. The workers appeal to a woman worker to join them. She says she won't, because they aren't raising her demand. What might that be? She says, why don't you ask for crèches where women work, so we can bring our children? A woman worker tries to enter a factory, carrying her child in her arms, but is stopped at the gate.

'Then what happens?' someone asked Safdar.

'I'm not sure,' he said. 'Let's see.'

The opening was pretty funny, till the point that the father breaks down Jogi's wage. After that, it was all talk and no drama. Safdar knew this, and said he needed to rewrite the whole thing. I thought it was clever that it took the cliché about street theatre – that it's a theatre of sloganeering – and used it to its advantage to move into the love story. The later scene, between Jogi and Ashsho, was funny too. Even as they rehearse the lines, you know that it's going to go awry, so when it does, as spectators you are gratified. Written in an over-the-top, melodramatic style that mimicked Hindi movies, it evoked much laughter. For us, listening to it the first time, it was funnier still because of the insider joke – the lovers were named after Ayesha Kidwai and, well, Jogi. We laughed spontaneously when we heard the sequence – and we knew that at least that part of the casting was already decided! There's another insider joke here, which I realized only later, after Safdar's death, when his articles were published. One of them, 'The Enchanted Arch', is a polemic against a playwright who, while chairing a session on street theatre in a conference, lamented that street theatre is only capable of sloganeering, and not of taking up important issues of life. Safdar's opening of the new play was responding to that, but playfully. It was delightful.

Later that evening, as we travelled back on the DTC bus, I asked Safdar who that man is who stops the play in the beginning.

'I don't know. A spectator.'

'Has something like this happened before, that a spectator has stopped a play and demanded that you do something different?'

Safdar laughed. 'No, no. Audiences love that you're performing for them. Only the police stop the play.'

He then described a scene that had been playing in his mind for a while:

A cop is on beat duty. He comes across a fellow doing nothing in particular. Who are you? asks the cop. I'm a pppppickpocket, stammers the man, trembling with fear. How much do you earn? asks the cop. Ffffifty rupees, says the man. Ah, nice, says the cop. Give me 25. He does, and the cop embraces him. Then he meets another fellow. Turns out he's a thief and earns 100 a day. The cop pockets 50, and embraces him. Then a third fellow, who turns out to be a drug dealer, and earns 200. The cop pockets 100, and embraces him. Then a fourth fellow, who turns out to be a worker and a trade unionist. The cop begins to beat him up.

'Nice. Where will this scene come?'

'Oh I don't know at all! Sometimes I get these ideas that are self-standing scenes; sometimes they find a place in a play and sometimes they remain orphans.'

That was that, and I didn't think any more of it. The following day, Safdar told us that he had written more of the play, and had also reworked the opening. Now, the play was stopped not by a spectator but a cop, who says that slogans are not allowed because they incite the workers, and it was his job to make sure the upcoming strike failed. Nobody dare as much as mention CITU's name in his area, let alone raise slogans, he says.

It was now the cop who suggested that the actors do a regular play with a love story. Safdar introduced Ashsho's mother as well into the scene. He reduced the initial exchange between Jogi and Ashsho, and heightened the comic parts when Jogi meets his future in-laws. When the love story brings up talk of the strike, the cop intervenes again to stop the play. The actors refuse and ask him to go to hell. He threatens them with dire consequences, and exits, saying he'll return with reinforcements.

'So, will he?' I asked.

'No, I don't think so. We'll move on to other issues,' Safdar said.

I thought this was not satisfactory. While working on *Moteram*,

Habib sa'ab had once spoken about 'Chekhov's gun' – the Russian writer's famous advice that if you introduced a gun in the first act, it had to be fired before the play ended. In other words, every element of the story must carry the narrative forward, and whatever doesn't, should be cut out.

I felt that the cop's threat to come back with reinforcements was an instance of Chekhov's gun – if it wasn't going to be fired, it shouldn't be there. At home that night, and the next morning, I agonized over how to engineer the exit of the cop in our play. It seemed to me that the only way for him to not return to the action was if he was driven out by the collective strength of the actors. But it was also clear to me that it was too early in the play for that to be convincing. More had to happen before the cop could be driven out.

I had an idea in the afternoon, and started writing an alternative scene – managing to finish it just in time for me to make it to the rehearsal. I was nervous and excited. I had no idea how the others would respond to the scene, and how Safdar would react. It was one thing to have a master like Habib Tanvir rewrite your scenes, it is another to have a slip of a boy meddling with your writing. I felt in my gut that Safdar wouldn't be offended or angry, but in my nervous state, I was prepared for the worst.

At the best of times, I wasn't a good reader – a goods train, in Habib sa'ab's evocative phrase, not a Rajdhani Express – so I asked Jogi if he'd read the scene for me.

'Safdar, Sudhu has written a new scene,' Jogi announced.

'That's great. But why isn't he telling us?' Safdar looked at me. My mouth was dry and no words would emerge. He smiled. 'Ah, you're stammering, is it? Jogi, you read the scene. Otherwise we'll be here till tomorrow morning.' Everyone laughed, I included, and Jogi started reading:

The cop stops the actors at the end of the scene where Ashsho's father breaks down Jogi's wage for him, and Jogi says he's going to join the strike so his wage can go up. This is the third time the cop has interrupted the action, and the actors are fed up. They announce to the audience that they can't do the play like this, and are folding up the performance. Then one actor – who plays Ashsho's father – says, hang on a minute, let me talk to the cop. He goes up to him and says, Mr Constable, I know you said that we can't even mention CITU in our play. But what if our play is against the CITU? Would that be OK? The cop thinks hard. Well, it is true that the orders from higher up are that even the name is not allowed, but if you're going to do a play against the CITU, sure, why not. He goes off into a reverie where he fantasizes that he will get promoted for this, and then, surely, it will only be a matter of time before he rises in the hierarchy and becomes the Deputy Commissioner of Police. Yes, go ahead, he says.

So the actors restart the play. The prime minister then was Rajiv Gandhi, who was obsessed with 'taking India into the 21st century', his favourite phrase. I can't any more remember the exact details, but he had made a speech about how workers ought to sacrifice for the greater good. I had written a scene where a neta delivers a version of Rajiv Gandhi's speech. All I did was to heighten the ridiculousness of his real speech. That made it funny, but funnier still was that the cop could no longer object to the play, since it was delivering the Prime Minister's message. By the end though, the actors are angry and stop the speech. The cop intervenes and threatens the workers that their slum would be demolished. A local neta now enters with a sidekick in tow, and the two, with the cop, threaten the workers with dire consequences. But the workers are now fed up and they rise as one to defend themselves. The neta, sidekick, and the cop have no option but to scoot. From here, the play would segue into the woman worker's scene, which Safdar was to write.

As soon as Jogi finished reading, Safdar jumped up, rushed to me, and engulfed me in a tight embrace.

'*Oye lale ki jaan, tuney to kamaal kar diya, dhoti ka phad ke rumal kar diya!* (You totally cracked it, man!)'

It was settled, then. The 'reversal' scene was immediately incorporated into the play, as was the slum scene. Safdar then read out the next scene he had written, about the woman worker who complains about not being allowed to enter the factory because she's had to bring her small child with her.

During the tea break in the rehearsal, Shikma whispered to me, 'You bastard. I know you wrote that scene only so he'd hug you.'

'Well, then you should've.'

'I know! But he wouldn't have hugged me. He's a good boy.'

Safdar took my scenes from Jogi.

'Is this how you normally write? So neat, hardly any cutting? Or is this your fair version?'

'No, I didn't have time to fair it out. And I don't know how I write. This is the first time I've written a scene.'

'Really? Amazing. My first drafts are full of cuts.'

'Your mind is too fertile, Safdar. You get too many ideas all at once. I got only one idea, and my Hindi is limited, so I don't have an alternative.'

We laughed and chatted about the women's scene.

'It's nice, Safdar, but it doesn't have punch.'

'So what would you do if you had to write it?'

'I'd never be able to! I don't know how they speak. But there's something in the woman here that reminds me of the old woman in the last scene of *Aurat*. I know she's not pleading here, but somehow it feels like it.'

'Hmm. Let me see what I can do.'

The next day, Safdar read out the new version of the scene. It began with a woman worker, Parbati, letting out a volley of invectives at being denied entry into the factory. She is feisty, combative, angry, willing to take on the male union leaders. And when we played it the first time, Mala hit the perfect note, her body a coiled spring.

The rest of the play came easily. Immediately following the women's scene was the contract workers' scene, where a union leader, Rampal, gets into a fight with two contract workers, Gulam Rasool and Raghavan, because they refuse to join the strike.

Safdar's choice of names alluded to the fact that the working class was composed of a large number of migrants. Again, it is Parbati who makes the male union leaders see reason. It worked well in performance. Workers saw the authenticity of their experience – the resentment that regular and contract workers sometimes felt for each other – without any sugarcoating, but the scene also demonstrated, simply and without preaching, the basis for unity.

I also liked the last scene of the play, in which a man enters with a red cloth draped around him. He appears to speak in favour of the strike, but it turns out he's not in favour of CITU's call for a seven-day strike, and is instead asking the workers to join a one-day strike. That is when you discover that underneath the red cloth is a pink cloth, and the man's revolutionary posturing is akin to the AITUC's. When workers tear off that cloth, we see a saffron, white, and green cloth, indicating the Congress's colours. But then he starts speaking some spiritual mumbo-jumbo, and it turns out that under the tricolour cloth is the saffron cloth of the Hindu Right. With a clever visual device, the scene exposed the shenanigans of the other unions, which ostensibly spoke in favour of workers' rights only to betray them in the end. Diwakar played the role with aplomb.

When I asked Safdar how he got the idea, he said he didn't know how exactly, but the character was inspired by Pandit Moteram Shastri. 'He also speaks the language of satyagraha to betray the freedom struggle, doesn't he?'

The play ended with a longish rhyming sequence that incorporated all the major demands of the strike. When I heard it, I felt it wouldn't work. There was no drama in it, so I wasn't sure if the audience would stay back for it. Safdar was confident, though. 'Wait and watch. It's going to be a hit.'

We had a large number of actors, and many roles were double cast. Ayesha and Nandita were to play Ashsho; Shikma and Shikha were to play her mother; Rakesh and Lamby, both tall, were to play her father; Jogi and I, both short, were to play Jogi; and Lalit and Vishwajeet were to play the cop. Some of the other roles were also double cast. The roles that were not were Brijender as the Sutradhar and Mala as the fiery Parbati. I pleaded with Safdar not to cast me as Jogi, but to have me as the cop. He would have none of it.

'Jogi is the central role – why don't you want it?'

'Because I can't play a worker. I'll be horrible.'

'But you played the father in *Aurat*. He's a worker too. You were good.'

'But I just know I won't be good here. Give me the cop. I'll be amazing.'

'Don't be silly. You're too slight. We need the cop to be intimidating.'

I begged, I implored, I tried emotional blackmail. But Safdar was adamant, grinning back charmingly. I was stuck with Jogi.

NOVEMBER 1988. Performing Chakka Jaam

The first performance of *Chakka Jaam* was on November 2, 1988, outside the Old Secretariat on Mall Road near I.P. College, where the Labour Commissioner used to sit. Hundreds of workers from all over Delhi were there. The mood was militant. The workers were ready for the battle ahead. As the play began, we knew we had a hit on our hands. The workers loved the over-the-top humour of the love story; they were delighted at the reversal of the anti-CITU play; they clapped when the neta, the sidekick, and the cop were chased away; they responded loudly to the contract workers' scene. As Safdar had anticipated, the last rhyming recounting of the demands worked beautifully, and in subsequent shows we found that one or two of the slogans Safdar had coined for this had become well-known among workers, and they had spread even to areas where we had not performed. The one scene that didn't work was the one inspired by Moteram's character. Workers found it confusing; but the reason, I suspect, was not that the scene itself was confusing, but because by now the emotional register of the play had shifted – by the end, the workers had been roused by seeing their enemies defeated, and to now have this dampener of a scene went against the grain of the play. Safdar decided to drop it after that first performance, and even though nothing else replaced it the play was none the poorer. On the contrary, it was leaner and sharper.

What was sensational was Mala's entry as Parbati. Her anger and fighting spirit spoke to not only the women workers, but to all workers. In show after show, I enjoyed waiting for that moment of Mala's thunderclap entry, because you could discern the wave that ran through the audience. I was reminded of the first time I had seen Mala in *Aurat*. The power of her performance had had a visceral effect on me. My hair had stood on end – and, as I learnt when I did interviews for this book, it had a similar effect on many others. Madan Gopal Singh, for example, spoke to me at length about Mala's performance. 'It was unlike anything I had seen. The line of her body, the way she held her arm, her voice. I was blown away.' It was the same in *Chakka Jaam*. Years later, Mala achieved the same affect in our play *Voh Bol Uthi*, a triptych of stories, in the last of which a woman worker takes on the patriarchy of the union leaders by demanding a separate toilet for women.

The *Chakka Jaam* campaign was special. Over the past three decades, I've taken part in maybe 4,000 street theatre performances. Of these, at least about one-third have been for working-class audiences – both factory workers and informal sector workers such as loaders, domestic workers, service-sector workers, and street hawkers. Never before or after *Chakka Jaam* have I experienced that kind of energy and enthusiasm. As the strike neared, the mood of workers became so militant that sometimes we had to take a long pause before delivering our next line, because the workers would cheer and join the slogans with great gusto.

The play captured both, the mood of the workers as well as the polemics of the campaign. Safdar had caught the pulse of the workers effortlessly. His writing seemed to flow from the workers' consciousness, and in turn enhanced it. Like *Machine*, *Chakka Jaam/Halla Bol* spoke to the lived experience of workers, and was in tune with the times.

A day before the strike, we took part in the intellectuals' and artists' march in support of the strike. Safdar played a major role in reaching out to his friends and acquaintances among intellectuals, artists, and journalists. The march started from Mandi House, went down Copernicus Marg, skirted India Gate, and walked up Rajpath to culminate at Boat Club.

A CITU leader gave a speech outlining the main demands of the strike, explaining the issues in a way that made sense to his middle-class audience. Professor Prabhat Patnaik was his usual lucid self, speaking extempore in sentences that seemed written out, painting an elegant picture of the inelegant current capitalist conjuncture. Students of the National School of Drama had also joined – Safdar had likely addressed them at the NSD a few days before – and their union president spoke, extending their support. Among the artists, I recall Bhisham Sahni speaking about how some of the greatest literature in the world had taken as its subject the lives and experiences of the poor, the marginalized, women, Dalits, workers, and peasants. The next day, which was the first day of the strike, citizens of Delhi woke up to an unusual sight – all major papers had covered the rally prominently, and for once a workers' strike was not spoken of in terms of traffic jams or loss to the GDP.

We were to perform in the Mayapuri Industrial Area after the march. Since we had a few hours to kill after the rally, we went across to Connaught Place, to the Central Park. Safdar was in an upbeat mood. He began singing Ghalib, while Jogi accompanied him on the dholak. As a crowd gathered, Safdar began explaining the verses. By the end, we had a couple of hundred people around us, some of them munching on peanuts, others just loafing about, taking in the mild early-winter sun. Before we wound up and moved on, Safdar addressed our spontaneous audience and told them about the upcoming strike. He explained the main demands briefly, in his easy, mellifluous Hindustani. He urged them to talk to others about it, and ended by raising a couple of slogans: '*Inquilab zindabad!*' ('Long live the revolution!') and '*Mazdoor sangharsh zindabad!*' ('Long live the workers' struggle!'). The crowd joined in.

We had to perform near the Town Hall in Chandni Chowk one day. Apart from the couple of performances I had missed because of my sister's wedding in early November, I had gone to every performance, whether I was to perform that day or not. When we reached Town Hall, we found that there had been some confusion among the play's cops, Lalit and Vishwajeet. Each thought the other was performing, so neither had come. Safdar said he would perform the role that day. Safdar was the default replacement for all male roles in Janam anyway – he would joke that he was going to change his name to Stepney Hashmi. He had replaced a couple of actors for one reason or another in the campaign already. I went to him and said I'd like to do the role. He gently refused. I begged and pleaded. I reminded him that I had always wanted to do that role, and now that an opportunity had arisen, he could not take that away from me. He kept parrying, hoping to dissuade me. I was having none of it. Finally, he had to relent.

I knew why he was refusing. He was afraid I'd stammer. I later learnt that he had taken Jogi, Brijender, and Rakesh aside and told them that since I was adamant he had to let me perform, but that if I stammered they'd have to handle the situation as best they could. They were thankfully more cavalier about it – also street smart, I should add – and asked him to chill. In the event, it went flawlessly. Not even a hint of a stutter.

As soon as the show was over, Safdar rushed to me and lifted me up in a tight embrace.

'You were superb! I really made a mistake by not casting you as the cop. Fabulous!'

'Are you talking about my acting or about the fact that I didn't stammer?'

'Your acting, idiot. You were really good. But now that you mention it, how come you didn't stammer? You haven't rehearsed it.'

'But I have, Safdar. I've rehearsed each line, each move, a million times. It's just that I did it in my head.'

'*Wah re mere Eklavya!* (Well done, my Eklavya!)'

As we walked to the bus stop, Shikma sidled up to me.

'Uff. Here we are, giving our heart and soul to our roles, day after day. We never get a hug. And you come along, imposter, and get it for one measly performance. Not fair.'

'I'm sure he sees your tremendous sacrifice in the service of art. It's just that he's a good boy.'

NOVEMBER 1988. The Strike

All the propaganda and campaign for the strike might well bring the workers on your side, but there won't be a strike if you go wrong on the day.

A veteran trade unionist from north Delhi, Kamal Narayan, who was referred to as 'Doctor saheb' – I don't know why, because he was not a doctor – used to have a formula for this: A successful strike, he would say, is fifty per cent propaganda and fifty per cent picketing. Till I took part in one, I had not realized that a picket is not a barricade – it is not a physical object that blocks the way – it is human beings speaking to other human beings, asking them to join the strike. I was struck that workers used the English word, and everybody seemed to know what it was. Picketing had to be carefully calibrated. The strike committee of each area, in consultation with workers, would choose certain points from where the maximum number of workers entered the industrial area. Some workers, along with activists like myself, would reach that point about half an hour before the entry time. Many owners would also be there, backed by a large posse of police. Then the bulk of the workers would start arriving.

Every morning, I saw a complex dance playing out. The workers would arrive, ostensibly all ready to go to work – bathed and combed, with their lunch boxes. But they would stand some distance away, not passing the picket line just yet. The owners and the police would insist that no worker should be forcibly prevented from going to work. The workers and activists at the picket would insist that any worker who wished to go to the factory would be allowed to. Then, in about 10–15 minutes, when sufficient numbers of workers had gathered – still at a distance, waiting and watching – the main leaders would arrive, seemingly out of nowhere. This would send a wave of excitement among the workers, who, emboldened as much by their own numbers as by the presence of leaders they knew and respected, would now storm past the police and owners and join the picket. The fiction they maintained was that they had come to work, but could not, because of the large number of striking workers. This large mass, now shouting slogans with great enthusiasm, would enter the industrial area in a militant procession. If the owners had the armed might of the police backing them, the workers had the strength of numbers.

I marvelled at how quickly the tables turned. In the beginning, I would find the police posse intimidating, and it would seem impossible to me that the strike would happen. Within half an hour, the police would be vastly outnumbered, and as we moved in an ever-growing procession through the industrial area, their job was to make sure that the owner didn't provoke the workers too much. We would inevitably culminate the procession some four or five hours later, in a park where workers and leaders from many different units would address the gathering. Some middle-class activists would also address the workers, congratulating them on their courage and thanking them for their inspiration. Even I was asked to address the workers on a couple of occasions. I was introduced as an actor from the play, which most of them had seen. Someone from the audience shouted: '*Joote maro*' – and the crowd roared back, '*paanch-sau-basath!*' Our play had hit the mark.

On the last day of the strike, the workers' march didn't culminate in the nearby park. I don't know if it was decided beforehand, but, taking the police by surprise, 5,000 workers spilled out from the G.T. Karnal Road Industrial Area on to the main road, and started marching. A kilometre or so down the road, I realized that we were no longer walking, but jogging. Soon, we were running. The march culminated at the Old Secretariat, a good four–five kilometres away, where the public meeting was held. The energy of that march – run, actually – was something to experience. It was explosive. Thirty-odd years later, the memory still gives me goosebumps.

The strike was spectacularly successful. As Indrani put it, in her report, 'Despite the persistent efforts by some of the other unions to downplay the impact of the strike, despite the series of contradictory statements emanating from the owners' associations, despite the massive deployment of the police and repeated lathicharges [canings], tear gasses and arrests, every day from the 22nd to the 28th of November, 1988, the industrial areas of the city witnessed huge mobilizations of workers, and churning unrest that penetrated all corners. For the seven days of its course, its impact could be underestimated, events and facts could be distorted and lied about, but its scale and sweep were such, that the seven-day strike could not be ignored by the media. ... The result – for a few moments, the mass of workers in Delhi were able to acquire a visibility in a city which otherwise continues to mete out the callous indifference to their concerns.'

In April 1989, the government announced a revision of the minimum wage, from Rs 562 to Rs 750 (the demand was for Rs 1,050). More importantly, it announced a biannual variable dearness allowance of 85 paise per point rise in the consumer price index for industrial workers. This mechanism for automatic revision ensured that Delhi has the highest minimum wage rate in the entire country today (though with Modi government's new labour code, it might all change very fast). This is the most important legacy of the struggles and sacrifices of millions of ordinary workers in the 1980s.

One reason for the concessions was the Congress's effort to shore up support for the upcoming elections. It didn't help. The Congress lost, and V.P. Singh became prime minister of a minority government in 1989, supported by the Communists on the left and the BJP on the right. The V.P. Singh government made some noises about giving jhuggi dwellers permanent-resident permits, but before anything could happen, the BJP pulled the plug and the government fell. A Congress government took over with Narasimha Rao as prime minister and Manmohan Singh as finance minister, and ushered in economic liberalization. Among other things, it severely crippled the working-class movement. Delhi has never since seen any working-class action on the scale and magnitude of the 1988 seven-day strike.

One day, after picketing and the public meeting, I met Jogi in Connaught Place. It was late afternoon, and I hadn't eaten anything since morning. I had no money, but Jogi, who used to play the dholak professionally at jagrans at night, usually had some.

'Let me treat you. Have you been to Kake da Hotel? No? Let's go there. We'll have some nice non-veg.'

So we trooped off to the Municipal Market opposite the outer circle of Connaught Place. Kake da Hotel was shut, which was unusual.

'No worries,' Jogi said. 'There are many places here. Let's go to the next one.'

Which was shut as well. And a third. And a fourth. We kept walking, perplexed, till we reached one where there were some people standing outside.

'That one seems open! Look at the crowd outside. Well, makes sense, since everything else is closed.'

As we got close to the crowd, wondering how we could get in, a couple of people came to us.

'*Laal salam*, comrade.'

They were part of the CITU-led Hotel Employees' Union and had seen *Chakka Jaam*. They were delighted that the two Jogis from the play had come to join their picket, which had ensured that all restaurants in Connaught Place were closed.

DECEMBER 1988. Dreams

A young member of Parcham, Ashutosh Doshi, who had sung with us in *Moteram*, had died when he was crushed by the moving bus he was trying to disembark from. That evening, we had a condolence meeting for him at Kajal's place in V.P. House. Safdar needed to get his picture enlarged and framed. He also needed to get the script of *Halla Bol* photocopied, which he had written up the previous night.

Safdar and I spent the day together. We first went to Mahatta's, the photographers, in Connaught Place. Safdar chatted with the owner, Madan Mahatta, who he seemed to know well. Mr Mahatta agreed to make an enlargement of the photograph immediately, when he learnt that it was for a young singer's condolence meeting. He ordered tea, Safdar and he chatted about this and that, and the photograph was ready in less than an hour. It was many years later that I learnt of Mr Mahatta's incredible photographic work as a chronicler of Delhi's modern architecture. From Mahatta's we walked across to Moti Frames in the Municipal Market. The proprietor used to be an old Sikh gentleman. Again, Safdar and he chatted with great familiarity. I later learnt that Safdar had helped the family after the 1984 anti-Sikh pogrom. He asked us to come back in an hour. Instead of getting the photocopies done from one of the shops adjoining Moti, we went to Shankar Market.

'You must be hungry. Let's get a dosa. And the best filter coffee in Delhi.'

'Don't tell me this dosa and coffee wallah is also your friend.'

Safdar laughed. He was. It was a little hole-in-the-wall establishment, where one ate standing. The guy seemed genuinely happy to see Safdar.

'We used to have coffee here when we were in IPTA. Have I told you how we were thrown out of IPTA? No? Really? Come, let me show you 33 Shankar Market.'

Safdar could tell a story. He regaled me with the entire saga that day. How they revived IPTA, how much he admired Shyamal Mukherji, how he was crushed when Shyamal died in the road accident, how they commandeered the office, how they got a taste of their own medicine when they were thrown out – their properties flying out of the first-floor window. All of it peppered with little anecdotes that had me in splits. Safdar was on a roll, and he had an eager audience. He told me stories of Janam's early days – including the one about Vinod Nagpal pacifying the unruly crowd in Amroha with his singing – all the while acting out the various characters, reciting lines from plays, singing songs. We picked up the frame from Moti, for which the old man refused to charge us.

'Oho! At this rate, I'll have to stop coming to you!'

'Give the picture to the boy's family. With an old man's blessings.'

'Well, when you say that, how can I insist? But next time ...'

'We'll see, we'll see. *Rab rakha, puttar.*' God be with you, son.

Maybe a year or so later, I went to Moti's. This time to get Safdar's photo framed.

'Did you know him?' the old man asked, running his fingers over the photo gently.

'Yes sir. Do you remember the last time he came here, in December 1988? I was with him that day.'

'Ah yes. It was for a condolence meeting. Who knew that ... *Rab achchhe logon ko sabse pehle utha leta hai.*' God takes away the good people first.

His eyes were moist. When I went back to pick up the frame, once again, he refused to charge for it.

But that day, Safdar and I still had time, so we walked from Shankar Market to V.P. House, enjoying the winter afternoon, Safdar still regaling me with stories. After a quick hello to comrades in the Party office, Safdar said, 'Aren't you hungry? Let's get a bite at the UNI canteen.' United News of India adjoins V.P. House.

After we ate, he started telling me about the dream he had for a cultural centre in a working-class area.

'We'll buy some land. We'll keep a part of it for gardening. We'll grow our own vegetables. We'll have a carpentry workshop. An electrical workshop. Equipment for video filmmaking. Editing room. I have many friends in the field. We'll ask them to train us. Then we'll offer training to local working-class youth. The working class must have the tools to tell their own stories. Some of the kids we train can then become trainers themselves. We'll all live together, all of us in Janam. It'll be like a commune. And we'll do theatre. Not like now, when we meet only in the evenings. We will do theatre all day. Train ourselves. Learn more. Become accomplished theatre artists. We'll train people from all over India in street theatre.'

'All this sounds great, but where will the money come from?'

'I'll earn it. I'm already getting offers to write for television and cinema, which I have to reject because I'm busy. If I take them, I can earn a lot.'

'But if you start doing this, who will do Janam?'

'You. All of you. There are so many of you. All young, with new ideas, so much talent.'

I must have appeared sceptical, because there was now a touch of gravity to his tone.

'I'm serious, Sudhu. I'm looking at Rakesh, Brijender, Shikha, Jogi, you, to be the new leaders of Janam. We'll all be there, of course, Mala, Lalit, Kalia, me, but you have to lead. I know you have directorial talent. You are a good actor. You can also write – your Hindi needs to be more idiomatic, that's all. And you understand organization. Rakesh can also become a director, I think. I'm going to involve him in my television work. Brijender and Shikha can be trained in organization. Jogi is a real talent, an unpolished gem, like Tyagi was. And there are so many others – Nandita, Joy, Lamby ...'

Less than a year ago, in the Lahore workshop, this is how Safdar had explained the idea:

'Now we are working towards a plan, which is in fact quite ambitious. We are working towards making our own theatre, in a working-class area. We are raising funds for this, and it will take two-and-a-half years or so. It is a huge amount to raise, in tens of lakhs of rupees. Our idea is that in a working-class locality in Delhi, we'll be setting up our own theatre, around 1990 or maybe one or two years later, where there will be provisions for all kinds of stages – proscenium stage, thrust stage, theatre-in-the-round. We'll then stop working on an amateur basis and become professionals – or wholetimers – and in the theatre we'll be setting up a repertory, which will by and large confine itself to working among the working classes. This theatre will also be a training centre so that people's theatre activists from other parts of the country, street-theatre activists also, will be able to come there from other parts of the country, and hold workshops. We'll invite other people to also hold workshops. And there we'd like to do all kinds of plays. For example, we'd like to do Greek tragedies and Shakespearean plays for the workers.'

He had also spoken to others about this. He had told Habib sa'ab of his plan. He had also spoken to Sohail, as well as to Pushi, who told him, bluntly, that it was a mistake to think that he could do film work as well as continue being active in Janam and the Party. Pushi was afraid that Bombay would seduce a valuable comrade away. Safdar didn't agree, naturally. Sitaram Yechury, current general secretary of the CPI (M), told me when I had interviewed him in 1998 that Safdar had given him a written note on the proposed centre at the end of December 1988. Yechury had promised to discuss the note upon his return from the Trivandrum Party Congress in January 1989. Brinda Karat also remembers the note:

'I had a very detailed discussion with him about his idea of creating an institution. He at that time felt that he had contributed whatever he could to the group. He was confident that the work would go forward. He felt that he wanted to contribute to the wider area on the basis of that experience. A cultural centre with multiple art forms. He was very keen on it. I distinctly remember the note he gave to the Party at that time. It was visionary. I had tremendous empathy and sympathy with what he was doing, but I felt that Janam needed him still. I said it was possible for a combination of these things to happen, and we were in the course of that discussion. He tried convincing me that the cultural centre was absolutely essential for a most lasting impact. The discussion was unfinished.'

Mala remembers that Safdar and she had once gone to Mangolpuri and looked at a piece of land. 'But the cultural centre was a dream. Something to be done at some time. But it wasn't something to be done immediately. When Safdar got an idea, he always had grand plans. This was a dream, a serious dream, but it wasn't a practical one. I think he realized that there was no way that this could be done so easily.'

What was far more concrete in his mind, Mala says, is the idea of a cultural festival in a working-class area. He called it 'Janotsav' ('People's Festival'), and he envisaged bringing leading artists with their work to the working class. This was to have been done in collaboration with mass organizations. Eventually, Janotsav did take place, in 1990, in Mangolpuri in west Delhi. It was organized by Sahmat. The cultural centre also came into being when Janam created Studio Safdar in Shadipur in west Delhi, in 2012. Today, it has become one of the cultural hubs in the city, alongside its next-door neighbour, the May Day Bookstore, set up by LeftWord Books.

DECEMBER 1988. The Last Month

We did an extensive review of the *Chakka Jaam* campaign in Janam's Executive Committee. The review report I wrote after the discussion notes that it was one of the most successful campaigns undertaken by Janam. We did 29 performances over 16 days between November 2 and 21. Twenty-seven of the performances were directly for the strike, mostly in working-class slums and industrial areas. In addition, we did a show in JNU, and one in Alwar, Rajasthan, though I can't remember what the occasion for that was. We reached 18,000–19,000 people directly, and collected Rs 3,641.77 as donations. Our expenses came to Rs 800, so we were left with Rs 2,841.77, of which half was donated to CITU. We also collected Rs 1,100 from two additional performances that were not for CITU. The review notes the role that Janam played in pulling together artists and intellectuals for the march in support of workers, and that this march had a positive impact in terms of press coverage and creating an overall feeling of sympathy for the strike.

The review goes into a detailed assessment of the roles

that various actors played. Since many roles were double cast, a comparative assessment was made. For instance, 'Joginder, Nandita and Rakesh did a better job than Sudhanva, Ayesha and Lamby in their respective roles', though it also notes that 'Sudhanva did a good job' the one time I played the cop. The only two actors who did all 29 shows were Mala and Shikma, and they maintained 'a high level of performance' throughout. Safdar stepped in for Riyaz and Brijender in two shows each, and 'did a very good job of it'.

Three people spoke before the performances – Mala, Vinod, and myself – and 'no less than ten comrades from Janam took direct part in the various actions during the strike'. Those who weren't directly in the play took no part in the campaign, and this is noted as an organizational failure.

What comes in for scathing criticism is the behaviour of the actors before and after performances. Not only was there little effort to interact with local comrades, 'we appeared to be just a bunch of middle- or upper-middle-class actors, who, apart from the time that we were performing, seemed to have nothing to do with the people for whom we were performing. ... This alienates us from the people from whom we draw our artistic and political nourishment'.

CITU Delhi Secretary Comrade Suraj Bhan Bhardwaj wrote to Janam appreciating Janam's role in the strike campaign. He also thanked us for the solidarity march, and for the two posters that Safdar had designed for the strike. Safdar told us that the mood of the working class was upbeat, and that CITU now wanted to intensify the struggle till the demands were met. He proposed that we redo *Chakka Jaam* by placing it in the post-strike context.

One evening in early December, some of us gathered at Mala and Safdar's house in Laxmibai Nagar to rewrite the play. We discussed the changes. Some of them were simple. For example, instead of Jogi telling Ashsho's father that workers are planning a strike, he speaks about the strike that had recently concluded. Safdar was in favour of keeping the 'reversal' idea of doing an anti-CITU play, but wanted us to come up with a new scene. So Jogi, Brijender, Lalit, and

I, snuggled up in quilts, each with paper and pen, stared hard into the middle distance and pretended to be writing. A couple of hours later, none of us had anything to show. Safdar, in the meanwhile, besides making tea for us, had produced an entirely new scene.

In the new scene, Jogi enters, battered and bruised after a beating from the cops, carrying a red flag. He is taunted by four characters, representing the other unions. So, says one, are you back to your senses? Enjoyed the beatings, asks another. Did they give you anything to eat in jail, says a third. So, you're a jailbird now, eh? All thanks to CITU, says the fourth. And so it goes, taunt upon taunt, with Jogi silent, sullen and angry. They ask him to abandon CITU and join any of them. Or, better still, join nobody. Why do you need a union, they say, when we are there to help you in times of difficulty. They pull at his flag. He is left holding the stick. Now Jogi turns. Don't you dare, he roars. Don't you dare touch the workers' flag with your soiled hands, you pimps, he snarls.

At this point, the actors intervene and try and stop Jogi. They remind him that they are supposed to do an anti-CITU play. Now, Jogi the actor and Jogi the character become one. No, he says, I refuse to do a play against CITU. This is my union, this is my flag. He exposes the role of the other unions when workers were fighting for what is just. He is a picture of defiance. He refuses to be cowed down even when the cop threatens him, or when the neta tries to scare him. At the end of the sequence, the cop, the neta, and the neta's sidekick have to beat a hasty retreat in face of the unity of the workers. The rest of the play remained essentially the same as *Chakka Jaam*.

Safdar called the new version *Halla Bol* ('Raise Hell').

Halla Bol is structured as a series of negations – the sloganeering play is negated and becomes a love story; when the love story threatens to stray into the strike, this is negated and we have a play ostensibly against the strike; this, in turn, is negated by the protagonist Jogi, who says he refuses to do a play against the trade union. Another set of negations begin at this point: When Parbati is refused entry to the factory because she's come with her baby, one section of the trade union leadership refuses to acknowledge that her demands (as well as that of the contract workers) need to be incorporated into the mainstream of the struggle. The views of this section of the trade union leadership are negated, and the demands of women and contract workers are incorporated into the scheme in the end. The play ends the way it was to have begun – with slogans. However, not only have the slogans been filled out and given flesh by the scenes that led to them, but even in the writing the slogans are not clichéd – they are written fresh for the play and the particular working-class struggle the play was a part of. Which is why they sound poetic, not like incantations that accompany mindless ritual, as slogans sometimes do.

The play makes delightful use of parody. When the police constable suggests – rather demands – that the actors present a love story, they break into a parody of an old Hindi film song. This sets the tone for the parody that follows. From the song, till almost the end of the Jogi–Father scene, the play uses stereotypes – the coy girl, the braveheart boy, the domineering father, the concerned mother, are all from Hindi film melodrama, but Safdar, in a parodic mood, inverts the stereotypes. Thus the coy girl is the one driving the relationship forward, the braveheart boy is scared stiff of the father, who in turn is somewhat slow in figuring out what is afoot, and the mother is sharp and wordly-wise. And, in the end, as the boy asserts himself, it is the father's turn to run scared. The whole thing is hilarious, and audiences would be in splits by the end of it. Previous Janam plays had word play and humour, but *Chakka Jaam/ Halla Bol* is the first play that was so uproariously funny. None of us, maybe not even Safdar, realized it then, but this was Habib sa'ab's gift to Safdar, and to Janam – the ability to take the germ of a humorous idea and follow its dynamic to its illogical end.

We started doing shows of *Halla Bol* in mid-December. On December 20, we travelled to Sardarshahar in Churu district, Rajasthan, where we performed *Aurat* and *Halla Bol* at a writers' conference. On December 31, Janam performed *Halla Bol* at Tehkhand Mode in Okhla Industrial Area. I had not gone to that performance because I was now pretending to prepare for my exams. Pushi and Safdar got into an argument that evening because Pushi wanted Janam to perform at a particular spot, and Safdar said no, we had performed there already and that a new spot should be sought. Safdar got his way, because, as Pushi says, 'He could be really stubborn.' Poor Pushi – his last two meetings with Safdar both ended in arguments.

That night, Lalit, Brijender, Rakesh, Jogi, and a couple of Lalit's friends came to spend New Year's Eve on JNU campus.

The next morning, on January 1, 1989, we left for performances at Jhandapur, Ghaziabad, happy and excited, unaware of what lay in store.

The Doubter

One way to characterize street theatre is 'theatre for social change'. Then, the question follows: What does street theatre change? This is a question that all of us in street theatre are repeatedly asked. What change have we brought about?

The short answer is: Nothing. It is not as if one does a street play and the people who watch it change suddenly, or decide to bring about change in their lives.

Like all short answers, though, this is a part-truth, and the situation is more complex than that. For example, suppose one does a street play on the issue of caste. Does caste suddenly vanish? No. Do people who watch it decide they won't be casteist anymore? No, not even that. OK, perhaps not everybody who watches it. Do at least some people stop being casteist? No, even that doesn't happen. OK, let's set our sights lower. Do some people interrogate their own lives in view of what the play shows them? Well, perhaps this might be the case – but for a small number of people. Certainly not enough numbers to change society.

Paulo Freire said, education does not change society.

Education changes people, and people change society. This can be appropriated for theatre as well, and for art in general. Theatre doesn't change society. It changes people, and people change society. But this is also not as true of theatre, or the arts in general, as it is true of education. Education can bring about a change in people, and people can change society, in a relatively short time. How short? It can be as little as a decade. For example, if an entire group of underprivileged girls start going to school, within a decade you might see society's attitudes changing, or at least shifting in a positive direction. Theatre and the arts take longer.

The medium length answer, then, might be: Theatre can change some people, and they in turn might play a role in changing society. But the causality is hard to establish, and in any case whatever change might happen takes longer, besides being propelled by myriad causes apart from theatre. Clearly, this is not satisfactory. If change is so hard to even establish, why do theatre for social change in the first place?

One of Karl Marx's most famous quotations is: Philosophers have hitherto interpreted the world in various ways. The point, however, is to change it. (From Marx's *Theses on Feuerbach.*) How do we interpret Marx's thesis? Is Marx posing a contradiction between interpreting the world – or understanding the world – and changing it? Surely not. It is self-evident that you cannot change something unless you understand it. Does Marx mean that the act of understanding the world automatically leads to changing it? In other words, is interpreting the world the same as changing it? No, even this doesn't seem right, despite how alluring this idea is to some intellectuals. Simply interpreting the world is not going to change it, no matter how accurate the interpretation might be.

What can theatre do, then?

One, theatre can give confidence. Amongst the biggest impediments to positive change in society is the belief that no matter what one does, nothing will change. This idea is surprisingly strong and tenacious, despite evidence to the contrary. We know that people have struggled for various values, and in a great many cases they have succeeded. The Indian people fought for freedom from colonialism, and they succeeded, even though it took a century, and the freedom we won eventually was not as thoroughgoing as many of those who struggled for it had imagined. Babasaheb Ambedkar, for example, was concerned that in our republic although one person equalled one vote, one person didn't equal one person. In other words, the formal equality of the electoral system, though a great and valuable advance, didn't result in equity in social and economic relations. Now, despite the incontrovertible evidence that the Indian people did get rid of colonialism by struggling against it, many people still say that there's no use struggling for social or gender or economic equity, because that will never come about.

This is what the ruling classes want us to believe. They want us to never have faith in change. Or, the only change they want us to believe is possible is the change that the rulers bring about from above. But change from below? No, no way will that succeed. This idea is often so pervasive in society that it prevents people from even changing what they can change relatively easily. Marx was right when he said that the ruling ideas of any age are the ideas of the ruling class.

But Marx also said something else: That ideas become a material force when they grip the minds of the masses. Bertolt Brecht expressed this same idea in his own idiomatic way. Faith can move mountains, the old adage goes. Faith, in this case, is faith in the idea of God. So if you surrender your subjectivity to an all-powerful entity, that entity will perform a miracle for you. Brecht turned this idea on its head. He said: Doubt can move mountains. In other words, that which appears immutable and immovable, that which seems permanent and 'natural' (in the sense of being formed by nature), is mutable and temporary, because it is a result not of nature, but of human history. What is made by human beings in history can also be unmade by them in the future. It is only when you subject that which appears permanent to doubt, that you realize, it is not permanent at all. Doubt gives confidence to people that they can win. Theatre can play this role; it can sow doubt, and thereby give confidence.

Two, by counterposing 'interpretation' and 'change', Marx is perhaps indicating that there can be two, mutually opposing modes of interpretation. One is interpretation inside a reality. The other is the interpretation that transcends a given reality. Many years ago, we had done a play called *Jinhe Yaqeen Nahi Tha* ('The Doubters'). The owner of a factory has got a bunch of workers to work for him when a strike is on. They are the strikebreakers. Realizing what's up, the striking workers cut the electric supply to the factory. The strikebreakers are trapped inside, unable to work, and they have to spend a cold night. To pass the time, they start to make up a story. They spin a yarn about a brutal king and his never-complaining slave. No matter how cruel the king is, the slave always submits. The story moves through three episodes, and in each, the depredations of the king take on ever higher levels. The strikebreaking workers discuss the story, and progressively reach the conclusion that the king is a tyrant without a shred of humanity in him. Then, at the end, one of the workers poses a question to the rest: If you had to choose to be one of the two, the king or the slave, what would you choose to be? Most workers choose the king, even though they despise him. One worker, however, chooses the slave. He is ridiculed by the rest, till a series of events make them realize that the question is itself false. In their lives, none of them have the choice to be the king. But does this mean that they have no choice but to be the slave? No. They can choose not to be the slave. In other words, they can choose to reject the exploitative system of which they are victims.

One way to read Marx's statement about interpretation and change, then, is in these terms: When the workers have to choose between being the king and the slave, they are interpreting reality from within the exploitative framework. When they realize that they cannot choose to be the king, but can also reject being the slave, they interpret reality by counterposing another reality – one that fundamentally alters the older, exploitative reality by going beyond it, by envisaging a new reality that may not exist now, but is the reality of the future.

Someone once called Communists exiles from the future; we live in the present, but are in the business of transcending it.

Theatre can help us see that transcendental future, not as a pipe dream or utopia, but as a concrete possibility, a realizable actuality. One of the songs that Parcham sang on January 4, 1989, when we performed *Halla Bol* at the spot where Safdar had been felled, was '*Tu zinda hai*':

Tu zinda hai, tu zindagi ki jeet mein yaqeen kar
Agar kahin hai swarg to utar la zamin par
You are alive, so trust in the triumph of life
If there's a heaven somewhere, then bring it to earth

It was a fitting tribute. For, Safdar was that, an exile from the future, Spartacus of the theatre, a non-believer whose doubt in the permanence of injustice imbued him with unshakeable faith that a just world could be created, here and now.

EPILOGUE

Ghaziabad used to be a massive district, comprising Ghaziabad city, Loni, Modinagar, Baghpat, Thekda, NOIDA, Dadri and Hapur. NOIDA and Dadri went into Gautam Buddh Nagar when that district was carved out. Subsequently, Hapur became an independent district as well. Ghaziabad district was left with two major industrial belts, Tronica City, and Sahibabad. Sahibabad itself has several industrial areas: Loni, Loni Road, Rajendra Nagar, Anand, Meerut Road, Bulandshahar, South of G.T. Road, Site IV (which includes Jhandapur), etc. Ghaziabad city is known for its technical and engineering colleges. Initially known for manufacturing engines and pumpsets, textiles, sugar, steel, and electronics, through the 1980s and later, the region's industrial output diversified with the arrival of companies such as Dabur, Hero Cycles, Godrej, Atlas Cycles, Coca-Cola, Delhi Press, Bhushan Steel, and so on (some of these, such as Hero, are shut now). Overall, Ghaziabad doesn't have too many large enterprises; it is mainly a centre of medium and small enterprises. It has also been home to two public sector enterprises, Bharat Electronics (BEL) and Central Electronics (CEL). Ram Bahadur, the other victim of the attack of January 1, 1989, worked at CEL.

Ghaziabad had a history of attacks on the working class. Herig-India is one example, and became the inspiration for Janam's play *Machine*. That happened in 1978. CITU, because it was the most militant of the trade union organizations in the region, had also faced attacks. A few years after the Herig-India incident, a CITU district secretary, N.C. Pal, was killed in his own house, though it is not certain if this was a result of his trade union activities. A few years later, another worker connected to CITU, by the name of Mann, was killed. Then Vijay Narayan Singh, who worked at East India Transformers, was killed. Finally, in the summer of 1988, a local CITU leader, Harendra Pal, was killed. He had led a strike at Precision Moulds and Dies (PMD), where the workers had unflinchingly confronted the police.

The attack on CITU and Janam was led by Mukesh Sharma, owner of a small enterprise called Indu Plywood. Safdar, at 34, was a young man when he was killed. Mukesh Sharma was 26. The 'property business', or the real estate market, is a refuge for criminals of all shades. Sharma had already acquired a bit of a name for himself in illegal land-grabbing, and had also diversified into running petrol pumps. Patronage by the Congress, the ruling party, and contesting the local election, were both ways to shore up his clout, which was essential to his business. His elder uncle was an elected sarpanch. The locals feared Mukesh, partly for what he was capable of on his own, and partly because he came from a family firmly entrenched in local networks of power and lawlessness.

Among his henchmen that day was one Surjit Nagar, later reportedly chopped into 50 pieces – for ease of stuffing into a gunny bag – by his own relations. There was a Karan Singh, who ran a ration shop in Jhandapur. It took the Indian legal system, our magnificent colonial legacy, merely 14 years, from 1989 to 2003, to confirm what the world knew: All the 14 accused – including two who had died in the meanwhile – were guilty of having committed the murders of Safdar and Ram Bahadur.

Every political killing is a public spectacle, designed to spread fear and terror. The question is, who is the intended audience? In the case of Dr Narendra Dabholkar and others who were assassinated, and of others such as M.F. Husain, who are attacked in various other ways, the intended audience is national. The attacks are planned to extricate maximum media attention – for the Hindu Right's twisted worldview, yes, but also for the attackers personally, as Malvika Maheshwari brings out in her study, *Art Attacks*. Often, the attackers alert the media and invite them to be spectators as they go about spreading mayhem. Safdar's killing, on the other hand, was meant for a local audience. Ram Bahadur, for them, was no more than collateral damage, and was given just as much importance as a speeding highway bus driver gives to the dog he crushes. The killers spent a long time in the area, strutting about, firing in the air, shouting obscenities, in a macabre choreography of terror.

Safdar was not assassinated, for that presupposes a specific target. His was a political murder. Mukesh Sharma and his henchmen were no evil geniuses; they were local thugs, protecting petty fiefdoms comprised of businesses such as land-grabbing, extortion, and black marketeering. Fear was the currency they traded. Which is why they came armed with guns, thick lathis, and iron rods. Their target was the workers' movement, which was a direct threat to their fiefdoms.

This was an instance of class struggle. Safdar was targeted because he put himself between the killers and his comrades in the class struggle. He offered his body, so others could be saved. If Janam's performance had started an hour earlier, as it was supposed to, they'd have probably missed us. But the attack on the working-class movement would have taken place another time, at another location, with other victims. Safdar's heroism saved lives on that winter morning.

The rapidity with which the news of the attack and Safdar's death went viral – before we knew that word, in an era without mobile phones and the internet – was stunning to me as it unfolded, for I was utterly clueless, in shock, unable to mourn, perplexed and scared at being looked upon as a minor hero, even if momentarily. There were protests all over the country, in towns and cities and villages. In some measure, this was because of Safdar's own personal contacts and friendships, which he had built up more or less effortlessly, with little expectation of payback and certainly no expectation of personal gain. Safdar was a natural organizer, he wasn't a networker.

At another level, the scale of the protests had to do with a decade or more of discontent boiling over – over economic issues, for sure, but also over the increasing evisceration of our social fabric by ideologies of hate based on identity. The scale of the protests was amplified by the fact of Safdar being a Communist, and his party, the CPI (M), along with its mass organizations such as CITU, AIDWA, and SFI, taking the message of his life and sacrifice to millions of people. Finally, the spread and scale of the protests were born of shock – how could a person be killed for simply doing a play? In that sense, it was that moment of liminality in the history of our republic, when we went from a certain naive innocence at the idea of an artist being killed on the streets, to a hardening of the arteries of our humanity, leaving us inured at rapes and lynchings of Dalits and Muslims.

But Safdar's life, and his death, show us that another rage is possible. Safdar's name and his face wouldn't have acquired an iconic quality had artists not banded together under the banner of Sahmat, and had Sahmat itself not been so innovative in responding to the growing brutalization of Indian society. Safdar died a hero, and his heroism was magnified by the creativity of thousands of artists and intellectuals who came together in his name to create a secular counternarrative to the religious right.

But Safdar's life also shows us how an artist can live in this world, not by embracing this or that identitarian cause, but by carrying within themselves a vision of human liberation transcending identities. A vision of liberation so glorious and boundless that it includes all the beings that inhabit this earth.

Akbar raja lajawaab tha, samajh mein uske aai
Ya to duniya sab ki hai ya nahi kisi ki bhai
Emperor Akbar was dumbfounded, for he at last understood
This world, it either belongs to all, or to none at all

CPI(M)
VOLUNTEER

TOP Janam performing on a makeshift stage of camel carts, early 1980s.
MIDDLE N.K. Sharma, Manish Manocha, Subhash Tyagi.
BOTTOM Arun Sharma, Rakesh Saksena, Lalit Ratan Girdhar and Moloyashree.

TOP Anil Chaudhury, Safdar, NK, Mukesh Kumar in *Aya Chunao*, Haryana, 1980. Photo: Surendra Rajan.

BELOW En route to Sardarshahar, December 20, 1988. Standing: Driver, Rakesh Sharma, Helper, Jogi, Sudhanva, Vijay Kalia, Tyagi, Raju, Moloyashree, Brijender, Vinod, Lalit. Sitting: Diwakar, Shikha, Prachee. Photo: Safdar Hashmi.

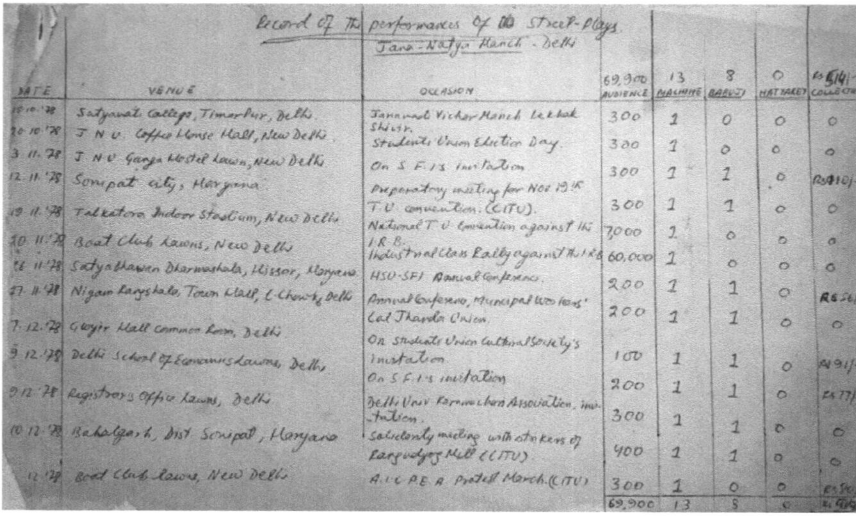

Record of the performances of the Street-Plays
Jana-Natya Manch - Delhi

DATE	VENUE	OCCASION	69,900 AUDIENCE	13 MACHINE	8 BABUJI	0 HATYARE	Rs 514/- COLLECTION
18.10.'78	Satyawati College, Timarpur, Delhi.	Janwadi Vichar Manch Lekhak Shivir.	300	1	0	0	0
20.10.'78	J.N.U. Coffee House Hall, New Delhi.	Students' Union Election Day.	300	1	0	0	0
3.11.'78	J.N.U. Ganga Hostel Lawn, New Delhi.	On S.F.I's invitation	300	1	1	0	Rs 101/-
12.11.'78	Sonipat city, Haryana.	Preparatory meeting for Nov 19th T.U. convention. (CITU).	300	1	1	0	0
19.11.'78	Talkatora Indoor Stadium, New Delhi	National T.U. Convention against the I.R.B.	7000	1	0	0	0
20.11.'78	Boat Club Lawns, New Delhi	Industrial Class Rally against the IRB	60,000	1	0	0	0
26.11.'78	Satyabhawan Dharmashala, Hissar, Haryana.	HSU-SFI Annual Conference.	200	1	1	0	Rs 56/-
27.11.'78	Nigam Karyshala, Town Hall, C. Chowk, Delhi	Annual Conference, Municipal Workers' Lal Jhanda Union.	200	1	1	0	0
7.12.'78	Gwyer Hall common Room, Delhi	On Students Union Cultural Society's invitation.	100	1	1	0	Rs 91/-
9.12.'78	Delhi School of Economics Lawns, Delhi.	On S.F.I's invitation	200	1	1	0	Rs 77/-
9.12.'78	Registrar's Office Lawns, Delhi	Delhi Univ Karamchari Association invitation.	300	1	1	0	0
10.12.'78	Bahalgarh, Dist. Sonipat, Haryana	Solidarity meeting with strikers of Rangudyog Mill (CITU)	400	1	1	0	0
[illegible].12.'78	Boat Club Lawns, New Delhi	A.I.C.P.E.A. Protest March. (CITU)	300	1	0	0	Rs 50/-
			69,900	13	8	0	Rs [illegible]

OPPOSITE, TOP TO BOTTOM Performance sheet, *Machine*, October-December 1978, in Safdar's hand; First performance of *Machine*, October 15, 1978. From left: Arun, Manish, Safdar, Tyagi, NK, Rakesh Saksena; *Machine* at Swatantra Bharat Mills, Delhi, May 1, 1988. From left: Safdar (sitting), Manish, Arun (sitting), Tyagi, Moloyashree (hidden), Lalit (sitting). In the audience: Vijay Kalia (with child on lap), Suraj Bhan Bhardwaj (behind Kalia, sitting, middle). Photo: Eugene van Erven.

ABOVE Moloyashree and Safdar, late 1970s and early 1980s.

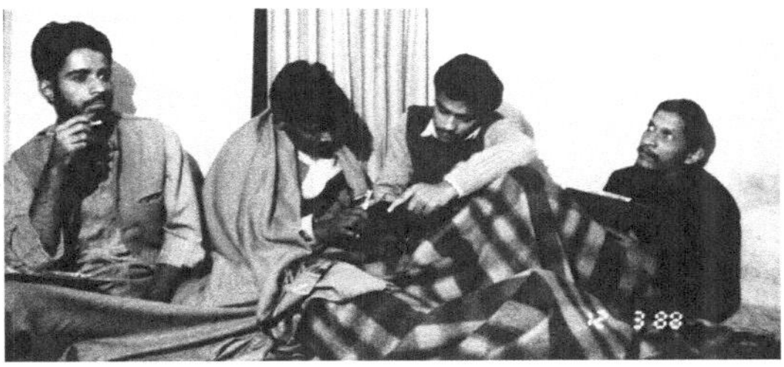

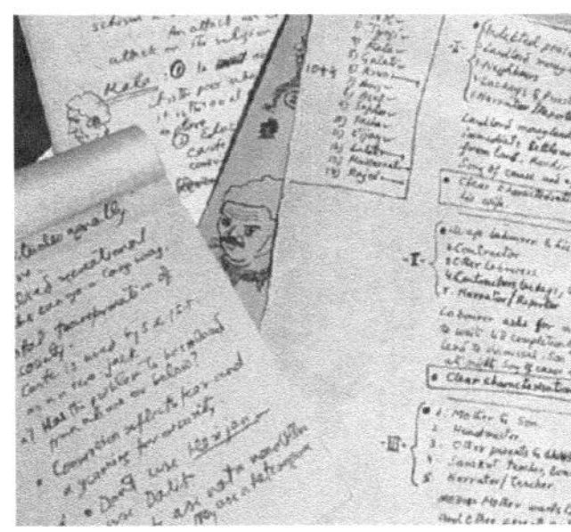

OPPOSITE *Aya Chunao*, Haryana, 1980. Photo: Surendra Rajan.
ABOVE (CLOCKWISE, FROM TOP LEFT) The Chamelijaan scene, *Moteram Ka Satyagraha*, September 1988. Photo: S. Thyagarajan; Safdar and NK with Rudraprasad Sengupta, M.K. Raina, Shombhu Mitra, unidentified person, Nag Bodas, Bhopal, 1983; Notes for the 'Harijan' play; Sudhanva, Sardarshahar, December 20, 1988. Photo: Safdar Hashmi; Shabana Azmi reading the protest note at the International Film Festival of India, New Delhi, January 8, 1989, as Kabir Bedi and Victor Banerjee look on. Screen grab from Sashi Kumar's film, *Safdar*, 1989; Mukesh Sharma's election poster. January 1989, Jhandapur; Parcham, early 1980s. Kajal Ghosh at the harmonium; Writing *Halla Bol* at Moloyashree and Safdar's home, December 3, 1988. Brijender, Jogi, Sudhanva, Lalit. Photo: Safdar Hashmi.

TOP The funeral procession, January 3, 1989.
BELOW *Halla Bol*, January 4, 1989, Jhandapur, Sahibabad. Tyagi, Jogi, Vishwajeet (sitting) Brijender, Moloyashree.

HALLA BOL

Written by Jana Natya Manch, Delhi
First performed in December 1988
Translated from the Hindi by Neeraj Malik

Actors sit in a circle. One actor starts the slogans. The other actors join him in a procession. They hold red flags and shout slogans.

NARRATOR: Workers, stand up for your rights! Comrades, stand up to resist!

SONG: Against oppression and exploitation, we raise our might
Hear our clarion call, we shall not cease to fight.
How long will you oppress us, how many imprison in your jails?
We shall fight, we shall resist, we shall surely prevail.

One actor gets up and blocks their way. He wears a police cap and holds a baton.

POLICEMAN: Stop, stop, I say! Stop shouting! (*Silence. The Narrator, unaware of the policeman, continues to sing. The policeman follows him.*) Hey, didn't you hear me? What did I tell you? Hey, Mr Revolutionary, shut your gob! Oh, you won't listen easily. (*Strikes him with the baton.*) You scoundrel, what are you up to?

NARRATOR: We are going to perform a play.

POLICEMAN: Pilay! You think I'm a fucking idiot?

NARRATOR: No, sir.

POLICEMAN: So?

NARRATOR: So what?

ALL: So what?

POLICEMAN: Is this the way to do a pilay? (*Waves his hands*) Shouting slogans, raising red flags, holding posters. Get lost this minute, you bastards. Or I'll put all of you in jail.

NARRATOR: (*Laughing*) Please believe us, Constable sir. We are only doing a play. You can ask all these people. We are all artists, actors of Jana Natya Manch.

ALL: Yes, yes. Jana Natya Manch of international fame!

All the actors try to persuade him.

POLICEMAN: Oh, I see. You were doing a pilay.

ALL: Yes, sir.

POLICEMAN: Alright. Go ahead then. Do a real good one.

NARRATOR: Yes, sir. Just move aside a bit. We shall start now. Come on, everybody. (*Resumes the slogans, the actors take up the song.*) Long live the revolution, CITU long live!

POLICEMAN: Hey, hey, what is this? Do your pilay; the pilay, I said. No slogan shouting.

NARRATOR: But, sir, our play calls for this action.

POLICEMAN: Your pilay calls for slogans? But slogans are not allowed in this area. We have strict orders ever since the seven-day strike took place. It's an order from the SHO saheb. Arrest anyone who even mentions CITU! Immediately, without asking for explanation!

NARRATOR: But we have to raise slogans in our play.

ALL: Yes, yes, Constable saheb. Slogans are absolutely essential for our play.

POLICEMAN: (*Shouting*) No, no. I will not allow it in my area.

NARRATOR: Then?

POLICEMAN: Then what?

NARRATOR: How do we do the play then?

POLICEMAN: You bastard! Do I have to explain, how? Do it as a normal pilay, with a love angle, with the lover courting his beloved, some song and dance, some jokes and comedy, some this, some that. (*He walks suggestively towards a female actor.*) Understand?

NARRATOR: Yes, understood.

POLICEMAN: What?

NARRATOR: A play about lovers?

POLICEMAN: Yes.

NARRATOR: But no slogans?

POLICEMAN: No slogans.

NARRATOR: All right, sir. As you order. We'll show you a play about lovers. So friends, Constable saheb does not allow us to do a revolutionary play, so we'll show you a play about love.

All actors confer. They make a formation of a garden. Two lovers are cavorting and dancing. They sing a parody of a popular Hindi film song.

CHORUS: Come, my beloved, come
Let us play hide and seek, come
In the lanes, and in gardens

Let's dance around the trees, come.

Jogi and Ashsho play hide and seek.

JOGI: Shall I come?

ASHSHO: No, no.

JOGI: Shall I come?

ASHSHO: No, no.

JOGI: Shall I come?

ASHSHO: Yes, my beloved, come.

JOGI: My beloved is playing hide and seek
There she is, behind the hut ...
There, I caught you ...

CHORUS: There, I caught you!

ASHSHO: Jogi?

JOGI: Yes, Ashsho?

ASHSHO: When will you speak to my father?

JOGI: Just wait a few more days, Ashsho.

ASHSHO: But why? You've been saying the same thing for two years. Wait a few more days, wait a few more days.

JOGI: Please try to understand, Ashsho. My salary is so meagre, how will I maintain you?

ASHSHO: But when will your salary increase? You told me that you'd know for certain after the seven-day strike. Jogi, I can't wait any longer.

JOGI: See Ashsho. This was such a big strike. Thirteen lakh workers kept the factories shut for seven whole days. Don't you see, the factory owners are totally shaken. Now we only have to intensify our struggle. You'll see, the government is bound to give in after our next action.

ASHSHO: Really?

JOGI: Yes, really!

ASHSHO: You swear!

JOGI: I swear!

ASHSHO: Swear by me!

JOGI: I swear by you!

ASHSHO: By God?

JOGI: By God!

POLICEMAN: Hey, hey! What's happening here? You bastards, you've started your propaganda for CITU even in your love story. I won't allow it.

NARRATOR: Oh, oh, Constable, sir. You really are the limit! After all, our hero is a factory worker. For seven days, he has fought so bravely under the CITU banner. How can he not talk about

CITU? And how many people will you ask to shut up? Today every worker is talking only about CITU.

POLICEMAN: No, no. Not allowed in my area.

NARRATOR: Meaning?

POLICEMAN: Meaning, in my area the lover will have to behave like a lover. If he dares to talk of anything else, I will arrest him on the spot.

NARRATOR: OK, as you say, Constable saheb. He will not speak about CITU but can't he at least talk about his salary?

POLICEMAN: Why should he talk to his beloved about his salary? Is he a lover or an accountant? If he wants to do a love scene, tell him to do it properly. Or else I'll show him how to do it.

NARRATOR: No, no sir. Please don't trouble yourself. He can do it. You can do it, mate, can't you?

JOGI: Yes, yes, of course. I will do it.

NARRATOR: Ladies and gentlemen, since Constable saheb has censored our play, we are again making some changes to the play. OK, come on, everyone. Let's start again.

ASHSHO: Jogi!

JOGI: Yes, Ashsho.

ASHSHO: You will speak to father today, won't you?

JOGI: Yes, Ashsho. I have given you my word. I'll do it.

ASHSHO: Good! And don't be nervous. Just be firm and assert yourself. Just like Comrade Nathu when he talks to the management.

POLICEMAN: What? What did you say, girl? What is this comrade-shomrade?

ASHSHO: Sorry, sir. Sorry ... Listen, don't be nervous. Be firm and assert yourself. Just like Lord Ram used to before King Janak.

JOGI: Don't you worry at all. I will just wrap your dear father around my finger, like this. You'll see the true mettle of your Jogi.

ASHSHO: Baba, Baba ...

FATHER: (*Off*) What happened, Ashsho? Why are you screaming like this?

ASHSHO: Someone is here to meet you.

FATHER: Must be a creditor. Tell him I'm not at home.

ASHSHO: No, no. He is not asking for money. It's someone else.

Father and Mother enter.

FATHER: Who is it?

Ashsho points to Jogi. Both parents circle around Jogi, scrutinizing him.

FATHER: Who are you, young man? I don't think I know you. (*Jogi is silent.*) Will you say something, or will you just stand here like a statue?

JOGI: Jogi …

FATHER: Jogi?

JOGI: Jogi – my name is Jogi. I mean Joginder, I mean … no, I mean Joginder Singh … meaning Jogi, Joginder … Jogi, Joginder …

FATHER: What is this Bogey, Bounder, Bogey Bounder? Don't stand there stammering? Tell me what you want with me.

JOGI: No, no. I mean, just like that. I mean I was just whiling away time. I mean, I'll go now.

FATHER: (*Holds him by the collar*) Where are you going, you scoundrel? Tell me, why did you come here? He must be a thief or some such.

Ashsho wails.

FATHER: Just shut up! What has come over you now?

ASHSHO: (*Crying*) He's not a thief!

FATHER: How do you know him?

ASHSHO: (*Sobbing*) I mean Jogi … I mean he … I mean he came to you to … I mean … O Amma! (*She hugs her mother. Both weep together.*)

FATHER: What the hell is going on? Can you speak clearly?

Mother pulls Father aside.

MOTHER: You are the limit! Whisper, whisper.

FATHER: Whisper, whisper …

MOTHER: Yes, and listen. Whisper, whisper …

FATHER: Whisper, whisper … whisper, whisper. (*To Jogi*) Oh, so this is the matter. You want to marry my daughter?

JOGI: Yes, I … I mean that's what I wanted to say.

FATHER: Stop this I mean, I mean. Come to the point.

JOGI: Yes, sir. I will treat her like a queen; her each wish shall be a command; she will never lack …

FATHER: Dispense with these filmy dialogues. Tell me what work you do.

JOGI: Sir, I work in a factory.

MOTHER: What is your designation? Are you the manager?

JOGI: No, madam. A little below that.

FATHER: Supervisor?

JOGI: A little lower.

MOTHER: Department-in-Charge?

JOGI: Just a little lower.

FATHER: Accountant?

JOGI: No, no … er … a little lower.

BOTH: A little lower? Are you a factory worker?

JOGI: Yes, Machine-man.

CHORUS: Yes, Machine-man.

FATHER: I knew it! My daughter would get proposals only from such down-and-outs!

MOTHER: Whisper, whisper.

FATHER: Whisper, whisper.

JOGI: So, sir. Should I take it that you agree to my proposal?

FATHER: (*Picks up his shoe, chasing Jogi*) Come here. Let me show you how I accept your proposal! You bastard, you worthless factory hand, you son of a beggar! You earn a measly wage of 562 rupees, and dream of marriage?

MOTHER: (*Chases Jogi, behind Father*) Look at your cheek. Do you think we'll destroy our daughter's life by letting you marry her?

Ashsho runs after them.

ASHSHO: Baba, oh Amma, don't beat him. Let go of him.

FATHER: Hit him with my shoe!

CHORUS: 562

FATHER: Slap him hard!

CHORUS: 562

FATHER: Kick him hard!

CHORUS: 562

FATHER: Go to hell!

CHORUS: 562

FATHER: Let me show you!

CHORUS: 562

FATHER: You'll never forget this!

CHORUS: 562

Suddenly Jogi stops, turns, and faces Father.

JOGI: Don't you dare raise your hand on me. Or else.

FATHER: I will, I will. I'll beat you a hundred times. 562 times.

JOGI: I'm warning you! Ashsho, tell your father to stop, or I'll teach your old man such a lesson …

FATHER: You bastard! You dare to threaten me? I'll mash you to pulp.

ASHSHO: Baba, take out your anger on me. Hit me. But please don't beat Jogi.

MOTHER: Come here, Ashsho. Don't meddle in men's affairs.

ASHSHO: Let go of me. And I'm telling both of you. I'll only marry Jogi. And I'll never marry anyone if you don't let me marry him.

MOTHER: Don't say such things, my dearest. Don't even utter such inauspicious words. And get this idea out of your head. How can you think of marrying this good-for-nothing factory worker of 562.

FATHER: Think rationally, daughter. With 562, how will he feed you and run a whole household?

MOTHER: Ashsho, anyone earning such a meagre salary is sure to kick the bucket in a year or two. Imagine, you will become a widow at such a young age!

FATHER: My dear, you don't know the state of Delhi factory workers.

MOTHER: Employed today, out tomorrow.

FATHER: Shutters down in one factory today, lock-out in another tomorrow.

MOTHER: Life spent in dirty slums. No water, no electricity.

FATHER: Place infested with criminals and no-gooders.

MOTHER: Facing police violence as a matter of routine.

FATHER: Spending nights in Tihar jail. (*Silence*) Use your brain, my dear. Forget this idea.

MOTHER: You know what marrying a worker means – choosing a living death.

ASHSHO: No, I can't live without Jogi. And I'll kill myself if you don't let me marry him.

Mother weeps.

MOTHER: (*To Father*) Whisper, whisper.

FATHER: Whisper, whisper. (*To Jogi*) Jogi, son, please understand we have nothing against you. You seem to be an honest, hardworking boy.

MOTHER: But we have to think about our daughter's well being. You understand?

JOGI: I have thought about it, Ammaji. I'll give up everything – bidi, cigarette, tea ...

FATHER: Don't be childish, son. How will a worker survive eight hours of hard labour if he gives up tea and smoking?

JOGI: I will stop sending money to my parents. I won't take the bus, I'll walk to the factory. I will take up another job in the evening.

FATHER: (*Mocking*) Of course! So I can bid goodbye to the world in two-three years!

MOTHER: (*Mocking*) So that my wife becomes a widow!

FATHER: All this is meaningless, idle talk. I have made my calculations. No one can live on less than 1,000–1,100 rupees in this city.

MOTHER: Even animals can't survive, let alone human beings.

JOGI: Yes, our Union also says that our wages should be at least 1,050 rupees.

MOTHER: And they are right.

FATHER: So, dear boy, take up a job that gives you at least 1,050. And we'll be happy to let you marry our daughter.

ASHSHO: But where will he find such a job?

JOGI: They all pay 562.

MOTHER: Son, why don't you talk to your boss and persuade him to increase your salary?

JOGI: You think it's easy, Ammaji? With great difficulty, the bastards gave us an increase of 73 rupees after two years. That, too, after a long struggle. This recent seven-day strike – it has brought pressure on the bosses and they are ready to increase our wages. Only the government is sitting quiet till now.

BOTH: So, don't give in. Intensify your struggle.

JOGI: But that's exactly what we are doing. Now all the workers are ready to join CITU and wage a long struggle under its banner.

Policeman intervenes.

POLICEMAN: Again! You are up to it again, you scoundrels! Just because I am not saying anything, you think you can take liberties. Come on, enough! Pick up your stuff and scram! Get out of here.

NARRATOR: Constable, sir, you had said no to shouting slogans and raising banners. See, we have put these aside. Now what's your problem, sir?

POLICEMAN: You good for nothings! How did I know that you are capable of inciting the workers even without raising slogans and banners? That's it now. I won't listen to a word more. Scoot! Just get out!

NARRATOR: Constable, sir. Why can't you get this simple thing into your head that a worker has to struggle to be able to live. If we do a play on our own lives, it does not matter whether we raise banners or not, or shout slogans or don't shout slogans. It boils down to the same thing. A worker's life is a big struggle. We have to fight to be able to live.

ALL: Have to fight to be able to live.

JOGI: And we have to fight to be able to love.

POLICEMAN: Oh, I see. Then you'll have to fight me to do your play. Who's ready?

NARRATOR: Go to hell! We refuse to do the play. The government has not imposed any Emergency, but you must start your censorship. Come on, friends, let's go. We will not do our play.

All move to pack up.

ACTOR 1: One minute! (*All pause. To Policeman*) You said that you will not allow the red flags, slogans, or any mention of CITU. But what if we do a play against all these?

POLICEMAN: Look, the SHO sir's orders are that there should be no talk of CITU. (*Starts to dream*) But if you do a play against CITU, then there is a good chance that I'll be promoted to the post of a Sub-Inspector ... Then Inspector, then ACP, and of course DCP someday soon ...

ACTOR 1: Mr Baton, sir! Please descend from the land of your dreams to this poor earth of ours. All right, so should we begin our play? Constable sir! ... (*Policeman in dreamland.*) ACP sir! (*Shouts*) Excuse me, DCP sir!

Policeman comes out of his reverie.

POLICEMAN: Yes, yes. Alright, begin.

Actors confer. The play begins. Jogi enters with the CITU flag. He is limping and crying in pain.

JOGI: We are the victims of hunger
We have no fear of death!
Lift the banner high!
Strike for freedom!

Four union leaders move in a circle around him.

ALL FOUR: What Jogi? Have you learnt your lesson now?

LEADER 1: Hope you enjoyed the batons of the police.

LEADER 2: Did they give you any food in the jail? Or did they make you starve the whole day?

LEADER 3: Poor thing. Got a real taste of what happens when you go with the CITU wallahs.

LEADER 4: Why talk of him? He's a small fry. Even their MP got beaten up in jail.

ALL FOUR: Ha, ha, ha ...

LEADER 1: Didn't we tell you not to fall into the trap of these CITU wallahs.

LEADER 2: But of course, you wouldn't listen! They misled you and you went in for a seven-day strike.

LEADER 3: And what did you get out of it? Zero!

LEADER 4: And to top it all, now you'll get a wage cut.

JOGI: Wage cut?

ALL FOUR: Of course. For full seven days.

JOGI: But the CITU wallahs were saying that we'll get a wage increase of 1,050, and a two-rupee per point dearness allowance.

LEADER 1: This is called 'leading up the garden path'. These CITU wallahs know how to serve their own interests by misguiding innocent workers.

LEADER 2: Why don't you ask them now? What happened to all their promises? They had said that they would end the contract system. What happened to that?

LEADER 3: They promised you housing, childcare services for women workers. What did you get?

LEADER 4: Not only that – they boasted that all anti-labour laws would be withdrawn, closed-down factories would be reopened, and police repression would end forever.

ALL FOUR: Ha, ha, ha. In effect, they had promised turning Delhi into a utopia for workers.

LEADER 1: Jogi, come to your senses now. You still have time. Have nothing to do with the CITU wallahs any more.

LEADER 2: Yes, join one of our unions. We have all joined together now.

LEADER 3: And if you don't want to do that, just quit all union activity. We are always there to help you if there's any trouble.

LEADER 4: Come, let us take away this flag. We'll tear it up and throw it into the dustbin.

ALL FOUR: Yes, do away with the flag. And you'll be rid of your troubles for ever.

They try to take away the flag. They pull at it. Jogi is holding the pole. He doesn't let go and pulls back the flag.

JOGI: Don't you dare! You pimps of the owners. Don't you dare touch the workers' flag with your soiled hands.

The rest of the actors stand up.

ALL: Hey, Jogi, what are you doing? We are doing a play against CITU. Constable sir is sitting here. Why are you intent on getting us all beaten up?

JOGI: No, I will not do a play against CITU. CITU is my union. The CITU flag is my flag. I know now that CITU is the only union which fights for the workers. In these last seven days, CITU has shown me the way to fight for my rights, to fight for a life with dignity. Where were these other unions when the police were showering their lathis on us? Where were they hiding when I was starving in the jail? The police were beating up women, arresting our leaders, and these people were quiet as mice. No, in fact, they were issuing statements against CITU in newspapers. They were stopping workers from coming out of the factories. I have seen the true character of these traitors. Now there is only one union for me – CITU. Now I am CITU. I will not speak one word against CITU. I am not afraid of the constable. I am not afraid of the whole might of the Delhi Police. They may beat me, torture me, but I will continue to say – Long Live CITU. Long Live Revolution!

POLICEMAN: You bastard! You've started your tricks again. You need a few lathis to bring you to your senses.

JOGI: Go on, beat me as much as you want. I will no longer be silent. The workers of this country will not remain silent. The worker is ready to lay down his life, why would we fear your lathis?

Sings.

JOGI: We are the prisoners of starvation
We have no fear of death.
Roll the drums of freedom
Raise the flag of Revolution.
Listen to the call of class struggle
Reverberating through this land.
Prepare, prepare, united we stand!

All the actors stand behind Jogi. Enter a local leader and his sidekick.

LEADER: Who's creating this racket?

POLICEMAN: So good you came, sir. (*Pulls Jogi towards himself.*) This bastard is making provocative statements. When I told him to stop, he turned on me.

LEADER: You bastard, you used to cower before me till yesterday. Now you think you can look me straight in the eye just because of your seven-day strike. You think you can threaten me with your red flag? Don't forget that it is because of me that you are allowed to live in your jhuggis. If I want, I can have the DDA send their bulldozers and demolish your whole basti in a minute.

SIDEKICK: Sir is right. It is because of him that we are living here today. If you hobnob with CITU, we'll all lose our houses.

JOGI: You call them houses. They are a pile of garbage.

The rest start to speak.

WORKER 1: He's right. Look at the muck around us.

WORKER 4: There's no difference between the water flowing in our gutters and our drinking water.

WORKER 3: Most of our homes don't have electricity.

WORKER 2: And those who have electricity have to pay regular bribes to the goons and the electricity people.

NARRATOR: There's no government hospital for miles.

JOGI: CITU has told us not to pay bribes for our houses to goons like you.

LEADER: You bastards, you'll learn only when houses are torn down. You'll be out on the streets. And don't come to me then saying

I didn't warn you.

ALL: Get lost! We know the likes of you. You speak one word more and we'll show you good and proper.

Leader, Sidekick, and Policeman run out. The rest of the actors raise slogans.

JOGI: We'll fight till our demands are met.

NARRATOR: We demand pucca houses from the government.

WORKER 1: Where there is no garbage or dirt.

WORKER 2: Where there is clean water and electricity.

WORKER 3: Where we have schools for children and hospitals for the sick.

WORKER 4: Where there are parks for our children to play.

CHORUS: We shall intensify our struggle till all our demands are met.

NARRATOR: Today all the workers of Delhi are united in their resolve. They are no longer willing to stay silent. They are fighting for a sustainable wage in the factories, they are fighting to protect their jobs. They are fighting for decent housing.

CHORUS: Everyday, everywhere, they are fighting for a life with dignity.

NARRATOR: And that's not all. The women workers of Delhi have also taken up the struggle. Here is one such woman worker.

All sit down. Enter Parbati with a child in her arms.

PARBATI: A thousand curses on you! I hope you die a dog's death! May your corpse rot! And the dogs piss on it! May your body be disease-ridden! The bastards think they can order everyone about. They refused to let me take my child with me. 'Children are not allowed inside the factory,' he says. You tell me, brother, what should I do with my child? Throw her on the garbage pile? You tell me, isn't this downright unjust? How is a working woman supposed to work if she can't take her child with her? My husband was looking after her till yesterday. Now he has got a job so I brought her along with me. That damned time-keeper stopped me at the gate. Said, there are orders not to allow children inside. Alright, so I'll just stand here at the gate. When the shift gets over, I'll tell the union people what's going on here.

The sound of the hooter. Workers come out of the factory.

PARBATI: Hey, Jogi … Rampal! I'll lose my job. The time-keeper didn't let me enter the gate today.

JOGI: But why? Why did he stop you?

SIDEKICK: Parbati, don't tell a lie. I saw everything. The time-keeper did not stop you, he only stopped your child.

PARBATI: This ass-licker has to pipe up every time to defend his masters. Should I have thrown my child on the street if I was not allowed to take her in?

RAMPAL: But why did you bring your baby with you?

WOMAN 1: Her husband has got a job. Where could she have left her?

PARBATI: Exactly. There is no one at home to look after her.

RAMPAL: I understand that, Parbati, but where would you put the child inside the factory?

PARBATI: She will just sit in one corner. The poor baby doesn't ever trouble anyone.

SIDEKICK: How can this be allowed? Today she has brought her child, tomorrow several others will do the same. Those who have children should stay at home.

PARBATI: You just keep your gob shut. Or I'll show you what I can do. I should sit at home? Will you feed my family and pay my salary every month?

WOMAN 2: I am also forced to leave my kid with the neighbour. The poor baby has to stay hungry the whole day.

WOMAN 3: My little daughter also spends the whole day loitering in the lanes, with nobody to look after her.

PARBATI: You people run the union. Can't you do something about our problem?

RAMPAL: But what can the union do in this?

PARBATI: Why can't you do something? There should be a crèche in the factory. Wasn't that one of our demands in the strike?

RAMPAL: Listen, Parbati. We have fought a long battle – a seven-day strike – for important issues, like a 1,050 rupee wage, two rupees per point dearness allowance, and for ending contract labour. The factory owners are feeling shaken now. We only have to intensify our struggle a little bit more and they'll have to concede to our demands. If we raise these trivial issues now, our fight will become weak.

PARBATI: Trivial issue? This is not a trivial issue, Rampal. It is a question of my job.

WOMEN: She's right. This was our demand in the strike.

PARBATI: Jogi, show me the campaign leaflet. It clearly says that the owners have to make arrangements for a crèche wherever women are employed.

RAMPAL: Jogi, please think carefully. I feel our struggle will weaken if we raise this issue.

SIDEKICK: Yes, he's right.

PARBATI: You shut up! Rampal, don't twist things. What kind of a CITU leader are you? It was CITU which had raised the demand for crèches. Our union also put forth this demand. That is why all of us women joined in. What do you say, sisters?

WOMAN 1: Yes, of course.

WOMAN 2: I joined the strike especially for this reason.

PARBATI: Isn't it a fact that our participation made the struggle stronger? You must be crazy to think that our fight will become weaker because of our demand.

WOMAN 2: Women workers demand ...

WOMEN: A crèche in every factory
A crèche in our workplace!

NARRATOR: Our struggle is against injustice!

All join in a procession.

JOGI: Gulam Rasool, Raghavan, won't you join the procession?

Both quiet.

JOGI: Come on, brothers. Everyone is joining. Even the women. You should also come.

Still quiet.

JOGI: Why, what's the matter?

RAGHAVAN: Comrade, we had joined the seven-day strike only because you asked us to. We were not going to gain anything from the wage increase. We are employed by the contractor, you see.

GULAM RASOOL: You know very well that the contractor refused to take us back when we tried to join duty on the eighth day.

RAMPAL: And you got back your jobs only because CITU intervened on your behalf. Don't you ever forget that.

RAGHAVAN: And later the contractor's henchmen threatened us. They said they would teach us a lesson if we ever joined in CITU's actions.

JOGI: That is precisely why I'm telling you to join the union. If you are isolated, they will crush you.

GULAM RASOOL: You may be right, brother. But if we join the union, the contractor will dismiss us immediately. Our children will starve if we don't get work. Come, Raghavan, let's go for duty.

Both start to leave.

RAMPAL: (*Advancing aggressively towards Raghavan*) You bastard, I'll see how you join work. I warned you, Jogi, don't trust these scoundrels. (*Fisticuffs*) They take away the jobs of permanent workers by agreeing to work for 250–300 rupees. (*Fisticuffs*) You can't trust them, they are like rolling stones. (*Fisticuffs*) I'm going to break your legs, you bastards, before the contractor gets to you. (*Fisticffs*) Let go of me, Raghavan.

RAGHAVAN: Who do you think you are? I'll be the one to break your legs.

Jogi separates them.

JOGI: Don't be insane, Rampal. I didn't expect such behavior from a responsible person like you. We have worked so hard to unite all the workers. Now our struggle is gaining strength and you are preventing out brothers from joining the fight. Don't forget that the factory owners are waiting for the slightest opportunity to create divisions among us. They will make the most of it. Use your brains. Gulam Rasool, Raghavan, come and join the procession.

Jogi goes to the contract workers.

GULAM RASOOL: But brother, you tell us what we would gain by joining your struggle. Whatever may happen, we will get only 300–350 rupees.

JOGI: There you go again. I told you earlier too – our charter says all workers should get equal wage for equal work.

CHORUS: Equal work, equal wage.

JOGI: Whose demand is this?

GULAM RASOOL: Yes, but ...

JOGI: Yes, this what the contract workers like you are demanding. You all work as much as the company workers but you get barely three-fourths of their salary.

GULAM RASOOL: Not only that our wages are less, but we don't get ESI, bonus, insurance, gratuity – none of these things.

RAGHAVAN: And we are shunted out like sheep and goats whenever it suits them. Even the Labour Office does not pay any heed to us.

JOGI: Precisely. That's why we want an end to the contractual system.

NARRATOR: Down with the contract system!

CHORUS: Weed out this disease!

GULAM RASOOL: Regularize the contract workers! Register them on the rolls of the company!

RAGHAVAN: We will fight for equal pay! We will fight for ESI, bonus, insurance, gratuity!

RAMPAL: You think they will give you ESI, bonus, insurance and gratuity so easily? We'll have to put up a united fight for each one of these.

JOGI: All the workers will have to stand together.

NARRATOR: Everyone will have to become a member of CITU.

WOMAN: United struggle for all workers.

PARBATI: Man or woman.

NARRATOR: Temporary or permanent.

RAMPAL: On the muster roll or on contract.

GULAM RASOOL: Those bastards will never concede this demand even if they agree to the rest.

JOGI: Why do you think so, brother?

GULAM RASOOL: Because all the workers are united on the rest of the demands. But this is only our demand. Tomorrow they may concede your demands and you'll conveniently forget us. We know it. Therefore, our best bet is to keep the contractor on our side.

WOMAN 2: Why do you say that, brother? This is not just your demand, it is our demand too. Women work as hard as the men but they get paid less.

NARRATOR: The owners do the same even to permanent workers in factories where the workers don't have a union. They make them sign on 562 and only give them 300–400 rupees.

RAGHAVAN: True, but there is no one to protect us till we are made permanent. Come, let's go, Gulam Rasool.

Both start to leave.

PARBATI: Gulam Rasool, Raghavan, stop. Only the workers can protect workers. Let go of your fear. Join CITU. That's the only way all of us can succeed.

SONG: Let us stand as one, my brothers
All for one and one for all.
Like a hundred sparks that make a fire,
Like a hundred streams that make a river,
Like a hundred lamps lit together.
We stand as one
All for one, and one for all.

All form a procession, including Gulam Rasool and Raghavan.

NARRATOR: Friends, we have presented before you a picture of the life of the workers.

CHORUS: But before we take your leave, we again want to tell you something.

NARRATOR: That the biggest need of the hour is to intensify our struggle for our rights.

CHORUS: We stand here together,
We who toil hard,
We who are the oppressed,
We who live at the mercy
Of contractors and factory owners,
CITU stands with workers,
CITU's voice is our voice.
It is the voice of every factory hand,
Of those who sweat and toil.
Put an end to closures and lockouts,

And retrenchments once for all.
Two rupee per point allowance,
To keep up with inflation.
Clean and decent living,
And, freedom from deprivation.
Take back all the black laws
That keep us in their thrall,
ESMA or NSA, we demand you repeal them all.
Crèches for all the working women,
No to contractors and middle-men.
End to police repression,
To daily beatings and threats.
We stand as one, we shall not rest
Till our demands are met.
We raise our banners high
To fight against oppression.
We workers stand together
With courage and resolution.
Narrator: We raise our banners high
To fight against oppression.
The workers stand together
With courage and resolution.

NOTE ON SOURCES

In writing this book, I have relied upon the memories of many comrades and friends, apart from my own. I interviewed the following people in 2019, unless otherwise mentioned: Aditya Nigam, Brijender Singh, Brijesh, Brijesh Singh, Brinda Karat (1998 and 2019), Jogendra Sharma, Jogi, Joy Sengupta, K.M. Tiwari, Kajal Ghosh, Kamla Bhasin, Lalit Ratan Girdhar, M.K. Raina, Madan Gopal Singh, Moloyashree Hashmi, Muralidharan, N.K. Sharma, P.M.S. Grewal, Rajendra and Madhu Prasad (2017), Rakesh Sharma, Rathin Das, Shohini Ghosh, Sitaram Yechury (1998), Sohail Hashmi (2017), Soman, Subhash Tyagi, Subodh Varma, Vijay Kalia, and Vishwajeet Pradhan.

Kavita Nagpal was interviewed in 2010 by Arjun Ghosh, whose *A History of the Jana Natya Manch: Plays for the People* (New Delhi: SAGE Publications India, 2012), is a valuable compendium.

There are two previous books on Safdar. His mother Qamar Azad Hashmi wrote a moving memoir, *Panchva Chirag*, published by Sahmat, New Delhi, in 1995, translated into English by Sohail Hashmi and Madhu Prasad as *The Fifth Flame: The Story of Safdar Hashmi* (New Delhi: Viking, 1997). Prabhat Upreti published in 1991 a memoir of his closest friend, *Safdar: Ek Adam Qad Insan* (New Delhi: Yatri Prakashan).

Quotes from Safdar's writings are from unpublished notes in the Janam archives and his private papers, and from articles collected in *The Right to Perform*, published by Sahmat in 1989. Eugene van Erven's long interview with Safdar is also included in this book. An updated and corrected version of this interview is published in *Theatre of the Streets: The Jana Natya Manch Experience*, published by Janam, New Delhi, in 2007. This book also includes Habib Tanvir's reminiscences of Safdar, under the title 'Janam Comes of Age'. Some of Safdar's writings are included in *Safdar: Safdar Hashmi Ka Vyaktitva Aur Krititva* (New Delhi: Rajkamal Prakashan, 1989). The volume also contains tributes to Safdar by Bhisham Sahni, Habib Tanvir, M.K. Raina, and Prasanna. Safdar's writings for children are available in beautiful editions published by Sahmat.

The Janam archives contain invaluable materials: letters, notes, programme brochures, organizational jottings, minutes books, etc. They also contain thousands of photographs and many hours of video. I looked through all photographs dated till the end of 1989, as well as all the video material featuring Safdar. Thanks to all those who made the photographs that comprise the archive – in particular, Surendra Rajan and Rathin Das, who made some of the most spectacular photographs of the early years of street theatre.

All Janam street plays quoted in this book are compiled in *Sarkash Afsaney: Jana Natya Manch Ke Chuninda Natak*, edited by Ashok Tiwari, and published by Janam in 2010. *Moteram Ka Satyagraha* by Safdar Hashmi and Habib Tanvir was published by Sahmat in 1991.

Quotes from articles by Babli Gupta, Javed Naqvi, and Kalindi Deshpande are from Janam's magazine *Nukkad Janam Samvad* (January 1998 and January–March 1999).

The details of the work of Theatre Union were provieded by Anuradha Kapur and Maya Rao on email.

Indrani Majumdar's excellent report, *Unorganised Workers of Delhi and the Seven Day Strike of 1988*, is published by the V.V. Giri National Labour Institute, NOIDA, and is available online.

Other sources directly referenced in this book are:

Rati Bartholomew, 'Samudaya's Jatha, Karnataka', *How*, vol. 6, nos. 1–2, January–February 1983

Bhaswati Bhattacharya, *Much Ado Over Coffee: Indian Coffee House Then and Now*, New Delhi: Social Science Press, 2018

Avik Ghosh, *Communication Technology and Human Development: Recent Experiences in the Indian Social Sector*, New Delhi: SAGE Publications India, 2006

Malvika Maheshwari, *Art Attacks: Violence and Offence-Taking in India*, New Delhi: Oxford University Press, 2019

Narender Pani, *Staging a Change*, Bangalore, Samudaya Prakashana, 1979

Zohra Segal, *Close-Up: Memoirs of a Life on Stage and Screen*, New Delhi: Women Unlimited, 2010

M.M.P. Singh, 'A Leader of Teachers: Kumaresh Chakravarty (1933–2017)', *Economic and Political Weekly*, vol. 53, no. 2, January 13, 2018

ACKNOWLEDGEMENTS

I now know what Shelley meant when he wrote about 'imagining that which we know'. Each telling of a story, even if it happened to you, is an act of imagination – the structure, texture, gestures, and nuance that make a particular telling are all imagined. Not only would others tell this story differently, even I would've told it differently a decade or two ago.

While books carry the name of their authors, every book is, to a greater or lesser extent, a collective creation. This is a book about a man of the theatre, and theatre itself is the quintessential collective art. This book would not exist but for Jana Natya Manch. Both its subject and its author have been shaped in all kinds of fundamental ways by their work in Janam.

But Janam is not simply an organization. It is people. A decade or so ago, Brijender attempted to compile a list of all those individuals who've been part of Janam. His list, if memory serves, included well over 500 names, and there were many who were doubtless left out – today, the list would be over 1,000. If I could, I would name every person on this impossible-to-compile list as a tiny token of my gratitude.

Instead, while telling the story, I've tried to name as many individuals who worked with Safdar as possible. To all those who were part of IPTA during 1970–73, and Janam during 1973–88, named and unnamed, my salute. You are the pioneers, you created the legacy that those who followed, like myself, have had bequeathed to us.

But there is an even larger number who came into Janam in and after 1989. They have been my comrades, colleagues, friends. It is impossible to name each of them. Instead, I name below all the people who've been part of the Executive Committee of Janam since 1988. I do this because they are the individuals that succeeding General Bodies of Janam elected to represent us, but also because organizational work, particularly in artistic organizations, is sometimes undervalued. The individuals named here, then, stand for a much larger number of people who have given their time and talents to Janam over the years. I remain personally indebted to them.

Janam Executive Committee members, 1988–2019 (with office bearer posts indicated in brackets): Abhay Shrivastava, Agat Sharma, Aishwaraj

Kumar, Anil Koli (Treasurer), Arjun Ghosh, Arun Sharma (Treasurer), Ashok Tiwari (President; Treasurer), Brijender Singh (Treasurer), Brijesh (President; Treasurer), Chirag Garg, Jogi, Joy Sengupta, Joyoti Roy (Treasurer), Kailash Negi, Karan Ahuja, Komita Dhanda (Secretary), Lalit Ratan Girdhar, Lovleen Misra, Manoj Karki, Moloyashree Hashmi (Convenor; President; Secretary), Naresh Parashar, Neel Dogra, Nidhi Kindra, Praveen Vadhera, Priyanka Monga, Rakesh Sharma, Safdar Hashmi (Convenor), Sania Hashmi (Secretary), Sarita Sharma (President), Satyam Tiwari (Treasurer), Shakil Khan (Treasurer), Sheela, Shehla Hashmi Grewal (President), Shikha Sethi, Shivani Chander, Soman, Subhash Tyagi, Uttam Halder, Vijay Kalia (President; Treasurer), Vikas, Vipul Mayank, Vishwabhanu.

I have had the joy of being associated with another remarkable institution, LeftWord Books. I was asked by Prakash Karat to set up our publishing operations, at a time when I was unsure of my future. That was in December 1998. Since then, I've worked with dozens of colleagues who've made LeftWord what it is – and enabled me to continue my activities in Janam. Again, they are too many to name.

However, I would like to name the current LeftWord team: Suvendu Malik, an absolute rockstar, the backbone of LeftWord; my editorial colleagues Vijay Prashad, Nazeef Mollah, and Shipra Kiran; along with Sreenath Hussain, Manoj Kumar, Shahid Ansari, and Purbasha Sarkar. I knew LeftWord was in capable hands throughout the two months I was writing this book. As was Studio Safdar, where Priyanka Monga handles her responsibilities as Programme Manager with efficiency and good cheer.

Vijay and Nazeef are both superb editors, and this book is much the better for their care and love. In addition, this book is lucky to have had Vinutha Mallya do a thorough and rigorous edit – she weeded out instances of the passive voice, dealt sternly with split infinitives, corrected my misuses of which/that, and pointed out instances where I was making unfair demands on the reader. It was a masterclass in copy-editing.

Several friends and comrades read parts or whole of the manuscript and offered incisive comments: Anu Yadav, Brijesh, Dipti Mahadev, Komita Dhanda, Moloyashree Hashmi, Neeraj Malik, P.M.S. ('Pushi') Grewal, Sania Hashmi, Satyam Tiwari, Shayoni Mitra, Vijay Prashad, and Vinutha Mallya. Wonderful readers, all.

Sherna Dastur is a dear friend and an extraordinary designer. I learn so much about design just by sitting next to her, watching her create magic. Over the years, she's done numerous covers for LeftWord. This book is designed by her.

Safdar spoke to me about joining the CPI (M) in autumn 1988. I did, the year after his death. The Party has been my beacon ever since. This book is a record of a small part of what I've seen, experienced, and learnt from the Party, and the inspiring work our comrades do in adverse conditions, day after day. In particular, the sections on trade union work owe a lot to what I've observed in the field. Red salute to them all.

I conducted a number of interviews as part of the research for this book. I am touched by the generosity and kindness of all the people I interviewed. Their names are mentioned in the 'Note on Sources'. Anuradha Kapur and Maya Rao were kind to respond to my requests for information.

Most of the interviews were heroically transcribed by my Janam colleague Komita at great speed. A couple were also transcribed by Nazeef.

I had originally envisaged a different book, one I was to co-author with Malvika Maheshwari, the author of *Art Attacks*. For reasons beyond our control, that was not to be. But I benefited by discussions with her, and she was generous with sharing documents from her research.

The trigger for arriving at the current shape of this book was provided, unbeknownst to him, by a conversation I had with Rajendra Prasad (Rajen) of CPI (M) and Sahmat. I am grateful for that metaphorical kick up my backside.

The Hindi translation of this book has been done by Yogender Dutt. He is the best in the business. Safdar would have approved. Neeraj Malik translated the text of the play *Halla Bol*, into English for this book, and helped me with other translations as well. My gratitude.

As soon as I announced on social media that I was writing this book, A. Mangai reached out to ask if she could translate it into Tamil. I was thrilled, having admired her own theatre and scholarly work for decades. I am similarly delighted that Kannada readers will read this book in translation by M.G. Venkatesh, another doyen of the street theatre movement. Malayalam readers will read the translation by Rubin DCruz, my friend and fellow publisher.

Githa Hariharan and Prabir Purkayastha have given their unstinting support to many projects I've been involved with.

Then there are those who help a writer just by being themselves. Rana has been an unwavering presence in my life for two decades or more, as were Mala's parents, Baba and Aparnadi, both sterling human beings. They'd have been pleased to see this book.

My mother, Kalindi Deshpande, was, at various points in her life, a Home Guard; expert rifle shooter; trained firefighter; probably the only woman to have driven a double-decker BEST bus on the streets of Bombay; speaker of several languages including Marathi, Hindi, English, French, German, Sanskrit, Kannada, Gujarati (and late in life she picked up enough of Bangla and Kokborok to conduct research for a PhD that death prevented her from completing); expert cook; gardener; theatre actor and director; writer; translator; street-theatre artist and playwright; feminist activist; and Communist. I'm sure I've left out a bunch of things, but you get the idea.

My father, Govind Deshpande (or GoPu, or GPD, or GP) had a more modest biodata. He was merely an expert on international affairs and a Sinologist;

pathbreaking Marathi playwright; cultural critic; columnist in the *Economic and Political Weekly* (or EPW, which his friends would joke should be called GPW); author; Marxist intellectual; and proficient in Marathi, Hindi, English, German, Mandarin, Sanskrit, and Gujarati.

Aai once asked me to write a book about my Janam experience; the only thing Baba ever tried to nudge me towards was a PhD. Aai, I wish I'd done this a decade ago; and Baba, here's my PhD. This book is for both of you.

She doesn't know this, but I've regarded my sister Ashwini as a bit of a hero. As an SFI activist and singer in Parcham, she first got me interested in activism, and nudged me towards Janam. Since then, she's been a rock in my life. Bhaskar and she have provided a happy and secure family for her daughter Ketaki to grow up in. Ketaki is a smart, sharp, insightful person, and I'm lucky to be her uncle – particularly because she gives me insights into Hindi films and online cultures, and because she bakes delicious cakes and cookies. Bhaskar and Ashwini are also mean cooks, by the way, as their friends well know.

Vijay Prashad has been my friend, comrade, twin, for the last two decades. Normally, he's the author, I the editor. This time, the roles are reversed. After writing this book in my head numerous times, I've finally committed it to paper. The particular shape of this book, its logic and argument, its style, and its politics, all owe more to Vijay than perhaps even he realizes.

And Mala.

She, more than anyone else, has maintained the excellent Janam archive; she is also a walking-talking archive herself; she created conditions that made my writing possible and shielded me from distractions; my work in, and understanding of, political theatre has been shaped by her in innumerable ways; I interviewed her formally a few times for this book, but really, I've been interviewing her for the last three decades; she has been my closest friend, companion, comrade, leader, lodestar.

This book is my tribute to her.

SAFDAR
DIED BUT NOT
IN
VAIN